# Romantic Suspense

## Danger. Passion. Drama.

### Operation Rafe's Redemption
Justine Davis

### The Suspect Next Door
Rachel Astor

# MILLS & BOON

OPERATION RAFE'S REDEMPTION
© 2024 by Janice Davis Smith
Philippine Copyright 2024
Australian Copyright 2024
New Zealand Copyright 2024

First Published 2024
First Australian Paperback Edition 2024
ISBN 978 1 867 29963 9

THE SUSPECT NEXT DOOR
© 2024 by Rachel Astor
Philippine Copyright 2024
Australian Copyright 2024
New Zealand Copyright 2024

First Published 2024
First Australian Paperback Edition 2024
ISBN 978 1 867 29963 9

MIX
Paper | Supporting
responsible forestry
FSC® C001695

Published by
Harlequin Mills & Boon
An imprint of Harlequin Enterprises (Australia) Pty Limited
(ABN 47 001 180 918), a subsidary of HarperCollins
Publishers Australia Pty Limited
(ABN 36 009 913 517)
Level 19, 201 Elizabeth Street
SYDNEY NSW 2000 AUSTRALIA

Cover art used by arrangement with Harlequin Books S.A.. All rights reserved.

Printed and bound in Australia by McPherson's Printing Group

# Operation Rafe's Redemption
Justine Davis

# MILLS & BOON

**Justine Davis** lives on Puget Sound in Washington State, watching big ships and the occasional submarine go by and sharing the neighbourhood with assorted wildlife, including a pair of bald eagles, deer, a bear or two, and a tailless raccoon. In the few hours when she's not planning, plotting or writing her next book, her favourite things are photography, knitting her way through a huge yarn stash and driving her restored 1967 Corvette roadster—top down, of course.

Connect with Justine on her website, justinedavis.com, at Twitter.com/justine_d_davis or at Facebook.com/justinedaredavis.

Dear Reader,

Well, here it is. That book you've been waiting for, asking for (okay, demanding), for *years*. I've heard you all, and so did a certain Mr. Crawford, but a more stubborn man I've never met. I interviewed him several times and got very male grunts and nonanswers. Each time I sighed and said to myself it clearly wasn't time yet.

It wasn't all his fault, mind you. It was also mine because I've always had it in my head that Rafe's story would be the last Cutter's Code book, and I was having so much fun with the series I didn't want it to end. But it's been made clear to me by you, the reader (and my editor as well, bless her), that you want more.

But I still had to convince Rafe. And to do that, upon recommendation from a writer friend who understands this weird aspect of writing fiction, I turned to the financial genius behind the Foxworth Foundation. To which Charlie Foxworth said, "It's about time you talked to me."

Despite Charlie's help, which was considerable, I was still iffy. (Hmm, I'm thinking maybe the problem was more *me* than Rafe...) So I went to the real source, the heart of it all, and I interviewed the star himself. And so it was Cutter who finally handed me the key that opened the door.

However you feel about the story, know that I worked harder on it than almost anything I can remember. It's a true labor of love, for a dog—and a man—unlike any other, and my readers, about whom I feel the same way.

Thank you,

*Justine*

# DEDICATION

Justine here, repossessing this space in this rather special book. Not for a goodbye to a much-loved furry one, but for a thank-you to one that only exists in my imagination.

When I wrote the first Cutter's Code book, I had no idea I'd still have this furry rascal in my head and heart seventeen books later. Twelve years, to the month, later. Yet here I am, and here you are, for which I thank you.

And I thank all the people who have contributed their own stories, some sweet, some funny, but always about the sad ending that inevitably comes for all dog lovers, for this dedication space. Sometimes I think dogs' lives are so much shorter than ours because they lavish all that love on us from day one. That doesn't stop me from wondering, When they can breed for size, colour, skills and temperament, why can't they breed a dog who will live twice as long? Heck, three times as long, and it still wouldn't be enough. But that's one thing I can promise about Cutter. There will never be one of those moments where we have to say goodbye because he has to leave us.

So this book is dedicated to all of the readers who have come along on this journey and who have fallen a little bit in love with a certain canine rascal named Cutter.

# Chapter 1

"Seriously?"

Hayley Foxworth knew she was gaping at her husband, but what he'd just told her made her doubt her own perception about many things. And judging by the way he grimaced and shrugged, and the uncharacteristic puzzlement in his ice blue eyes, he was as blown away as she was by the phone call he'd just gotten.

"So it seems."

"Your sister," she enunciated carefully, "your I-don't-have-time-for-such-things sister, is dating a former senator turned power broker with...questionable ethics? And they're coming here? Tomorrow?"

"She's coming here," Quinn said, gesturing to include the Foxworth headquarters building. "He's coming to the city, probably to broker some of that power."

Hayley grimaced in turn. She'd put her long, autumn colored hair in a loose braid today, and now she tugged at it distractedly. She had an opinion, a strong one, about the man in question, Maximilian Flood, often referred to in opposing party quarters as Maxi-million. Her dog, Cutter, must have sensed her mood, because he nudged her hand with his nose. She gave him a quick pat on his dark head but kept her eyes on her husband.

"And she had Ty call and tell you?"

He nodded. "All he knew was that she'd said there was good reason."

"Sometimes," Hayley said with a shake of her head, "your sister plays it a bit too close to the vest. Are we supposed to meet Flood?"

"He said she didn't say."

"And you didn't ask?"

He shoved a hand through his dark hair. "More a case of I didn't want to know. You know Charlie," he said dryly.

"Apparently not," she retorted, "because I can't imagine her with someone like Max Flood. I always hoped someday she and Rafe—"

She broke off abruptly. She didn't want to put into words what she'd always hoped. Quinn's gaze locked onto hers.

"So did I," he said softly.

She drew in a long breath and let it out in an equally long sigh. A moment later she heard a small whine, and looked down to see Cutter looking up at her with an expression she could only describe as worried.

"I know, sweetie," she said as she stroked his head. And for once the sense of comfort the dog always gave was somehow lessened. As if the dog was distressed himself, and had no comfort to spare. He nudged her hand, then her leg, almost knocking her off balance. "Your only failure."

"Don't know if it could be called a failure when he never really got a try."

The dog's dark head moved again, first nudging her leg insistently, then his amber-flecked gaze shifting. Hayley looked that way just in time to see a tall, lean, dark-haired man leaving through the back door she hadn't even heard open.

"Rafe," she whispered, and Quinn froze. She hadn't even realized he'd been there, and apparently the former sniper had moved so quietly Quinn hadn't, either, which was saying something.

Cutter, however, had clearly known. Had been trying to tell them. She'd known the dog had gone over to the hangar to greet him when they'd first arrived, but she hadn't realized Rafe had apparently come back with the dog.

They stood there, staring at the now closed door, wondering how much the Foxworth operative—and their dear friend—had overheard. Anyone else, it wouldn't matter. But Rafe… The man they never mentioned Quinn's sister to, except when it was unavoidable.

"Do you think we'll ever know?" she asked. "What happened with them?"

"Not if he has anything to say about it," Quinn said.

"That's just it. He has absolutely nothing to say about it."

Quinn grimaced as he nodded in acknowledgment of the truth of that statement. "He's as stubborn as—"

"Your sister?"

Quinn let out an audible breath. "At least."

"Funny how the guy who can hide any trace of his feelings about anything else…" Her voice trailed off.

"Can't keep a lid on it when it comes to Charlie?" Quinn asked. "I've noticed."

"Well, at least you don't have to decide whether to tell him," she said with a wry twist of her mouth.

Quinn looked startled, then smiled at her. "Leave it to you to find the bright side."

"I just wish Rafe and Charlie had found it," she said softly.

Quinn reached out and pulled her close. Cutter walked over to the door Rafe had left through and plopped down rather dejectedly. Quinn held her for a long time, and she leaned into him in turn. Finally, as if he'd gotten some signal undecipherable by humans, Cutter got to his feet and headed for the front door. He raised up to bat at the control pad with a front paw, and the door swung open. Hayley knew where the dog was headed.

"He's probably the best thing for him right now," Quinn said. "We'd just make him clam up even tighter."

"Yes," Hayley agreed with a sigh.

She hated it when a friend was in pain and there was nothing she could do about it.

It was worse when that friend refused to admit he was in any pain at all.

She should have paid more attention in drama class.

That was Charlie Foxworth's uppermost thought as she looked out the window of the small, elegant private jet. But she hadn't, because she'd had no interest at all in the onstage performances. No desire to be in the spotlight, with all eyes fastened on her, watching every move, every gesture.

The backstage stuff, now, yes, that had intrigued her. And was why she'd shifted to the stage crew almost right away. The process of building sets, of recognizing how to make something look like something else from an audience viewpoint, preventing any midperformance accidents like a prop missing, or a fake wall falling over. Making it all work behind the scenes—that was what had appealed to her. And still did.

But now here she was, having to act as if she were up front on that stage, having to keep up a facade, pretending to be someone she was not. Having to pretend to feel something she didn't feel. Having to appear infatuated with this man—years older than she was, even if he didn't look it—when in fact she loathed him.

And there was a lot more than applause at the final curtain at stake here.

*It will be worth it.*

She had no doubt about that. Putting an end to three years of searching, of hunting. Finally nailing the guy who had betrayed his word, his country, and most important to her, nearly gotten their team—and Hayley, the woman who had changed her brother's life—killed.

No, her doubts were more personal, as in how long could she keep up the pretense of being enamored by this guy, charmed by his practiced manner, impressed by his easy wielding of power. A power subtly emphasized by the presence of the man who now sat a discreet distance away, yet still facing them. The man who was watchful even now, as if he took no one at face value, even his charge's new…whatever she was. The man she'd seen that first night at the glitzy party, ever present, ever watchful, ever silent, always within reach but never intrusive.

He'd been introduced to her merely as Ducane, although she'd later heard Flood use the name Cort to address him. When she had noticed the wedding ring he wore and found herself wondering what kind of woman it would take to live with this kind of man, a jolt of realization hit her. They looked nothing alike, but there was something about him, some inner quality of strength, intensity and utter control that reminded her of the one man she was forever trying to forget.

"He's rather intimidating," she had said to Flood that night.

"That's his job," the former senator had said dismissively, confirming her guess that he was a bodyguard.

A wise decision, she'd thought, for anyone this high profile.

A necessity, for anyone this high profile involved in unsavory dealings under the surface.

And frankly, she found Flood's unctuous aide, Alec Brown, now seated in the far corner seat, a lot more bothersome. The man was always around, usually at Flood's elbow, and assessing what good anyone they encountered could be to them. Not that Flood didn't do the same, but he was much better at hiding it.

She'd also wondered how long she could put up with that spotlight Flood not only drew but craved, savoring every time he was recognized, photographed or approached with that deference he expected as his due.

"I didn't put in all those years in the Senate to simply fade away," he'd explained. "I have plans, big plans. I'd love to share some of them with you, Lita."

She'd chosen to use the first name Lita—along with Marshall for the last, randomly chosen—on her manufactured ID not just because it had a faintly ethnic sound to it that she knew would fit the man's carefully constructed public image, but because it had been her college roommate's name and she would instinctively react to it if she heard it, in a way she hoped would seem natural. She'd had to use the manufactured ID because if he ever found out who she really was, things could get very ugly very fast. He was many things, including dishonest, corrupt and immoral, but he was not stupid. And he would instantly put together the name Foxworth with that witness protection operation he'd been paid big to sabotage.

And if he did...

*The guy sold crucial info to one of the largest drug cartels, to help them take out the top witness against them. Do you really have any doubts what he'd do to you?*

No, she didn't.

She knew her brother was not going to be happy with

her following this lead personally, without even consulting him, let alone letting him in on the planning. Such as it was. But she'd already had her suspicions, the chance had so unexpectedly appeared, and they'd been hunting this guy for so long, she didn't dare pass it up. She'd had to move and move fast, and Quinn was just going to have to accept it. She'd waited to tell him in person, because it would be harder for him to argue her point face-to-face. Plus, they'd be on his turf, one of the deciding reasons for her. Once she'd found out where Flood was going, she couldn't help feeling it was meant to be.

Quinn could adapt on the fly, he was good at it, one of the best. They both were, because they'd had no choice.

She felt an echo of the old, long-ago grief. That day, when they'd learned a horrific act of terrorism had orphaned them, was etched so deeply into her mind and psyche that she knew it would never fade completely. She thought of it every time she got on an airplane.

Of course, she hadn't spent a lot of time on planes like this. True, she'd spent time on small planes, like the Foxworth plane Quinn had insisted they needed to sometimes reach more remote areas in the Northwest. The Piper Mirage had the benefit of being one of the first ever propeller-driven planes with a pressurized cabin, so she'd seen the attraction. The Northwest was full of mountains, after all.

But as useful as the plane Quinn's team member Liam Burnett had dubbed Wilbur was, this little jet was in another class altogether. Elegantly appointed, sleek inside and out, the six-seater private jet included a lavatory and what the manufacturer called a refreshment center, but she, after perusing the contents, would simply call a bar. At least on Max Flood's version of the aircraft.

Even as she thought the name he was there, back from pacing the small open space near that bar, his phone in one hand held up to his ear, a drink in his other hand. The "crucial" call he'd had to take ended now, he sat in the seat next to her.

"It's begun," he said, his booming voice unrestrained here in this place where he thought it safe, where he thought no opponent would overhear.

*Little do you know, Mr. Flood.*

"What has?"

"The speculation."

There was satisfaction in his voice, the sound of a master planner who was seeing yet another strategy come together. She recognized the feeling—she felt it herself when a major plan worked as she'd envisioned.

"Speculation?" she asked, although she suspected she knew what he meant.

"We were seen at the airport."

She had been right. He hadn't had a headline in at least three days, and that just wasn't acceptable.

"I have to keep up the high profile to maintain my ability to get things done," he'd told her that first evening when she'd asked him, with a shy flutter of eyelashes, how he tolerated being in the public eye all the time.

*Get things done. Right. Like getting a payoff from the head of a huge drug cartel. Gotta pay for this jet somehow, right, Max?*

She tried to rein in the voice in her head, because it made it harder to maintain the necessary facade. But she couldn't quite stop herself from wondering if he'd had the same tone of satisfaction in his voice when he'd seen all the sympathetic headlines after the death of his wife in a car accident a few years ago. By all accounts Alondra Flood had been a good, kind and smart woman, involved in several worthwhile charitable causes, including a couple that were important to Charlie as well. The marriage had seemed pretty solid, publicly at least. She had no idea if Flood had actually loved his wife, but she was certain he hadn't been above using her death to his advantage.

His phone rang again, and he excused himself as he got up and walked back to the more open space where he'd been pacing before. He might be flirting madly with her, and putting on the big show of wealth and influence, topping it off with this flight on his private bird, but he wasn't sharing anything of real importance with her. He was very careful, about everything. Which was only to be expected, after just a few days of knowing her. It was unexpected enough to end up here on his plane.

*I have to fly to Seattle next week, for some meetings.* He'd sounded as if he regretted leaving and looked at her as if she were the reason. He was very smooth.

*It's a beautiful part of the country. I have friends there.* She'd carefully avoided saying family. And as she'd hoped, he bit.

*Then you should come with me. You could visit them while I take care of business.*

She'd put on a show of being doubtful, gotten his assurance—so very charmingly—that he would not push her into anything she wasn't ready for, and she had finally agreed.

She hadn't expected the private jet. And she should have. She should have assumed all his talk about regulations to save the planet was bull.

Or at least, that those regulations did not apply to him.

*Rules for thee, not for me...*

Yes, taking this man down would be worth the effort. And with the full might and resources of Foxworth behind her—she'd built a lot of them after all—she would get it done.

# Chapter 2

*I always hoped someday she and Rafe—*
*So did I.*

He couldn't get the exchange out of his head. None of his usual tactics worked. So Rafer James Crawford simply stood next to the helicopter named Igor and let it batter him.

He'd sensed, on some level, that they knew. Knew something, anyway. Not much got by Quinn, and even less got by Hayley. They might not know the details, but they knew enough. Enough to assess and, as much as they ever did to someone they cared about, to judge.

And they did care about him. He knew that, too. For a long time it had been an odd feeling, one he wasn't comfortable with. He didn't feel…worthy of them caring as much as they did, and he'd always told himself that if they knew the whole story, they wouldn't. But he also knew Quinn carried more than his own share of haunting memories around, and yet here he was, happier than

Rafe had ever seen him. Which Rafe was glad about; no one deserved it more.

But he himself didn't deserve any amount of happy.

Charlie did, though. She deserved to be happy. She worked as hard as or harder than any of them, in the areas none of them understood as well as she did. She had such a knack for knowing when and where to invest, and more importantly when to pull out. Among the many other things she had a knack for.

Including turning him inside out.

It had been a pipe dream from the get-go. It would have been so much easier if he'd stood strong, but he'd weakened, and instead of some vague whisper of unrequited longing, he was lugging around vivid images of something that never should have happened. He never should have let himself—

With tremendous effort, he refused to let his brain careen into the old memories. Memories he couldn't seem to shed.

It was crazy, with everything he'd been through, everything he'd done in his life, all without turning a hair, that she could still do this to him after all this time. He'd spent years in war zones, he'd plunged into battles with as little as ten minutes' warning, he'd made shots some considered impossible, others miraculous. He'd saved lives, a lot of lives, enough to make the fact that he'd done it by taking enemy lives bearable. It didn't haunt him, it had simply been a job he excelled at. It didn't keep him awake at night, because it had had to be done. It didn't send his mind careening down dark, ugly paths, because the fighters he'd saved got to go home to their families.

No, only one thing could do all that to him. One gorgeous brunette with more energy than an entire platoon and blue eyes deep enough to drown in. As he once almost had, before he'd pulled back, before he'd turned his back on the most wanted but least possible thing in his life.

*It would be wrong, and not just because she's Quinn's sister. You have no right to a woman like her. And she has the right to a better man.*

He leaned back against the chopper's solid side panel. The one that carried a carefully tended bullet hole, a souvenir of the mission where Quinn had met the love of his life. The mission that had almost ended up with them all dead thanks to the betrayal of a traitor they had yet to find, three years later. A case anyone would admit had gone cold.

But cold cases were a quiet cause of his. And he'd yet to give up on that one. Someday they would find the man who had sold them out, who had told the drug cartel where to find them. And he would personally see that the man paid.

But even that wasn't enough distraction at the moment. An image of Max Flood popped into his head. Smooth, polished, handsome, with just a touch of gray in thick, brown hair swept artfully back from a still young-looking face that Hayley suggested, long before this, had seen the edge of a plastic surgeon's scalpel. He'd had a rather meteoric rise at a startlingly young age, going from a two-term mayor of a midsize coastal city at twenty-five to a senator with apparent ease. But he had startled people when he'd declined to run for a fourth term in the powerful position.

At least, he'd startled people less knowledgeable and informed than Foxworth.

Rafe had a memory of being at one of the gatherings at Quinn and Hayley's home that he usually tried to dodge, but this last one just a few months ago had been to welcome Foxworth operative—and his friend—Teague Johnson's little sister home and into the fold, after she'd run away at age seventeen thinking her beloved big brother had been killed in action overseas. He remembered the news had been on in the den, and he'd retreated there for a bit of a break from the celebration. He'd found their consulting attorney, Gavin de Marco, there, watching a report on Flood's retirement from office.

They listed the causes he'd espoused, his wins in Congress—including a few that Rafe privately thought had done much more damage than good—and then spoke in hushed voices of the sorrow he'd endured after the death of his beloved wife a couple of years before. This, they concluded, was what had driven him to retire. Even Rafe had to admit he'd felt bad for the guy then, although the public display of grief had seemed a bit over-the-top. But maybe that was because he was a much more private kind of guy.

When the piece had concluded with some more rather fawning adoration, de Marco had snorted in unconcealed disgust.

"Not buying?" Rafe had asked, genuinely curious about what the world-renowned attorney thought of the man.

"He became a senator to build his power infrastructure. Now he figures he's got it in place, it's time to start pulling those behind-the-scenes strings."

"More power than he'd have as a single senator," Rafe had said, unsurprised and pretty much agreeing with the assessment.

He also remembered de Marco looking at him with a slight smile. "Exactly."

And Rafe couldn't deny that having a man on the level of de Marco, who genuinely had walked away from a career most in the world would envy to do what he thought was right, give him that approving look meant a great deal.

And now here he was, having to face the fact this scheming, backroom-style politician—because he had no doubt that de Marco had been right—was coming here to continue his wheeling and dealing.

And that Quinn's sister—he'd long ago found that thinking of her that way helped a little—was coming with him.

*With* him. Because she was dating him.

A faint nausea rose in his gut, as if just the thought had literally turned his stomach. If that was who she wanted, the kind of man she wanted, then it only proved he'd made the right decision. This, finally, should crush this chronic problem of his once and for all. They had been hot, short and impossible. When reality had finally caved in on him, leaving him in shambles, he'd known that. He'd made the best decision and walked away, her protests ringing in his ears. He'd set her free to find someone worthy of her. And had braced himself for the day it happened.

He hadn't been braced for this. Couldn't quite believe it. Couldn't believe that Charlaine Foxworth would really, truly want that...that...

The string of invective that ran through his mind was not helpful. But right now he wasn't sure anything could help.

He slid slowly down the side of the helicopter until he was sitting on the ground beside it. His left leg protested the sharp bend, as it always did. He ignored it, as he always did.

He heard the faint click of the hangar door as it was nudged open. When no one spoke he knew who it was. And looked up to see Cutter heading straight for him. The dog always seemed to know. And seemed, to Rafe at least, to spend a lot of time and energy trying to ease that chronic ache in his leg.

Among other chronic aches.

"You can't fix this one," he murmured to the dog, who sat beside him and rested his chin on that leg, looking up at him with those dark, amber-flecked eyes. "But you sure manage to make the leg feel better." He reached out to stroke the dog's dark head. "Or make me think you do."

He didn't remember exactly when he'd started talking to the dog so much. Crazily, he wanted to say it was when the animal had started demanding it with that unwavering stare. And it didn't really matter. It wasn't like the dog was going to tell anyone he'd been babbling like...like an almost normal person.

But that was all Liam's fault. The other Foxworth Northwest operative who was their in-house tech guy—and who had been hired by Quinn after he'd been caught trying to hack the Foxworth website—had one day mentioned how, as a kid, he'd often talked to the dogs his family raised just to test how things sounded. It worked, somehow, to say things to a living thing that paid attention to you, even if it didn't understand what you were saying.

Of course with Cutter, there was no guarantee at all that he didn't understand every word. And everything he didn't say, too.

He knew how rattled he was when he realized he was serious about that thought. But he wasn't sure how else to explain the dog's almost unnatural awareness of...well, everything. The rest of Foxworth had long ago progressed to simply accepting his instincts. He himself had learned better than to doubt the dog on a case, to doubt the uncanny accuracy of his judgment about cases, circumstances and people. More than once the dog's actions had tipped the case in the right direction, sometimes even blown it wide open.

So far, Cutter had never been wrong. About anything.

Including his other weird, unexpected skill of somehow knowing when two people needed to be together. As if love, or fate, or whatever, had a scent only he could pick up, or threads only he could see. Even Rafe, soured as he was on the subject, as absurd as he'd always thought the idea of soulmates was, couldn't deny that the couples the too-clever dog had brought together seemed rock-solid. Starting with Quinn and Hayley.

Cutter made a soft little sound as he nudged Rafe's hand, urging him to stroke again. Sometimes it simply amazed him how this creature he'd seen, when necessary, turn into a fierce, snarling attack dog, could be so gentle. How he could tell when people needed the comfort he could offer, comfort that somehow seemed to come simply from petting him. Comfort that eventually overwhelmed even Rafe's bone-deep skepticism, and he had to admit that stroking the dog's soft fur relieved...something. Whether it was the mental side, which then eased the physical, or the other way around, he didn't know.

He only knew it happened.

And as Cutter nudged him again, practically crawling into his lap now, he knew he'd needed it at this moment perhaps more than he ever had. Not because of the pain in his leg, but the pain inside, whenever he was face-to-face with the simple fact that Charlaine Foxworth existed.

Only when the image of the dark-haired beauty slipped back into his mind did he realize Cutter had done it again. He'd given him a side trip to take, pondering the dog's unexpected skills and the results, distracting him enough to get his breath back and at least reach for some equilibrium.

"Saving me again, boy?" he murmured.

Cutter whined slightly, something else he did rarely. In fact, did only when the person he was helping—because Rafe didn't even try to deny that anymore—was in a very bad place, physically or mentally. Or both.

This time he reached out and scratched the loving animal behind his ears, which he knew was a favored caress. It wasn't a long reach, not with the dog actually in his lap, now that his legs had straightened out into a more comfortable position. He bent his head to stare at the miracle worker. Cutter reached upward in turn and swiped his tongue over Rafe's chin.

The experienced former Marine, the battle-hardened warrior, the deadly accurate long-range sniper, felt his eyes sting at the simple, loving gesture. And had the thought that the human race would be a lot better off if people would learn from dogs.

# Chapter 3

Charlie looked out the window again as the small jet flew westward toward the distinctive landscape that was the Pacific Northwest. It wasn't the water that would soon be in sight ahead that always caught her attention. In St. Louis, she lived within sight of the Mississippi, and no water in the country was more—just as, perhaps, but not more—significant than that. No, it wasn't the fjord of Puget Sound that struck her most, or the islands that dotted the chilly waters, or the towering evergreens along so many of the shorelines. It was the mountains that surrounded the area, the knowledge that some of those mountains were living volcanoes that could still erupt, and that one had not all that long ago.

She was used to the flats, sometimes seemingly endless, stretching out as far as the eye could see, marked by no more than an occasional slight undulation in the earth. With few exceptions, flat was the rule, and any break in it the exception and unusual enough to be considered a landmark. And there were tall trees, yes, but they were usually birch, maple and the occasional pecan tree. Not that there weren't maple trees here as well, but the landscape was dominated by the trees the state was nicknamed for. And very, very unlike what she was used to.

Very unlike what her brother, Oliver, had been used to, and yet...

She remembered so vividly the day he'd called her. He'd flown out here to set up a new Foxworth office, the first of a planned two on the west coast. It had taken longer than expected, but she'd put it down to the complications of working in a new territory.

"We're set," he'd told her. "Ready to go operative."

"Good. Any problems I need to know about?"

"No. The headquarters is done, the outbuilding nearly so. Met with Teague Johnson, and he's a good fit."

"We'll need more operatives."

"I know. I've...partially solved that."

"Somebody new?"

"In a way." She recalled the deep breath he'd taken then. "I'm staying, Charlie."

"What?"

"I'm going to do my bit from here."

"But you can't—"

"I love this place, sis. I have from the moment I got off the ferry on this side."

She remembered, through her shock, that he'd quickly written off the city of Seattle as a place for them and had widened his search, settling on a small town—or village, actually—on the other side of the sound.

"Quinn—"

"I know, it seems crazy to you, but it felt like coming home, just as much as coming home from overseas when I left the Army did. Maybe even more. All I could think was...so this is where I'm supposed to be."

That fanciful thinking from her practical, ever-efficient brother had given her pause. The certainty in his voice had put the cap on it. And less than two months later it was done—her brother had relocated, leaving her and their small staff to run the main offices of the Foxworth Foundation. And a little to her surprise, as technology progressed—and their resident genius, Tyler Hewitt, had been on the cutting edge of some of it—it had worked.

Quinn had built a great team there. No matter how she felt about one particular member, it was undeniable. The later, unexpected addition of Liam Burnett, the young hacker Ty had caught trying to breach his own considerable firewalls, to the team had completed the four-man roster.

Quinn being Quinn, he'd then quickly set about building goodwill and relationships, establishing the Foxworth mission in the area, and gathering others who believed in the idea of helping the little guy in the right fight the big ones who wanted to stomp him down. With each case that goodwill grew, with each success their pool of helpers widened. Because Foxworth didn't take any payment for their help, except the kind that couldn't be bought—the willingness to somewhere down the line help someone else as they had been helped.

And then, on their biggest mission up until that time, Quinn had encountered Hayley, and his life was changed forever, in the best possible way. So maybe it was meant to be. She was sure Hayley's frighteningly smart dog would think so. She wasn't much on imputing human characteristics onto animals, but that remarkable creature had made her think about it more than once.

A chill rippled down her spine as the thought of that mission, and what had nearly happened, crashed into her musings, erasing all else. She pushed back at the onslaught. Forced herself to remember instead the first time she'd met

Hayley. She'd purposely come on strong, knowing what her brother had probably told the woman.

*So you're the one who thinks she can tame my brother? I don't want him tamed. I love him as he is. And he loves me. So if you hurt me, you hurt him. Don't.*

She'd known in that moment just how right it was, that her beloved brother had found a woman to match him.

The memory served its purpose, and the chill receded. She gave herself an inward shake. She needed to focus on her own mission, on why she was here. The man coming back to sit beside her again.

The man she suspected was the mole they'd been chasing for three years.

"Sure you don't want to blow off those friends and come with me?" he asked as he fastened his seat belt and indicated she should do the same, as they would be landing soon. "I could introduce you to a lot of movers and shakers."

She put on her best smile. "Oh, I couldn't do that. I haven't seen them since the last time I was here, over a year and a half ago."

"What was that trip for?"

"A wedding," she said, carefully omitting that it had been her brother's wedding. As far as Max knew, she had no family, and she intended to keep it that way. A man who would do what she strongly suspected he'd done wouldn't hesitate to use any leverage he could find, if there was something he wanted.

"And that's who you're going to go see?"

"Among others, yes."

Others. She had a lot of new others to meet. Teague's wife, Laney. Liam's wife, Ria. And Gavin's fiancée, Katie. She never would have expected Gavin to leave St. Louis, either, and yet here he also was, in this so very different place. All of them happier than ever.

A happiness she was certain she would never find.

And that fact could be laid at the boots of one person, and one person only. The one person she hadn't allowed into her thoughts about this trip. The one person she couldn't allow in, because it would shake her concentration.

*Shake? How about destroy?*

"—after you've finished your visit."

She snapped back to the present, a present that confirmed the thought she'd just had. Rafe Crawford was deadly to her focus.

And her heart.

The heart she would never again risk, because of him.

"That can wait," Quinn said.

"It needs to be done. I'll just pick up the parts—"

"They can ship them."

Rafe had to consciously relax his jaw muscles. "They're just down in Salt Lake City. Only take two, maybe three days."

"And they can ship the parts in the same amount of time. Try again."

Quinn was looking at him as if he knew exactly what was going on. And maybe he did know. Just because he'd never discussed it with him didn't mean Charlie hadn't. And it would be like Quinn to never mention it, even if she had. Unlike his interfering dog, Quinn was a big believer in letting nature take its course.

Then again, Hayley seemed like a mind reader half the time, so maybe that was where Quinn was getting this.

"All right," he said, his voice rougher than he would have preferred. "Then I'll be at the airport. Wilbur needs some attention."

This, at least, was true. The plane—that Liam had named after one of the Wright brothers, just as he'd named Igor after the man who'd pretty much invented helicopters—hangared at the small airport about thirty miles south, a few miles from the Naval shipyard, did need some regular maintenance done. A lot of the time they got the crew there to do it, but if things at Foxworth were slow, as they'd been in the three weeks since their last case, he did it himself.

"Is it that bad?" Quinn asked quietly. "That you can't even be in the same room with her?"

His jaw tensed again. "Maybe it's her…companionship I can't be around." It was a dodge, he knew it was, but it was better than admitting Quinn had been exactly right. There was no way in hell he could stomach seeing her with a man like that.

*Be honest, if nothing else. With any man.*

"Can't blame you for that," Quinn said, surprising him. "But he's not coming over with her."

*But she came here with him…*

With one of the greatest efforts of his life, he closed the door—no, mentally slammed it—on that twisted, beaten part of him. For good. Because if that's the kind of man she wanted, it just proved he'd done the right thing all those years ago.

"Are you ordering me to stay?" he asked flatly.

Quinn studied him for a long, silent moment. Then, finally, he let out an audible breath. "No."

Relief flooded him. He had such respect for this man, not just for the incredible soldier he'd been but for what he'd built out of his massive, personal grief—and what Quinn had done for he himself, pulling him out of a morass that likely would have been the end of him—that he would have obeyed. He would have hated every minute of it, but he would have done it. And he knew that Quinn knew that.

Which was likely the reason he hadn't, in the end, made it an order.

And so Quinn Foxworth saved him once more. This time from coming face-to-face with the one thing that haunted him more than anything he'd ever done—or not done—in his life.

# Chapter 4

"So what is it you're hoping to accomplish here?" Charlie asked, trying to make her voice sound simply interested.

"Adjusting relationships, mostly," Max said with that wide, practiced smile. "These are people I've dealt with before, but things are different now."

"Because you're no longer in office?"

"Yes."

She considered her next words carefully, and put on her most innocently curious expression and as much concern as she could manage into her voice when she spoke. "Are you worried these people won't deal with you any longer, now that you're not...in an official position to help them?"

He smiled again, and this time it was as if she were a student who'd correctly answered a question. "That's exactly what I'm here to clarify with them. That without the constraints of office, I can help them more than ever."

*For a price, no doubt.*

"At least you left on your terms," she said, trying to sound proud of the fact that he had retired, not been booted out.

He flashed that camera-ready smile that he so often used. Be it friend or foe, that smile was always handy. Friend, and it was welcoming, grateful and all things warm. Foe, and it was amused, belittling and pitying. And the man had it down, she had to give him that.

*Which one did you wear when you were selling out Vicente Reynosa? When you told the cartel when and where the only witness against them would be moved and by who? When you made the deal that almost got my brother and his team killed? When you almost got the only man I—*

She cut off her own thoughts sharply. It did no good to think of that now. She was nearly certain she knew what the man beside her now was. And the more time she spent with him, the more certain she became that the connection Ty had found was real and solid.

They'd been down many dead ends in this search before, too many. They'd spent time and resources, had actually come across more than a couple of people who had done illegal or hideous things and ended up making them face their crimes, but none thus far had been the man they truly sought.

But her gut was telling her Max Flood was. She never claimed to have the instincts her brother had, both innate and honed by years in the military, but when it came to business and businessmen, as this man essentially was, her instincts might be even better. And if she were looking to make a genuine investment, one that would benefit the Foxworth Foundation's continuing work, she would rather stuff the money in a mattress. Better yet, under Cutter's bed, because he'd keep it far safer than Maximilian Flood would.

"I'm very glad you decided to come with me," he said with that charming smile, yanking her out of her ruminations. She'd best stop that, because the inward anger she was feeling was going to show. She called up the practiced mask she used in financial negotiations. She had to make him believe she was flattered, pleased to be here with him. Just as she'd had to occasionally convince a start-up or already successful business that Foxworth was exactly the quiet partner they needed.

"It was so kind of you to offer the ride in this lovely plane of yours. It's much more convenient and pleasant."

His smile widened. She bit back an additional comment about the state of commercial air traffic these days, because Ty's in-depth dive had told her he was not only on the board of one of the major airlines—added the week after he'd retired from the Senate, so clearly long planned in advance—but was a large investor as well. Hidden well, many layers deep, but that was the kind of thing Ty Hewitt excelled at; there had never been anything yet hidden so deep he couldn't find it eventually. One of the best things she'd ever done was to pull that guy out of the downward spiral he'd been in after his parents had been murdered and put him to work on bringing the people responsible to justice. That had resulted in a genius talent who was loyal to Foxworth to the bone.

The talent who had found, buried deep, the link between a shell corporation Flood was connected to and another shell that, even deeper down, was the "legitimate" front that washed the cartel's drug cash. The link of a sizable transfer of funds the week before Foxworth had set out to transport the one witness who could take down that cartel. And had.

But that hadn't been enough for Ty. He'd kept going. And eventually, on one of the several deep-dive searches he'd done, he'd made a connection that sealed the deal for her.

Charlie let a bit of the pleasure she felt over that show in her smile. If Max thought she was enamored already—which he likely would, given his assessment of his own charms—all the better.

"Once I'm through with these meetings, we can spend some time together," Max said, responding to that expression on her face.

"That would be lovely," she said. *I hope I spend it watching them take you away.*

"And of course, you'll come with me to the big party Friday night," he said, as if granting an award to a lesser being.

"I would be honored."

She managed to get it out fairly evenly, despite the faint nausea that churned at the idea. She could only imagine some of the people who would be there. As if being with Flood wasn't bad enough. Adding in some of the likely guests at that exclusive gathering, it would be enough to make her truly want to vomit. There might not be a shower long enough or sufficient soap to make her ever feel clean again if she had to spend too much time among those top feeders.

She let out the smile inspired by their uncle's long-ago phrase, which he'd coined to describe the ones at the top, who fed upon those below them, who in turn fed on the next level down, and then the next, until you got down to the last ones fed upon, the everyday folks who had no power or influence worth taking or using, the ones who were not users but only used.

The kind of people Foxworth now helped.

"You go have a good time with your country friends," he said, managing to keep it to just a touch of condescension in his voice, "then I'll introduce you to a different group of people."

He didn't say "better," but she heard it in his tone and read it in his expression. And she knew that to him, anything that wasn't wall-to-wall skyscrapers with a Starbucks on every corner was "country," and anyone who voluntarily lived there had to be what he'd call a hick.

"Sounds fascinating," she said. And meant it, in the same way watching a gathering of sharks was fascinating.

Yet again his phone rang, only this time they were close enough to landing that the pilot had given the seat belt notification, so he stayed put as he pulled it out and answered, although he gave her a sideways look. She wondered if his careful responses, mostly yes, no, and "It can wait until I land in a few minutes," were trimmed because of her presence, within earshot.

To show him she was paying no attention to his private call, she took out her own phone as if to make a last check for messages before they had to put them into airplane mode for the landing. As far as Flood knew, she was a mid-level advisor at a small financial firm; they'd stuck close to her real life experience so she could believably field any questions tossed at her. And if he had checked, as she suspected he or someone on his still sizable staff had, they would find a comfortably successful business that made good money for their clients.

There were no messages, and she'd known there wouldn't be, because this was not her actual daily use phone. That one, with her real name and contact list, was safely locked up at home, while she carried this one in the name of the non-existent Lita Marshall, with a list of contacts that didn't really exist, either. It had been carefully tailored, the business side populated with fake names that would ring through with a warning to Ty if dialed, and the personal side with almost all female names, since her story to Flood had been that she had no family left—she didn't want him to have that leverage—and was not in a relation-ship at the moment.

Any call to one of the numbers listed would take her someplace else, depending on the name. And any call she made to any of those private numbers would trigger an alert telling them what was incoming, and to speak as if she were truly Lita Marshall.

So she only had to remember the system she and Ty had concocted. Tina Hartford—the T.H. matching Ty's initials—would reach Ty's private number. Luna Bick-ford would reach Quinn, the initials she would happily tell him stood for Little Brother. Heather Cox was for Hayley's maiden name of Cole, and Lea Dallas was for their resident tech guy, Texan Liam Burnett, who'd worked well with Ty before. Teague Johnson was Marnie Johnson, the last name being common enough to keep, and the first name an anagram of Marine. The plan she hoped Quinn would go along with when she explained was, if anyone other than she herself called any of the guy's numbers, they'd react as a relative or significant other of the fake woman, and then get Hayley on the line to cover.

She refused to think about the other name Ty had in-sisted be included, and that she couldn't insist be excluded without explanations she did not want to and would not make. So she'd picked Raine because it seemed appropri-ate, and kept Crawford as a reminder not to ever let down her guard.

All of this preparation was, of course, useless until she had the chance to tell Foxworth Northwest about this new system in person, away from any of Flood's nationwide army of connections and informants. Ty had told her the man had an impressive crew monitoring and tracking all sorts of phone, internet, website and email activity. On one level it could be passed off as just being a good representative of his constituents, and knowing what they wanted and cared about.

But Flood's network went far beyond that, digging into things he had no business knowing. Violating privacy to an extreme that had brought this about, the switch in phones and her not telling her brother what was going on until she could tell him face-to-face. Once everyone was read in, then they could proceed.

To cover her actions, she actually wrote a text to "Tina" to let Ty know they were about to land. He answered quickly with Can't wait to see you! and a smiley emoji that was very un-Ty-like, but very fitting for the fictional Tina.

For a moment she allowed herself a bit of pride at what she'd helped build. That people who'd suffered as she and Quinn had—losing their parents at such a young age and then having to watch as the cause of it walked free after some backroom deal between people who didn't care who was hurt—that people who'd tried to fight for what was right and been outnumbered or out-influenced, that Foxworth could help those people, meant so much to her. She and Quinn had found a calling few had in life, something that was more fulfilling than anything else she could imagine. It didn't make up for the loss they'd suffered, but it made the loss mean something.

And she'd helped build it.

*You've got the money brain, Charlaine. Use it.*

Uncle Paul had told her that when she'd graduated high school. He always called her by her full name, he said to honor her parents, his brother Charles and his wife, Elaine, for whom she was named. She appreciated the thought, even if she much preferred Charlie, if only for the assumptions it frequently led to, assumptions she then had the fun of blasting to pieces.

His advice had sent her on to college to learn just that—

how to make the sizable insurance payout their parents had made certain of, and that their slightly awkward but honest to the core uncle had refused to touch for himself even as he provided them a home, do nothing but grow in the long run. It just seemed to come naturally to her, that knowledge of what to do, where to invest and, probably more importantly, when to pull out.

And because of that, Foxworth had grown from one office helping a few people a year to five helping dozens, from small but personally crucial things to much bigger things. Like Quinn and his crew taking down a sitting governor for murder.

She was proud of him for that. But then, she was proud of him for just about everything he'd accomplished. Especially his priorities, and that he'd considered the recovery of a treasured locket holding the image of a child and her deceased mother, and getting it back to that child, just as important as any other case. She'd like to think she had a part in that, in making him the amazing man he was, since she'd been the closest thing he'd had to a mother since she'd been fourteen when their lives had been nearly destroyed.

And now she was going to hand him a gift he richly deserved. The name of the mole they'd been hunting for three years.

The man who was sitting smugly beside her right now.

# Chapter 5

If he worked a little slower than usual, maybe even took a break now and then, he could stretch this maintenance work out to two or, if he did a full exterior cleaning, even three days.

Rafe rubbed his stubbled jaw as he considered it. He had been in such a rush to get away he hadn't bothered to shave. Now he looked up at the sleek little aircraft. He didn't mind flying in this. Airplanes, after all, essentially wanted to fly by design. And unless interfered with by an outside force—weather or man-made—or an inside one in the form of a bungling pilot or poor maintenance, it would fly. Even if that meant gliding to an unplanned and perhaps ungraceful landing.

Igor the helicopter, on the other hand, wanted to tear himself apart.

"With Wilbur, you enjoy the flight," Quinn, who flew them both, had once said. "With Igor, you enjoy having survived the flight."

Rafe did a mental inventory. He had both his go bags in the trunk of his slightly battered and surreptitiously powerful car. One a standard backpack with survival necessities, the other what he called his gear bag, and others called his arsenal. He could easily sleep on the plane. He was too tall to enjoy sleeping in one of the seats, even reclined, but he could sack out on the floor easily enough. It wouldn't be comfortable, but at least he could stretch out. He'd slept in worse places. Much worse.

As for eating, the stuff available in the airport lounge would get him by during the day, and it so happened the place whose retro decor made him smile wasn't too far away. He could easily live on Crazy Eric's burgers for dinner for a few days.

*Maybe stretch it out into a week, huh, Crawford? You want to be sure she's not only not at headquarters, but not even in the state, maybe?*

The self-directed derision made him regain his focus on the matter at hand. So, feeling he'd solved the immediate problem, he went back to work. The winterization process wasn't due until November, but that didn't mean he couldn't do a few things now. He knew Quinn, knew that he'd never take a plane out in any season without having checked it out completely himself, but he also knew Quinn counted on his help keeping the plane airworthy. Especially in winter when things like the deicing system, heater and carbon monoxide detector were crucial. Quinn was not one to let a little weather stop a flight that needed to be made, so Rafe made sure to have the oil changed out to a more winter-suited type, and that the fuel tanks were full to prevent the buildup of condensation.

But that was for weeks from now. Right now he just needed enough to do to keep him here until the threat was over. And that quickly he was back in the morass he'd just climbed out of.

*Just when did you become such a coward?*

He laughed silently, sourly, his head ringing with the bitter tone of it. He knew exactly when he, the guy they'd hung a boxful of medals on, had become just that, a coward. When he who had faced down battalions could no longer find the nerve to face down one single human being.

But knowing didn't help him get past it.

Nothing helped. And he was convinced now that it would stay that way. The only real solution would be to leave Foxworth. And he couldn't, wouldn't do that. Foxworth had pulled him out of a hole so deep he'd almost been lost forever. So he considered the pain, the embarrassment of admitting his own cowardice, simply the price he had to pay for this job with colleagues he trusted completely and for a man he admired beyond all others.

Determinedly he reached out and opened the top of the rolling toolbox.

"All right, Wilbur," he muttered aloud. "Let's get to it."

Cutter was the first to greet her when she arrived.

She knew Quinn or someone would have come to pick her up, but she didn't trust that Flood didn't have someone watching her. And so she'd rented a car on the city side—it seemed rideshare had yet to spread thoroughly on this more rural side of the sound—and taken the ferry over.

Normally she would have relied more on her admittedly prodigious memory than the vehicle's GPS to get her here from the landing, but for that same reason she'd taken the most convoluted route she could, until she was certain no one was following her. So it had taken her twice as long as it usually would have to reach the inconspicuous dark green building masked by a thick stand of almost matching evergreens. Those tall, majestic conifers she was so unused to back home, except perhaps when their much shorter cousins appeared for sale at Christmas.

She hadn't even gotten out of the rental before the front door swung open. She remembered how crazy she'd first thought it—that they'd installed an access pad on the front door mainly for the dog, who had learned what it was and how to operate it by batting at the pad with his front paws in a matter of a minute. It had been her first inkling that what they'd told her about the dog—which from a distance, without having ever met the animal, had seemed like something out of a fanciful kid's movie—was actually true.

She'd been even more doubtful about them seeming to accept that the dog had some sixth sense about finding people who needed Foxworth help. But after about the fourth or fifth case file she'd read, she'd had to admit every person he'd brought to them had been a prime example of the reason they'd started the foundation.

Her feet had barely hit the gravel of the parking area before Cutter was through the door. The dog seemed to remember her, even after the twenty months—nearly two years!—it had been since Quinn and Hayley's wedding. He came charging out of the headquarters building, dark head up, reddish-brown tail wagging in welcome. She'd never had a dog herself, so didn't quite understand why the sight made her want to smile.

And when he skidded to a halt in front of her, tongue lolling happily as he looked up at her expectantly, almost smiling—gads, she was getting as bad as they were, attributing human characteristics to a dog—she wasn't able to resist bending to pat him on the head.

With a little snap it came back to her the moment her fingers touched the soft fur. That unexpected warmth, the soothing feeling of…comfort, somehow, as if everything would be all right.

She'd noticed it when she first met the animal, and Hayley had told her pretty much everyone felt it, and that was why she'd gotten Cutter certified as a therapy dog to visit local hospitals and nursing homes. That had gotten Charlie thinking about therapy dogs, and why they seemed to work. Which had in turn led her to making a sizable Foxworth donation to a local charitable group who trained and arranged for them to work with injured veterans. In a moment of whimsy, she'd done it in the name of Cutter Foxworth, and had sent the resulting donor acknowledgment to Quinn as a joke. Her brother hadn't laughed. He'd merely told her with a nod, "Good idea."

"You are the most interesting creature," she murmured to the animal, who sat giving her a rather intense look with those dark eyes that seemed flecked with tiny spots of gold. Just as she remembered from that last day she'd been here in this surprisingly lovely, peaceful place.

She hated that it had been so long, but the wedding—that beautiful, heartfelt ceremony so full of love and joy—had been a strain for her, and she'd needed some recovery time after she'd had to table her own feelings about the best man.

Except the one time when she hadn't been able to keep her emotions on a leash and had let out a snide, "You're the best man he could get?"

His quiet retort had chilled her. "I'm nobody's best man."

That exchange, in the moments before the ceremony had actually begun, could have been overheard by anyone there had it been any louder. And that alone had enabled her to rein it in. Not for anything would she ruin this day of joy and beauty for her beloved brother.

Not even to dig at the man who'd walked away from the possibility of the same thing for them.

The man whom she dared hope was not here now.

"I'm sure there's a reason you didn't want us to come get you?"

She straightened quickly to look at the tall, strong, dark-haired man approaching. The man with icy blue eyes that always made her heart give a little kick, they looked so much like Dad's. Sometimes, when she hadn't seen her brother in person for a while, she forgot just how impressive he was.

"Glad to see you, too, brother mine," she said, smiling to see him despite the circumstances.

He smiled back at her and enveloped her in a warm hug. Then he put his hands on her shoulders and held her where he could look into her face. His smile faded. "What is it, Charlie?"

She drew in a deep breath and let the words tumble out. "I found him, Quinn. I found him."

# Chapter 6

Rafe was ankle deep in parts and tools and oil when his Foxworth phone sounded an in-house communication. His first reaction was to freeze in place. He just stood there for a moment, his jaw tight as the signal echoed in his ears. The three-bladed prop, looking like what it was, ready to chew the air—or anyone in its way—on command, took up the edge of his vision. It was a long moment before he turned away.

Then he started toward the wheeled tool chest that stood open next to the sleek nose of the small aircraft, where he'd set the phone. He had the sudden, stupid wish that it was at the far end of the over six-thousand-foot runway. Three times what the Mirage needed to take off, but a small fraction of the distance he was wishing for now.

He set down the socket wrench he held with much more care than the tough tool needed. He grabbed the rag from atop the chest and wiped at his oily hands. Thought about buying another minute or two by washing his hands before picking up the unwelcome device.

*Always on a tether, always reachable, never alone.*

With a sharp reminder that that tether was his connection to the man who had saved him from what likely would have been a steady downward spiral, he dropped the rag and tapped the phone's screen. A text message came up. Short, blunt.

Return to HQ. Now.

Quinn was never wordy with these things, but that was brusque even for him. Possibilities started to slam into his mind, each one worse than the one before. He assumed Quinn's sister had arrived. Had she brought Flood with her, after all? Was he supposed to come meet the power broker and—he almost gagged on the thought—be polite?

Or was something else going on? Had she brought bad news? Some kind of financial trouble for Foxworth? As sharp as she was in that area it was hard for him to believe she'd made a mistake of any size. But then it was hard for him to believe she ever made serious mistakes.

Except one.

*Yes, her biggest mistake was ever thinking you were something you aren't.*

But then, she'd always thought that. Even when they were kids. She'd thought he was...like them. Steady, strong and basically balanced.

He knew better.

It was hard for him sometimes, to even remember those early days. Back when the Foxworths had lived down the block, when they ran into each other at various locations and functions. It seemed a dream now, those long-ago days before a terrorist had blown up so many lives, including Quinn's and Charlie's. Charles and Elaine Foxworth had always been kind to him, welcomed him into their home. Back when life had been simple, and admittedly pretty easy.

At least at their home; his own had been decidedly less comfortable. His mother had done her best, but a single mom's life was never easy. Had it not been for Charles Foxworth he would never have known what the influence of a stable and loving husband and father could be.

When they had both been killed in that horrible terrorist attack, he'd vowed to do something, and as soon as he'd been old enough he had. He'd enlisted in the Marines, determined to strike back, and had found his life skill, his calling. And if he ever wavered, if the fact that that calling was essentially to kill ever bothered him, he simply took the day he'd last seen them alive, cheerful and loving, and mentally juxtaposed it with the gruesome, smoking aftermath of the attack that had killed them and so many others.

He had no idea how long he'd been standing there lost in that haze when a second buzz from the phone snapped him out of the miasma that only trying to avoid thinking about Charlie could plunge him into. He looked down at the screen again.

That IS an order.

His gut tightened. Whatever was going on, Quinn didn't say that lightly. He sent back a single word.

Copy.

He did the tasks of putting away tools and supplies, securing them, then the plane, and at last the hangar itself as if by rote, the main part of his energy diverted into trying to control his racing imagination. This was not a problem he usually had, and again, only Charlie could bring it on.

It was only when he was back in the car and headed out of the airport that the other possibilities hit him. Was there some other reason she was here? Did she have some other bad news? Was she maybe…sick? Had she gotten some horrible health news?

He couldn't even process that one. The idea of Charlie, strong, smart, tough, fearless, and utterly gorgeous Charlie Foxworth brought low by some disease seemed as impossible to him as if the Mirage had blown up while just sitting there quietly.

The memory of the last time he'd seen her in person crashed, unwelcome, into his mind, as clear and vivid as if she were standing before him now as she had then. Her incredible dark hair tumbling down in thick waves, only slightly controlled by a sort of tiara thing that matched that sleek, silky blue dress, the same blue of the wedding decor, as she served as Hayley's maid of honor to his best man. A blue that made her already bright blue eyes glow in a way that had made his pulse kick up to ridiculous levels.

Only by focusing on his ceremonial task—and the pure love and joy glowing from both Quinn and Hayley—had he gotten through that day. Especially walking with her arm in arm down the aisle formed by the chairs laid out neatly in the meadow on that day, a day fate had gifted the bride and groom with what the locals called a severe clear winter day, bright, sunny, almost gilded. Only appropriate, he'd thought at the time, since no one deserved it more than those two. And after all, wasn't people getting what they deserved, good and bad, what Foxworth was all about?

"We set this aside today," she had said to him in the last moments before the ceremony had begun. Ironically, as she demanded peace she had sounded determined enough to fight him if necessary. It wasn't necessary, because he'd agreed completely.

"Yes. Today only Quinn and Hayley matter."

And they'd gotten through it. He knew how well when Hayley had whispered to him, just before they'd left for their honeymoon, "Thank you for the best gift of all."

He'd blinked at her. "What?"

"The truce."

He'd looked away then and repeated what he'd said to Charlie. And meant it. This was their day and they were the only ones who mattered.

Only after they'd gone and the guests had cleared out had he been left to deal with memories inspired by knowing instinctively what an amazing honeymoon these two would have. Because it would probably be as intense, as amazing, as incredibly hot as a certain three months of his own life had been. Months that had begun—

A rabbit darted across the road, and he barely managed not to hit it. It snapped him back to the present.

*Focus, Crawford. If you were on a mission you'd probably be dead already.*

The fact that he'd almost rather be dead than face Charlaine Foxworth again was something he tried to ignore.

# Chapter 7

*Damn it.*

Charlie didn't swear often, but she couldn't help it this time. She also couldn't quite believe that even now he had that effect on her. Just watching him get out of the silver coupe down at the far end of the drive and start walking toward the headquarters building had her pulse in over-drive. It was the same effect he'd had on her since Quinn had brought him to her as a potential Foxworth operative.

The very first hire, in fact, after they'd decided they needed more than just her and Quinn to get everything they wanted to accomplish done.

After the tragedy that sent them to live with Uncle Paul, they'd lost track of the neighbor boy. They'd had enough to do to survive what had happened and adjust to their new, painful reality. She knew Quinn had missed his friend, but it had taken a back seat to simply surviving the hideous truth of their lives now. And the more time that passed, the more unreal that sweet, innocent life before had become.

That had made the shock when Quinn had come face-to-face with him more than a decade later even greater.

"It was Rafe," he'd told her, shock echoing in his voice over the phone on the overseas call.

"Rafe? Crawford? The boy from down the street?"

"Yes. He's the Marine sniper who saved us, on that mission that went haywire. He took out nearly every man in that nest we stumbled into, giving us time to get clear. And he did it from so far away they couldn't even begin to find him."

Inwardly she was still processing exactly who that expert sniper had been, but had managed a tone of mock horror when she'd said, "Is this my Army-to-the-core brother, admitting a Marine is good?"

The horror she felt at her beloved brother coming that close to death was anything but mock. She remembered the incident all too well, how the intelligence had failed them completely on where the terrorists were hiding, and they'd practically walked right into their hideout.

She knew how, after that harrowing incident, Quinn had pushed to meet the man who'd pulled off those deadly accurate shots that had saved them, the man who had volunteered to do it simply because he was in the area and was their best chance. Then only to discover it was the childhood friend he'd lost track of, the boy from down the block…

A boy who had never had much effect on her—then—at all. He'd just been a friend of Quinn's she found slightly less annoying than his other friends. Mainly because he was quieter, apparently by nature. And that nature was also apparently well suited to selective killing of the enemy, an idea she couldn't deny gave her a little chill.

"He's better than just good," Quinn had told her. "He's got his name on the highest level sniper trophy there is, twice. He got banged up on his last mission, almost lost a leg, and he's still working through that. But he's functional, and if I know him he'll stay that way, whatever it takes."

She'd felt the same pang she always did when she heard one of the country's warriors had paid such a price—which was why veteran's organizations were one of Foxworth's primary interests—but that this was someone she knew personally made it...well, more personal.

Then Quinn had delivered the decisive words. "Charlie...he enlisted because of what happened to Mom and Dad. He said they were always so nice and kind to him. He felt...it was a way to pay them back a little."

She'd had no words for how that made her feel. And a couple of years later, when Quinn was thankfully safely home and they were building the Foxworth Foundation into something their parents would approve of, he had come to her with the idea of hiring Rafe, who was also back home now. Back home, but not doing as well.

"We need more help, and he..." Her confident, fearless brother had hesitated then, and that was enough to make her zero in on his next words. "He needs this. We need him, especially if we're going to build out the way you want to, but he needs this, too. He could probably get a job with any private security firm in the world, with his record, but...he needs a cause he can believe in, before he goes completely off the rails. I can't explain it, but I know Foxworth is right for him."

She would have agreed to hiring him without the argument, simply because of what he'd done, saving her from losing the last of her family. And it was only later that Quinn had told her how he'd found Rafe after a long search, in an encampment of homeless vets under a bridge. Although Rafe himself hadn't fallen quite that far, having a small, rented room, it had only been a matter of time. Quinn had told her he barely recognized the man from that surprising reunion overseas, not with long, shaggy hair and a beard sporting a couple of spots of silver gray. But he'd recognized the haunted gray eyes and knew the look of a man who carried too many lingering memories.

But the Rafe he'd finally reintroduced to her had been a different man altogether—tall, rangy, clean-shaven, the only trace of civilian about him the couple of strands of dark, thick hair that tended to drop down over his forehead. That he'd once been the kid she remembered didn't even seem possible. Until she looked at his eyes. She had remembered those seemingly fathomless gray eyes, which even as a kid had seemed too old for his young face.

The possibility of putting his skills to use helping people who deserved it, people who had been wronged by another, or by the system itself, had clearly put new life into those eyes. Eyes that had an entirely different effect on the grown-up her. And the grown-up her had, as she never had with anyone before, reacted to him on three fronts—mentally, emotionally and, to her chagrin, physically—before he'd ever said a word. And when he did speak, that low, rumble of a voice had tipped her over the edge.

And for the first time in her life she had wanted, on a primal level.

And damn him, she still did. Even after what he'd done, the way he'd thrown them away as if what happened between them was no more than the fling he'd cuttingly called it. And when Quinn had headed here to the Northwest to set up this office, Rafe had gone with him. And stayed, demonstrating without saying a word that he wanted to be as far away from her as he could. He'd denied it, said he liked it here because it was about as far from desert as you could get. But she'd known that was only part of it. Known he hadn't wanted to be in St. Louis any longer because she was there, and as long as he was working for Foxworth, they would have to be in almost daily contact.

So she'd lost him first, and then Quinn had fallen in love with this cool, damp, forested place and decided to stay and she'd lost him, too.

As the thought formed and the emotions tried to well up yet again, she felt a nudge on her hand. She looked down and saw Cutter, looking up at her with an expression she could only describe as concerned, ridiculous as that was. Automatically she stroked the dark fur of his head. And couldn't deny the calming effect of it.

Calming enough for her to mutter to herself, *Well, aren't you just a puddle of self-pity?*

With an effort she buried all the tangled emotions. This was too important to let her stupid, apparently inescapable feelings get in the way. She gave Cutter another pat. "Thanks," she said, feeling a bit silly even as she said it. For all his undeniable cleverness, he was a dog, after all. But this must be why he'd succeeded at being a therapy dog.

*And a matchmaker?*

She nearly laughed out loud when that popped into her mind. She might have to admit the dog was smart, well-trained and had great instincts, but the matchmaker they talked of was a bridge too far. Or was it? Since she'd last been here, Hayley's brother Walker and her best friend, Amy, had married. Teague and Cutter's groomer, Laney, had married. Liam had married the schoolteacher he'd met on a case. Most shocking of all to her, after working closely with him before he, too, had decided to stay here permanently—what was it about this place?—even Gavin was engaged.

And that wasn't counting all the cases where people they'd helped had ended up with what Hayley called—without a trace of whimsy—their soul mate in the process.

The bemusement she felt at the idea helped her regain some modicum of equilibrium.

"Shall we give you two a few minutes alone?"

She didn't quite jump at Hayley's quiet question; she'd heard her coming down the stairs from the office/meeting room level, where she assumed Liam and Teague were still gathering information. Still, she hadn't expected the offer. She'd never admitted even to her brother what had happened between her and Rafe. But then, Hayley had an uncanny way of sensing what other people were thinking or reacting to. Almost as uncanny as her dog.

She turned to meet her sister-in-law's gaze. It was kind, understanding and gentle, as it always was when she knew someone was troubled. She had come to both love and respect this woman who had made her brother's life so much more simply by loving him.

"I think it would be better if you didn't," she said wryly, not denying or admitting anything. But Charlie suddenly and unexpectedly wished she'd confided in this warm, caring woman long ago. Perhaps she could tell her how to rid herself once and for all of this stupid, energy-wasting infatuation with a man who didn't want her.

It was not, as some would assume, an ego thing. She was more than used to men who were drawn by her looks, and she knew just how shallow a connection that could be. But she believed, with all her heart, that she'd found a connection so much deeper than that with Rafe. It had been as if her soul had been healed at last from the devastation her parents' tragic, horrible deaths had wrought.

And then he'd walked away. No, he'd run. To this far edge of the country, where he'd stayed except when a case demanded he return. And even then he went out of his way—sometimes far out of his way—to avoid having to be in the same room with her, and even farther out of his way to avoid being alone with her.

What would he do now? Try to dodge yet again? Or maybe just give her that cool stare that could turn a room to ice. The stare that always left her trying to convince herself it wouldn't be quite that cool unless he still felt…something.

She had no idea which way this would go, and she determinedly decided it didn't matter. Just as Quinn and Hayley's wedding had been, this was more important than their personal clash. And given he'd been one of the ones under fire thanks to Flood's machinations, he would likely see it the same way.

He'd better.

"All right, not alone, then," Hayley said. "But keep in mind Cutter doesn't like it when two of his family are at odds."

"Neither do I," she said, as close as she could come to admitting she was not now and had never been happy with the state of affairs.

And that she'd even thought the word *affair,* even in a totally different context, irritated her. But then, she'd never thought of what had happened between them as simply an affair. For her it had been much more, it had been dreams made reality, a happiness she'd never even dared hope to feel.

It had been Rafe who'd thrown it away so lightly.

*Which makes you an idiot, for believing in some foolish, little girl fantasy of a happy ending.*

She heard Quinn coming down the stairs from the office level. Resisted the urge to flee up to that third floor herself, right now. She felt Cutter's nose nudge her again. She petted him again, just to see if it would have the same effect. It did; she felt the calming, the soothing. It just wasn't enough to cancel out the boil that was beginning inside her.

It was enough to steady her, though, and that would have to do.

She murmured a thank-you to the animal, even as she felt a little silly doing it. Cutter swiped his tongue over her fingers, giving her the strangest feeling he understood both the thank-you and how she felt giving it.

Then, as if he'd sensed she was as composed as she was going to get, the dog trotted off to open the door.

# Chapter 8

With all the years he'd spent expecting the unexpected, he would have thought the expected wouldn't have much effect.

He was fiercely, bloodily wrong. As he had ever been when it came to this one thing, this one person.

She wasn't as beautiful as ever. She was more beautiful. He'd seen her like this before, on the very rare occasions she emerged from the low profile she preferred. Those had been the worst, and after that brief, scorching three months with her he'd tried to avoid being around for those. Not simply because it hurt to look at her when she went all out and with glamorous makeup, her hair in impossibly glorious waves, and wearing some sleek, silky dress that reminded him of the body beneath it, but because he knew how well the outside masked the brilliance of the brain behind it.

She wasn't wearing the formal clothes now, but it didn't seem to make any difference at all. Even the simple black dress was beyond elegant on her, with the added distraction of baring a length of those long, fit legs.

The sight of those legs slammed him back into the past, to the day shortly after he'd started at Foxworth, when he'd encountered her in the local gym where he worked to keep his mangled leg functional. The injury had been much fresher then, and he hadn't yet learned to compensate for it as well as he eventually did. He'd walked by the training room—okay, limped—and heard her voice, asking a question of one of the personal coaches. He'd been unable to stop himself from looking through the open door. It had been quite a vision—a tall, willowy woman in snug black leggings and a red, abdomen-baring workout top that did little to disguise lovely curves. Her long, dark hair was pulled back and up into a practical tail, yet still hung past her shoulders.

She was utterly, totally absorbed with the hand weights she was using, under the coach's close direction. Focused, intent, determined. And the results showed in the body he couldn't help admiring; she was taut, fit and strong, yet as feminine as any woman he'd ever seen.

He reacted exactly as he had the first time he'd seen her, when Quinn had brought him into the Foxworth offices. Everything male in him had suddenly awakened after a long, long sleep.

That she was the long-ago girl from down the street had made him feel a little weird about the sudden kick.

That she was Quinn's sister made him feel almost appalled.

But that day at the gym, she'd looked toward the doorway, almost as if she'd sensed his presence. Their gazes had locked, and a small smile curved her mouth. That incredible mouth.

She'd looked at him as if she were happy to see him.

As if she were happy he was there.

As if she were as...interested as he was, in an eternal male/female way.

And all the time and effort he had put into quashing his own inappropriate response—she was as much his new boss as Quinn, after all—hadn't had much effect. No matter how hard he had tried to write it off as the oft-discussed back-home-at-last effect.

Then had come that night when, with Quinn out of town, he'd had to accompany her to some fancy function, even though he'd only been with Foxworth for a couple of months. He'd groaned inwardly when she'd come out wearing an amazing blue dress that clung to her slender but curved shape, and bared enough of her toned, sleek legs to make that groan even harder to suppress.

It was a private party, she'd explained, but it was for the head of the company that had been the most lucrative investment she'd ever made. This man's work had made the launch of the Foxworth Foundation possible.

There had been so much admiration in her voice when she spoke of the man, he'd wondered if there was more than business between them. But when he'd tried to tactfully—well, tactfully for him—ask if he should leave them alone, she'd answered, "Don't you dare!" and then laughed and said Mr. Trent was much more likely to be interested in him than her. Which, she'd added with a rather intent look, she could understand.

He did his best to forget that look. And to remind himself he was there as more of a bodyguard than anything else. He'd put on his most civilized demeanor, even though it was a bit rusty from lack of use, and pretended his way through most of the evening. And it had worked...until he'd come up behind her chatting with another woman, one he privately felt had overdone the glamming up a bit.

"Your escort this evening is quite something," the woman was saying.

"That he is." There had been an undertone in her voice he couldn't quite put a name to.

"He looks a bit…dangerous."

"Only when necessary," Charlie answered, and it felt strange to hear the words he'd often heard Quinn say coming from her. But then she had smiled and half turned to look at him, telling him without words that she'd known he was there. "And that's why I think the world of him," she'd said softly.

For a moment he couldn't breathe. Or had forgotten how.

"Not to mention he's sexy as hell," the other woman quipped, giving him a visual up and down that, oddly, had no effect whatsoever.

"That, too," Charlie had agreed softly.

That had nearly put him on his knees. And that night it had begun, the fiery, impossible three months that were burned into his memory so deeply that he knew he'd never be free of them.

And he wondered how twisted it was that sometimes, when the other memories, the horrible ones, rose up, it was the images from those months he used to hold them back.

The feel of Cutter's cold nose bumping his hand snapped him back to the present. He wondered how long he'd been standing there, staring at her, those images parading through his brain with vivid impact.

He summoned up a countering image, that of the smooth, polished former senator who, as far as Rafe could see, Gavin had been utterly right about.

*He became a senator to build his power infrastructure. Now he figures he's got it in place, it's time to start pulling those behind-the-scenes strings.*

And Rafe wondered what strings he was here in the Northwest to pull.

Or maybe he was just here to please the new lady in his life. Charlie.

He nearly laughed out loud at the thought, if only because he doubted the esteemed Senator Flood would use such an unsophisticated name. It was probably Charlaine all the way.

He gave Cutter a scratch behind the ears in thanks for the dog's returning him to the here and now. The reality he had tried so hard to avoid.

"Upstairs," Quinn said, a bit sharply. "This is all hands on deck, and—"

He stopped as Cutter let out one of his distinctive barks. Gavin's, Rafe recognized. Quinn really did mean all hands. He'd already seen both Teague's and Liam's cars parked outside. And a practical little sedan that looked like a rental, but hardly the kind of rental he'd expect the new girlfriend of someone on the level of Flood to be driving.

*But exactly what Charlie would rent. Ever-practical Charlie.*

And a bit belatedly he realized that this wasn't sounding like a social occasion at all. Charlie always did seem to slow down his thought process. But upstairs meant business, and Gavin meant serious business.

He watched as the lawyer, dynamic and commanding as ever, came in, Cutter escorting him happily. As if the dog knew that the gathering was now complete. Gavin greeted him with a nod, but Charlie got a hug. Rafe had gotten used to the high power attorney being here, and had almost forgotten he'd been in St. Louis with Charlie for longer.

"What's up?" Gavin asked.

"We're meeting upstairs," Hayley said. "Quinn will brief everyone there."

In the end, he and Charlie hadn't even spoken before they all headed up. He felt a jab of inwardly directed scorn as he resorted to using his leg to make sure he was the last one on the stairs; it wasn't bothering him much today at all. Which had him wondering not for the first time how much of the pain he usually felt was just from dwelling on it. Because it seemed if there was enough distraction around, he barely thought of it at all.

And there was no bigger distraction than Charlie Foxworth. Not for him, anyway.

It had been a while since the entire Foxworth staff—except for Ty, who never left St. Louis—had been gathered under one roof. If he included Charlie, it had been since Quinn and Hayley's wedding. And again he wondered if this case, whatever it was, had something to do with her, or if she was only here because she happened to be in the area with her new, high-profile boyfriend.

He kept his grimace turned inward. The idea of this woman who worked to avoid the limelight, at least the public kind, taking up with a man who craved it practically beyond all else, except maybe power, simply did not compute, as Liam would say.

Rafe could tell from the way that Quinn stayed edgily on his feet while the rest of them took the seats he indicated around the big meeting table that this was something big. And when they were all seated and looking at him expectantly, Quinn finally got to it.

"My sister brought us a present," he said.

Rafe's brow furrowed. He glanced around the room. Hayley, as he'd expected, showed no surprise. Obviously neither did Charlie. The rest of them all waited silently for Quinn to get to the crux of it. He did, in two words.

"The mole."

And in those two words, all his perspective abruptly shifted. The memory of that near escape flooded him.

The mole.

The one who had almost gotten them all killed, including then innocent bystanders Hayley and Cutter.

*My sister brought us a present.*

Flood? He was the mole? It fit. Oh, it fit. He was just the type.

And when he should be feeling jubilation that he'd finally been found, all Rafe could really feel was an overwhelming swell of relief that Charlie hadn't really fallen for a man like that.

And what that said about him would have to wait. Right now, there was a very large payment to extract. And he planned on being a central part of that.

Whether Charlaine Foxworth liked it or not.

# Chapter 9

Charlie laid it out in her usual way, systematically, chronologically, although it was taking a bit more effort than it usually did for her. She told herself it had nothing to do with Rafe sitting across the table, not looking at her but tapping the table in that habit he had. It was simply that she was jet-lagged. She was her usual organized, focused self, just a little tired.

Another of those taunting memories arrowed through her mind. The day they'd talked about the differences between them.

*I admit, I'm a bit of a control freak.*

*Probably comes from not having any control at all after your parents were killed.*

She'd never thought of it quite like that before, and his quick—and probably accurate—assessment had startled her.

*Do you always assess things and people, and so quickly?* She'd given him a smile then. *And accurately?*

*You want to control circumstances. I'm all about adapting to changing circumstances.*

Because he'd had to be, she'd realized then. It was not only what made him the best sniper, it was what had made him able to adapt to the injury to his leg, most days ignoring it completely despite the fact that she knew it always ached a little and sometimes ached a lot.

She had to pull herself out of the memory and back to the present. Her explanation of why she hadn't told them anything before she could do it in person seemed a bit garbled to her, and she wondered if her thinking had been a bit garbled as well; Ty was the best, and if he said a system was secure, it was. But she realized she was, perhaps, getting a taste of what it felt like in the field when the adrenaline kicked in. Quinn had always told her one of the first things it affected was judgment, and she believed it now.

*Adapting to changing circumstances...*

"I probably overdid it on the secrecy thing," she admitted, "but I confess I also wanted to tell you in person, so you could see how sure I am. That said, I still think we shouldn't mention him by name in any communications."

"Agreed. Better safe than sorry," Quinn said. "The...subject has his fingers in pies all over the place." He glanced upward. "I assume you found a particularly interesting pie?"

Ty was on the big screen on the wall above the table now, ready with the explanation of how he'd found what had set her on this trail. He started with the money trail, as Quinn had taught him in the beginning. How that had led him to Flood, which had in turn, eventually, led him to the final pieces of the puzzle.

Quinn listened to the details of the discovery of the pay-off. "So it was a ten-million-dollar transfer between two shell companies, one leading back to the cartel and the other to the subject, all about ten layers deep?"

"Yes, sir," Ty said. "And it was two days before the mission to move the witness." Taking his cue from Quinn, he carefully didn't mention Vicente Reynosa by name, either.

"And the subject—" Charlie used her brother's term "—announced his plan to retire at the end of his term as soon as the transfer cleared. But there's more. Ty, go on."

"Okay. We knew this wasn't really proof, the payment was buried so deep, we couldn't prove it had actually gone to the subject. Only to a company he's an owner of. Which is why my boss—" he flashed a grin at Charlie "—went for the personal contact when the opportunity came up."

He hesitated then, as if he thought Quinn was going to chew him—or her—out for making that move without consulting him first. But her brother only nodded. "While you did...?"

Ty gave his best nonchalant shrug. "I...er, hacked his calendar."

"Find an interesting appointment, did you?" Quinn asked, one brow raised.

"Actually, when I went way back, I found an evening with no appointments at all, something almost nonexistent for him. Just a blocked-out square at ten p.m. I thought that was strange, so I dug some more."

"Into?" Hayley asked, looking as if she could barely suppress a smile.

"Um," Ty began, then said, "Security cams. Since he was a senator, there were a bunch, near his office and home. And it seems like they keep the footage forever. Anyway, I found that night, and he left his DC townhouse at nine forty-five. On foot. Only his aide with him."

"At night in DC?" Quinn asked. "No security?"

Ty nodded. "That's what got me wondering. So I tracked him as best I could with other cameras, and...ended up with this."

The screen switched to a somewhat grainy black-and-white image that appeared to show a construction site of some sort. Ty's voice came through. "This was right down the street from Flood's place. Keep watching."

They did, and the two men they'd seen leaving the townhouse came into view. After a moment, a third figure emerged from the shadows of the construction site. The men were clearly expecting him and began a conversation. Charlie had watched this video repeatedly, so she spent the time when it was running watching her brother. She saw his jaw tighten in the moment Flood handed over something small enough to be hidden in his hand.

"We're guessing that's a flash drive," Charlie said.

"All right," Quinn said when Ty was back on screen. "Hit us with the rest."

"I did some facial recognition, and the closest match was this guy." An image of a face popped up beside Ty. Quinn immediately leaned toward it.

"The tatts." It was Rafe who said it.

"Yes," Quinn agreed.

The inked-in signature of the cartel Vicente Reynosa had lost his entire family to, and who had nearly cost her what remained of her own.

"He's the top US lieutenant in the cartel," Ty said. "And the clincher is this meeting also took place two days before the witness's scheduled transfer."

She heard a couple of muttered oaths. One she knew was Rafe, the other could have been either Teague or Liam.

"Two days," Quinn said. "Not much time to prepare."

"Lucky for us," Teague said.

Not having that tactical mindset, she hadn't really realized this, and it made her shiver a little now. If it had happened sooner, if the cartel had had more time to prepare their across-the-border operation…

Quinn looked thoughtful for a moment before asking Ty, "Any sign of an effort to repossess that payment?"

Ty grinned suddenly. "You mean after they failed miserably at taking you guys out and ended up going down?"

Quinn chuckled. Charlie wasn't sure his taking a bullet to the arm and Cutter getting clipped was failing miserably, but in the end she supposed it fit. The biggest drug cartel going up against a small, private team of four—plus the unexpected gift of support from Hayley and her dog—and losing had to have been a downer. The trial and hearings that had followed, with Reynosa's testimony, had blown things up completely.

But unfortunately not deep enough that it had reached Flood. Then again, Flood had protections the cartel could only dream of.

"That's what they get for taking out his family," Quinn said, his voice flat and uncompromising.

"Seems stupid," Ty said. "They destroyed their leverage against him by killing them all."

"I don't think that was the plan, from what the witness said," Quinn answered. "They just didn't know he'd gathered his family together to try and evacuate them when they blew up that house."

Ty's brow furrowed as it sometimes did when he, from the relative safety of his rather expansive tech lair, came face-to-face with a real-life tragedy. He snapped out of it quickly and returned to Quinn's original question.

"I had the same thought and looked, but no sign of even an attempt to take back the payoff. Do we think there's enough of their organization left to even try?"

"I suspect they've rebuilt a bit by now," Quinn said. "But maybe not enough to try that."

"Or maybe they decided having our subject in their stable, so to speak, is worth it," Liam said.

"They'd own a chunk of him, for sure," Teague agreed. "If word ever got out he was in their pocket—literally— he'd be done for."

Quinn's mouth quirked rather sourly. "Time was, I'd agree. But the cover-up apparatus is so powerful these days, it could go away completely."

"Then maybe he should go away completely," Charlie said, sounding just as sour as her brother had looked. That earned her a startled glance from the man in the room least likely to be startled by anything. And for the first time since they'd sat down here in the meeting room he actually looked at her. And stopped the quiet but incessant tapping of fingers on the table he'd been doing.

For a moment silence reigned in the meeting room. Then, holding her gaze with those steely gray eyes, he said quietly—too quietly, "Happy to oblige."

And that quickly she was back in the past again, in her office in St. Louis, in the final interview before she agreed to hire him. Even then there was something about him that had reached beneath the usually calm, composed exterior she'd built in the years since she'd had to become the responsible one in a futile effort to take on the job of parenting her brother.

Bottom line, he rattled her, she didn't like it, and so had pressed hard. And had been a little surprised, given it was an employment interview, when he'd struck back.

*I'm concerned about you making the adjustment from shooting to kill to...not. Are you going to be able to do that, Rafer?*

She'd used his full name intentionally, formally, to remind him this wasn't some reunion of childhood acquaintances but a serious job interview. And she couldn't deny her tone had been a bit...snarky. His answer, on the other hand, had been cool and dismissive.

*People like you, safe here in your little world, don't want to even admit people like me exist, let alone that there's a need for us.*

She admitted to herself later she'd deserved that. But at the moment she'd struck back as if he'd slapped her. Something she never, ever did.

*Get off your high horse, Crawford. I know perfectly well that you and men like you—and my brother—are the reason I'm able to have the life I have.*

It hadn't been long before he'd proved himself quite capable of doing what was asked of him, and no more. On a case they'd been pulled sideways into a gang retribution murder in a back alley, he'd managed to shoot out every car window and mirror—including the one bare inches from the would-be killer's head—without actually hitting the guy, but terrifying him into giving up. And Quinn had told her it was done so rapidly it must have seemed like full-auto fire to the guy, when in fact it had been single shots.

He'd also explained that, in fact, it was harder to shoot not to kill, because it so limited your target zone. Something she'd never thought about, and that had made her even sorrier about the way she'd snapped at him that day.

She realized suddenly that the meeting had gone on while she'd been lost in the quagmire her mind made of the past. A past that she was apparently unable to keep where it belonged. And for her to admit that, she who had always prided herself on being in control—probably to make up for all the things she couldn't control—was both chastening and a tad humiliating.

"—how did you manage to connect with him?"

It was Hayley, and clearly directed at her. She gathered her scattered wits and answered as calmly as she could. "I saw he was going to be at a fundraising party in the city. So I wangled an invitation."

"Hence the new name, I presume?" Hayley asked.

"Yes. I couldn't chance that he wouldn't recognize the Foxworth name, after the witness and then the whole thing with the governor." Their name hadn't been widespread after they thwarted the effort kill the federal witness, although Flood likely had known it. And Quinn had managed to keep them pretty low profile in the case that had taken down former governor Ogilvie, but they had been mentioned here and there, and politicians tended to pay attention when one of their own went down. Especially for something like murder.

*And especially if they're the same kind of slime themselves.*

"So how did it go down at the party?" Quinn asked.

Back in control, she looked at her brother. Since they were sitting next to each other she was able to keep Rafe in her peripheral vision when she answered.

"Oh, that was the easy part. He made a pass at me."

The tapping on the table that had resumed stopped again. But he didn't look at her. He just sat there, staring at his own fingers on the table as if he'd suddenly grown an extra one. It was all the reaction she got, but it was enough. And she went on so smoothly she was almost proud of herself.

"That gave me the best opening I could ever get, and I knew I had to grab it. We'll never get a better chance at him."

"So you played into it, let him think you were receptive?" Hayley asked.

She looked at her sister-in-law, grimacing. "It wasn't easy, but yes."

"And he bought it?" Quinn asked.

Hayley grinned at her husband. "Look at her. Of course he did."

Charlie smiled with satisfaction. "He did. He thinks I'm

smitten with his looks, charm and power. So now I can use that to get what we need to take him down."

Quinn looked from her to his wife and back. "Sometimes," he said slowly, "you women scare the hell out of me."

"Keeps life interesting, don't it?" Liam drawled, grinning.

"Where is he now?" Teague asked.

She shifted her gaze to the other former Marine at the table and made sure her voice hadn't changed at all. "He has meetings scheduled for the rest of the week. He thinks I'm visiting friends in the area. His official fundraising meeting isn't until Saturday, but we're supposed to reconnect on Friday night for a big power cocktail party." She sniffed. "Early, because he wants to introduce me to some people."

"As what?"

Rafe's words weren't just chilly, they were icy. And even after all this time, he had the power to infuriate her with a single sentence. With two words.

She barely noticed that everyone else at the table had gone still. That Cutter's head had come up sharply. Quinn's head turned as he gave his operative—nice, distant word there, operative—a look she couldn't see from her angle.

Charlie had to work to keep her expression even. Which irritated her all over again. She should have been long over this by now. With one of the greater efforts of her life she kept her voice casual. She had to keep her gaze on her brother to do it, however.

"He knows me as Lita Marshall, an executive with an investment firm, which, if he checks, has existed for several years," she said, answering Rafe's question literally but avoiding what she knew had been the intent.

She didn't elaborate on the investment firm front, knowing they were all familiar with the company that existed only in the Foxworth computer system. "Ty has planted a full backstory for Lita," she went on. "Including some details and connections that should keep the subject intrigued for a while. He's already intrigued enough to accept my suggestion of the Puget View Hotel for a venue." She focused on Quinn. "I presume Mr. Linden will be willing to help?"

Quinn smiled quietly. William Linden and his missing family had been one of their first cases after opening Foxworth Northwest. The new branch of the Foxworth Foundation had then consisted of him and Rafe, but they'd pulled off a dramatic rescue of the two young children who had, terrifyingly, witnessed a murder and been taken by the street thugs who had done it. Thugs who had connections to a sex trafficking ring, which was where those two would have ended up. They'd had to move fast, strike hard, and they had, catching up to the crew just as they'd been meeting with the leader of the ring to hand the girls over.

And Mr. Linden happened to be the manager of the luxury Puget View Hotel.

"I'm sure he will," Quinn said. "In fact, I'm guessing we can even get Cutter in as a security or a service dog."

Charlie nodded and smiled at the dog before she went on; she was not one to argue with the success rate this dog had piled up.

"I'm sure I'll have to pass muster with those powerful friends of his Friday night first. It will be difficult—I do find him repugnantly smooth and inherently arrogant—but I can act that much."

"Because it's that important," Hayley said quietly.

Charlie looked at the other woman and saw total understanding in her steady gaze. Quinn had gotten very, very lucky.

*Luckier than you will ever be.*

# *Chapter 10*

"So what's the plan?"

Rafe grimaced inwardly. Sometimes Liam's bright energy was annoying. And since he'd gotten married a couple of months ago, it had downright exploded. Enough to get on his nerves.

Nerves that were already a bit raw.

*A bit? Keep telling yourself that, Crawford.*

He'd made himself stop tapping on the table when he'd realized Charlie had noticed. So now that hand was massaging his leg, pressing hard into the spot that usually caused the most pain. It hadn't been too bad today, but he was going to aggravate it just sitting here if he didn't ease up a little.

"We need to go slowly," Charlie said. "Can't do anything to make him suspicious. Ty will keep digging for more, something more out in the open than what we have, but we can't be sure he'll find anything."

"Agreed. The subject is too careful. Nor is he stupid," Quinn said.

"Also you need to be aware he has a personal bodyguard. A man named Cort Ducane. He's always armed, and more than capable." She held Quinn's gaze for a second, then Teague's. Him she barely gave a glance. "He reminds me of you guys. I have no doubt that he can be lethal if required."

"Would he consider it required if the subject simply ordered it?" Quinn asked.

Charlie let out a long breath, obviously considering. "I don't know."

"What else do you know about him?" Hayley asked.

Charlie was silent for a moment, probably to mentally organize her thoughts, then laid it all out. "He wears a wedding ring and is constantly fiddling with it. That might mean trouble on the home front. But he has been nothing but scrupulously polite to me, the few times we've spoken. I once saw him when no one else was around, and he looked...weighed down. But it vanished the moment he realized I was there. I asked him if he liked his work, hoping to get him to say something about his employer, but he only said it was what he does."

"Sounds like a guy who's not ecstatic about his job," Liam said.

"Or like a guy who doesn't blab to strangers, even ones that look like her."

Rafe hadn't really meant to say that, or at least not that sharply, but Liam's overflow of happy was starting to get to him. And yet again everyone at the table went still for a moment. He could feel Quinn's gaze fastened on him, and knew he'd been out of line and was going to hear about it.

He'd have been better off just maintaining the silence he'd always been known for. It was just that everything seemed to blow up when he was around Charlie. He lost his reticence, he lost his judgment and above all he lost his cool. And he couldn't seem to do a damned thing about it.

Fortunately, Ty jumped back in as an image popped up on the screen, of a serious-looking young man in uniform. "I ran a check on the name. That him?"

"It is," Charlie said with a nod. "Longer hair now. And his eyes are much more strikingly green than in that picture."

*Strikingly green?* Rafe felt a sudden jolt, and it was all he could do not to look at her.

*I love how your eyes shift color, get stormy dark when you—*

He chopped off that memory with the biggest mental axe he could summon as Ty went on.

"Marines, as you can see, so maybe Rafe or Teague can ask around."

It was only a headshot so Rafe couldn't tell how tall he was, but he looked solid, fit and...determined. He wasn't sure how that last made him feel, given the circumstances, but there it was. Cort Ducane looked like a man who would get the job done. Striking green eyes or not.

He wondered if the guy knew the truth about his boss. If he knew he'd set up three other vets for destruction, two of them fellow Marines.

"What I found," Ty continued, "showed a pretty clean record. Two tours overseas, a couple of combat ribbons, left as a first sergeant eighteen months ago. One minor disciplinary ding."

"For what?" Quinn asked.

"Punching an officer."

Quinn blinked. Teague looked up at the screen at the same time he himself did. "Punching a superior officer is a minor ding?" Teague asked.

Ty grinned, as if he'd known that was coming. "In this case, yeah. The officer in question gave a statement for the defense, as it were. Said he had it coming, he'd been out of line in something he'd said."

Quinn leaned back in his chair. "Well, isn't that interesting."

It was. Rafe found himself more curious about that officer than the man they were discussing. That is, until he reminded himself the man was Flood's bodyguard, and if Charlie was going to continue this farce she'd begun, she was going to be too often within reach of the guy. And she thought his eyes were striking.

He gave himself a mental shake, made himself focus. She was obviously pretty determined to continue. And nobody knew better than he did that getting Charlie Foxworth to change course when she was convinced she was right was a futile exercise. That didn't make the idea of her spending time with a slime like Flood any more palatable. Especially up close and personal time.

How personal, he didn't want to even speculate. Didn't want to, but as was usual for him around her, he couldn't seem to control his imagination. Him, a guy who dealt in what was, not what he wanted it to be, not some fantasy that would never be real, couldn't be real. That couldn't be, because the bottom line never changed.

He was who and what he was, and no match for the likes of Charlaine Foxworth.


"She really gets to you, doesn't she?"

Rafe slowly turned his head to stare at Liam. "Sometimes," he said slowly, "I fear for your life, Burnett."

Liam only grinned at him. "And when you give me that death's head stare, I know I'm over the target."

He went back to staring out the window, focusing on the bald eagle pair that had taken up their frequent spot in the big maple on the far side of the meadow. The same pair that had seemed to give a soaring salute to the marriage of Hayley and Quinn by an uncannily timed flight over the ceremony just as the minister made the pronouncement they were husband and wife. Rafe knew he would never forget the way they swooped into view, circled overhead, dived, rolled, soared again and then vanished into the trees.

The memory made his throat tighten, as it had then. He'd known they had it, that something that practically shouted they were meant to be, but that eagle flight had pounded it home to him in a way nothing else could have.

And then he'd glanced at the woman opposite him, impossibly beautiful in that royal blue dress that made her look like the royalty the color was named after, had seen the sheen in those eyes that matched the dress. And it had nearly broken him. Because the last time he'd seen tears in those eyes, he had been the cause. He'd hurt her, badly.

But he'd saved her from worse.

And that was the one thing that enabled him to keep going, keep functioning. He'd hurt her, but he'd saved her from even worse pain.

*Don't worry about it, Crawford. You made me what I am, utterly focused and committed to Foxworth. In a way, you're why it is what it is today.*

She'd said it to him the day of the wedding rehearsal, said it in a cool, unruffled way that rattled him even more. She'd said it as if she'd really meant it, as if he were, in a twisted sort of way, partly responsible for why Foxworth was what it was. Because he'd hurt her so badly she'd done nothing else but make building Foxworth her focus. Her obsession.

"—don't like it."

Quinn's voice snapped him out of this morass, the latest in the string of useless reveries.

"It's the only way," Charlie insisted. "I'm in, and he doesn't suspect a thing. It would be foolish for me to walk away now, when we don't have enough yet to take him down."

"I know," Quinn said, but he clearly wasn't happy.

"Don't trust me, bro? Think I'll mess it up?"

"I think for all your genius, this isn't your bailiwick," he said flatly.

"Oh, believe me, I know that. And normally I'd leave all this undercover, secretive stuff to you. But three years of trying that got us nowhere."

"And you," Hayley said cheerfully, her tone breaking the tension with an almost audible snap, "grabbed a chance and put us where it could have taken three years longer to get the old way."

"Exactly," Charlie said, smiling back at Hayley.

"Now," Hayley said, briskly this time as she looked at her husband, "I'll call Ty and have him put that fake ID machine to work again for us, while you make some calls and get us into that soiree Friday night. And since you've got the hotel contact, get Rafe on the security team. And Cutter, if Mr. Linden is willing. Teague, Liam, you'll look great in formal staff attire."

The two men looked at each other with very visible eye rolls. But they were smiling.

Rafe had to look away again. Those two women... They were incredible. Impossible.

Quinn might be the spine, he, Teague and Liam the ribs maybe, but those two...

They were the brain, heart and soul of Foxworth.

# Chapter 11

"I used to wonder if you left the main office because of me," Charlie said, looking at her brother over the rim of her wineglass. "If I was just too hard to work with."

Quinn lifted a brow at her. "I left for the exact reasons I told you then. Not," he added with an upward quirk of one side of his mouth, "that you're not a pain in the butt to work with."

"Thanks," she said, lifting her glass in a mock toast just as Cutter came through the dog door and joined them. He'd been out, Hayley had explained, making his rounds to check on the neighborhood. And the neighbors loved it, said they felt safer knowing he was keeping an eye and nose on things.

They'd come back to Quinn and Hayley's home after an exhausting day hammering out a plan. A plan that, Quinn had warned her, would no doubt have to change on the fly since in the field a plan was a great thing until reality kicked it in the teeth.

"Reality?" she'd asked.

Unexpectedly Rafe had answered, in that wryly amused tone she hadn't heard in so long. That she had missed so much. "The fact that the other side doesn't know or follow the plan."

She glanced at him, but looked back at Quinn before she'd said, an edge in her voice, "I think I'm capable of at least a little thinking on my feet."

"I'm sure you are capable," Quinn had said. "After all, you already do what Rafe does."

That had startled her into gaping at him. "What?"

Quinn shrugged. "You both plan and figure trajectories with what data you have. For you it's financial things, stocks, bonds, whatever. For him it's weapons and bullets."

At that she'd had to glance back at Rafe. The man was staring at Quinn as if he felt the same way she did about the analogy. A little stunned at how much sense it made.

She'd been more than relieved to come to this quiet refuge her brother and Hayley had made here, the charming, lovely but understated home amid tall trees and assorted other greenery. For someone used to all the trees turning autumn colors by now, the green was…refreshing. Somehow the spots of color that were here, on various maple and oak trees, stood out even more against the green.

"I have to admit," she said now, "there is something quite appealing about this place. I didn't realize what a difference always having green trees around could make."

"And not a tornado in sight," Quinn said cheerfully.

"You get them," she protested.

"Sure. Once a year, maybe, just to remind us what they are."

Hayley laughed at them both. "We prefer natural disasters of the earthquake or volcanic variety."

Charlie laughed right along with her sister-in-law, and

as some of the pressure inside eased, said to Quinn, "You do know, brother mine, how lucky you are?"

"Oh, I've gone way beyond luck," Quinn said, turning his head to look at his wife. "And ended up in paradise."

Hayley actually blushed slightly, and that she still could at a compliment from her husband Charlie took as simply further proof that these two were just as perfect together as she'd thought from the moment she'd met her sister-in-law for the first time.

Later, after a wonderful dinner and a second glass of wine, Hayley excused herself to go do something Charlie suspected was merely a way to leave her and Quinn alone together. Well, alone except for Cutter, who showed no inclination to leave. As if the three of them had planned it this way.

She knew her brother well enough to see that he wanted to say something, but was having to work up to it. And that in itself was rare enough that she knew it had to be something personal; if it was strategic or tactical, he'd never have hesitated.

"Out with it, little brother."

Quinn's mouth twisted upward at one corner, as it did every time she used the appellation. "Yeah, yeah," he muttered. Then he took a visible breath and met her gaze. "Are you ever going to tell me?"

"Tell you what?"

She was glad it came out evenly, with just the right amount of normal curiosity. But just as he couldn't fool her, she couldn't fool him anymore, either. Not like she'd been able to when he'd been a kid, when she'd tell him everything would be okay when she herself had no idea if they'd ever come out of that long, dark tunnel.

"No games, please. You know what I mean. You and Rafe."

"There is no me and Rafe."

"But there was."

"*Was* being the operative word."

She saw that register. Understood why. Because she'd never really admitted to him before that there had been something more than a working-for-Foxworth connection between her and Rafe.

After a moment of wearing his processing-new-information expression he asked, "What happened?"

She drew herself up straight on the couch. Her instant reaction was a fierce resistance. She shouldn't have done it, shouldn't have admitted even as much as she had. Shouldn't have—

Her runaway train of thought cut off as Cutter, who had been sprawled on his bed near the fireplace, came quickly to sit beside her. He plopped his chin on her knee. With those dark eyes looking up at her, she couldn't deny what he was obviously asking for, so stroked his head.

And there it was again, that sense of comfort. Looking down into those eyes, she found herself soothed enough that her anger at her brother for asking—and at herself for answering—faded. Enough for her to meet his gaze and answer in a much different manner than her initial jolt of irritation would have dictated.

"I loved him. He didn't love me."

Quinn looked as close to gaping as her cool-headed brother ever did. "What?"

"How else should I interpret him saying, 'This isn't for me,' and then walking out of my life for good?"

"He...said that?"

"He did say that. And nothing else about it, ever. Not a word. But I obviously wasn't enough for him." And that was not something she was used to thinking, she who had fought hard every minute after their parents had been killed to be enough. Enough to fill the void they'd left behind.

Quinn sat, wine forgotten, staring at her. But she could tell by the look in his eyes that he wasn't really seeing her, that his brain was working, assessing, considering options, as he always did.

Finally he asked, "Then how do you explain the way he reacts around you? The way he reacts to just seeing you on a video call? Hell, the way he reacts when he just hears your name? That's not somebody who doesn't care."

"Someone who feels guilty for ending it like an ass?" she suggested sweetly.

Again he went quiet. And in this conversation that did not bode well for her, she found herself tensing, as if she were waiting for the timer on a bomb to reach zero. Cutter, who had settled at her feet, was suddenly up again, nudging her hand, practically demanding she pet him. As if he'd sensed the rising pressure within her somehow. And when she did stroke the dark fur of his head, she felt it again, that soothing calm.

She'd read the reports, knew what Quinn and Hayley had told her about the dog's aptitude for just about any job they gave him, but this aspect was the one that surprised her most. She never would have expected a dog that could be as fierce as any trained military or police dog, or as playfully funny as any household pet, could also have this knack for comfort. He was taking jack-of-all-trades to new heights.

And she knew she was dwelling on that to avoid thinking about the way she'd just poured her guts out to her brother. The brother whose mind she could practically hear working.

"Did you never think," Quinn finally said, speaking carefully, "that maybe he thought he wasn't enough for you?"

She stared back at him. For a long moment she was at a loss for words, hardly a frequent situation for her.

"How," she finally said, just as carefully, "could he possibly think that? He's not only integral to Foxworth and works as hard at keeping things running—and I don't mean just machinery—as anyone, but he's a freaking war hero."

"Right on all points. And no one knows that better than me. After all, he saved my life and the lives of my entire platoon. And I'm the one who has to practically force him to take time off—which for him means working on machines instead of a case—now and then."

"Then—"

She stopped when Quinn held up a hand. "If I've learned nothing else from my lovely wife, it's to realize that we all have emotions. Even those of us who have them buried so deep they rarely ever surface. And that, being emotions, they don't always have a basis in truth."

"What are you saying?"

"That the people who bury them the deepest—like Rafe—do it for a reason. Maybe he does it because he feels he's not any of the things you just said."

It sounded so impossible to her she nearly rolled her eyes. "So they just put his name on the Hathcock Trophy twice on a whim?"

"Oh, he knows he's good at that. If he didn't, if he wasn't, we would have lost him long ago."

"I did lose him long ago."

She rarely ever acknowledged loss aloud, hadn't since they'd lost their parents so young. As if hiding it, not acknowledging it could somehow make it not real. She'd known even at fourteen it didn't change anything, but she'd gotten into the habit and had never quite been able to break it.

She knew that, and knew he knew it, too, so she wasn't surprised when her brother went very still.

"And," he began, so quietly she knew that, Quinn-like,

a bombshell was coming, "you're doing exactly what he's done. You bury yourself in your work, devote every waking hour—which is far too many I'm guessing—to Foxworth, and above all you don't let anyone in past a certain point."

"And just when did you become a shrink?" she retorted, stung. Probably because he was right.

"I haven't. I just recognized it, once it was pointed out to me. About me, I might add." He gave her a wry smile then. "That's why I recognize it in you."

She studied him in turn for a moment. "Hayley," she guessed.

"Exactly. So take it seriously, because she's almost always right about things like this."

"I know." It was nothing less than the truth. Her sister-in-law had the most uncanny knack for understanding people that she'd ever seen. She let out a long breath. "You truly have landed in paradise, little brother."

"Don't I know it," he agreed.

"I'm glad." She meant it. She loved him deeply and was more than glad for him. He deserved every bit of the happy he'd found with Hayley.

She just knew it wasn't in the cards for her.

And later, when she lay sleeplessly in the cozy, comfortable guest room of her brother's home—with Cutter, surprisingly, snuggled beside her as if he realized she needed the kind of comfort he could provide—what Quinn had said played back in her mind in a seemingly endless loop.

*Did you never think that maybe he thought he wasn't enough for you?*

It still seemed impossible to her. How could a man like Rafer Crawford possibly think he wasn't good enough for…anyone?

Difficult, yes, with his reticence and the fact that you

practically had to pry what he was thinking out of him. But she'd always assumed it was simply because he had so many awful memories in his head. She knew all about those; although as bad as hers were, she guessed they were nothing compared to his, by sheer volume if nothing else. And eventually he had actually begun to open up with her.

*Yes. Right before he walked out on you.*

And that night had been the capper on her collection of awful memories. Him breaking what had been the most powerful kiss of her life, saying those blunt words, then turning and walking away, out her front door and out of her life.

She'd been foolish enough to believe something else must be wrong. Something he was keeping secret.

Then she'd resorted to thinking he'd just been in pain, because his limp had been a little worse that night.

Then she'd told herself there had to be some outside reason he'd ended them. Something she could fix, some way she could make it right. She only had to find out what it was, and she could fix it, then he'd come back.

It had taken a while for her to realize it was none of those things. And a while more for her to admit it wasn't anything she could fix.

She then had spent a long time waiting for him to wake up, to realize it had been a mistake.

That had morphed into just…waiting.

But the longest time of all was how long it took her to understand he was gone forever.

# Chapter 12

Rafe checked his gear bag for a third time, because he didn't trust himself at the moment. Not when he hadn't slept more than a couple of hours at a time since he'd overheard that conversation between Quinn and Hayley. Not with his brain careening around in all directions, only to keep coming back to the thing he least wanted to think about.

The truth of that brief idyll years ago.

She had to have known he'd been right to walk away. She was too smart not to have known. It had been a mistake from the beginning, she had to have seen that. And if she hadn't seen it then, surely she had by now.

And the fact that she still dug at him every time they faced each other in person or otherwise? That he didn't understand. Reactions like that usually meant the person felt…something. Cared enough, even if in a negative way, to not just move on. She should treat him as she did any other member of the Foxworth team, and yet she still, after all this time, acted as if he in particular needed to be the recipient of her barbed wit.

Maybe it was as simple as she was giving him what he deserved. What she knew he deserved, probably better than anyone.

Except himself.

Quinn had to have told her. Rafe knew Quinn knew he'd been teetering on a crumbling edge. His long, shaggy, neglected hair, his rough, untrimmed beard, and the fact that he probably weighed twenty pounds less than he had back when Quinn had hunted him down to thank him for taking out that terrorist nest, had been sign enough. The guy Quinn had found under the bridge that day was not the kind of guy who deserved a woman like Charlie Foxworth. And she was too smart not to know it. He'd spent their last month together expecting to hear her say the inevitable.

Except she hadn't. So in the end he'd had to do it.

*The right thing. You had to do the right thing.*

The refrain wasn't helping any more now than it had then. Even knowing the truth of it didn't help.

He zipped up the bag and slung it over his shoulder, ready to take it out to his car. The plan was that he would get himself and Cutter to the other side and report to the head of hotel security. Liam and Teague would report to the head of the hotel staff. Quinn and Hayley would check in to the suite they'd reserved, then pick up their invitations to the gala, secured through the event coordinator upon the order of the manager, who had given them carte blanche after they'd saved his family.

That had, in fact, been Rafe's first case out of this office. The first one after he'd left the St. Louis headquarters. Left Charlie. Left her to continue to make it possible for them to expand, to help more people. Left her to work sixteen-hour days, including weekends, the schedule Quinn had been worried about but got only "I'll take a break when we're solid" in response.

Well, they were more than solid now. Much more. They were well funded, and all five branches were set up, staffed and working well. And it was all because of Charlie, because of those long hours and her brilliance with finance and investments.

*In a way, you're why it is what it is today.*

The words she'd said the day of Quinn and Hayley's wedding, right here in the meadow, rang in his head now. Among the many things he didn't want credit for, that probably topped the list.

His Foxworth phone sounded a message. The screen read merely, Final meeting in fifteen.

*Time to get your brain in gear, Crawford.*

He took the gear bag out, stowed it in the locker in the trunk of his car, secured it, then closed the trunk and locked it as well. He heard the sound of the front door opening, and a moment later saw Cutter racing toward him. The dog greeted him with a sniff and a soft *whuff*, but then promptly circled behind him and nudged.

"In a hurry, dog?" Another nudge. "Everybody pouring themselves some of Hayley's great coffee, huh?" He wasn't sure what she did to it, but she'd gotten even his need-the-spoon-melting-stuff taste buds to like the richer flavor.

Cutter trotted ahead, head up in that mission-accomplished way he had. The dog had trained them all, at least in his ways. And given how often he'd been the crucial factor in making a plan come together, none of them would really complain about him trying to run everything else in their life. Although he did wish the dog would stop putting on that damned matchmaker hat of his whenever Charlie was around. Which thankfully wasn't very often.

*But she's here now. And will be for a while.*

He watched Cutter trot ahead and bat the pad beside the door to open it. He wasn't looking forward to this. But he had no choice. And this was the most important cold case on his list. He'd just have to focus on that and ignore the rest.

*Right. Like Charlie Foxworth is ignorable in any way.*

Or Cutter, for that matter. Not when every time he and Charlie were in the same vicinity, the dog started his routine of trying to get and keep them together.

When Charlie was safely tucked away in St. Louis he didn't think about it. He'd convinced himself the dog knew better than to try his tricks with him. But now he was the one who knew better. Cutter had just been waiting, biding his time. He'd no more lost sight of the goal then Rafe had been able to stop reacting to Charlie like a starving wolf.

He stepped inside just as the door started to swing shut. Cutter was already into the seating area in front of the fireplace. And then he heard a voice, speaking softly. A voice he knew all too well. The others might be already upstairs, but Charlie was down here, standing in front of the at the moment inactive fireplace. No, pacing in front of it, as she spoke into her phone. Not the Foxworth phone, but the personal one she'd said was a burner Ty had set up under her fictitious name.

"—of course I will," she was saying, in a light, cheerful tone he'd never heard directed at him. A pause, then a light laugh that seemed the tiniest bit forced to him. But to someone who didn't know her well, it probably sounded fine. "Max, dear, you worry too much. I'll be there in plenty of time." And that wasn't forced at all. Which made his nerves start to hum. Another pause, another laugh. "I miss you, too. Can't wait until tonight. See you soon!"

She ended it gaily. Stood there holding the phone for a moment, obviously unaware of his presence. While his nerves went from humming to buzzing. Loudly. As if he could actually hear it in his ears.

"Can't wait until tonight, huh?" The words broke from him before he could stop them. She spun around, clearly startled. "You sure you want us to take 'Max, dear' down?"

"What?"

"Maybe you'd prefer we stay out of your...budding romance? Or are you already past the budding stage?"

He didn't know what was driving him, other than the image his brain insisted on forming of her sleeping with the traitor. But the look that came over her face then told him just how far over the line he'd gone. Her eyes were even icier than her expression.

"Were it not for the fact that I'd have to explain the blood, I would punch that insulting mouth of yours right now." She held up the phone she'd been using. "This soul sucker aside, what I do, when and with who is not your business. You threw away that right long ago, *Mister* Crawford."

She dropped the phone onto the coffee table. It hit with a crack. She ignored it, turned on her heel and headed for the stairway.

It stung, but he knew he'd had it coming. Charlie would no more get genuinely involved with the mole who had set them up than she would disown her beloved brother. It had been stupid to even suggest it, no matter how his gut had reacted to that cheerful, excited tone she'd used on the phone. He'd insulted her on a primal level, and if she had punched him, he would have deserved it.

And she was right. He had thrown it away. He'd thrown them away. And that it had had to be, that it was the only possible outcome, didn't ease the pain of that even now, years later.

Snipers were supposedly capable of utter and complete concentration, shutting out anything that didn't affect their potential shot. Yet when she was around he felt constantly distracted. Snipers were also touted to be among the most patient people in the world. And he was…except with her. She rattled him like nothing else could. Got to him like nothing else could.

And he hated that she still could, after all this time.

# Chapter 13

Charlie wished that she had punched him. Even now, as she stood upstairs looking out the window, her right hand curled into a fist. But if she'd punched him as hard as she'd wanted to, she'd probably have broken a finger. And it wasn't worth that. There had been a time when she would have sacrificed a lot more than a finger for him, but not anymore.

On a case he'd get her all, as any Foxworth operative would. Personally, he'd get from her exactly what he'd given her. That chilly remoteness and…she would have said heartache, except she wasn't sure his was capable of pain anymore.

She smothered a sigh. She remembered again when Quinn had first proposed hiring Rafe. He'd warned her that Rafe was closed off, withdrawn. He'd told her they would get his best work but not to expect him to open up and be a friend, not like the friend he'd been back when they were kids in the neighborhood. That he'd seen too much, had to do things that scarred a person.

"So have you," she'd protested then.

"It's different," he'd insisted. "Snipers are different. Set apart. In some quarters they aren't even allowed to call them that, they just say they have overwatch. Or in his case, long-range overwatch. They're essential, but scary. And they work alone, unless they're with a spotter."

"Is that why he's so closed off, as you say? He wasn't that way as a kid."

"Probably partly."

She'd thought then about the skinny kid who had hung around their house a lot, because apparently his wasn't the most pleasant place to be. She'd found out later why. But then she'd only asked her brother, "You're okay with asking him to do more of it?"

"I'm okay with asking him to be our backup, our last resort. And to act defensively, not offensively." He'd given an admiring shake of his head. "Rafe is quite simply the best. Talk about cool under fire, he's the personification of it."

"You mean like that joke that was going around about a reporter asking a sniper what he felt when killing a terrorist, and he shrugged and said, 'Recoil'?"

"Not sure it was a joke."

"And we…need this?"

"If we're certain of our mission." He'd given her that very Quinn look then, that steady, determined look. Then he'd said quietly, "If you're going to fight the good fight, you need warriors."

A glimpse of movement near the trees across the meadow snapped her out of the recollection. She focused on it just in time to see an eagle flare its wings to land on a sturdy branch. A branch where a second eagle was already perched. The same pair that had made that dramatic flight at Quinn and Hayley's wedding? She'd read somewhere that they mated for life.

*I guess you're better at it than we humans are.*

But now, when Quinn called them all to the table, and Hayley took her seat beside him, she knew she had to amend that thought. Because there was no doubt in her mind her brother had found his life's mate.

"All right," Quinn said, "we all know this is mainly a research and observation mission. We're nearly positive this is our mole, but we don't have enough evidence to prove that to anyone outside. So we're all clear on that, right? That we're looking to find evidence, not take action?"

The people around the table nodded, although Liam said, "Can we add a 'yet' to that?"

Quinn smiled at the question. "We can," he affirmed.

"Good," Teague agreed.

Hayley smiled as widely as Quinn had. Charlie thought she even saw Rafe's mouth twitch slightly. But all humor vanished when Quinn went on.

"If we're right that this is the guy, he's gotten others killed. Those three feds who were hunting for where they had Reynosa stashed walked into an ambush. Because somebody knew they were coming." He zeroed in on Charlie. "We all need to remember that."

"Oh, I do," she said. "And I won't be in the least surprised if, when all's said and done, it turns out he's got a lot more to answer for. His tentacles are far reaching and widespread."

She'd kept Rafe in her peripheral vision when she'd answered her brother, but he didn't react. Not even a blink. So the armor was back up. Ironic, given he was the one who'd insulted her with the suggestion she was sleeping with Flood. Just the idea of being intimate with that man nauseated her.

Of course, that thought only brought on a string of memories of the only man who had ever made her feel that mating for life was possible for her.

"All right," Quinn said briskly, "let's get into the details. Hayley and I will be hitting the cocktail party rather than the fundraiser for a couple of reasons."

"For me," Hayley said dryly, "it's because I don't want to be among those who'd actually donate to the guy."

Quinn grinned at her. "That, too. But the main one is that there will be people at the fundraiser we know might recognize us. But also because it's Flood's job to schmooze everyone at the party so donors will give more at the fundraiser. I want to see who he thinks will be receptive. And any other connections he might make in a more informal setting."

"Does he drink?" Liam asked, looking at Charlie.

"Not when he needs not to, from what I've seen. And Alec Brown, his personal aide, once said he can nurse a glass for an entire function. He's many things, including probably evil, but he's not careless."

"Noted," Quinn said. "Now, Hayley and I have a suite reserved. That'll be our on-site fallback position if necessary."

"You'll all get key cards once we're there," Hayley added. "Liam, Teague, you're set?"

"Ready," Liam said. "Comms gear will be masked until we're inside, just in case. I'll get you all the earpieces."

"I don't know if his paranoia has reached this level yet," Charlie said, "or whether he could even demand scans and security checks of every guest, given he's not really the host."

"We're prepared anyway," Quinn said. "We don't want to blow it at this early stage. Better safe."

Of course. She should have realized. She should also, she told herself, leave this to the experts. While she'd had some training in self-defense—at Quinn's insistence—she was nowhere near as proficient as her brother on this front.

She knew all the ins and outs of her world, but Quinn was the expert at fieldwork, and she would bow to that expertise. And be glad it was her brother she was acceding to, and not…someone else.

"Everybody have the Flood crew fixed in your mind?" Hayley asked. Charlie had shown them the photo of Alec Brown, who was always at his side. And of course Ducane, whom she'd labeled as security and added a note reading "don't take him lightly."

"That the guest list?" Teague asked, nodding toward a printout on the table in front of Quinn.

Quinn nodded. "Ty got it last night. Didn't want to push Linden too far and get him in trouble. We went over it this morning. You should have photos to go with the names shortly. No one unexpected, although a couple of unknowns that could be aliases. Or not."

Charlie started to speak, then stopped herself, remembering what she'd just lectured herself about.

"Open floor, go for it," Quinn said. "You've had the personal contact with the subject."

"This is just a feeling I've gotten about him," she began, more carefully than she usually would, now that she'd acknowledged and accepted she was out of her depth here. "That he's careful to keep anything that might be subject to scrutiny private. Very private. He might meet someone with questionable connections in a back room, but he won't be seen with them at such a public gathering. He's too conscious of his public image and the benefits that brings."

"And too shrewd about his future plans?" Hayley asked.

"Exactly," Charlie answered.

"Noted," Quinn said with a nod. "So aware, but not the top focus. Okay, transceivers are ready."

He slid a small box across the table, and a smaller one to her. Liam had cleverly hidden her earpiece in a pretty set of earrings she wouldn't have minded wearing anyway. They had a curve that rested against her skull above her ear, and that was where the sound conduction device was. She would hear communications in her ear, but nothing would actually be in her ear. These days, earbuds were the rule rather than the exception it sometimes seemed, but Flood was very observant. Her hair would have covered her ears, anyway, but as Quinn had said, better safe.

"Charlie," Hayley said, "want to give us the details of your cover ID, in case we overhear anybody talking about you?"

"You mean gossiping about the esteemed Maximilian Flood's new lady friend?" she asked dryly.

"Pretty much," Hayley agreed with a grin.

She really did like her sister-in-law. And she was sure Rafe hadn't reacted at all; he'd been staring at the table since he'd answered Quinn. And the finger tapping, well that was just Rafe.

"Lita Marshall, granddaughter of immigrants who made good, and daughter of parents who lean his way politically. Ty even planted a donation to his first senate campaign from them."

"Nice touch," Quinn said.

"We thought so. She's also a widow."

"Oh, even nicer touch," Hayley said.

Charlie nodded. She'd been certain Hayley, with her keen sense about people and the way they reacted and responded to things, would get it. "Her fictional husband died four years ago."

"The same time his wife was killed," Hayley said. "So you not only play the sympathy card, you also get people—including him—thinking how much in common you two have."

"Exactly. I thought it would feed the publicity, once

Flood and Ms. Marshall were seen together." Her mouth twisted in the manner of someone who had a distasteful task ahead, as she indeed did. "And we were, at the airport in St. Louis. He seemed quite pleased with the speculation that's already begun."

"Saw that early this morning," Liam said. "Or rather Ria did. She doesn't know what our case is, of course, but she saw the blurb online about the former senator and his new lady." He grinned his slightly crooked grin. "First thing she said was, 'Someone should warn her.'"

"I already like her," Charlie said with a smile at the young Texan.

They went over all the details, in detail. Charlie mostly listened. She knew each Foxworth team had their own way of working, the tone set by the team leader. Since here it was Quinn, she was more familiar, but she was still well aware she was the outsider. And it was obvious they were in essence the proverbial well-oiled machine. In fact, sometimes the verbal shorthand they clearly all understood took her a moment to translate.

Finally Quinn wound it down, saying, "I'm hoping we can wrap this up for good while he's here, but if we can't, I at least will be following them when they leave."

All the others talked over themselves, volunteering. Except, she noticed, Rafe. Would he just quietly wait for Quinn's orders? Or was he assuming he'd be one who went along, because of his...unique skills?

When they had covered everything, a glance at the time told Charlie she needed to go, and she stood up. "I have to get back in time for my appointment with the hair stylist and manicurist at the hotel beauty salon," she said with distaste in both her tone and her expression. And she carefully avoided looking in Rafe's direction when she added, "Dear Max wants me to look especially impressive tonight."

"Your debut as an official couple?" Hayley asked.

She truly did get everything, Charlie thought. "I think so, although he hasn't bothered to tell me so."

"You're supposed to be so delighted you won't care," Hayley said dryly.

Charlie couldn't hold back a snort of laughter. Yes, she did so like this woman.

Cutter walked with her to the top of the stairs, then glanced back toward the others, who had also gotten to their feet. He seemed to be looking at Rafe rather expectantly.

*Don't even try with us, furry one. It's over and done, blown to bits, shattered, or whatever other cliché you want to use.*

Finally the dog's seeming sense of propriety won out, and he escorted her politely downstairs and to the front door, opened it, then went with her out to her rental car.

And on her way to the ferry to make her way back to the city, she confirmed her earlier thought. She needed to spend more time with her sister-in-law. She didn't have a lot of female friends—she got bored and thus ran out of patience too easily—but she had a feeling Hayley would keep her on her toes. Hayley had known tragedy as she and Quinn had, and Charlie had a suspicion she had as little patience with people obsessed with mundane, insignificant things as she herself did.

Yes, she definitely needed to spend more time here with Hayley. Or maybe this cool, green, admittedly beautiful place was simply growing on her. She found even the thought hard to accept. She'd been inclined to hate the area because it had taken her brother away. And had cost her any hope of mending things with Rafe.

But now she was beginning to wonder if there was something…elemental about it that simply drew people of a certain nature. Which she had assumed she was not.

She almost laughed at herself then, imagining how her relocating here would be interpreted. As if Charlaine Foxworth, known throughout Foxworth as tough and no-nonsense, had succumbed to pure emotion.

*Not going to happen.*

That vow made, she began to brace herself for the task ahead.

# Chapter 14

"You look utterly striking."

Rafe rolled his eyes at Hayley's compliment as he stood in what the hotel rather grandiosely called the parlor of their suite, while she adjusted his bow tie. He'd never been much good at tying the, for him, unusual kind of neckwear, but Hayley had a knack. As she had with so many things.

She suddenly stopped, a quiet sort of smile curving her mouth. "I remember the last time I did this."

"So do I," he said softly.

It had been the day of her and Quinn's wedding, and the first time he'd been in a tux. She'd looked up at him then, and the sheer happiness in her eyes seemed to spill over, even into him a little. It made him ache a little inside just to look at her now, and think about what she'd brought to Quinn's life.

"You're the best thing that could ever have happened to him." Even he could hear the slightly husky note that had crept into his voice.

"I'm happier than I've ever been," she said, still looking up at him. Then she reached up and patted the now properly knotted tie. "So happy that I want everyone around me happy."

He went very still, his brain scrambling for a way to tell her to back off without being curt or rude.

"I'm not asking you to kiss and make up, Rafe. Just to clear the air so it doesn't feel like we're going to have a bomb go off every time you're in the same room."

*Kiss and make up.*

Just the thought nearly made him turn on his heel and walk away. Only the fact that it was Hayley stopped him. He didn't know if it had just been a figure of speech or if she knew. Maybe she had figured it out with that sometimes impossible-seeming instinct of hers. Or maybe Quinn had figured it out and told her; there were few, if any secrets between the couple.

Maybe Charlie really had told her brother. Told him about the iceman, as she had once called him. And he wondered, as he had occasionally, if Quinn was the only reason he hadn't been kicked out of Foxworth back then. If she'd wanted him out. He wouldn't blame her. Maybe it would have been better if Quinn had. Sometimes he thought it would have been better for everyone if he'd been one of those who'd never come home, if he—

"Stop it!" Hayley's sharp, snapped command startled him out of a morass he hadn't revisited in a while. But he was even more startled when she hugged him fiercely. Her voice was quieter but no less urgent when she said, "I hate it when you get that look in your eyes. You're crucial to Foxworth, and you're even more crucial to us, Rafer Crawford, and don't you ever forget that."

He couldn't speak, couldn't find any words to say what he wanted to express. So instead he hugged her back, and after a moment murmured, "I'm fine. It was just a…flash." And when she pulled back far enough to look up at him, he said simply, "Thank you."

After a moment she nodded and stepped back. "I'd better finish getting ready for tonight, and you need to meet with the head of security shortly, right?"

He nodded. It was mainly to introduce him—and Cutter, who would be playing security dog—to the regular hotel team who'd be working the event, so they'd recognize him if anything happened. Mr. Linden, the hotel manager, had presented the idea of the dog to Flood, and had done it hitting Charlie's suggested points about precautions, protection, and rich people wanting to feel safe, and it had worked perfectly. Given the state of the city these days, he would have been surprised if it hadn't.

"Cutter's going to draw attention," Rafe said, thinking that if Flood's security was anywhere near competent, they'd recognize the lethal capabilities of the dog.

"Yes. Which means they'll be paying less attention to us and more to him," Hayley said. "Besides, try changing that dog's mind once it's made up."

"No, thanks." *I know all too well what he's like when he's set on something.*

"Oh, and something else you should probably know."

*Uh-oh.* He recognized that tone, that Hayley's-about-to-nuke-you tone. "What?" he asked warily.

"We've made it official. If anything should happen to Quinn and I, Cutter goes to you."

He felt as if she'd punched him in the gut. Yet all Hayley did after that shock of an announcement was smile widely as she left to finish her own preparations for the evening.

Him, take Cutter? Of all the people… Teague and Laney would be better, surely? Laney was the dog's groomer after all. Sure, when not with Quinn and Hayley, Cutter probably spent more time here at headquarters with him than anyone else, but...

At the same time he couldn't deny he didn't mind the thought. Of course it would be a big responsibility, taking care of a dog this smart, this capable of getting into and downright causing trouble. He'd have to—

He'd have to be around to do it.

His mouth quirked. She was nothing if not clever, was Hayley Foxworth. What better way to ensure he didn't go off some deep end if something indeed happened to them than to saddle him with the dog who had brought them together?

A glance at his watch told him he'd better leave now to meet the head of security. He started toward the door, and as he turned he caught a glimpse of himself in a mirror on the far wall. He never looked at mirrors unless he was shaving, so it caught him a little off guard. Especially in the formal wear. He'd never worn a tuxedo in his life before he'd come to Foxworth, and then it was only the one time.

*You look utterly striking.*

Hayley was too nice. He looked...different, now that he'd buy. Barely recognizable even. But he had to hope she was wrong, because striking implied attention getting, and that was the last thing he wanted. Ever, but especially while working. It was not in a sniper's nature to be out in the open, attracting attention.

Of course, if this devolved into something where his shooting skills were needed, it wasn't really going to matter.

"You just take your time, honey. I know you want to impress."

*The guests? Or you?*

She knew which one she'd put her money on. She was positive he thought he was the one she wanted to impress.

The rest of this rich donor crowd tonight was just a side benefit.

He leaned in to give her a kiss. She turned her head at the right moment to make sure it landed on her cheek. It didn't rattle him. She had the feeling it played right into his plan. She'd even overheard him discussing with Alec how to play it up, that they were two bereaved people who were taking it very slow and carefully.

"Great idea, sir. People will eat it up."

No wonder the guy gave her the creeps.

Flood thankfully then went to ready himself. If it wasn't for the circumstances, it might be funny that he usually took longer than she did. Creams for his skin, to keep that youthful look of energetic leader, and that thick sweep of hair he was so proud of and combed straight back, probably to show off the fact that he still had a full head of it, unlike many of his contemporaries who were already losing theirs.

*Or pulling it out after having to deal with the likes of him.*

She cut off the thought. She had to stop letting those ideas form because it was too hard to hide them. And hide them she must. Even if it did make her cringe inwardly when she tried to believably coo over that famous head of hair.

True, the reason her prep had taken longer today was also the hair. She'd wanted the full effect of the curved, shiny waves of hair that had attracted him in the first place, the cause of the first compliment he'd given her when he'd approached her at that party back home. Normally she preferred to let her hair just fall in its usual way, smooth and straight down well past her shoulders. But he'd fallen for the full mass of waves, which were far more trouble than they were worth to her on any normal day.

But today wasn't a normal day. And there wouldn't be a normal day until they had their mole put down.

She tugged, pulled and sprayed until she was happy with the mane she sometimes hated. Then she slipped on the dress she'd chosen. With dear Max's input, of course.

*If this was real, if we were real, I'd ask him to zip it up for me.*

The thought caused a near painful clash in her mind, repugnance at the thought of Flood doing that, and the pure, overflowing delight she'd felt back then, when Rafe had done the same. More so when he'd been unzipping her. When his fingertips had brushed the bare skin of her back, all it took to send a fierce shiver through her.

*Be honest, at least with yourself. He's the real reason you're going to all this trouble. You know he'll be there, in the room, and you want to show him what he threw away.*

Not even to herself could she deny the truth of that. It made her a tiny bit unsteady just realizing he was here in the same hotel, let alone that he'd be there tonight, camouflaged as part of the hotel's security staff.

She took a last look in the mirror and had to admit the dress, with its figure-skimming cut and gold fabric with just a slight sheen, was flattering. She wasn't comfortable with the diamond necklace—it erred just slightly on the side of flashy to her mind—but Flood had given it to her to wear tonight, saying it had been his mother's.

She'd done her homework before making first contact, and knew there were photographs out there of the rather imperious woman wearing it. And she was sure some internet sleuth would find them and point this out after this event. She wouldn't put it past Flood to have asked her to wear it for precisely that reason. All a carefully constructed and timed progression of events to keep his name out there, for whatever his next grandiose plan was.

Lastly she put on the simple—thankfully, given the necklace—gold earrings. Liam had managed to make them match, even though only one functioned as a transceiver, putting an extra bit of gold metal on each that curved over her ear and touched her head behind it, conducting the incoming sound on the activated side. And he'd sworn they would pick up her voice fine, even if she had to whisper.

She glanced at the time. They were due to go live in less than a minute. She spent those last seconds sliding her feet into the heels she'd picked out not only because they matched the dress, but because the heel wasn't so high that she'd be taller than Flood. He didn't like it when men were taller than he, but he really didn't like it when women were.

She heard a familiar voice in her ear just as she got the second shoe on. Liam's Texas drawl was barely discernable but his voice as crystal clear as he'd promised. "Check-ins, please,"

They'd worked it all out and decided going by number would be the simplest, since there were going to be six of them on the channel, plus Ty when necessary, who with a laugh had insisted on being called Data.

"Data, you there?"

"Here. I'll be monitoring and recording only, unless otherwise indicated."

She, however, was designated Focus. She'd picked it both for being the person closest to the subject, and because it was something she could say to indicate whoever she was with was of interest, and if overheard, pretend she was merely telling herself to focus despite the noise of the gathering.

She said it now. "Loud and clear," Liam responded.

"One." Her brother's voice was also clear and strong.

Each of them came through. Hayley, Teague, Liam himself and lastly the low, rough-edged voice she'd been edgily waiting for.

"Five."

Even as he said it she remembered the exchange he'd had with Liam that she'd overheard.

*How'd you end up last? I've got the least time here, so it should be me, shouldn't it?*

*I'm last because I'm the last resort.*

His voice had been flat. Accepting. A bit weary. And she'd felt an unwelcome tug of concern.

"We're live," Liam pronounced now. Then added, in a lighter tone, "Just remember we're on voice activated now. We can all hear everything going both ways, so anything you say can and will be used against you at the earliest opportunity."

She could picture everyone smiling at that. Well, almost everyone. She may not have worked with a team like this often, but she could already see what a valuable asset each was in their own way. Including Liam's humor lightening the stress.

When she came out of her bedroom in the luxurious suite, she found the one exception to that no-taller-than-Flood rule waiting in one of the side chairs. When it came to his security, Flood thought the bigger the better, and Ducane was a tall, broad-shouldered man. He immediately stood and greeted her with a respectful nod. She didn't miss that he'd looked her up and down first, and decided to try and pry a bit more out of him. After all, she had some experience with laconic, reticent males. And this one reminded her of the one she was trying to stop thinking about.

But it was her job to talk to everyone, so the group could hear the voices and connect them to names. She was going to have to be careful, because thanks to the voluminous

Foxworth research, she already knew a great deal about all of them, and she could all too easily get herself in trouble by betraying that.

So she took a deep breath and smiled at the man before her now.

"Hello, Cort," she said, labeling him for the listeners. "Will I pass muster, do you think?"

"Only with living, breathing people."

She didn't know which surprised her more, that he'd said more than three words, or that they were undeniably a compliment. And she couldn't deny either that the knowledge that Rafe had heard it gave her a little kick of satisfaction.

"Thank you," she said, and he looked away as if he regretted saying it. *Oh, I do know another like you, Mr. Ducane. Which has me wondering exactly who and what you used to be.*

Charlie quickly decided giving him options would be more likely to get him talking than a straight-out question. So even though she already knew the answer, she asked, "Is your background police, or military?"

She thought he looked surprised, she guessed because she'd asked at all as much as anything. And it worked, because he did make the choice.

"Military. Marines."

Charlie didn't think she'd mistaken the tiny note of pride that had crept into his voice. She'd hoped for it. Even Rafe had never lost that. And that small sign made her go on.

"Are you one who would prefer not to be thanked for their service?"

Now she was sure about the surprise. And she guessed this wasn't a man who surprised easily. Kind of like someone else she knew. "Uh...it's not necessary, but no."

She smiled at him then, meaning it as she did for any veteran. "Then thank you."

For just a moment, he smiled back. Then Flood was there and he was back to all business.

"You look lovely, dear Lita," Flood said, smiling.

"And you look like a man to remember," she said, choosing her words carefully as she always did with him. Then, for the listeners, she added, "I like the gold bow tie. A nice, subtle way to stand out."

He seemed pleased—almost puffed up—that she had noticed, although she was sure he'd done it to match her dress. He offered her his arm and she took it, ignoring the distaste that rippled through her. She'd done things that made her stomach churn before.

But never one more important than this.

She knew he had timed their entrance after everyone else had arrived, for maximum impact. Wondered briefly what it must be like, to spend every waking moment calculating such things, always looking for the best way to impress, to be memorable, to inspire people to trust you no matter how little you deserve it.

And she couldn't help but feel a little disappointed that it seemed to work so well. But then perhaps it was just that like attracted like, and the kind of person who would react that way was the kind of person he attracted.

*Nothing like hanging around a politician to make you lose faith in humanity.*

And he drew that humanity like flies to something rotting. He introduced her to each person, sometimes merely politely, sometimes more effusively, and on a couple of occasions with some over-the-top fervor. Tailored, she supposed, by what each person was worth to him. She carefully repeated each name as she acknowledged their greetings, so that the team clearly had them all.

She knew they'd register the difference in tone and approach, and Ty was probably already searching out connections, data on why one person was more important to Flood than another. Money or influence were the obvious ones, but with this guy there was no limit to what he might search out.

As Flood was talking to one guest he deemed worthy of more attention, Charlie scanned the big ballroom. It was glitzy, as expected, and the wait staff was quick, efficient and unobtrusive. She spotted Teague, with the typical towel draped over his arm, serving a tray of appetizers. Liam was apparently assisting the bartender, although she suspected his location was mainly to enable him to monitor the electronics allowing them to communicate. And on the floor beside the entrance doorway, mostly hidden by a purposely long tablecloth on the table holding the guest register, Cutter was in what Hayley called his sphinx pose, upright and alert, and although she couldn't see anything but his front paws, she guessed his ears and nose were twitching as he took everything in.

And then her scanning came to an abrupt, almost slamming halt as her gaze snagged on the man just a few feet from the dog, scanning just as she had been. He wasn't looking her way, so for a moment she simply stared. Tall, lean, dark haired and looking impossibly elegant in that perfectly tailored tuxedo, if she hadn't known she would have pegged him for someone who fit into this wealthy crowd of highfliers perfectly.

Charlie remembered her earlier thought, about him being here.

*...camouflaged as part of the hotel's security staff.*
Camouflaged?
Not looking like that he wasn't.
It was going to be a very long night.

# Chapter 15

It was strange how, after all this time, he still knew the instant she had walked into even this huge room. It was as if the entire atmosphere shifted. It was like a low-grade hum, and it happened no matter how hard he tried to shove her out of his mind. His heart. His soul.

If he still had one.

In that gold dress she looked like some gorgeous trophy an ordinary guy could never hope to even get close to. Wondered if that was the not-so-subtle message Flood was trying to convey, that she was a prize he'd won. She certainly looked the part.

He forced himself to look away, telling himself he was on a job and needed to do it. That it wasn't because he couldn't stomach the way she smiled and greeted everyone Flood introduced her to as if she were honored, when in fact it should be the other way around.

He scanned the room methodically, noting and assessing anyone he recognized from the guest list, coordinating with the rest of the team who were doing the same. Some present were the known quantities they had researched, some were familiars from the city, many of the rest unknowns. He also watched Cutter for his reaction; the dog's sense about people was uncanny. The dog was acting as if he liked none of them, but neither did he give any signal that he'd sensed an enemy.

Except for Flood, but they already knew that. But Cutter had never met the man before, so it had to be that instinct again that had his lip curling at the guy. Rafe wondered what the dog would have done if Charlie hadn't been with him. Cutter gave the aide the lip curl as well. Or maybe he was just too close to Flood. It was hard to tell.

He went back to scanning before his thoughts could stray again. Some people stood out more than others, whether by their own effort to do just that, or simply by way of their own sort of presence. He quickly spotted Quinn and Hayley, looking as if they fit here, elegant and putting out that classy air they did so well.

*Because they are. Pure class. The real kind, not the kind too many of these people here just paint on.*

Teague was doing a fine job, whenever one of them spotted someone from the list that they'd wanted a closer look at, of approaching them with his tray and doing the best assessment possible in that limited interaction. If he thought it was worth more, he relayed it to One and Two, and Quinn and Hayley made sure to approach and make contact.

So far, nothing unexpected had turned up. Just the expected self-important types. Or more generic types who hung out at this kind of thing. Like the already drunk man who had just careened into him. That was what he got for stepping too far into the muck—what he was mentally calling this gathering of what they themselves called movers and shakers. He should have stayed on the perimeter.

Rafe stepped back. The guy tried to salute him with his glass, but only made the contents—Scotch, if he had to guess by the aroma—slop over the rim.

"Oops."

Even the muttered apology was slurred. Rafe kept his eyes on the room, the drunk only in his peripheral vision, knowing too well that this could be a distraction technique. But nothing else out of the ordinary—at least, ordinary for this kind of gathering—seemed to be happening, at least not here in the main room. A verbal check with the team confirmed it.

"Five, that's a known quantity to my colleague here," Liam's voice murmured in his ear, indicating that the bartender said the drunk was just that.

"Copy," Rafe acknowledged, shifting his gaze back to the drunk.

The man stopped moving, although still swaying a bit. He seemed to almost focus for a moment as he met Rafe's eyes. He hadn't said a word and yet the drunk stumbled back a couple of steps, then darted away as fast as his unsteady gait could manage. It was almost amusing, if Rafe had been in any mood to be amused.

*It's some deep down human instinct. People recognize when they're looking at lethal force personified.*

Teague's words, spoken long ago—on the case where he'd first connected with his now-wife, Laney—popped into his mind. He didn't know why it happened, but Teague was one of the smartest guys he knew, and a former Marine to boot, so he believed him. So perhaps, drunk as he was, the guy had still recognized that Rafe was not a man to cross.

*Especially now, when I'm stuck here in this swamp.*

He moved to his right, out of the crowd, and went back to scrutinizing the room's occupants. It was definitely a crowd now; they were nearly at capacity, which made their job that much more difficult. Especially difficult for him, because he loathed being in a swarm of people. He'd always said it didn't take trees to make a jungle, and nothing proved it to him more than a group like this.

He wondered how long he had before the ibuprofen he'd taken would wear off. He rarely resorted to that, but he'd be on his feet for a long time tonight, and he didn't want his leg putting up a major protest at some critical moment. If he was moving, it was fine, but just standing around like this really got to him.

He became aware of another man approaching from the left a split second before Teague's voice came through, saying, "Five, on your port."

"Got him," he acknowledged quietly.

This man most definitely was not drunk. When he turned his head to focus on him, a pair of steady, green eyes met and held his gaze. He immediately recognized the bodyguard. The man Charlie had said barely spoke, yet who had been so blown away by her appearance tonight that he'd admitted it.

Not that he could blame the guy. Not when, if he didn't know better, he himself would swear that damn gold dress was glowing, the way it stood out in this throng. Or she did.

Cutter's head turned slightly, and Rafe knew the animal had sensed the approach. He didn't react as if it were a threat, but more like he somehow knew this was a man to pay attention to.

As Flood's bodyguard got closer, Rafe recognized the expression of a man who was trying to figure something out. That did not bode well. Nor did the first words out of his mouth.

"I know you."

"Don't think so," Rafe said, rapidly assessing.

He assumed the man was armed, although his formal wear was well tailored enough to hide a sidearm. There was no sign of a comms device, not even one as subtle as Foxworth's, so apparently he worked alone.

His assessment was interrupted when the man's eyes widened just slightly. "Crawford. You're Rafer Crawford."

Well, that was unexpected. Rafe wasn't sure what to say, so said nothing, merely waited for the man to say more, so he could assess how much trouble this was going to be.

"I saw you shoot, in the competition at Fort Gordon. Watched you blow away the Army, even the Rangers, the National Guard, all of them."

"Did you," Rafe said neutrally.

"And you brought those clowns down a peg at the USASOC competition. Upheld the pride of the Corps." Ducane's mouth twisted wryly. "Then you left and we lost to the freaking Coast Guard."

He well remembered that last time at the United States Army Special Operations Command's international sniper competition. But he'd gone downhill a bit sharply and in a hurry after he'd left the Marines, and only much later heard about the victory of the Coast Guard team. He'd dealt a bit with the Coast Guard since he'd come to Foxworth Northwest, and had to admit his opinion of them had moved up several notches, so it didn't sting the way it once might have.

"Good is good, whatever the uniform." He gave the man a steady look. "Or without."

The Marine-to-Marine acknowledgment done, Ducane asked, "So is it true, that old rhyme about snipers? The 'One shot, one kill, not luck, all skill' thing?"

He'd heard it a hundred times but managed not to roll his eyes. "Only part that matters is the end."

"'Kill first, die last'?"

"Exactly."

The man grinned then. "Cort Ducane. An honor to meet you." Rafe shook the offered hand, but quickly. "What are you doing here?" the guy asked.

Rafe half expected Quinn to pop up with a suggested answer, but apparently he trusted him to come up with something. *Great.*

"I suspect sort of the same thing you are," he finally said.

Ducane grimaced. "Kind of what's left to us."

Rafe nodded. "Only choice is who you do it for, the good guys or...the not-so."

"Mmm."

He registered the noncommittal answer, and after a moment of silence said, "You look like a guy who's not sure he chose the right one."

"But you did?"

There was something in the man's gaze that made him dig deep for an answer. "I'm prouder of what I do now than anything I did in uniform."

Although it was much more Hayley's skill, he didn't think he was wrong in seeing regret with a touch of envy in the other man's eyes.

"Well, it's an honor to meet you."

Rafe only nodded. He was never sure what to say at times like this.

"Thanks for that, Five," Quinn said in his ear as Ducane walked away.

"Beautifully done." Hayley's voice held a note of pride that almost embarrassed him.

"Indeed." Charlie. Funny how the compliment from her felt...different. "That's the most I've heard that man say since I met him."

Again he remembered Ducane's reaction to her and hastened to blot it out. "I don't think he's happy with Flood."

"Who could be?" Charlie clearly must be far enough away from the subject to speak freely at the moment.

"Turnable?" Quinn asked, getting back to business.

"Maybe."

"Might be worth pursuing, if you get a chance."

"The thought occurred," he agreed. And meant it. He'd recognized that look in the other man's eyes.

It was the same as he'd seen in the mirror, in the days before Quinn had found him and offered him the lifeline of Foxworth.

# Chapter 16

"Have I told you that you look lovely this evening? You're making quite an impression, Lita dear."

Charlie managed, barely, not to pull away when Flood came up behind her and put his hands on her shoulders, leaning in to speak softly into her ear. She thought if she heard him talk about making and giving impressions one more time she might blow it all and slug him. She knew it was supposed to be a compliment, and that in his world it likely was.

But not in hers. No, in the Foxworth world, reality mattered, not impressions. What people did, not what they said. What they were really like, not what they looked or acted like.

Now, if he'd told her people were impressed with her brain power, that might be different.

She inwardly laughed that thought off as soon as it occurred. Nothing could change her opinion of this man

and the world he moved in. Or swam in, with all the other
sharks.

*Might be an insult to sharks. At least they don't gener-
ally try to hide what they are. Especially the teeth.*

She used the internal laughing at her own thoughts to
make her voice light. It was a little harder to inject a certain tone of appreciation, but she managed it. "Thank you,
Max. I'm glad. This is quite a gathering."

"Yes. A couple of very promising new potential donors."

"I'm sure you'll nudge them out of that potential category," she said, trying to make it sound as if that was
something she appreciated. Inwardly, she made a mental
note to take a look at that donor list when she got home, to
compare against the Foxworth investment portfolio. She
didn't want to have any financial dealings with people
dimwitted enough to believe in this man.

She had to suppress a wave of disgust. The longer she
spent in this swamp he lived in, the more she hated it. And if
she wasn't careful, eventually it was going to show. This was
the man who had been on an investigative committee privy
to information. Information on Foxworth moving star witness Vicente Reynosa, which he had then sold to the cartel.

But that part of that memory always made her smile.
Never had a case of the wrong place, wrong time turned
into such a case of a perfect match. She had only to look
at her brother and his wife to see that.

Flood took her smile as approval and murmured a suggestion of what they might do later on tonight.

Charlie felt her cheeks heat, and Flood gave a low
chuckle. "Not ready yet, I see. That's fine, honey. I find
it charming that you're capable of being embarrassed by
that. And that blush will charm others as well. You're indeed a prize, Lita."

Fortunately for her, someone approached him then, and

he straightened up to turn and shake hands. She doubted very much he would be as pleased if he knew the real reason for her embarrassment was that the entire Foxworth team had heard his suggestion.

Including Rafe.

By now it was clear what people were assuming, that she and Flood were definitely a couple. Some were congratulatory to him, saying they were glad to see him coming out of his grief, and they sounded almost sincere. Others were merely assessing, as if trying to gauge how much influence she might have with him, to decide if it was worth spending any time and effort on her.

Frankly, she preferred the latter, because it meant she didn't have to try and gauge in turn how sincere anyone was; she knew up front they were cut from the same cloth as Flood. The kind who would do as he had, if they had the chance. Selling out justice for the payment that had insured his newly started political action committee began with enough money to buy the people they needed would be seen as smart and admirable in some quarters.

The fact that only the cartel's soldiers had died was down to luck, and the pure skill of her brother and his team. Just thinking about how close they'd come to disaster that day three years ago burned away all the irritation and purified her cluttered mind, making the goal here once again paramount.

She purposely but subtly nudged Flood toward a knot of people near the entrance to the ballroom, not because she knew any of them or wanted to meet them, but because she wanted to see Cutter's reaction again. There was no way he could have known Flood was their target, and yet…he had.

The guests moved farther into the room. The dog stayed in his hiding place, unnoticed except by the most alert.

*Because they're all staring at Rafe in that tux...*

If only they knew how...lethal he was. To her, it radiated from him. But was that only because she knew him?

*You don't know him. Not really. If you did, you'd understand why he left. You wouldn't still be wondering, after all this time. Wondering what you'd done wrong, what sign you missed, why he wouldn't even give you a chance to fix whatever it was that had driven him away.*

She only heard Cutter's low growl because she was listening for it; to anyone else it would have been buried in the ambient noise of the party. But beyond the edge of the tablecloth she saw his ears and his nose, both aimed at Flood, so she knew that was who he was reacting to.

The dog was as smart as her brother said he was.

Rafe didn't even look at her. He just kept scanning the crowd.

"Their security team is impressive," Flood whispered to her, "but I have to admit the dog makes me nervous."

*If you knew what he probably wants to do, you'd be beyond nervous. I wish he was free to do it.*

But Cutter was also incredibly well trained, so his reaction never went beyond that low sound of warning. The sound that one predator might make to another, warning them off.

She spent another ninety minutes or so being introduced to even more people—and trying not to notice how closely Rafe was watching her. After what Flood had said, or just doing his job? She couldn't tell, and couldn't dwell on it and lose her focus on what was happening.

At last, Flood said he wanted to make a final circuit of the room. Relieved at that word *final*, she pleaded needing to get off her feet for a bit to avoid going with him. He'd allowed it, indulgently, and walked her over to a chair.

*Thank you so much, your highness.*

She grimaced, covering it by rubbing at a foot that indeed wasn't happy at being this long in heels, even non-towering ones. She watched as he started on his tour, indeed acting as if he were royalty and should be treated as such. And for the most part, the guests complied. Which made her feel even more out of place here. Along with not liking to think that there were truly this many people who believed in this man and his policies.

There were a few, though...

"Focus," she identified herself softly. "Are we tracking those who look...less than impressed?" That word again.

"One, yes," Quinn came back. "They've been noted."

That, she suddenly realized, explained the times she'd heard someone say "Note" followed by a name. Had they explained this earlier and she'd missed it? Had she been so distracted?

"And Four's making a list to be followed up on," Hayley added.

Charlie wondered what kind of clever method the Texan had come up with to do all these things at once. He and Ty had a friendly competition ongoing over which one could out-tech the other, and as frighteningly good as Tyler Hewitt was, she wasn't always sure Liam Burnett couldn't beat him. At least at some things, like this live, ongoing interaction.

As if the mention of his call name had triggered it, Liam spoke. "The subject's a big tipper, by the way. He dumped a hundred in the tip jar here at the bar."

"Shows where his priority is," Quinn said. "People do things drunk they'd never do normally."

Finally Rafe spoke, in that wry, ironic tone that seemed to say life and most of the people in it were just a big joke. She wasn't sure he was wrong. "Like commit to donations?"

"Exactly." She could agree with him, when he was right.

"Three, I can confirm on the tipping," added Teague. "He just dropped a twenty on my tray, along with some others. Times all the staff, that's a chunk of cash."

"Plus he wants good word of mouth among the peons," Charlie said. "Of course, then he'll turn right around and undermine them with his political policies, but in his view they're too dumb or blind to notice."

"Easy, Focus. Your animosity is showing." Her brother sounded more teasing than serious, and the sound of that tone so well remembered from throughout her entire life did a lot to help keep her temper in check.

As Flood continued to work the room one last time, she wondered how on earth she was going to get through that fundraiser tomorrow. She'd hoped he wouldn't expect her to be there, since he was the one people came to see and listen to, but he'd informed her that her presence was required. She gathered her function was to sit among the donors and listen raptly to his speech, and make appropriate comments to the person sitting next to her, who of course would be one of the biggest fish Flood wanted to reel in. He'd made sure of that.

"Just pour on your usual charm, Lita," he'd said. "You're such a help."

She had only smiled, but had wondered what he'd do if she'd sighed and said, "My only goal in life is to help you," while fluttering her eyelashes at him. Because it felt like that to her, as if she were acting as much as some on-screen performer. Probably felt like it more, because they likely didn't hate everything about what they were doing.

*I'm prouder of what I do now than anything I did in uniform.*

Rafe's words had taken her breath away for a moment. And she'd felt a burst of pride herself, pride in what she'd helped build. It was leavened with satisfaction in the simple fact that they helped people, both clients and their own people, by giving them work they could say that about.

Cort Ducane appeared before her, once more reminding her of Rafe in the quiet, almost stealthy way he moved. And she reminded herself yet again these mental plunges into the past had to stop.

"Are you ready to leave, Ms. Marshall?"

"More than." She let the pure truth of that creep into her voice. And she thought she caught the corners of his mouth twitch, as if he were stifling a smile. "Is he finally done?"

The smile threatened again, she was sure this time. "He will be ready to leave momentarily."

"And he needs me for the grand exit," she said.

"Easy there, Focus," Quinn cautioned in her ear. "We're not sure he's not tasked to report everything you say to him back to his boss."

She hadn't really thought of that, although she should have. But ever since his exchange with Rafe, she'd been looking at Cort a little differently. And in this case she had to agree, because he looked as if he wasn't quite happy with his current position.

As if he were perhaps not completely Flood's man.

"Sorry," she said, putting on the most pained expression she could manage. "I'm a bit cranky. My feet don't care for these shoes."

"Understandable," he said, rather gruffly but kindly. "I'll escort you back to Mr. Flood."

So Flood had sent him to be essentially an errand boy. As if anyone who worked for him was expected to do anything he asked. She wondered how he felt about that.

"Thank you, Cort."

She always used his first name, despite him always calling her Ms. Marshall even though she'd told him to call her Lita. She guessed that was a case of Flood's orders far superseding her own preference.

They walked toward a knot of people near the double doors at the far end of the room. She knew that Flood would be at the center of that knot, because that's where he preferred to be. Making his last, charming bid for their trust and probably inviting a few more to the fundraiser tomorrow.

She felt an odd sort of tickle at the back of her neck. And she knew if she turned her head she would find Rafe staring at them as they crossed the room.

She didn't do it.

# Chapter 17

The only thing better about this fundraiser than that glittery function last night, Rafe thought as he settled the earpiece and took up a position inside the ballroom door again, was that he didn't have to wear the tux. This suit was bad enough. But he had to look the part, so he wore the ridiculously expensive thing Hayley had insisted they all have, just for assignments like this.

"You're lucky, dog," he muttered to Cutter, who had taken up the same station as he had last night. "You get to wear the same thing every day."

Cutter let out a low woof, as if he somehow knew he shouldn't draw attention.

"Got this undercover thing down, don't you?" Rafe said, smiling despite himself as he went back to once again scanning the room and its occupants. Both looked completely different. Gone were the sparkling lights, and the equally sparkling cuff links and jewelry.

*And glowing golden gowns.*

He knew it was bad when he sunk into alliteration.

This afternoon—they'd had to give people a chance to get over their hangovers, he supposed—the room was much more businesslike. Rows of chairs faced a slightly raised stage with a lectern adorned with a microphone and the logo of Flood's new PAC.

This was clearly going to be a speechifying event, and he hoped he could stay awake after a fairly sleepless night. They had slept—or in his case tried to—in shifts in the suite, with someone always awake and monitoring things just in case. He knew Quinn was taking extra care, with his sister being on the front line, and he certainly wasn't going to argue with that.

But when his turn came to hit the rack, all he could think about was that barely audible suggestion Flood had made, about "Lita" sleeping in his bed that night.

He knew he'd been both over the line and very wrong when he'd made that nasty accusation about her relationship with Flood. He'd seen too clearly now how much she detested the man. Others wouldn't, but he knew her. Probably better than anyone except her brother. And he knew she detested the man for more than just what he'd done to Foxworth, selling them out for that big chunk of cartel cash.

There had been no reason at all to think she would ever even consider sleeping with the dirtbag.

Which left him with only one explanation for his reaction, and it was one he didn't want to face. He never had wanted to face it. The simple fact that he'd never, ever gotten over having to throw away the best, the only real relationship of his life was something he'd acknowledged but never really dealt with. When it surfaced he shoved it back down again, into the mental box labeled No Choice.

He hadn't had to do that this much since…the last time

Charlie had been in town, Quinn's wedding. Thankfully, for him, she'd been unable to attend either Teague or Liam's weddings, although she'd arranged their honeymoons and sent strikingly appropriate gifts. But he knew she wouldn't miss Gavin's, not after they'd worked so closely together at the St. Louis headquarters. So she'd be back soon regardless. Gavin had even joked about having her as his best man. And if that came to be, she would pull it off, and with flair. Because she always did.

Unlike himself.

When there was half a continent between them, it was a lot easier to keep her out of his mind. But when she was here, in the same room, he wondered if he'd made any progress at all. Hell, if she was even in the state he was fairly sure he would be a mess. And for a guy whose life had so often depended on total concentration, he seemed incapable of it when she was around. And no amount of shoving thoughts aside, of focusing on something else, of reminding himself he hadn't just burned that bridge, he'd vaporized it, seemed to help.

"Status, everyone?" Quinn's query brought him out of his useless haze.

"Focus, en route in a couple." Charlie's voice was barely a whisper, indicating she wasn't alone, but whoever else she was with—he didn't doubt who—wasn't so close she couldn't respond at all.

"Three, on duty." Rafe knew that Teague and Liam were playing ushers today, escorting attendees to their seats along with a couple of regular hotel employees.

"And Four," came Liam's response.

"Five plus—" the plus to acknowledge Cutter "—in position," he said. And smiled wryly at the fact that, in essence, he was a door monitor. Ticket taker.

*You've done worse. Much worse.*

Most of the seats were full when the speeches started. He knew he didn't dare actually pay attention to what was being said, or the occasional bursts of applause at some of the ideas that were being promoted would make him want to walk away. Especially when he thought about the huge amounts of money that would likely end up in the coffers of this PAC, to promote those ideas and causes. To buy politicians who could get it done.

And line the pockets of the administrators, of course.

He cleared one latecomer, a woman who looked for all the world like somebody's doddering grandmother, but who had scanned him up and down and rather sassily said that the decor had definitely improved around here.

Then he set his brain to tune out the drone and focus on any unexpected sounds. One person came toward the room from the lobby, looked around and apparently realized he was in the wrong place and went back the way he'd come. A couple of people in hotel uniforms went past, barely giving him a glance. He was watching to be sure they kept going when he realized that hum in his head had started again. He knew before he looked down the wide hallway what he was going to see. Braced himself.

And there they were, Flood with his best game face—that too wide, too disingenuous, too practiced smile, baring too white, too perfect teeth—and on his arm, looking up at him with a fatuous expression he'd never seen on her face in all the years he'd known her, was Charlie. Flood couldn't see through that? Couldn't see it was a facade? Was he blind, or just utterly convinced of his own appeal?

*Maybe Ms. Foxworth is just that good at it.*

He yanked his mind back to the job at hand. There were two others with them. Brown, Flood's personal aide who seemed glued to his side even more than "Lita," and of course Ducane, at the moment scanning their surroundings in a way Rafe recognized. It was instinctive for him to assess the biggest threat, and there was no doubt that in this group it was Flood's bodyguard.

*As long as you don't count the biggest threat to you, personally.*

When they reached the doorway, he heard Cutter, from his spot under the table just a couple of feet away, let out a very short, muted sound.

*Recognize him from last night, do you? Or just reacting to the evil?*

Rafe made eye contact with Flood and nodded as he stepped back to let him pass. He thought about making the typical welcoming gesture of waving him into the room, decided he couldn't stomach it and didn't. Flood looked back at him for a moment, then his gaze flicked to Ducane. When those muddy brown eyes came back, Rafe could almost see the thought process going on. Flood had clearly linked him and Ducane, probably as the same sort. Quinn had said from the beginning the man might be pompous, self-important and evil, but not stupid. He also noted Cutter's presence again, a bit warily, but kept moving into the room.

Ducane gave Rafe a nod, even acknowledged him with a quiet, almost respectful "Crawford" as he passed.

Charlie never even looked at him. Which was just as well. He went back to playing sentry. All business. Unmoving. Unfeeling.

It was that damned gray suit.

She remembered how Hayley had insisted they all have both formal attire and expensive-looking business attire, and at the time it had made perfect sense; the work Foxworth did required them to blend into all sorts of environments. She'd okayed the expense without a second thought, because of the sense it made.

But that dark gray suit that matched his eyes perfectly rattled her.

*And don't you dare think about him in that tux.*

"—in the purple."

She suddenly tuned back in to what Flood was saying. She saw where he was gesturing, spotted the stocky woman in the rather bright pantsuit. "Mrs. Kline," she murmured, glad yet again of the research Ty and Liam had done, giving her images to put with almost every name on the list.

"Yes," Flood said, sounding pleased, she supposed because she'd recognized the woman whose family name was at the top of that most special list of donors, the ones who kept giving with the most digits to the left of the decimal. "Chat her up if you can. Turn on the charm."

*Right. As if there's a switch.*

Even as she thought it she knew what he meant, because she'd seen him do it time and again. She even knew the stages, spotting and recognizing someone, assessing their value to him, which then determined just how much of that charm he turned on.

She wondered if he'd ever had a genuine, not self-interested interaction with…anyone.

The knowledge that the answer to that was likely *no* made her faintly nauseous. Only the fact that when this was over she could walk away and cleanse herself of the taint enabled her to say sweetly, "Of course, Max."

And while what he'd done to endanger her people was more than enough reason, she knew more about him now. Knew that he was the antithesis of everything she believed in. She wanted to take him down for more than that very personal betrayal. And take him down Foxworth would.

She was going to greatly enjoy it when they did.

# Chapter 18

"You did a wonderful job at the fundraiser, Lita dear. And you were spectacular at the party Friday night." He stopped short of rubbing his hands together in glee, but Charlie guessed it was a close thing.

She should have eaten something before she had that Sunday morning coffee. Or else it was just Flood making her queasy.

She pasted on her best smile. "Thank you. I'm glad everything went so smoothly."

She couldn't deny that it had, at least from the Foxworth point of view. More importantly, she was as certain as she could be that neither Flood nor any of his people knew they'd been under observation the entire time.

"It did." He didn't quite crow. "We made a lot of excellent contacts."

That, she supposed, had been the royal "we," since she'd met no one she'd care to contact after this was over. Except maybe the sharp waitress who had replied to her co-worker's comments on all the expensive clothes by saying "Money's all they've got."

*Truer words. Take that away, and there's nothing left of them.*

She knew some would say that was easy for her to say, but those same people would likely be shocked at how little salary she and Quinn made as the heads of Foxworth. Every one of their operatives made nearly as much, and to their minds it was all well-earned.

*No operation goes well unless all the parts are oiled, fit right and work together.*

She felt the little tremor she always felt when Rafe's voice echoed in her head. She'd asked him once why he liked working on machinery so much—it seemed odd to her, for someone with his particular skills. At first all he'd said was that it kept his mind busy. But after a moment he'd added that the two skills, shooting and mechanics, were correlated in his mind, that the calculations on a long shot were brother to the logic of machinery.

And then he'd said the words that had become a mantra as they built and expanded Foxworth. She'd never told him that. But then, there were a lot of things she'd never told him. Because he'd walked out of her life and never given her the chance. But he'd agreed completely with the goals of Foxworth, and was not only Quinn's trusted friend, but had become one of their best and most effective operatives.

From the beginning the plan had been to deal in goodwill as much as money, taking nothing from the people they helped except their help in turn for someone else down the line. She'd been able to finance that, building on the financial legacy their parents had left them, and she was proud of that. But it had never been done for personal wealth, although they could have taken a lot more out of the portfolio than they did. But she and her brother had agreed long ago that they didn't want or need the wealth and flash.

They didn't want or need the Maximilian Flood life-style. In fact, both she and Quinn found it repulsive, and agreed that it would dishonor the upright, principled people their parents had been to use the inheritance they'd left them to live that kind of life.

"Speaking of that," Flood said, "why don't you plan on visiting your friends today, one last time before we leave?"

*Speaking of what?*

She'd been tuned out again. Lost in memory. For someone who was rarely caught off guard, she'd spent more time scrambling in the last three days than in recent memory. And when she could least afford it. Focus had obviously been the right choice for her call name.

She was the center of this operation, and that she wasn't that often in the middle of it didn't excuse not paying attention. Not to mention his words had sounded more like an order than a suggestion. And that pricked at her already on-edge nerves. "I thought we were—"

"I know, dear," he interrupted smoothly, "but something's come up. I have an unexpected meeting I need to take later today."

She got a grip on her edginess and went for the innocent voice. "With someone helpful?"

"Someone who was once helpful," he said.

*Interesting differentiation.*

She tried to gauge how far she could go, all the while thinking that if she was going to do this fieldwork regularly she needed more practice. And again she thought of Rafe, who on an earlier case had gone to that steely cold place in his mind when she'd done something as simple as confronting a driver who had been paid to run down their client. Maybe he'd been right, and she should stay in the office.

Still, she decided she could risk poking a little and asked, "And could perhaps be helpful again?" She tried her best to look concerned as she added, "Or are they going to be asking you for help in return?"

Something flickered in his gaze, and she had the feeling the concern had been just the right touch. As if he thought she wanted to protect him, which would put her right where he wanted her, solidly in his camp.

*Dream on, Flood. You're the only one I want in a camp. A prison camp.*

"I'll find out this afternoon. Now, I don't want you to have to worry about getting a car on such short notice, so Ducane will drive you in the limo."

*You really want me out of the way, don't you?* It had to mean he didn't want her to see who he was meeting with. Why? Was there some possibility she might recognize the person? She didn't know anyone here, outside of her brother and the Foxworth-related people. She knew she needed to try for more info.

"Won't you need it to get to your meeting?" She tried her best to make it sound as if she were concerned about inconveniencing him, furrowing her brow as she spoke. He apparently bought it, because he gave her a munificent smile.

"No, but I love that you're worried about that."

She smiled. Maybe she was a better actress than she'd ever given herself credit for.

Or maybe Flood was just that in love with himself that he assumed any common courtesy was out of consideration for his own wonderfulness.

But his answer told her some things. That the meeting would be here at the hotel, or that the person requesting the meeting would be providing transportation, or that Flood would find his own way, uncharacteristic as that might be.

And it told her that he didn't feel his bodyguard's presence was necessary, told her that he was confident whoever he was meeting with did not have ill intent toward him.

She just hoped it didn't also tell her Ducane was assigned not only to drive her, but to watch her.

She decided to test that. "He can just drop me off at the ferry, and Heather can pick me up on the other side," she said, using the name programmed in for Hayley's temporary number, figuring if for any reason Flood decided to check on that he'd get a female who knew she was supposed to be Heather if a call came to that number. "I'll check the ferry schedule. When's your meeting?"

That sounded innocent enough. She'd have to know that, right?

"One o'clock," he said, apparently unconcerned.

She called up the app and checked the sailings. "There's a boat leaving at about a quarter till. And coming back—"

"You can take your time. Whenever you get back we'll pack and head for the plane. It's the least I can do for dropping this on you at the last minute."

She smiled at him as widely as she could manage, given she was fairly certain the first thought that had hit her had been correct. That he wasn't being nice, he didn't want her around while he had this meeting. She wasn't sure what that told her, but that kind of caution had to mean something.

"I'll call Heather right now."

As she spoke she pulled out the phone. She half expected Flood to insist that Ducane take her all the way, perhaps secretly ordering him to meet and assess these friends of hers. She wouldn't put it past Flood to run backgrounds and practically audition anyone around a woman he was considering as a good front woman for his campaign for power.

He didn't stop her from making the call. But neither did he walk away to leave her to do it in private. So he was being cautious, but not paranoid. But still, as they'd agreed, they would handle these calls as if they were being monitored, because too much was at stake not to. At least now that the Foxworth team was in the game, she no longer worried about him having her surreptitiously followed, requiring a rental car and a meandering route. She knew nothing would get past them, and if she was being followed, they'd know it.

Hayley answered on the first ring.

"Heather? It's Lita."

"I didn't expect to hear from you so soon," Hayley said.

"I know, but something came up and Max has to make an unexpected meeting with someone—" she put a little bit of emphasis on the words and hoped Hayley picked up that she didn't know who "—today, so he suggested I come see you again before we leave tonight."

"That's wonderful!" Hayley exclaimed. "I wish Marnie and Lea weren't staying in the city tonight, but they have tickets to watch a play."

Charlie had to stifle a smile. Her sister-in-law was amazingly quick on the uptake, so easily letting her know Teague and Liam would be staying in the city to watch Flood's antics, whatever they might be.

"I'd love to see them again, too, but as long as I get to see you it will be worth the trip. Max is so sweet to suggest it." That one about choked her, but she got it out. "He's even going to have his security man drive me to the ferry landing in Seattle."

"Ohh," Hayley cooed, "he must really like you, Lita."

"I hope so. If I take the twelve forty-five boat to the island, would you be able to pick me up at the ferry landing there?"

A valid question, given that the woman she was talking to was in a suite one floor below where she stood right now.

"Of course, we'll make it work. Can't wait to see you again."

"Ditto," Charlie said, soothed by Hayley's easy assurance she would somehow get it done. She supposed Hayley could take an earlier ferry and then just wait on the other side for the one she would be on.

*I'm surprised Quinn hasn't asked for a speedboat.*

She grinned at that thought and let it show, figuring it fit the moment. But she wouldn't be mentioning the idea, or Quinn would likely agree. Not that they couldn't afford it, but she was a bit more sensitive about big money now that she'd spent a little time around the backroom dealing it accomplished.

After they'd ended the call she gave Flood the remnants of that grin.

"Thank you for thinking of this."

He smiled as if her gratitude were no more than he'd expected. And deserved. She wondered if there was a pill to control nausea that was strictly situational, not medical.

And she also wondered, not for the first time, how her brother and the other Foxworth operatives did it, dealing with the bad guys day after day, without going stark, raving mad.

# Chapter 19

"An unexpected meeting?" Quinn asked, stopping his pacing of the central room of the hotel suite.

Hayley nodded from where she sat on the sofa in the main room, stroking Cutter as he lounged beside her like any well-loved pet. "She implied she didn't know with who, and with the way she was talking I'd say the subject was right there, listening."

Rafe's gut knotted in the same moment Quinn frowned. As if he'd somehow sensed it from across the room, Cutter's head came up and the dog looked at him.

"Suspicious?" Quinn said in a thoughtful tone.

"Or simply assuring himself she truly appreciates his kindness," Hayley said with a grimace. "She said something about how sweet it was of him to think of us getting together again, and she sounded so…not Charlie. I think she just said it so he would hear how she talked about him to her friend."

Quinn's expression shifted to a quick smile. "She thinks pretty good on her feet."

"Runs in the family, obviously," Hayley said with a return smile.

"Including you."

Rafe didn't know if in their mutual adoration they'd forgotten he was here, or if they just knew better than to ask for a sane opinion from him when Charlie was involved. He suspected it might be a little of both. And it wasn't that he begrudged them, not at all. It was just that sometimes they seemed so complete that simply being in the same room with them felt like an intrusion.

"All right," Quinn said then, in the brisk tone that meant back to business, although he had one more compliment for his wife. "That was a good live call, about Teague and Liam. They can keep their cover of hotel employees going a while longer, but we'd likely be recognized after the party."

Finally he looked at Rafe, who shrugged in understanding. "And Ducane would recognize me. Sorry about that."

"Sorry we've got someone good enough to be famous years after he left the service on our team? Hardly." Rafe grimaced at the word *famous*, but Quinn kept going, the decisions now coming rapid-fire. "We'll keep the suite for Teague and Liam's use. Rafe, since you're the most recognizable to Ducane, you and Hayley take your car and head to the other side on the first ferry you can make and wait for Charlie. Better take Cutter, too, since he's probably as recognizable as you are, now."

Rafe said nothing, just nodded.

"What are you going to do?" Hayley asked.

"I'll make a costume change, as it were, and get on the boat ahead of Charlie so I can watch her board and make sure she isn't being followed. I'll leave our car on this side so I can be on foot and free to move at all times. Hayley, on the other side you can wait for her in the normal area where people wait for arrivals."

He shifted his gaze to Rafe. "You take a position with a visual on the ramp where you can watch the walk-ons disembark, and look for the same thing. Once we're sure she's clear, we four will head to headquarters and connect with Teague and Liam on comms and see what the subject appears to be up to."

Again he only nodded. Quinn had a great tactical mind, so he rarely if ever questioned his calls.

As they started to gather their things to put the plan in motion, Hayley spoke, as if she were musing aloud. "I wonder if his meeting is with some big donor who couldn't make it to the party or fundraiser."

"More likely someone who doesn't want to be publicly connected to the...jerk," Rafe said as he put the formal wear and the suit in the garment bag Hayley had opened and hung on a door. If it had been up to him, it would have gotten stuffed into a backpack without much care, so it was probably a good thing the bag was here.

"That could well be," Hayley agreed. "Not like the subject is a genuine public servant."

Quinn snorted. "He doesn't care about serving, people or the law. He only cares about power. And he was in DC long enough to see who truly has it."

"And that money, like what he's here raising, is the way to buy it," Rafe muttered.

"Exactly," Quinn and Hayley agreed in unison. And they smiled at each other in that pleased way Rafe always saw when they were so perfectly in tune. Which was most of the time.

Okay, maybe he did envy them a little.

Charlie wasn't sure what to do. Which usually only applied to her in one situation, one involving a certain Marine turned Foxworth man. But while the man behind the wheel right now was also former military, she had none of the emotional entanglement to deal with, so she was able look at him more clearly. He had that same demeanor her brother, Teague and, yes, Rafe had, but once she had tamped down those emotions she realized he resembled Rafe more. Not so much physically, but in the haunted sort of look in his eyes.

He had the same sort of almost tangible alertness, always aware of surroundings, the kind of what she called mental radar that made him good at his job. Good enough for Flood to hire him. It was the kind of thing they looked for when considering adding someone to Foxworth. The kind of thing that radiated from her brother.

And from Rafe.

She yanked her mind back to business before it could stray down that overused path. The wireless transceiver that was back on her ear courtesy of the—again, thankfully plain—gold earrings was live, so she knew Quinn and the others would hear, although Rafe and Hayley had shut down the voice activation for the trip on the ferry, since they'd be staying outside in the car with Cutter, and it got a bit noisy out there.

She thought about the exchange Cort had had with Rafe, and wondered if she could—and should—give that a nudge.

Deciding she'd never have a better chance, she asked, "Do you miss the Marines, Cort?"

They'd been driving along in silence, so he seemed surprised when she spoke. Just as he'd been surprised when, after she'd again insisted on sitting up front with him, she'd told him she wasn't comfortable treating him like a taxi driver. But he'd conceded. Which gave her a clear view of that near-constant spinning of that simple gold ring on his left hand.

"In some ways, ma'am."

"Ma'am? Ouch. Now I feel old."

He gave her a startled glance. "I meant it respectfully."

He sounded almost worried. What did he think, she was going to complain to Flood and get him fired? Was it his assessment that she already had that much influence with the man? That was interesting. And perhaps encouraging.

"You're obviously not old," he said then, and a bit of that worry crept into his voice.

"Not that getting old is a bad thing," she said, in an exaggeratedly similar tone, as if she were afraid she'd offended.

Again he glanced at her, and she made sure he saw her grinning. And he let out a half chuckle that was obviously relieved.

"You're..."

"Nice?" she suggested, still grinning as he cut himself off.

He'd acted as if he'd forgotten for a moment that, from his point of view, he was talking to his boss's...whatever he thought she was. He had to know they weren't sleeping together, because he'd done a security sweep on her room in the hotel suite when they'd first checked in, and she'd made it pretty clear with a couple of comments. She was playing this game for keeps, but that didn't mean she wanted people to think she was the sort who'd jump into bed with a man like Flood just because he was a power broker. Or because he was, to some, good-looking. Personally she found him more than a little over-the-top. And even if that appealed to her, the cold calculation that always seemed to be in his eyes would have clinched it for her.

"Yeah," Cort said, not looking at her. "Nice."

She didn't have Hayley's knack for hearing what people didn't actually say, but she still got the feeling that, had he been free to say it, there might have been a "What are you doing with him?" attached to that.

*I'd like to ask you the same thing.*

She knew she couldn't, but maybe...maybe she could turn that around. And neither Quinn nor Hayley had said anything to stop her yet.

"How did you end up working for Max?" She felt a little chill as she had to stop herself from saying Flood—or "the subject"—which would hardly fit her role.

He gave a one-shouldered shrug and didn't look at her. "I needed the job. His people offered it."

"Max didn't interview you?"

"He asked...one question." There was a long, silent moment that, on instinct, she let spin out. Then Cort spoke again, in a very different tone of voice. "He asked if I'd ever killed to get a mission done. I said yes. He said, 'Good.' And that was the interview with him."

Something about that tone tickled at her brain, but she kept analyzing the very telling exchange he'd just described. She wasn't surprised. She'd always known whoever had sold them out had to have a callous, self-centered attitude. But she had to admit she was surprised at how effective his cover persona was.

*Or maybe how blind his voters were.*

It was when she hit that point that what she'd heard in Cort's undertone coalesced into a word. *Warning.* He'd been warning her, or rather Lita. He'd related that story, something that Flood would no doubt be very unhappy that he'd done, to warn her that Flood was not who she thought he was. He'd taken a calculated risk, for her sake.

His hands shifted on the steering wheel, and she caught the glint of the ring on his left hand.

"Your wife is a lucky woman," she said quietly as they reached a stoplight.

His head snapped around. Since they were stopped he didn't look immediately away, and she saw his surprise replaced by a look of pain so harsh it made her own heart quail.

"Lucky? She's dying, so no, not lucky."

She couldn't completely smother her gasp. His earlier words echoed in her mind. *I needed the job.* The job? Or the money that Flood was no doubt willing to pay for someone who would kill to protect him if necessary? Money for his wife's care? According to what Ty had found, he'd left the military before he would have gotten any retirement from his service. Maybe to come home when she was diagnosed? If nothing else, this explained the constant fiddling with the wedding ring.

"That's why he's doing this." The voice in her ear was barely a whisper, but she knew it had been Rafe.

"Agreed," her brother said.

"I'm so sorry," she said to Cort, meaning it with all her heart. "I had no idea."

The light had changed, and he must have seen it out of the corner of his eyes, because he turned his gaze back to the road ahead.

"No reason you would." His voice was gruff now.

"I wish I had. I'd have at least been more...tactful."

"You were being..."

"Nice?" she suggested again, but in an entirely different tone than before.

Again he flicked her a quick glance. She wasn't grinning now, not after this, but she was smiling. Sadly, letting a bit of the regret she felt show.

He didn't speak again until they were at the ferry landing. He'd insisted on finding a parking space and walking into the terminal with her. When she had paid her fare and was ready to head for the boarding area, she looked up at him, ready to thank him. But something in his expression made her wait a moment again.

"You are nice," he said suddenly, as if he'd been trying to hold it back. "Maybe too nice. For his world, I mean."

And suddenly she had a decision to make, how much to say, what to say that would leave this door open, but not give too much away. He'd risked this job he so badly needed to warn her yet again, which told her a great deal about him.

"You're very observant," she finally answered. And then, just as she turned to go, she looked back and said with full sincerity, "Thank you, Cort."

She could almost feel him watching her go. And her last thoughts before she took her first step onto the big green and white vessel were that she'd been partially right. Their circumstances might be tragic, but Cort Ducane's wife was lucky to have him.

And that Foxworth needed to look into that situation.

## Chapter 20

Rafe, Hayley and Cutter had caught the first ferry after the decision was made, before Charlie and Ducane had even left the hotel. That would put them in position well before Charlie made her crossing.

"This'll give you plenty of time to scout out your spot," Hayley had said as they drove down the ramp on the home side, as Rafe thought of it. "We'll have to turn around and come back on the arrivals side when Charlie's ferry gets close."

For a woman who'd never even thought about such things before Quinn had dropped into Hayley's life, by essentially kidnapping her, she was definitely a pro now. And a crucial part of Foxworth.

It had occurred to him then he'd never told her that. Not that she didn't know, but she'd never heard it from him. And after all the times she'd gone out of her way to let him know how much she valued him and his contributions to the team, it seemed rather petty that he hadn't.

Surely he could manage to say that much, at least? It would probably come out sounding boneheaded, but still, he should try, shouldn't he? They'd gone to monitoring only on comms when they'd gotten on the noisy boat, so it wasn't like anybody'd hear his stumbling effort. So he did try.

"You went from knowing nothing about what Foxworth does to being an essential part of the team so fast... I don't think I've ever seen anyone learn as fast as you have."

He knew by the way she reacted, with a startled look, that he should have said it long ago.

"That's quite a compliment. Especially coming from you."

He gave her a wry smile. "I believe you once told me that more than a sentence at a time from me was a compliment."

She grinned, that expression that always made Rafe thankful Quinn had found this woman who so completed his life.

"I did," she said. "And it's true. I take it as a measure of trust."

"It is," he said.

"And maybe someday, you might even trust me about other-than-work things."

Well, that was a shot over the bow he hadn't expected. He was very glad they'd turned off voice activation. His gut was telling him any answer he tried to make would get him in trouble, so he stayed silent, focusing on driving as if they were back in the city instead of this place where encountering five cars on the road counted as heavy traffic.

He heard a movement from the back seat and Cutter's head appeared between them. And Rafe would swear the look the dog gave him was a bit disgusted.

Cutter was different, a law unto himself, and even among the Military Working Dogs he'd served with, Rafe had never seen his like. It had taken him a while to trust the dog as the others did, but he'd proven himself time and again, and now he trusted the dog completely. Tactically, anyway.

The problem was that other talent he seemed to have. How could he trust that when Cutter kept trying to shove him and Charlie together?

They had found their parking spot and settled in before Charlie's ferry had even left the dock. And it hadn't been long before Liam's voice sounded in his ear. "Four here, going voice activated again. All copy?"

"One copy, ready to roll." At the sound of Quinn's voice, Hayley smiled.

"Two copy," she said. "We're in place."

Rafe acknowledged he copied just before Teague chimed in to say the same.

"Focus," came Charlie's voice over the earpiece, spoken softly, as if she were telling herself to do so. Since she'd be inside the ferry cabin, extraneous noise wouldn't be such an issue.

Rafe mentally ran through what he and Hayley had worked out on their own ferry ride. Hayley would stay by the car in the line where people waited to pick up walk-ons, as someone normally would, while he took up his position opposite the ferry landing. From there he could see the foot passengers offloading through the long balcony egress, as they called it.

The plan was that Charlie would disembark the traditional way, but he would also keep an eye on the lower level, where some people tried to use the same route as the vehicles, just in case. He would use the camera with a telephoto lens that was in the permanent gear locker in the trunk to watch the stream of people, as he often did in such public circumstances, simply because it was less suspicious than watching with binoculars. And would make him harder to recognize for anyone who might be following her and could remember him from last night, or the party.

When Charlie had started the conversation with Ducane, his voice was clearly audible since they were in the same vehicle. He had listened to the conversation, at how she gently worked at Ducane, getting him to say some things he probably never would have. And he felt certain now that he'd been right: the man might be working for Flood, but he didn't like him much.

He'd felt a jolt when Ducane said his wife was dying, making any bit of irritation at how easily Charlie lured the man vanish instantly. And Hayley had gone immediately into action, pulling out her Foxworth phone and beginning to text. Since she could just speak to anyone on the team, it had to be someone else.

"One, we're pulling away from the dock," Quinn said, snapping Rafe out of the memory of that sad conversation and back to the present. "So far, no sign of a tail."

"Agreed," Charlie said. "I'm going to keep moving. And silent."

"Yes," Quinn agreed.

They had planned this as well. It would be much easier to spot a tail if the tail had to move to keep her in view. True, they were on a boat, but it was a big one full of people, and she could lose someone if she really wanted to. Especially with Quinn there to run interference. The silence was another precaution, just in case she was being followed. They didn't want anyone Flood might have managed to sic on her thinking she was talking to anyone.

"I'm having Ty look into the situation with Ducane's

wife," Hayley said. "Maybe we can give him another way to go."

Rafe turned his head to look at his boss's wife. She saw the movement and met his gaze. "Prove my point, why don't you?" he said softly.

The look she gave him then had him wondering if maybe he should try to talk more, more often. An idea he never, ever thought he'd have.

When the big green and white vessel came into view in the distance, he headed out to the place he'd picked, lugging the big camera. When he got there it was still too far out to really see faces, so he gave it another few minutes, then tried again.

He spotted Quinn first, on the upper level, leaning casually on the railing while other people were already lining up at the ramp. He looked as if he were simply waiting for the crowd to thin out before he headed for the passenger ramp himself. Rafe didn't see Charlie yet, but he knew Quinn must have her in view.

Once the boat had docked the pedestrians started to move. Knowing Quinn had the exit covered, Rafe focused on the line of people already off the boat and headed either toward the town's main street or the parking area below him. It was a bit difficult with the partially enclosed walkway, but with the powerful telephoto lens he saw well enough. He saw none of the other people they'd had photos of, but that didn't mean Flood didn't have someone they didn't know about.

He spotted Charlie simply by the way she moved in the instant after Quinn said, "Focus is off the boat."

"I have her," Rafe said, keeping any hint of another spin that could be put on those words out of his voice. He wasn't so successful at keeping it out of his head.

He watched her as she pulled out her cell phone and put

it to her ear, as if making a call to whoever was going to pick her up, as many others were doing.

"Focus, I'm clear," she said into the transceiver. "Nobody looked twice at me."

*Ha. Any guy with a pulse was looking at you. And more than twice.*

"Focus," Hayley said, "Two is on the way to meet you." A decisive bark echoed in his ear. There was a pause before Hayley added, a grin almost audible in her voice, "With an escort. We'll be waiting at the door."

"One en route as well. Five, status?"

"Heading back. Focus still in view." Somehow that half step of distance he gained using the assigned code name let him speak evenly.

He emerged from the trees just as he spotted Hayley and Cutter—leashed at the moment in this place that required it—at the door to the passenger terminal. A moment later Charlie was there, greeting her sister-in-law like the friend she was supposed to be meeting, holding the cover to the end. But it wasn't all a cover, he knew that. Knew that Charlie and Hayley had bonded, both over their love for Quinn and an appreciation for different but equally sharp minds.

And then Quinn was there, and they headed for the car. His car, for which Hayley had the keys—no fancy electronic fob for his old beast—since he'd left to take up his overwatch position. He started that way, having to pause to let other vehicles pass in the parking area as arrivals began to leave. A large SUV passed, blocking his view. When it was clear the other three and Cutter had already reached the car he always thought of as camouflage. Not simply because it was an every-other-car-on-the-road model, but because the tired-looking silver coupe was a sleeper. It might look like it barely had enough gumption to get out of the way, but he kept that engine tuned and ready, and more than a little souped-up. It might look tired, but it had energy to burn. It would beat any—

His thoughts stopped as if he'd plowed that car into a brick wall. Because Quinn, Hayley and Cutter had just piled into the back seat. Leaving him the driver's seat. And Charlie the passenger seat right next to him.

His next stride wobbled a little, and for once it had nothing to do with the old injury to his leg. Jaw set, he kept going. It was only a half-hour drive back to Foxworth headquarters, he could do this. And with luck they'd be discussing tactics, where to go from here. He wouldn't have to say a word, or even look at her.

He was a row of parked cars away when Quinn's voice said, "Three and Four, we're off the boat. We'll keep comms live, but there's that dead spot for about three minutes."

"Four, know it well," came Liam's voice, sounding just as sour as he would expect the tech-reliant Texan to sound.

"Three, copy," Teague said, sounding amused. "Activity kicking up here. Will report anything of interest."

By then Rafe was at the car, and he got into the driver's seat. Hayley had already put the keys back in the ignition so he started it up immediately, with satisfaction at the low, steady purr of the motor.

He glanced at Quinn in the rearview mirror. "Any change?"

"No. Back to headquarters."

He nodded and pulled out of the line of cars. He was glad of the traffic in the at-the-moment busy lot, because it gave him an excuse to keep his gaze elsewhere than on the woman beside him. Too bad it wasn't so easy to ignore the whiff he got of whatever perfume she was wearing.

Something rich smelling, that he didn't like nearly as much as the lighter, breezier scent she used to wear.

*And that he'd known up close and personal.*

He heard rather than saw Cutter shift his position in the back seat. The dog plopped his head on the center console, just far enough forward that Rafe could see his head with his peripheral vision. Automatically he reached out to scratch behind the dark ears. And his hand collided with another that had apparently done the same.

He had the crazy thought that he would have known it was Charlie even if he couldn't see her, just from the shock that went from his fingers straight to his chest. It was all he could do to just remove his hand and not to yank it back as if he'd touched a searing hot engine.

She did yank her hand back. And instantly went back to looking ahead through the windshield. The dog let out a long, weary-sounding sigh.

"I admire your perseverance, dog," Quinn said from the back seat, his tone wry.

"He's never given up before, and I don't expect he will now." Hayley's tone, by contrast, was almost cheerful. Or amused.

Personally, he didn't find anything the least bit funny about any of this. And judging by Charlie's rigid posture and determined staring, she felt the same way.

*At least we agree on something.*

They'd been on the road back for nearly fifteen minutes when Teague's voice sounded again. "Three to One, pic incoming. Request ID, if you know him."

"Copy," came Quinn's response from the back seat, now hitting both ears simultaneously.

It couldn't have been more than thirty seconds before Quinn spoke again. "Where?"

There was no mistaking the change in his tone, and it

was sharp enough that Rafe looked at him in the mirror again. He had that intent look that matched the edge.

"In the hall near the ballroom. He looked familiar, but I couldn't place him."

"I can," Quinn said flatly. "He is—or at least was—an aide to a certain former governor. One we suspected but couldn't prove helped hide the body."

Rafe went still. Ogilvie? An aide to the former governor they'd helped take down for murder? The disgraced man who, just over a year and a half later, was hiding out in his basement, still managing to stall off a trial, no doubt calling on every lawyer and judge he'd purchased over the years, using all the dirt they knew he'd collected on others, for any tactic that would keep him out of prison?

"There's more," Teague added, his voice telegraphing tension.

"Go." Quinn's voice was clipped now.

"The subject's aide was with him."

Flood's man Brown, meeting with Ogilvie's? They were the same ilk, so it shouldn't be a surprise, but Rafe was still a bit stunned.

"Well, that makes this a whole different ball game," Liam, still on the other side, drawled over the earpiece.

Indeed it did.

# *Chapter 21*

"Do you suppose," Hayley said in a musing tone, "that the governor called the subject for help? He's running out of ways to stall his trial."

"Gee, after only twenty months?" Liam drawled.

Rafe grimaced at the truth there. The guy should have been in prison long ago. But then, there were a lot of people he thought should be in prison that weren't.

"Could be," Quinn said with a nod. "The subject and his influence is the level of help he'd need."

"Any connection between them before now that we know of?" Teague asked on comms.

"No, but I didn't look for that. I'll start digging now," Ty said. "If you're done with me for the moment, that is."

Quinn nodded. "Go for it. We'll be monitoring you, but we're back on house comms for now. Three and Four copy?"

Teague and Liam chimed a copy, acknowledging they'd be the only ones on the earpieces for now, so if they needed someone at headquarters, they'd have to run up a flag first.

"And Data?" Quinn said. "Great work."

Ty flashed a grin before the screen went dark. For a moment it was silent in the room, and on the earpieces, which they now pulled out.

"Well," Hayley finally said, "hasn't this gotten even murkier."

"Birds of a feather," Rafe muttered. "Politicians."

"And he's a consummate one," Charlie said, to his surprise not giving him the side-eye for speaking at all.

She reached for the remote control Quinn had set down on the table. Rafe already knew they had the same system back in St. Louis, but he would have guessed it anyway from the way she handled it, quickly calling up a recorded video that again lit up the screen.

"Ty pulled this off a news site's archive. It's a press interaction that happened the week after his wife was killed. It's what gave us the idea for who Lita should be."

The video image was shaky at first, then settled. Maximilian Flood stood on the steps of some impressive building before a gaggle of reporters who seemed to radiate adoration.

*So much for impartiality.*

But he had to admit the guy was pretty. Even more on camera than in person, which he figured meant…something. If nothing else, the guy knew how to use that charisma he had.

"There is nothing," Flood began, "that can describe how I'm feeling right now. My wife was such a determined, brilliant woman. My life will never be the same without her."

*Now there were some carefully chosen words…*

The reporters began shouting questions at him, which seemed tasteless under the circumstances, but Flood didn't seem to mind. He answered some about the tragedy of the accident, then quickly turned it political with a declaration he would be making traffic safety a cornerstone of his policy push. More questions were called out, including one asking if he would ever marry again. Rafe marveled at the tactlessness, just a week after the woman's death, but any sympathy was destroyed by the sad smile that looked a little too practiced, and the not-so-surreptitious wipe at his eyes.

Rafe studied him. If he hadn't chosen politics he could have made it in Hollywood. But Hollywood was openly fake. Politics hid the fakeness, but changed the world. And in this man's case, not for the better.

"I doubt I could ever find another woman like my Alondra," Flood said, a catch in his voice that matched the sad smile. "If I ever even try again, it would have to be someone who understood how I'm feeling now."

Charlie hit the pause button. "That's when Lita Marshall was born. Or rather, Ty built her."

"Good call," Quinn said.

Hayley made a face at the screen. "He's very good at this."

"Good enough to get away with what he did for three years," Quinn said, distaste clear in his voice.

"But no longer," Charlie said, satisfaction in hers.

"We owe Ty big-time for this one," Rafe said.

"Yes, we do," Charlie and Quinn said simultaneously. The brother and sister laughed at each other, and for a moment the mood lightened.

There was no way, Rafe realized, that Charlie would deny the great work Ty had done just to argue with him. Anything else, maybe, but not the value of any of the Foxworth people. She didn't even deny his own worth to the Foundation, and she hated him.

"So that clip was four years ago," Charlie said. "This was four days ago."

She pressed the play button on the remote. The scene switched, Flood again, this time against a backdrop Rafe recognized as Lambert Field, officially known as St. Louis Lambert International Airport. The rest was the same, a gaggle of reporters tossing questions out at Flood. Only this time the smile wasn't sad, it was wide, white toothed and engaging. And he ended the brief session with a statement no one had even asked for.

"Today I'm happier than I've been in years. And soon I hope to introduce you to the woman who's made that possible."

"Nicely played, sis," Quinn said.

"Congratulations," Hayley said. "Thankfully, for that not being really true."

Charlie laughed. "Thankfully, indeed. Many's the time I've had to fight throwing up, just being close to him."

Rafe spoke before he could stop himself. "At least you're out now."

Charlie turned to look at him then, her vivid blue eyes puzzled. "What?"

He realized Quinn and Hayley were looking at him as well, and wondered what was wrong. Of course she was out. One of them, Teague or Liam, disguised as hotel staff, could get her stuff if she was worried about it, but she had to bail, and now.

Still no one spoke. His brow furrowed, he shifted his gaze to his boss. "She can't go back now. If Ogilvie and Flood are talking—and you know he's at this meeting—then there's a chance Flood will find out who she really is."

"*She* is sitting right here." He looked back at her just as she practically snarled out, "Do you really think he hasn't checked me out, and that Ty didn't lay the groundwork well enough to withstand that?"

"Do you really think Ogilvie hadn't pried into Foxworth deep enough, trying to save his own ass, that he didn't find you?"

"Even if he did, he'd never connect me to the name Lita Marshall."

"Never mind the name, do you think he never found a photograph of you? That he won't eventually see you and make the connection?"

"What could he have found, my old college graduation picture? Because that's about all that's out there."

He knew that was true. If nothing else, Charlie had never wanted to be in the limelight, and avoided it as much as possible. But that didn't change the bottom line, not for him.

"And you look just the same," he said.

She stared at him. He stared back. He was vaguely aware neither Quinn nor Hayley had said a thing yet, but at this instant it didn't matter.

"Why, Mr. Crawford," she said, far too sweetly, "if I didn't know better, I'd take that as a compliment. But I do know better, so I have to assume you're just being an ass."

She didn't add "As usual," but it rang in the silence as if she had. He didn't care. Only one thing mattered right now. But she had to realize it would be beyond foolish to go back, it would be downright dangerous.

"Don't be stupid. Flood is one step away from knowing who you really are."

"Considering how stupid Ogilvie is, more like ten steps."

"If Ogilvie's after Flood's help on his case, what could be better than warning him you're Foxworth?"

"There's no reason Ogilvie would know or guess. He's never seen me in person. And even if he had, it was never like this." She made a gesture that seemed to encompass herself from head to toe. "This is as much a disguise as if I were wearing a mask. I don't ever go to this much trouble."

*But you used to.*

A memory hit him like a punch to the gut. Charlie, the evening they'd gone out on a date for the first time. Her eyes had been bright and vivid, emphasized by whatever makeup she'd skillfully applied, and her hair had been a dark, shining, sleek mass that went down past her shoulders. She'd been wearing a silky bright blouse the same color as her eyes, a short black skirt and heels that brought her mouth—luscious and tempting with a shade of lipstick he had no word for—within easy reach.

He'd about had a heart attack the moment she'd opened the door.

The memory made his voice both harsh and fierce. "You're not going back there."

For a moment she simply stared at him. But he could almost see the anger boiling up in those eyes. He should have known better. He did know better. Charlaine Foxworth did not respond well to autocratic commands.

"Shut up, Crawford." She somehow made the barely-above-a-whisper demand as much of an order as his words had been. "I already told you, you gave up any right to boss me around long ago."

A movement and a loud, oddly pitched howl made them both jump.

Cutter, on his feet and now between them, looked up at them both with the canine equivalent of a glare. He'd never heard the dog make such a sound before, something that sounded both mournful and angry.

"You're right, Cutter."

Quinn's snapped-out words had the same sort of edge. He was on his feet, which told Rafe how out of it he'd been; he hadn't seen that either the dog or the man was about to move until it had happened. Hell, he'd barely been aware that Quinn and Hayley were still there, seeing and hearing it all.

"Rafe, you're with me. Hayley, don't shoot her."

"Tempting though it may be," his wife answered, and Charlie looked the slightest bit abashed.

He followed Quinn outside, where a blast of cooler air hit him. He needed it. He'd gone too far, slipped the leash, and likely had reached the point where his usefulness was outweighed by the irritation factor of putting up with him. He once more hadn't been able to keep that lid on when she was around, and he was about to find out the price. He'd feel humiliated if he wasn't wondering what the hell he would do if Quinn cut him loose.

Quinn turned to face him, and he inwardly braced himself.

"I have never seen you lose sight of the mission before."

Because he never had. Until now. Until her.

"And I never would have expected it," Quinn went on, "on this of all missions."

That one hit hard. *Stabbed with the truth, Crawford?*

This of all missions indeed. To take down the man who had nearly helped orchestrate the death of them all. Three years they'd been hunting him, he'd lost track of how many false starts there had been. Until now.

Until Charlie found the real one, the man who'd sold them out.

And he, the man with a reputation for cool, the most patient of the most patient faction of the military, had lost all of that.

He said nothing, because he had nothing to say. No words could change this. Just as it seemed no amount of time could move him past this. His reaction in there had been gut level and automatic. He knew perfectly well—

and better than anyone except Quinn—how Charlie would respond, and yet he'd said it anyway. In the form of an order that would get her back up like nothing else could.

Because, as she'd said, he had no right. He'd thrown that away. That he'd done it for her sake didn't matter. She didn't know that, and never would. The reason behind that was a secret he'd take to his grave. He could handle her hating him. He hated himself, after all. He deserved it.

He couldn't handle her knowing why he deserved it.

With one of the greatest efforts of his life, including those on the battlefield, he met Quinn's gaze. "I'll save you the trouble and quit, if you want."

Quinn blinked. "Quit? What the..." His boss—and the man he admired above all others—shook his head sharply. "You're not quitting, damn it. Get your head out of your ass, will you?"

"I..." Words failed him. As they so often did.

Quinn rammed his fingers through his hair, then put his hands on his hips. "I don't know what happened with you two. I only know you've known her as long as you've known me." Suddenly, unexpectedly, Quinn reached out and grasped his shoulders. "You're family, Rafe."

Rafe blinked this time. How often had he thought that, that the Foxworth's were the family he'd never had? Even before he'd been foolish enough to fall for Charlie, he'd felt...included. As he never had before. But he'd always thought it was just him. Just a fanciful idea he had, that would never occur to them.

"She's set on this, and she's right. She's the best chance we have of taking this guy down." Quinn's fingers tightened, almost dug into his shoulder muscles. "I don't care what happened between you. I'm trusting you to set it aside when it comes to protecting my sister."

Rafe stared at the man who had given him this life, who

had given him the chance to put his skills to work in ways that only helped people, who had given him a place to belong when he never thought he'd have that again.

The man who had trusted him with his life and the lives of those he loved more than once.

Rafe knew in that moment he would keep that trust. He'd do whatever it took not to lose this man's respect and high esteem. He should have known he couldn't quit. Not on Quinn Foxworth.

And especially not when Charlie was in danger. He would never be able to tolerate not being there.

*You gave up any right to boss me around long ago.*

Was she saying he'd once had that right? That the indomitable Charlie Foxworth would have once granted him that? The idea jolted him to the core. But it didn't rattle the one thing he was certain of. He needed to be involved, to be close, even if it was so close his skills were of no use.

He needed to be close enough that he could step in front of a bullet for her.

That was what family did, wasn't it?

He spoke quietly, carefully, making it clear he meant both the assent and the respect.

"Yes, sir."

# Chapter 22

Damn Rafe for planting that seed.

Charlie spent the entire trip back to the city wrestling with what he'd said. Not just the thought that someone connected to Ogilvie might figure out who she really was and tell Flood, but the fact that he'd demanded she not go back simply because of that narrow possibility. The fact that he'd demanded at all.

The very idea that he thought he had the right.

That was almost enough to distract her from the task ahead. She had to force herself to, ironically, focus. She had to play this as if nothing had changed, as if this were just a vacation, as if she appreciated the chance to see more of her "friends," as if she were still just as impressed with Flood as she'd made him believe she was. Still, she'd contacted Ty before they left and told him to replace her actual photo wherever it might be out there with a "newer" one that wasn't really her at all, that looked close enough to be believable yet with at least one noticeable difference. Knowing Ty, he'd have that done before they got to the other side.

She hadn't put the wireless transceiver back in her ear yet. She needed to think, and this ferry ride was going to be her only chance.

Of course the fact that Rafe was on the boat just yards away didn't help. He didn't even need to be in sight, just knowing he was here somewhere had her in an uproar. And wouldn't all the people who said Charlaine Foxworth was the toughest woman they'd ever known, that she was smart, savvy and above all cool under stress, laugh to see her now? In a stirred-up mess because one man was somewhere on this nearly five-hundred-foot-long boat.

She got the full measure of how distracted she was when a woman in the row that backed up to hers and one seat over spoke.

"We're live again."

Charlie barely managed not to jump. She knew it was Hayley's voice but had to force herself not to look over her shoulder to be sure. She turned her head just enough to see that Hayley, dressed today in casual leggings and with her hair up in a perky ponytail, looking very little like the stylish woman who'd attended the party, had her phone up to her ear, to make it seem as if that's where the comment had been aimed. They had obviously risked this because she hadn't responded to a roll call on the system.

Embarrassed now, she put the earring back on and settled it into place. Funny how just about every episode of embarrassment she'd suffered in her entire adult life could somehow be traced back to one person.

She thought about muttering "sorry" into the transceiver, but since Rafe was no doubt live and tuned in—he would never miss a check-in—she did not.

"Focus is here," was all she said.

"Copy," came her brother's voice back. "Three reported subject's security has left the hotel, headed for the garage."

Did Teague never miss anything? "You think the subject isn't coming? He's sending him for me?"

"That's our guess. And according to Three he doesn't look happy about it."

"Reduced to a chauffeur, I'm not surprised," Charlie said.

"Just got some info on him from Data." Since that came from Hayley, who was still sitting less than two feet away, she heard it with both ears. "Or rather, on his wife. She's here in the city, in hospice care. Stage four cancer, last treatment option failed."

"No wonder he needs what the subject's willing to pay," Quinn said, sounding grim. "Five, Focus, you two have the best chance with him, so if the opportunity arises…"

She didn't like the linking even with call names, so it was an effort to keep her voice neutral when she said, "Yes. I'll keep working on him."

"Copy," Rafe answered, his tone seemingly unconcerned by the juxtaposition. *Why would he be concerned? He made his decision long ago.*

Her cell phone rang. "Hold on, the subject is calling."

"Ah. The official explanation," Hayley said.

"Probably," she agreed. "Answering now," she added by way of warning before she swiped to answer the incoming call, mentally prepping herself to put on her best happy voice. She put the phone to her free ear.

"Max? Is your meeting over already?"

"No, I'm sorry, Lita dear—" he was starting to say it as if it were one word, Litadear "—we're running long. I'll send Ducane to pick you up."

*Or keep an eye on me?*

"Are you sure you don't need him there?" She tried her best to put worry into her voice.

"I need you safe more," Flood said, so practiced she would have sworn his concern was genuine if she hadn't known better.

"All right," she said, although thanks to her newly planted paranoia she wasn't certain it was. "That's sweet of you," she added, and it almost gagged her.

"I'm afraid we may have to delay our departure until tomorrow," Flood said. "Will your boss be all right with you being away a little longer?"

He sounded so troubled she almost bought it. Wondered what he'd say if she said no. *My boss is unbending and occasionally tyrannical. And nothing like the accommodating, easygoing woman you think you know.*

She'd only been that once in her life. Only once had she ever been willing to accede to another's wishes, just for the joy of being with them. Only once, and she knew to her bones she never would again.

"I'll call and ask, but I'm sure it will be all right." She decided to go for the empathy play, since it was his favorite. "This is the first time off I've taken since my husband... well, you know."

"Of course I do, honey," he said, his voice fairly dripping with well-practiced compassion.

"I know. You're so understanding, because you've been there, Max."

"I think it's partly why we work so well together," he said, sounding now as if he were reassuring her. "Now, sadly, I need to get back."

She went for a lighter tone for her much more serious question; they needed to know what this meeting really was. "Did this turn into a negotiation? If it did, I feel for them. I've seen you at work."

"In a way, it has," he answered, sounding pleased now.

"And it will come out as it should. I'll see you soon, Lita dear."

For a long moment after the call ended, Charlie stared at the phone in her hand with distaste. "I feel like I need a shower."

"He does drip a bit," Hayley agreed wryly. She had stayed in her seat, and Charlie had tilted the phone to be sure she could hear Flood's side of the conversation.

"Curiouser and curiouser about who this meeting is with," Quinn said. "Especially after his aide met up with the gov's."

"Three here," Teague said. "All I've been able to find out is if the meeting is happening here at the hotel it's not in a publicly accessible space. And the subject isn't waiting in his suite. He's down in the coffee bar, socializing."

"Four here. I'm trying to get into the hotel records, to see who may have rented a new room or suite just for today."

"One, I copy," Quinn said. "We should be on-site in about an hour."

*Assuming the boat doesn't sink.*

The phrase that formed in her head startled her. She wasn't normally a pessimist, but this case was getting to her. They'd been hunting this mole for three years, had thought they'd been close at least twice before, and instead had discovered their then-target was, while a despicable human being, not the one who'd sold them out.

And this was the first time she'd ever run with a gut feeling instead of facts, figures and solid intel. That kind of information had sent her to the party where she had met Flood, but it was the chill that had enveloped her, the sudden involuntary tensing of every muscle the first time she looked into his eyes that had convinced her this was their true quarry at last.

She'd never told anyone, not even Quinn, about that,

even though her brother had more than once admitted sometimes he just had to go with his gut. She was a facts and numbers person, not an instinct and gut-feeling person.

Until now.

But then, her gut had been in turmoil ever since that day when she'd done that video meeting with the Northwest crew on their last case. She hadn't meant to blow up—she never did—but seeing Rafe sitting there, never even looking at the screen, at her, she'd just lost it. She'd turned an official briefing into something personal, in front of clients. To the point where her imperturbable brother had put an abrupt stop to it.

That was when she'd known she had to deal with this once and for all. And she'd been planning to do just that when Ty had come up with the lead on Flood.

*Life is what happens while you're making other plans...*

She didn't remember who'd first said it, but she knew the truth of it, now more than ever. She'd always been able to bury herself in planning, researching, crunching the numbers. She loved her work, she loved and believed in Foxworth's mission, but outside of that...life had gone on, often without her.

Rafe had barricaded himself behind an impenetrable wall of brusque reserve. She had barricaded herself behind an equally impenetrable wall of work and withdrawal. All begun on the day he'd walked out of her life forever.

And she still didn't know why.

She bit the inside of her lip, hard. *Focus! That's your call sign, but it's also an order, as of now.*

By the time they reached the dock, she thought she had herself convinced. And like some of the actors she'd seen while working backstage, she mentally prepared herself for the character she must now become again.

"Five has overwatch. He'll be last off, with the car and Cutter," Quinn said.

She knew her brother was worried that they didn't have anyone to cover from the ferry landing side, since Teague and Liam were needed at the hotel. And there, too; they had the front doors and garage area covered, but there were other exits. This office might really need another body here, along with that speedboat.

"Two, stay on her," Quinn continued. "I'll get off first and scope out the terminal, and her ride. Hold back until I report."

"Two, copy," Hayley said.

Charlie knew the couple had been noticeable at the party and the fundraiser, so were keeping a low profile. Although she herself thought there was little chance Quinn would be recognized by anyone they were watching, even if they had seen him at the party. He'd skipped shaving, and today had on worn jeans, a T-shirt, zip-front sweatshirt and a Mariners baseball cap. No one would connect this rather scruffy guy with the elegant man in the tux from the party.

She was on her feet and moving before her mind could stray to images of that other unexpectedly elegant man in a tux.

The man who even now watched over them all.

# *Chapter 23*

$R$afe had to call up every bit of his much-vaunted concentration to shut out everything except the job at hand. This time it was to keep them all safe, as it usually was. Lately, at Hayley's insistence, he'd been up front more on cases, even handling a couple on his own. And they hadn't been disasters, although he was fairly certain they would have gone more smoothly if someone else had run them, or if the whole team had been on the job.

But the outcomes had been right, and the good guys were still standing and breathing, so he counted them as wins.

*The whole team's on this one, and you're still antsy as a prairie dog who's spotted a coyote.*

He knew why. Just as he knew he should never have blown up the way he did. Now, or the case before this one, or a couple before that. But when Charlie was involved, all his should-haves seemed to fly out the window. Along with his common sense.

Back then, he'd spent what seemed like days on end telling himself over and over that she couldn't want him, not this dynamic, brilliant, gorgeous woman who could have her pick of any man she wanted. But all that was blown away when they touched, blown right out of his mind. Because when they touched they didn't just strike sparks.

Together, they were an inferno.

With an effort he pulled back from that precipice. He watched as the woman he couldn't get out of his head got up from her seat and slowly, casually started toward the line of people ready to disembark. He saw Hayley do the same, keeping a short distance behind but still where she could reach Charlie within a couple of strides; Quinn had taught her well.

He moved forward, to where he could see toward the dock, yet still keep the two women in his peripheral vision. He quickly spotted Quinn, already off the boat and headed down the covered ramp to the terminal, eyes scanning the crowd. As soon as he knew Quinn had the front covered, he took up a place in line behind the women, but close enough that he could still see them both, his height an advantage now. As was, apparently, the icy stare he'd been told he had. Nobody objected but rather quickly stepped aside when he hustled by some slow walkers to keep the two in his line of sight.

When they hit the terminal, Hayley veered to one side and he to the other, as they'd planned. Charlie kept going straight, scanning the crowd for her ride. There were only three or four people facing the oncoming tide of passengers, and Ducane stood out like a misplaced statue, tall, steady and radiating whatever it was that made people also give he himself a wide berth.

*It's something you and Quinn both have, that air of competence that could turn deadly, if necessary. It's why*

*people—at least the ones who are awake—react to you
the way they do.*

Hayley had told him that back when they'd been re-
hashing the case that had begun all this, the case that had
nearly gotten them all killed, but had brought her and her
impossible dog into their lives. The case they were so close
to finally bringing to an end.

"I have Focus in sight from the landing," Quinn said in
his ear. "And the...chauffeur." Rafe grimaced inwardly,
guessing how a man like Ducane probably felt about
being ordered to essentially be just that, a driver for the
boss's girlfriend. His stomach knotted automatically at
the thought, and he tamped it down just as Quinn added,
"Five, get the car."

"Copy."

They'd planned this out, too, that Quinn would watch
until Charlie met up with the driver. She would stall Ducane as long as she could, strolling through the terminal,
stopping for coffee, giving him and Rafe time to get to the
car to follow them to the hotel. And as much as he didn't
want the balance upset, Rafe had to admit another body
to play chauffeur for them would be handy about now.

"Or you need to learn how to drive, dog," he muttered
to Cutter, who was on his feet in the back seat, clearly
knowing things were about to start. The animal let out a
low, huffing sort of sound, and Rafe nearly laughed at himself when he realized he was putting the words *You think
I couldn't?* to it.

The dog's skills—of all kinds—aside, Cutter had done
more to give him back a sense of humor and whimsy than
anyone ever had. After all, it took a sense of humor to accept the fact that he'd had a paw in matching up not just
their clients with their soulmates, but everybody on the

Foxworth team. Except him, of course, but that was only to be expected.

But with the others, he couldn't deny the dog's part in all of it. His skill in knowing people who belonged together was right up there with his scenting and tracking capabilities, his instincts about suspects and situations, and his ability to go from friendly, tail-wagging pet to ferocious fighter in a split second.

But neither he, Quinn, Hayley nor Cutter could do much once Charlie got into that car alone with the person Flood had sent.

There was no rushing getting on or off a ferry unless you were in an ambulance. You went in the order and to the lane the crew directed. In this case, one of the raised, outside ramps which made for a good view but wasn't much help to him right now. He sat tapping a finger on the steering wheel as Cutter let out a low, impatient woof from about an inch behind his head.

"I know, dog," he muttered.

He tried to tell himself that the chances of Ogilvie's man seeing Charlie and recognizing her were slim to none, but it didn't matter. Because for him, any chance, no matter how slim, was too much. But he also knew Quinn had been right when he'd said she was their best shot at Flood, and that she was—stubbornly—determined to be part of it.

And a stubborn Charlie Foxworth was a force to be reckoned with.

Charlie knew perfectly well why this man unsettled her, that he reminded her of Rafe. But she knew he wasn't really like that infuriating man. After all, he'd married his love, and was clearly devastated that he was losing her. She felt such a qualm that she vowed whatever Foxworth could do to help they would do, no matter how this turned out.

But right now, she had a trek through city traffic to get through, and that meant time to do something constructive. Like pry, looking for the spots to aim at.

With no small effort, she put everything—and everyone—else out of her mind. All that mattered right now was finding out how much—or how little—this conscripted driver knew. And doing it in a way that wouldn't give anything away.

This time Ducane didn't resist her getting in the front seat. She hoped that meant he was comfortable with her not riding in back, or maybe it just made him feel less a hired driver.

"Thanks, Cort," she said. "Although doing this seems a waste of your skills."

He gave her a sharp sideways look. She smiled, and he seemed to relax a little. Charlie pondered what to ask next. She knew she'd have to be careful, since from the viewpoint of Flood and his crew, she had no way of knowing exactly who Flood was meeting with. And they could be wrong about that, too. Just because the man Teague had seen had once worked for the disgraced former governor didn't mean he still did.

*Eggshells. Just remember you're walking on eggshells.*

"It's such a change," she said, nodding back toward the ferry, "coming from that side back to the city."

"I've never actually been over there," Cort said, glancing back toward the sound.

"It's different," she answered. If the situation had been different, she might have waxed more eloquent, because she was truly beginning to see the pull the place had.

*Rafe says it's as far as you can get from a desert without living on an iceberg.*

Quinn had told her that, back when she'd been trying to talk him out of staying.

She corralled her memories once more, thinking more than ever that Focus had been the right call name for her. She'd made a career and built Foxworth on her ability to do just that, but now…

"Are you from Seattle?" That seemed innocent enough.

"No. I'm from Tumwater. That's down south," he explained.

And very close to the capital of Olympia. Not for nothing had she studied the map before getting here. She thought back over the research Ty had done. Hadn't Ogilvie himself also claimed the distinctively named town as his home? Hadn't he even gone back there, after they'd taken him down? Was he perhaps a friend? Had that been how Cort had gotten the job, through Ogilvie to Flood?

"I think I've heard of it," she said, going for her best trying-to-remember tone. "Didn't somebody famous come from there?"

"Olympia Beer," Cort said with the best smile she'd seen from him.

Charlie laughed, but inside she was thinking how hard it must be for him to be away from his wife right now. She gave herself an inward shake, telling herself she couldn't let sympathy divert her course.

"Focus, this is Data," came Ty's voice in her ear. "The gov left that town before your guy was born, and your guy was still in the military when he came running back."

*And that is why you got that big raise, my friend.*

"Hometowns aside," she said to signal she'd gotten the message, "how did you get roped into playing taxi driver?"

"I don't mind. It's better than listening to—" He cut himself off sharply.

"Relax," Charlie said with a smile. "All that political yammering bores me to tears, too."

That got her another wide smile. Cort went silent then,

his expression looking as if he were thinking. Thinking hard. She occasionally glanced into the side-view mirror, but only once caught a glimpse, several vehicles back, of what she thought might be her brother's dark blue SUV that he'd left on this side. She mused for a moment about the vehicle juggling that was apparently part of life here, mainly so she wouldn't be thinking about the vehicle she hadn't seen even a trace of, Rafe's silver coupe.

They'd nearly gotten to the hotel when, stopped at a red light, Cort looked at her.

"I know you're...involved with Senator Flood. In a relationship with him, I mean."

Something in his voice made Charlie answer very carefully. "I don't know if I'd call it that. It's too new. For me, at least."

"Oh." Again he went quiet. But when they arrived at the subterranean parking structure and pulled to a halt at the entrance to the hotel, he turned to look at her again.

"Look, don't take this wrong, but...be careful." Charlie tilted her head, waiting, hoping her silence would draw more out of the man. "I only meant," he started again, clearly worried now that he'd gone too far, "things aren't always what they seem."

"I think with politicians, that's mostly a given," Charlie said dryly, and a look of relief flashed across Cort's face. "Heard some things, have you?"

"I... Some."

"That happens, when to them you're just a tool to be used and ignored otherwise." She knew that one had hit home by the flash of irritation in the man's eyes. And that made her decide to take a calculated risk. "They are a pretty ruthless bunch," she said.

"Yes." Cort sounded relieved, as if he were glad Charlie

understood. "They tend to assume they can get away with anything. It's like they think they're…"

"Invulnerable? Untouchable?"

"Exactly," Cort said.

Charlie kept her gaze unwaveringly on the man's face, watching for any reaction at all as she said, "I think they're where the phrase 'Getting away with murder' originated."

Those bright green eyes widened. Not in shock, but almost in relief. As if he were indeed relieved that he didn't have to explain what he'd meant. It wasn't concrete evidence, but Charlie's brain and gut were in agreement; it was as close as confirmation as they would get. This meeting was with Ogilvie.

Flood was in a private meeting with a murderer.

# Chapter 24

So Flood was meeting with Ogilvie.

Rafe knew there was still a chance that the presence of Ogilvie's man at the hotel was a coincidence, but after hearing this his gut screamed it was the truth.

Just as Charlie's apparently did.

It was hardly a surprise, a murderer and a would-be murderer having a meeting. Given what Flood had done in the Reynosa case, facilitating the death of that witness and if necessary the Americans protecting him, meeting with a man who'd successfully done the same with an opposing candidate was nothing unusual.

The question was, what did Ogilvie think Flood could do for him? He already had a team of attorneys who'd managed to keep him out of prison for well over a year, nearly two, by doing that legal dance they did so well, using any and every delaying tactic known to the profession.

They'd known from the beginning that the destruction

of his reputation and future prospects, and perhaps a slap on the wrist from the courts, might well be the only price the former governor would ever pay. And given the man's pride and what had been grandiose future plans, perhaps it was enough.

But it also had become obvious to anyone with a functioning brain that he was stalling, desperately. Because Brett Dunbar's case had been rock-solid, and no matter what they threw at him the detective never wavered. The man had more integrity than they could ever destroy, and they had tried. In the court of public opinion, the most important from a slippery politician's point of view, he'd already been convicted. And it had cost him everything he treasured most.

Funny, Ogilvie had succeeded in having someone murdered, Flood had tried and failed, yet in this moment Rafe wanted Flood more. Ogilvie had been a case, yes, but Flood was...personal. If the cartel he sold them out to had had more notice, or been more efficient on foreign soil, they would all be dead. And none of what Foxworth had accomplished in the three years since would have happened.

Then there was Cutter. He never would have gotten to know the incredible animal that even he, the most pragmatic of realists, had had to admit was special. Uncanny. And a few other words he never in his life would have expected to be using about a dog.

The dog he now knew would be his, if something horrible happened to Quinn and Hayley. And if the worst were ever to happen, there was nothing that would convince him to go on more than that dog. Which Quinn and Hayley obviously knew.

And here and now...there was Charlie. Making this case even more imperative. And yeah, personal.

He heard the sound of a car door opening, then a few

seconds later heard it again. He supposed the man had gone around to open her door for her, since she thanked him.

"You'll be going to see to Max, now?" she asked.

"Actually, no. I'm to wait here until he gets back to the hotel."

*Back?* Rafe straightened sharply. And in his ear he heard Teague swear. "He slipped past us."

"You couldn't cover it all." Quinn clearly wasn't happy, but just as clearly didn't blame the two men trying to cover the entire hotel.

Rafe listened to the background noise change as they went inside. Then again as they reached the elevator, with at least two other people. There was no further conversation between them, other than a brief exchange where Charlie told Ducane he didn't have to take her all the way to the door, and him replying those were his orders.

The background changed again as they stepped out of the elevator, clearly alone now. But still no exchange of words until they reached the door of Flood's suite. Rafe heard the sound of rustling, then the click of a door unlocking.

"Here we are," Charlie said, "so mission accomplished."

"Yes, Ms. Marshal."

"I really can't get you to use my first name, can I?"

There was a brief pause before he heard a low, respectful, "Have a good day, Ms. Marshal."

There was the sound of the room door closing. "So, here I am, all alone," Charlie said, as if to herself.

"Four to Focus, it's still clear," Liam said. "I slipped in when you were in transit and swept the room."

"Thanks, Four," she said, normally now.

So Flood still wasn't having his own suite monitored. Rafe wasn't sure if that was because he was confident of his cover, thought no one would dare, or just made sure nothing suspect was ever said in the rooms. He'd half expected him to at least have Charlie's room bugged, but apparently not, because Liam's little gadgets weren't just top-of-the-line, they were groundbreaking. And Foxworth's alone.

Did that mean he trusted "Lita" that much already? Or did he simply have that much faith in his facade and assume she would never see through it? Or would never look, because he was such a prize?

*Underestimate her at your peril.*

One corner of his mouth twitched as he thought the words. Because if nothing else, and despite all that had happened between them, he had never, ever doubted that Charlie would not be easily fooled. It was why he'd known that in time she'd see him for what he was, and that if he didn't walk away, eventually she would.

And if she ever found out the truth, she'd hate him for it.

*She already hates you. But at least she doesn't know how much you deserve it.*

"He was relieved. I could see it in his face, he was relieved I had the measure of the man," Charlie said now.

"So how long before he starts to wonder why you're with the bastard?" Quinn asked.

"He already knows I'm being...cautious."

*I know you're...involved with Senator Flood. In a relationship with him, I mean.*

*I don't know if I'd call it that. It's too new. For me, at least.*

He shoved the memory of that exchange aside as he pulled into the parking garage beneath the hotel. Went back to a question that had occurred to him earlier. And asked, without aiming the question at any one person, "So sending him to get Focus... Was he worried about her, or was it about getting him out of the way?"

"I'd say both," Hayley said. "But probably more keeping him in the dark. The subject only hired him a couple of months ago, so he probably doesn't trust him enough to have him know the whole truth, at least not yet."

"Good call," Charlie said, sounding a bit sour. "Even he has to know you can only buy so much loyalty. And I could see by my chauffeur's expression that deep down he knows he's scum. He just doesn't know how bad he is."

"And he doesn't have the option to walk away like he once might have had," Hayley added. "Not with his wife's situation."

"So, y'all, can we guess why the subject would want him gone at this particular moment?" Liam's drawl became exaggerated when he was being sarcastic.

Rafe knew of one reason, and it wasn't Charlie's—Lita's—welfare. It was because Ducane was from here and would likely recognize the disgraced former governor by both sight and name.

"One and Two, we're back on-site," Quinn said, reminding him he hadn't done that.

"Five, same. With…" He realized they had never really given Cutter a call name.

"We could use Fuzzball," Hayley said, in that tone that was just a little too sweet. "That way we'd have Focus, Five and Fuzzball, all together, one happy family."

He didn't miss the point she'd made, leaving the other "F" out of the combo. Normally he'd let it ride, but as was usual for him when it came to anything connected to Charlie, he couldn't. But he could try for humor, as if it meant nothing. Couldn't he?

"Four, are they ignoring you?" he said.

"Leave me out of it," Liam came back quickly, almost pleadingly.

Rafe wanted to roll his eyes and let out another word that

started with the same letter, but they were live on comms and he couldn't, wouldn't.

He heard a sound he immediately recognized as a Foxworth phone signaling a text message, but since it had come through the earpiece he didn't know whose phone it was, other than not his. A moment later Quinn spoke, answering that question.

"Data thinks he knows where they are. He found a car rental arranged by the hotel concierge, at about the right time, and in the name of the subject's aide. He got into the vehicle's GPS and has the location where it has been stationary for a couple of hours. In Tacoma."

"Which is conveniently about halfway between Seattle and Tumwater," Hayley said.

"Data's already going into our old files, in case the gov is still driving the same vehicle he had back then, to see if he can get into it, too," Quinn said.

"Focus, are we paying him enough?" Hayley asked.

"He says more than," Charlie answered, smiling at the question. "But that may be because of the big raise I just gave him."

"Good," Quinn said, "because he just came back with results already. Apparently it's the same car he had on our case."

*Couldn't afford a new one with all the legal bills, I hope.* Rafe's thought again told him how personal this one was; he usually didn't get vindictive, once the client had been taken care of.

Of course, this time the client was Foxworth.

"And he says he's done with the photo, too." Hayley this time. "New one is in place at all sites that had the old one. I looked, and it's good. Very close, but she has short hair and a bigger nose."

It took him a moment to figure out that she'd acted on

what he'd said when they were…fighting. Again. Always. She'd shown no sign then that she thought he might have a point, but yet she'd taken action. He wasn't sure how that made him feel.

"Since nobody's here at the moment, I'm going to look around a bit."

Charlie's voice came through as nonchalantly as if she'd said she was going to look out the window. Rafe had to clench his teeth to keep from blurting out an order not to. Just because Flood was apparently in Tacoma didn't mean someone else wouldn't show up at any moment. They didn't know for sure where Brown was, for one, and until they knew that for certain, she damn well should be more careful.

But he'd been recently reminded of how well she took autocratic orders. Especially from him.

"They're moving." Quinn's voice broke in on his thoughts. "Leaving Tacoma. According to Data, each headed back the way they came. Focus, according to traffic, you've got half an hour, thirty-five max."

"Copy. No papers left behind that I can see. I presume anything crucial is in that lockable case he makes his aide lug around."

Silence stretched out, although he could hear some rustling. As if Charlie were moving things, doing a real search. And if someone Flood had left behind walked in on her…

"Well, now I know that in private he's a slob," came her voice, with a wry note in it. "This bedroom's a mess."

"Probably used to having people pick up after him," Hayley said, in much the same tone.

Rafe heard the exchange clearly, registering the likely truth of Hayley's guess even as he tried to deny the blast of relief he felt that Charlie truly hadn't known this about their target.

Another long stretch of silence except for a bit more rustling. When they reached the half-hour point, he was wondering what else she could possibly be doing.

"Pockets and drawers are a bust as well. I'm going to—"

"Three to Focus, get clear. You've got incoming." Teague's voice was sharp with warning.

The split second before she said, "Copy," felt like much longer.

"It's the aide," Teague said, and Rafe wasn't really surprised Flood had left Brown behind to watch things. Probably including his Lita. "He's on the phone, heading for you pretty fast."

The silence before she said, "I'm back in my room," felt like the longest of his life. "Is he still on the phone?"

"Yes," Teague answered. "And at the door now."

"Hold traffic, please. I'm going to try and listen before he realizes I'm here."

Rafe heard a slight click, guessed it was Charlie opening her bedroom door. Then, in the background, he heard a male voice, in what was clearly one side of a conversation.

"—remember that, with the governor. And over there is where they found the body?"

There was no sound of a reaction from Charlie, but Rafe's gut knotted up enough for both of them. She needed to get out of there, but he knew she wouldn't. She was just too damned stubborn.

Then came the words that clinched it, for him, anyway.

"You think it's the same Foxworth we ran afoul of? Yes, I'll look into that right away."

The faint click told him she'd closed the door. And that she knew they'd heard what they needed to hear.

They knew now that Ogilvie had told Flood that the

Foxworth Foundation had been instrumental in taking him down and destroying his career and reputation. And that their Northwest office was in the very place Lita had gone to visit. The same area where Ogilvie had buried the body of the political opponent he'd had murdered.

From there it was a short jump to connect them to his own failed effort three years ago. It was a fairly distinctive name. So no matter how low a profile they tried to keep, thanks to the media and the internet, enough information was out there that Flood would eventually be able to verify the same Foxworth had foiled the cartel in their effort to murder the one man brave enough to testify against them. Ironically, only the fact that Vicente had, in the end, testified and the cartel had been taken down had allowed Flood to survive and keep his position—and the buckets of cash they'd paid him to get his government colleagues to look the other way.

But most of all, what they had just heard was tantamount to an admission that Flood had indeed been the one behind that fiasco three years ago. That he truly was the mole they had been hunting all this time. They'd had little doubt left, but that little bit had been blasted away now.

And now they had to assume he'd soon know for sure they were the same Foxworth. The ones that stood against everything he dealt in: bribery, collusion, influence peddling…and selling out his own country. Not to mention soliciting the murder of American citizens.

And if Flood—or Brown—dug deep enough, long enough, he might just find something. Ty had replaced the recognizable photo, but the internet was forever. And although the chance was slim, any chance was too much for Rafe.

He knew Charlie would say Flood could never put it together in time to stop them. He also knew the timing didn't matter, not to him. Because once Charlie was in Flood's crosshairs, all that was left was to pull the trigger. He had no doubt the self-preservationist Flood would do just that. Quite literally if necessary.

It was one thing when he or Quinn or the others risked their lives. They were trained for it. Charlie's genius was in other areas, involving numbers and finance. And Rafe knew, as they all knew, that if they lost Charlie, they'd lose the very foundation of Foxworth, the one person who enabled them to do what they did, to fight the fight they fought, to do the good they did.

They should pull her out. Except she'd never do it. This was as close as they'd gotten, as they would likely ever get. She might be a numbers person and not a field operative, but she would never quit, not on this. Even if it meant risking her life.

As for what he personally would lose if Flood succeeded...

*Nothing you didn't already throw away, Crawford.*

But he would not let it happen. If it meant he had to take Flood out himself, so be it. After all, that's what he did. Why they kept him around.

The fact that he could end up in prison himself did not escape him. But he didn't care. Not when it came to this.

Not when it came to Charlie.

And what that said about him was the one thing he couldn't face.

# *Chapter 25*

Charlie arranged the scene carefully, seating herself at the room's small table, with her feet up on the second chair, and the tablet she'd bought specifically for this trip—she wasn't about to bring a laptop Flood or his minion might be tempted to snoop into—open to a reading app and showing her halfway through a current bestseller she frankly didn't think much of.

But she wasn't reading. Her mind was racing as she stared unseeingly at the words on the screen. They couldn't suspect she was connected to Foxworth, at least not yet. And there truly wasn't much out there about her, her distaste for the limelight had seen to that. And Ty had now changed what few pictures of her were out there. Sure, somebody could dig into the Wayback Machine and find the originals, but it would take time for the idea to even occur.

So she had time. She didn't have to bail, not just yet. But maybe soon. She had to find the proof they needed before that happened.

The tap she'd expected came on the bedroom door. "Yes?" she called out.

It opened, and Brown stood there. She gave him her best smile. "Alec, hello. Is Max back?"

"On the way," the man said, and she didn't miss the way he'd scanned both her and the room as he said it.

"Oh, good. I hope his meeting went well."

"Yes and no. He's a little…edgy, so I'd tread carefully, if I were you."

*Thankfully you are not.* "Thanks for the heads-up. I know he deals with such big things, it must be nearly over-whelming sometimes."

"Only when he has to do business with people who don't know who they're dealing with," Brown said, and there was no mistaking the acid edge in his voice. The tone reminded her of when she'd overheard that brief exchange before they'd left St. Louis.

*We don't want to have to take another chance like we did before.*

*That was an emergency. It required extreme measures.*

Brown had had the same edge in his voice then—although Flood had been calm to the point of being blasé with his answer—as he had now, and she had no idea why either time. And she didn't like not knowing.

Ogilvie had clearly told Flood about Foxworth's involvement in his downfall, and they had to assume Flood had remembered the name from his own experience, even if it hadn't involved him firsthand. But had Ogilvie told him because Flood had great influence, or because he knew about Flood's prior encounter with them and so they had a common enemy?

Her best guess was that Ogilvie had been asking for Flood's help with his defense, perhaps asking him to look into Foxworth in an effort to discredit them and their part in his arrest.

*Good luck with that.* It wasn't ego that made her think that, it was the simple fact that Foxworth ever and always made absolutely sure of their footing before they took aim and fired, as Quinn put it.

"He's told me you've been with him for years. I admire your loyalty," she said to Brown, wondering what tale Flood had spun to so completely win over the man. Or perhaps they were both cut from the same cloth, and that's all Brown needed to know. She had the feeling that if she ever heard them discussing long-term goals, their aims would probably turn her stomach. "Are you sorry he left the Senate?"

Brown looked at her for a moment, as if pondering if he should answer. Finally he shrugged and said, "He can get more done this way."

*By circumventing the process? I'll bet.*

She watched him go and for a moment simply stayed where she was, her mind racing. So many pieces had tumbled together in the last hour she wasn't sure where to start. How on earth did Quinn and the others make decisions when they were in the field and had to act fast, had to make those decisions on the fly, and sometimes without much concrete information or evidence?

Once more her mind flashed back to when Quinn had told her he'd found Rafe and wanted to hire him. Before she'd seen the tall, rangy, impossibly appealing—to her, anyway—man their childhood friend had become.

"Do we really need…a sniper?" she'd asked, then immediately regretted it; after all, the man had saved her brother's life by being just that.

Quinn, knowing her well, had cut through to her real doubts. "He made decisions, to pull the trigger, that ended with him killing people. Right decisions, in combat, against an enemy, as he was ordered. And that doesn't bother him. But he made two bad ones, in his mind, anyway. I disagree, but the fact that they haunt him to this day tells me what I need to know about him."

"Bad decisions?"

"Once it was based on faulty intel on where a couple of terrorist leaders were holed up. He thinks he should have guessed it was wrong. The real bad guys came up behind them and killed a couple of the team before he could shift and take them out, and he blames himself."

"But if that's what the intelligence he was given said…"

"Exactly. Not his fault."

"What was the second time?"

"Following an order to shoot he suspected was a mistake, that it was the wrong target, but he followed it anyway. Turned out to be a woman trying to get away with her child. Kid wasn't hit but the mother was."

She remembered even now how awful that story had made her feel. And learning later that the mother had survived she was sure hadn't changed Rafe's reaction much. A memory had popped into her mind, of the skinny, lanky boy they'd once known, quiet even then, but ever and always watchful. And even then, those stormy gray eyes of his had made her feel as if he were seeing more than just what was before him. That had never changed.

And once he'd seen what he needed to see, he'd make his decision and take the action he'd decided on. Even as a kid, he'd done that. And now, here she was struggling with making the simplest of decisions, like what to do next.

She didn't think Brown suspected her of anything, not really. Flood had warned her when he'd first introduced them that the man required a great deal of time and ex-

perience with someone before he would trust them. She'd
merely nodded and said, "Sounds wise."

And had meant it, which Flood had clearly seen because
he'd given her that approving smile that reminded her of
nothing less than a school teacher smiling at a pupil who'd
given a right answer. It wasn't the first time she'd sensed
he was testing her, but that was when it had first occurred
to her that he was, in essence, schooling her. For a life
with him? Or simply how to not cause him any problems?

"Three to Five, you're on scene?" Teague's voice in her
ear brought her out of her assessing. Irritation sparked
through her when she realized she was holding her breath,
waiting for the response, the sound of Rafe's voice.

"East side." She took a breath. "With... Fuzzball sidekick."

"You sure you're not the sidekick?" came Liam's drawl.

"Pretty sure I am."

For a moment Charlie just stood there, marveling at the
simple, teasing exchange she'd just heard. Hayley had told
her that Rafe tolerated Liam better than anyone, probably
because the young Texan simply refused to get ruffled or
irritated at his taciturnity. She'd once known that Rafe.
Once upon a time, he had unbent with her enough to make
her laugh out loud with his wry and unexpectedly humor-
ous observations on just about anything.

Once upon a time.

And it had been as fleeting, or as unreal, as the fairy tale
those words implied. Three months of a bliss she'd never
expected to find, a kind of joy she'd thought had died in her
when her parents had been blown up by a terrorist bomb,
an interlude that had made surviving worth it.

And he had thrown it away.

The bottom line never changed, no matter how often

she thought about it, or how long she managed to go without thinking about it.

"—spotted his security just outside the main entrance. Waiting for the subject no doubt, but Data says he's still a good fifteen minutes out, maybe more with the traffic he's seeing. Might be a chance to work him a bit."

"Copy. En route."

"With the sidekick?" Liam asked. "Always a good icebreaker."

"With Fuzzball," Rafe confirmed, then added, "If I leave him in my car, he's likely to drive off with it."

She smiled, but with a small sense of shock at the continued joking. And then a feeling of warmth. Clearly he felt comfortable enough here to let the humor that had once so startled her emerge. Despite it all, what had happened—and not happened—between them, she had never wished Rafe ill, even though she didn't understand why he'd done it.

*Did you never think that maybe he thought he wasn't enough for you?*

Quinn's words echoed in her mind now. And the answer was still the same. It had never occurred to her that he'd walked—hell, run—away because he didn't think he was enough for her.

She knew she had a bit of a reputation. Yes, she was smart, and didn't think it was ego but only fact to add a "very" in front of that. She was very good at what she did, and had always had to work at having patience with others who didn't or couldn't see what was so obvious to her. She'd found a way to deal, by trying to find out what others were good at, like her brother's tactical skill, dedication and courage, or Ty's tech genius, and focus—that word again—on that.

With Rafe, when they'd connected after all those years since childhood, she'd started out knowing that he was among the very best at what he did. What she hadn't known, had never expected, was that he made her pulse race and her heart give an odd little flutter every time she saw him. And when he'd eventually let that sense of humor show, she'd been beyond charmed, she'd been head over heels. And that was something that had never happened to her, before or since. Nor would it ever again. She wouldn't be a fool twice.

But she would find out why.

## *Chapter 26*

Rafe saw Ducane's gaze shift from him to Cutter, then back again. Damn it, the guy's eyes really were an unusually bright green. He steadied himself inwardly, knowing he was going to have to use a tactic he rarely did. He was going to have to talk to the guy.

"He yours?" Ducane asked.

"My boss's." He let his mouth quirk slightly. "Both my bosses, actually."

"You've got two?"

He nodded. "Best people a guy could ever work for."

Ducane frowned. "So you don't work for the hotel?"

"Only temporarily. Helping out. Along with my side-kick here." He nodded down at Cutter.

"Seen dogs sort of like him," Ducane said, studying the animal, who looked back at him steadily.

"Only less fluffy?" Rafe suggested.

Ducane smiled at that. And as if the smile were a cue, Cutter stepped forward, nudging the man's hand. As most people instinctively did, Ducane bent and moved to stroke his fingers over the dark head. Rafe immediately shifted his gaze back to the other man's face, waited a silent moment, then saw what he'd expected, that look of bemused wonder.

"Almost scary, isn't it?" he said quietly.

Ducane looked up, met his gaze. "What...?"

"I don't know what it is he's got, only the effect it has." He gave a half shrug, then dived ahead with a truth he'd given up denying early on when it came to this dog. "Sometimes, I'm not even aware I'm feeling bad until he does that and makes me pet him."

Rafe heard a sound in his ear, but it wasn't a word and he couldn't be sure who'd made it.

"So you're saying he knows, even if you don't?" Ducane asked.

"Exactly."

"So he's what, some kind of therapy dog?"

"Not just that. Name anything you'd want a dog to be, and he's it. Soothing, intuitive, devilishly clever, goofily funny and, when necessary, deadly serious."

In the pause while Ducane absorbed this, Hayley said cheerfully, "Nice. Cutter in a nutshell."

"Serious like when he was playing guardian at the gate the last couple of days?"

"Exactly. You do not want to cross him when he's working."

"Ex-MWD?"

"Don't know. He just kind of dropped in out of nowhere and stayed." *And we've all been the better for it.*

Ducane looked back at him. "So, these people you work for, you really...like them?"

"I do. And admire and respect them." He studied the other man for a moment, then went for it. "Everything and everyone you wish others would stand and fight for, they do."

Ducane's expression only flickered for an instant, but Rafe knew what he'd seen. Distaste. So he knew his own boss was far less than that. Maybe he even knew he was the exact opposite, fighting only for himself. But did he know how little Flood cared about anyone else who might get hurt—or killed—in the process? Did he know he himself would be jettisoned easily and without second thoughts if Flood so decided?

"Nice," Ducane said.

"If you're in a bad situation because you had no choice, or you're in the right but up against impossible odds or unbeatable forces, they'll find a way to make it right. Maybe not the way you imagined, but in a way that's undeniable."

Ducane was listening intently. "What if it's a situation that…can't be fixed?"

"His wife," Hayley said instantly, warning him to tread carefully.

"They're not miracle workers, although sometimes it seems like it. But they will take whatever it is and make it as easy as is possible."

"What if it's…inherently unbearable?"

"Then they'll help get you to the other side." He purposely said the "you" as if he meant it specifically, as he indeed did. "Even if it's only to remove every other worry you have."

Ducane let out a harsh sound that was half laughing, half despairing. Rafe recognized the tone, he'd heard it in his own voice, back before Quinn had found him and pulled him out of it. Teetering on the edge of despair.

Rafe wished he could ask Hayley for help. She was the genius at reading people, at knowing when to push and when to back off. Even as he thought it, her voice came through his earpiece.

"Give him something, something you have in common."

"Merland," Charlie said suddenly, unexpectedly.

Rafe was stunned for a moment. He'd almost forgotten he'd told her about the officer who'd passed on intel without vetting it, that had led to the deaths of two men he'd been handling overwatch for.

That he still felt responsible for.

But she was right. It was a door, and it felt like the right one, with this man.

"I had to take an order from an incompetent ass once," he began, then grimaced before going on. "Well, more than once, but this time it cost the lives of two good men I was responsible for. When I got back to base, I wanted more than anything to hunt him down and send him to join them."

Ducane's gaze sharpened. "Did you?"

"No. He wasn't worth ending up in Leavenworth for. But I did stand as a witness against him, and got to watch Mr. High-and-Mighty-Privilege go down in flames and shame. It was worth it. The boss doesn't always win. Even with power behind them."

Ducane shook his head slowly. Rafe saw the despair creeping into his expression. In that moment Cutter moved again, and the anguish faded a little as the man stroked the animal. After a moment, clearly steadier now, he looked up at Rafe again.

"What if that job for...that person, was the only one that would pay what you needed?"

Ducane wasn't even trying to hide it now; this was personal, this was him and he was letting it show.

A new voice came through. Gavin. "You've got his attention, Rafe. Now offer him the bait, but slowly." If anyone would know about that, it was Gavin de Marco. They'd called out the troops to help. For which he was grateful; this was not the pond—or swamp—he usually swam in.

"Talk to him the way someone would have to talk to you, to get you to listen," Quinn put in.

*Like you did, when you pulled me out of the pit?*

Quinn had been utterly calm back then, not pushing but merely offering another path, and promising he would be there every step of the way. Without the background he and Quinn had had together, the basis of trust, he'd have to be a little more careful, but...

"Is he really the only one?" Rafe asked Ducane.

The man let out an audible breath. "I needed to move fast. There were...things I had to do, to pay for." He seemed to realize suddenly how that could sound, and quickly added, "Nothing illicit, I just... It was personal."

"So your employer was the only one you could find in a hurry who would pay what you needed."

Ducane nodded.

"And now that you've been working for him a while, what do you think of him?" The man shrugged, giving a half shake of his head. Guessing he was still wary of saying what he really thought, Rafe did it for him. "Personally, I don't like him much. I don't know if it's the slippery slime of the swamp, or the smell of it that puts me off."

Ducane's gaze shot back to his face. "It clings, doesn't it," he said, almost in a whisper.

"It does. Now my boss, he's solid gold. Even if he was Army."

"He was?"

"Ranger. But I don't hold it against him. Just rag on him now and then."

A brief grin flashed across Ducane's face. Which seemed the right moment to make the final strike. And he found he really, really didn't want to blow this. He felt for the guy, and he wanted to help him out of this mess. Especially before Foxworth took it all down.

"You want out of that swamp, Ducane?"

His expression gave the true answer, but he shook his head. "Can't afford it."

"Don't be so sure."

"You don't understand. There's more to it."

Yes, there was. And it was something he couldn't let Ducane know, that he already knew about his wife. Just as he couldn't speak the name Foxworth, the one thing that might convince the man, given he was local and had probably heard of them during the Ogilvie chaos.

But it also might give away the entire operation here and now, and before they had Flood nailed.

"They're on our street now," Liam warned in his ear.

Over Ducane's shoulder he saw Brown coming out the hotel's main doors. The man glanced toward them, flicked his gaze to Cutter and stared for a moment with his brow furrowed. Rafe's breath caught. Recognition, yes, but… more puzzlement.

It made him uneasy, because they still didn't know why Flood had told Brown to stay here. They'd figured Flood went dressed in ordinary, casual clothes as a sort of disguise, given he was usually dressed up to the hilt, but they hadn't expected him to go alone. The only reasons that made sense were that this meeting was strictly personal, or too clandestine even for the trusted aide, or… Flood didn't trust either his own security or his new lady, and had left the only one he did trust to watch. And if it was the latter, it only meant one thing to Rafe—Charlie's position was indeed precarious.

Then Brown turned away, to look toward the street entrance to the garage. In almost the same instant Rafe heard Liam again. "They're almost to the driveway."

Rafe grabbed the few seconds he had left to hand Ducane a card, on which was printed only a phone number, a special Foxworth phone number, the otherwise blank cards printed for exactly this kind of situation. Then, as he spotted the rental car approaching, he spoke, as seriously and convincingly as he could.

"We can find you a way out of that trap you're in."

Ducane gave a sad shake of his head. "It's hopeless."

Doing something he almost never did, Rafe acted on impulse, reaching out and grasping the man's shoulder as he spoke one last time, almost solemnly.

"Hopeless is what we do best."

# Chapter 27

Charlie sat on the edge of the bed, forcing herself to take deep, calming breaths. She didn't need to compose herself because Flood was on his way back, she was ready for that. Eager for it, in fact. She wanted this case over and done, wanted the man disgraced, publicly vilified and hopefully locked up.

No, she needed to compose herself because she'd just heard compelling and undeniable evidence of how much Rafer Crawford had changed since that day Quinn had brought him into the office in St. Louis. He'd been hesitant, uncertain about what his place might be in this foundation his childhood neighbors had begun. And, she'd sensed even then, more uncertain that he could fit in at all.

*While you sat there and stared at that tall, lean, powerful guy with the impossible stormy gray eyes and wondered how the gangly kid you remembered had turned into such a hunk of gorgeousness.*

She'd never had that kind of reaction before. She'd seen

it before—and uncomfortably often aimed at her little brother—in other women, but had thought herself immune.

Boy, had she been wrong. It had taken her a while to get past always connecting him to that kid she'd known, but reading through the military record they'd pulled, re-membering what Quinn had told her about him being the sniper who had saved his life and the lives of his platoon, seeing his name on that world-famous trophy, helped.

But a few times watching him move, looking into those eyes, feeling the incredible warmth when he gave her one of those rare smiles... Yes, those things pushed her way beyond the boy from down the street.

And now she knew just how deeply he was embedded in Foxworth, not only the workings but the philosophy. When he'd spoken to Cort, the pure truth and, yes, passion in his voice had been clear. He not only completely believed in what they were doing, he'd allowed it to show when he ap-proached the man. He'd played it perfectly, and that was something she had to admit she wouldn't have thought he had in him.

*Because he'd been such a blunt weapon with you? Be-cause of that you assumed he couldn't deal with anyone subtly or carefully?*

She stood up abruptly, knowing she had to prepare for Flood's return. But then what Quinn had said rammed into her mind, distracting her yet again.

*...how do you explain the way he reacts around you? The way he reacts to just seeing you on a video call? Hell, the way he reacts when he just hears your name? That's not somebody who doesn't care.*

Was that it? Had he been so abrupt, so cold when he'd walked away, because he cared...too much? But if that were true, why had he walked away at all? If—

The sound of voices—including that smooth, well-oiled

one that made her skin crawl—from the main room of the suite yanked her back to reality.

*Focus, indeed. Before you blow this whole thing.*

"Subject has arrived," she said quietly.

And she settled in to play the part of a woman blind enough to be fooled by the likes of Maximilian Flood. But what she heard when she again quietly opened the bedroom door stopped her in her tracks.

"—saw that Ducane was pretty deep in conversation with that hotel security guy with the dog."

"Was he, now," Flood said, in that tone she'd come to know meant he was adding new factors to his never-ending calculations. Calculations that were always about what impact something new might have on him personally, the rest of the world be damned.

Charlie heard Quinn mutter something and whispered back, "I'm going to try and cover for them." She shut the door behind her quietly, so she could say she'd been on this side of it, not eavesdropping.

"He's still here?" she asked brightly as she walked toward the two men. "I thought maybe he—and the dog— were hired on just for you, Max."

Flood turned to look at her, smiling that smile she didn't believe was any more than one layer of skin deep. "Perhaps they're to be here until we leave."

"That makes sense." She smiled. "Cort knows him, or at least of him. That must be why they were chatting." Both men's gazes narrowed, and she went on cheerfully. "I gather he's rather famous in military circles. Won some trophy or other a couple of times."

The furrow in Flood's brow cleared. "I see. Been chatting a bit with Ducane yourself?"

She let out a little laugh. "Chat? Hardly. He treats me with kid gloves. On your orders, I presume." Flood smiled again. "I did ask him, though. Because the dog caught my attention."

His smile widened. "So you like dogs?"

"Love them," she said earnestly. *Especially that one, who has saved the day so many times. And tries so hard to get through to that stubborn partner of his...*

"Then we'll have to get one, eventually. It's always good PR."

How like him, to think of it that way. Trot the dog out for photo opportunities, then shove him back in the shadows until the next time. But then, that so often seemed the way politicians did it, up to and including presidents.

Of course the bigger point in what he'd said was that "we" part.

"Are you hungry?" he asked. "Would you like to get a late lunch?"

"You didn't eat at your meeting?"

Something flickered in his eyes, as if the thought of the meeting irritated him. "I was not hungry," he answered, and the same emotion sounded in his voice. She was a little surprised he let it show, and hoped it was a sign he trusted her.

"I am hungry," she said, weighing the options. "Heather and I didn't eat, either. We were too busy reminiscing."

He smiled indulgently. "Then let's go downstairs. I hope you don't mind if Alec joins us? We need to discuss the logistics of our return trip."

"Of course not," she said, although the guy made her edgy. As did the words about the return trip. She knew Quinn would have her back until this was done, following them wherever, and that they'd pull in everybody from all their locations if necessary. But she wanted this *over*. Three years was long enough for Flood to have gotten away with this.

"Let me just clean up a bit, then," he said, and headed for his room of the suite.

Charlie took the first deep breath she'd allowed herself since she'd stepped out of the bedroom.

"Nicely done, Focus," Hayley said in her ear.

"Agreed," Quinn added. "Cover for both security man and Five."

"I'm not so sure I convinced the aide," she whispered. "He still looks suspicious. But then, he always does."

Brown was busy on his phone. Not texting, he was doing more reading. But she didn't like the glance he gave her as she wandered that way. She kept going past him, toward the large windows of the suite that faced toward the water, as if that had been her goal all along. But she didn't miss how he turned the phone so she could not get even a glimpse of what he was doing. He'd often done the same with his laptop, either quickly closed what he was working on or slapped the lid down any time she got anywhere close, even though she'd made no effort to see.

Not that she hadn't wanted to spy. The very way he acted made her curious. She herself was careful, but Brown carried it to the point where the word that popped into her mind was paranoid. Maybe that was his job, to be paranoid on behalf of his boss. Flood didn't come off that way. Maybe this was why—he had his aide do it for him.

She stared out through the glass, across the buildings of the city, and the expanse of Puget Sound beyond. At home if she looked out a window toward water, it was the Mississippi in the distance. From the office it was the Gateway Arch. Ironic, she supposed, that she worked in the shadow of that monument called the Gateway to the West, yet so rarely headed that way. But now she was here, less than a hundred miles as the crow—or the eagle, as Hayley would put it—flies from the Pacific, and she couldn't deny the pull of it.

She saw smaller boats here and there, and to the north two

of the iconic green and white ferries, passing each other on their journeys east and west. She found herself envying the people on the westbound ones, knowing where they would land, not too far from the Foxworth Northwest headquarters.

*What is it about this place? Quinn, then Rafe... What kind of hold did it get on people?*

It was a puzzle. Especially since she, the quintessential big-city girl, was feeling it, too.

The restaurant in the hotel wasn't crowded, although she had the feeling if it had been there would have been a table found for them, anyway. Most places that catered to people of Flood's standing made sure there was always a prime spot available.

Throughout the meal, she felt as if she were trying to pick her way through a minefield. Flood seemed on edge, and Brown more so. But Brown had always been worse at hiding his feelings. Finally she worked up her most concerned expression before asking, "Did your meeting not go well, Max? You seem a little glum."

His gaze narrowed for a moment, but then he shook his head. "Just something unexpected," he said.

Considering the man never went into a meeting without knowing exactly what was going to happen and how he would turn it to his advantage, this was a rather amazing admission. As was the fact that he let any concern show at all.

Quinn seemed to have the same thought, because she heard him mutter in her ear, "Didn't think he allowed the unexpected."

*He didn't expect any of you to survive the cartel, either.* It was all she could do not to smile at the thought. But she put concern in her voice when she spoke.

"Will it be a problem for you?"

And that quickly he was back to his polished self. "I won't let it be. I'll have a solution before we leave."

"If you need to stay longer," she began, almost hoping he'd say yes. She wanted this to go down here, on her brother's home turf.

Not because Rafe was here.

Her words got her a wide smile. "I may. There are... some details to work out. And someone awaiting a decision from me."

That sparked her sometimes overactive curiosity, but she said only, "That's fine. I've been thinking I'd like to see more of the area, so I'm sure I can stay occupied while you handle what you need to handle."

"You're so understanding, Lita dear."

*Oh, I understand. More than you know. But you will. Soon.*

As they finished the meal off with some rather fluffy coffee drinks, he surprised her. "We should see some of the sights now. You feel up to a walk?"

She hadn't expected that. And if she had to bet, she'd say they'd encounter some sort of news media outside. Flood would want to make one last splash before he left. Perhaps that was what Brown had been working on upstairs, leaking that the Senator would be strolling around downtown.

She managed to smile. "Of course. Any place in particular?"

"Since it's not far, less than a mile, I thought we'd walk down to the Great Wheel."

She tried her best to act as if she'd just brightened up. "The Ferris wheel? Sounds lovely. Isn't the aquarium near there?"

Flood laughed. "I should have known. My lady does have a soft spot for the creatures of the world. Of course, we can do that. It's very close by. I'll call for Ducane to accompany us."

"Let me just run up and change into walking shoes," she said, getting to her feet in an effort to show eagerness.

Flood started to rise. "No, dear, finish your coffee. I'll just do this quickly so we can get going. I read that they have sea otters! I love sea otters."

That seemed to decide him, and he was still smiling as he sat back down. But when she reached the door of the hotel restaurant and glanced back, Brown was getting to his feet. She moved quickly to be out of sight, and then headed at just short of a run toward the elevators while talking.

"Focus, I think he's sending Brown to follow me. Can someone stall him?"

"Got him." Rafe's answer was short and almost lazily certain. He said something else she couldn't hear, and she realized he must be talking to Cutter.

"One, copy. Focus, what's up?"

"Brown doesn't have that locked case with him. I think it's still up in the suite. Now I just need somebody who can pick a lock."

"Four here, I think that'll be me," Liam said, and she could almost hear his grin.

"Go," Quinn said. "Three, watch the approach."

"Copy," Teague said.

"Focus, I'll meet you there," Liam said.

She made it to the elevators, found one that was waiting on the ground floor, stepped inside and quickly pushed the button for the suite's floor. In the couple of moments it took for the doors to slide shut, she saw Brown round the corner, and less than two strides behind him came Cutter, then Rafe.

*Try and get past them, Mr. Oh-So-Cool Brown.*

Because despite everything, there was one thing she was certain of: if Rafe Crawford was determined to stop you, you'd be stopped.

She knew that firsthand.

# Chapter 28

"Got it."

Liam's voice held a touch of triumph even through the earpiece. Rafe considered it well-earned, given he'd gotten into that locked case in just over a minute.

"Yes, I rented the damned car, but there was no accident, and no damage."

Brown, the caretaker of that case, was glaring at him now. And his voice had taken on an edge that matched. To which Cutter reacted with a low sound that was more aware-ness than threat, but Rafe didn't think Brown realized that. Which was fine with him. He smiled inwardly as the man took a half step away from the dog.

He heard Liam again, a semi-profane exclamation. Then some rustling, and a few clicks.

"A few irrelevant papers, and a flash drive," Charlie said, instantly making sense of the sounds in the background, Liam pulling his ever-present small laptop out of his pack.

Custom built by the man himself, Rafe guessed the thing could run the country if he cut it loose.

He put on his best businesslike voice, letting only a tinge of irritation through, as he thought any qualified security man might at having to deal with something like this.

"I'm sorry, sir, but the rental company says there is. If you'll just step over to the concierge desk, I'm sure this can be straightened out quickly."

"I don't have time for this," Brown snapped. And looked as if he regretted his tone when Cutter made that sound again. "Is that dog of yours under control?"

"That dog will do exactly what he's supposed to do, exactly when he's supposed to do it," Rafe answered, with a smile that succeeded in making Brown look nervous. He left out the part where Cutter sometimes made that decision on his own.

"Five, you're enjoying this too much." Quinn, who had stayed in place to monitor Flood, sounded as if he were smiling himself.

"Hoping you have to take him down?" Teague suggested from his position near Flood's suite, to warn if anyone seemed headed that way.

He couldn't deny he was enjoying it. Brown was exactly the kind of self-important jerk he enjoyed taking down a peg or three. But the real goal was the most self-important jerk of all, the one who had nearly gotten them all killed with his treachery. And for that, Rafe would rein in the urge.

Liam spoke again. "It's encrypted. It's going to take a few minutes longer. Five, keep stalling."

Rafe thought fast. "Come with me, please, sir. I'm sure the concierge will be at her desk and we'll get this straightened out in no time." He put the slightest emphasis on the "at her desk." And Hayley didn't miss it.

"Two will make sure she's not," she assured him.

"Do you know who I am?" Brown demanded.

*Ah, there it is. The punctured ego.* "I know you're the man who rented and returned a seriously damaged vehicle, and the man who didn't report said damage. There are a couple of laws involved there."

"Are you threatening me?" He sounded so incredulous Rafe nearly laughed.

*Promising, jackass. Promising.* "Of course not, Mr. Brown. I just know you wouldn't want this to somehow rebound on your boss, so you'll want to get it straightened out right away. Perhaps they have the wrong information, or a record got switched." He gave it a beat. "Unless of course, there's something you're not telling me?"

The man was clearly furious, but gave in. They started back toward the lobby, Brown pulling out his cell phone as they went.

"No calls until this is resolved, I'm afraid," he said, putting everything he could manufacture of regret into his voice. It wasn't much.

"You can't stop me from using my phone! You're not a cop."

Cutter definitely growled this time. Rafe smiled. "Do you really want to play that card, Mr. Brown?"

"This is ridiculous. We'll have your job when this is over."

"Now who's threatening who?" Rafe asked mildly.

That seemed to shut him up, temporarily at least. They kept walking, although he was going much slower than the clearly angry Brown wanted to. Indeed stalling.

Then Hayley's voice came through again. "Two to Five, you're clear."

When they turned the corner from the elevators back into the lobby, he saw that the concierge desk was indeed vacant.

So did Brown, and he turned on Rafe quickly. "I do not have time to wait around to straighten out what is obviously a clerical error. The senator has plans, and I have to be there."

*Plans like walking his new lady around in public to be followed by a gaggle of media? Not enough headlines this weekend already?*

He clamped down on his temper. "I'll find out where she is."

He estimated Brown would last maybe three minutes before he threw caution to the wind and stalked off in a snit. He reached out and picked up the phone on the desk and faked a dial. Asked the dial tone for an ETA, then hung it back up.

"She was with another guest. She's on her way now," he told Brown. It wasn't true, of course, Hayley would keep her occupied, somehow, until they got an all clear or the woman insisted she had to get back.

He figured this had bought them another maybe five minutes at most. He had to hope Liam was as good as ever with that tech crap.

Even as he thought it he heard the young Texan exclaim, "In. It's downloading now."

A moment later Charlie spoke. "Looks like financials of some sort. There's a lot."

"Copy, Focus. I'll have Data stand by. I'm headed toward the elevators to send as many as I can up to the top so he'll have to wait. Five," Quinn added, "try not to kill him."

"Mmm," Rafe murmured, mentally adding, *Tell that to your dog.*

Brown lasted another two minutes. "I have to get upstairs." He glanced at Cutter. "I'll stop by here on my way back to meet Senator Flood."

Rafe let the name-drop echo for a long moment, watched the man's puzzled expression as he again didn't react to it.

"One, every elevator's headed up."

That would only buy them an extra thirty, maybe forty-five seconds. But it might be enough. Or it might not. And Charlie was up in that room. He didn't want to think what might happen if Brown walked in on her and Liam with that case open and the laptop madly copying all those files.

He couldn't order—he knew better than that, despite his occasional gut reaction—her to leave, even though Liam would be better equipped, and armed, to handle the situation. Quinn could, but he couldn't suggest it with Brown still right here, glaring at him again. He couldn't do it until Brown actually left, anyway. It had to have occurred to Quinn, though, so maybe he would—

"Did you hear me?" the now thoroughly irritated man demanded.

In that moment Liam yelped. "Got it. We're clearing out. Less than a minute.

He breathed again. "Did you say something worth hearing?" he asked.

On that the man turned on his heel and strode away. Cutter watched him go, nearly trembling with eagerness to go after him.

"Sorry, buddy. I know you wanted a bite," Rafe told him, not even caring at this point if Brown heard him.

He watched as the aide impatiently slapped at the controls on three different elevators. Saw him back up to where he could watch the indicator lights on all of them at once.

He seemed more than just irritated. He seemed worried. It was normally Hayley's bailiwick, to recognize that, but in this case it was obvious even to him. And he wondered why. Wondered if perhaps he was regretting having left the case up in the suite, even locked. And Rafe didn't like what that had to mean.

"Five, I still have eyes on him. He's beyond edgy." He hesitated, but when it came to Charlie's safety, there could be no hedging. "He doesn't want her alone with that case. He doesn't trust her."

"One, copy. Question is does he not trust her specifically, or does he just not trust anyone?"

"Two also copies. My guess is a little of both. My question is, how much of the suspicion is his own and how much is the subject's?"

Leave it to Hayley to nail it down. But was Flood really that good an actor? Because if the demeanor of being head over heels for Charlie was fake, it was a damned good fake.

*Or maybe you just can't imagine any man* not *being head over heels for her...*

"He's a career politician," Quinn said dryly, as if that answered everything. As perhaps it did. Personally he thought the words career and politician should be mutually exclusive, but apparently the example George Washington had set had been too hard to follow.

A pair of elevator doors slid open. Brown dived for them. "He's got a ride."

The doors slid closed. Ten agonizing seconds ticked by where the only sound he could hear was the hammering of his pulse. Then Liam. "Clear." Rafe breathed again. "Focus on her way down, Four on the way to base. Files will be on the way to Data within five."

Liam heading for their own suite meant they'd be down one on surveillance, so Rafe had already made the decision to stay where he was until Charlie was back down to ground level when Quinn gave the order for him to do just that. Then he'd keep eyes on her until she was back in her brother's sight line.

*I don't care what happened between you. I'm trusting you to set it aside when it comes to protecting my sister.*

Quinn's figurative slapping some sense into him rang in his head. And now that it was real, now that it was happening and she needed that protection, he knew it had never really been in question. If Charlie was in danger, he would do what he had to to protect her. No matter what.

He heard the faint chime of an elevator arriving. Cutter was back on his feet, looking toward the sound. The door slid open and she stepped out. Cutter's tail began to wag. He gave a little tug on the lead, clearly wanting to go to her. *I know the feeling, dog.* But he held the animal back.

She spotted him immediately. More likely them, since she was smiling and that had to be for Cutter. She started walking toward them, with that graceful, purposeful walk that had always seemed to imply—to him, anyway—that she had important places to go and even more important things to do. Because Charlaine Foxworth was indeed a force to be reckoned with.

And yet all he could think of as he watched her, dressed in a sleek pantsuit that somehow managed to be sexy rather than just utterly businesslike, and was a deep greenish blue that somehow made her eyes look the same shade, was of those days—and nights—long ago, when looking into those eyes as he was buried in that lusciously sleek, curved body had been closer to heaven than he had ever expected to get.

And closer than he would ever get again.

## Chapter 29

Charlie smiled widely when one of the two otters—both female, according to the sign—who, after a burst of play with her companion was now lolling on her back in the water, turned her head to look straight at Charlie. She hadn't been lying about that, she did think they were among the most adorable creatures on the planet. And when this one moved its paw almost as if waving to her, she couldn't help laughing out loud.

Flood, as usual, was over with the knot of media people Brown had arranged. She could hear him, but did her best to tune him out; he was using that voice and tone that she hated, that pontificating tone that made it clear who was the important one of the group.

She glanced at Cort, who had come over to stand a discreet couple of feet away from her, apparently at Flood's instruction. As usual, he was alert and scanning the crowd regularly, but now he was smiling. Whether at the otter or her response to it, she didn't know. Or, really, care.

"Can't help it," she said to him. "They're just too darn cute."

"They are, Ms. Marshall."

She thought about asking him how his wife was doing, but didn't want to nip the conversation in the bud if he was relaxed enough to maybe actually talk. She tried to think of something else, hoping all the practice she'd had with the laconic Mr. Crawford would pay off.

She glanced toward Flood, who was shifting the discussion to his pet political projects.

"Amazing how they turn out just to hear the same old, same old."

"I never try to understand the workings of the media mind," he said with a grimace.

She laughed again. "I knew I liked you, Mr. Ducane."

He almost smiled. She saw him fighting it.

As the otters went back to playing, rollicking and rolling in the water, she heard the inevitable begin from that small gathering, the questions about Flood's late wife and his new love. Ducane shifted subtly, so he was more directly between her and the media as some began to notice her, apparently recognizing her from the few photographs that had already hit.

"I appreciate that," she said to her guardian, very quietly.

He gave her a glance, as if he hadn't expected her to notice, but only nodded.

Eventually the otters, after all that play, seemed to have decided it was time for a late afternoon nap. They were now both floating quietly on their backs, eyes closed and paws resting on their chests.

"Now, that looks peaceful," she said.

Ducane's eyes flicked toward Flood, then to the otters, then to her. "Yes," he agreed. Then, after a moment's hesitation, he asked quietly, "Does it bother you? When they talk about his wife?"

"No," she said, honestly. "From what I know, Alondra was as lovely as her name." *And too good for the likes of Flood.*

The smile broke through this time at her words. "Do you know what it means?"

"Alondra? No."

"It's Spanish for lark, my mother's favorite bird."

"That's lovely. You speak Spanish?"

He nodded. "My mother was born in Puerto Rico."

"What's her name?"

"Solana. It means sunshine."

"Nice as well."

She studied him for a moment. This was the most conversation she'd gotten out of the man, and she couldn't resist pressing on, hoping that somewhere would be the key that would help him get free of Flood.

"May I ask how you ended up Cort?"

Again the brief smile. "It's short for Cortez. My mother's maiden name."

She smiled back, liking that. "And your father?"

"Straight back to Great Britain for generations, before one of them ventured here and wound up in South Carolina." His mouth quirked. "Spelling got a lot simpler along the way."

"Lucky for you," she teased.

"Very," he agreed.

Charlie was pleased to see him grin, a full-on grin. He seemed like a different man, at least in this moment less rigid. Less haunted. And she renewed her determination that Foxworth would find a way to help him. He didn't deserve to go down when Flood did because of something out of his control that had put him in a desperate state.

"You two having a nice time?" It came from just a couple

of feet away; apparently the media interaction had ended. Flood's voice, with the tiniest edge of accusation in it, shattered the easy mood.

Charlie didn't miss the flash of tension in Ducane's eyes. And Hayley's voice sounded in her ear, saying, "Focus, I do believe he's a tiny bit jealous."

*That Cort would dare to smile at me? Okay, grin, but still...*

But she needed to defuse the situation, quickly.

"Oh," she said, as brightly and airily as she could, "we were just laughing at these poor otters, napping afloat after getting tired out after playing all afternoon. Not a bad life." *If you don't mind living in a zoo...*

Either her tone or her words seemed to work, and Flood relaxed. He slipped an arm around her, and she managed not to recoil, instead converting the urge to pull away into leaning in. Ducane had moved back several steps and turned his attention to the other aquarium visitors.

Thinking a bit of flattery might not be amiss, she added, "Unlike you, Max. You always seem to be working."

"That's how things get done," he said. "But I'm ready for an evening off. Dinner here at the hotel tonight, I think. Alec and I need to go over some things for tomorrow."

"Have you made that decision you mentioned yet?"

"I believe so, yes."

"I have faith in you, Max. You'll do what's best." *For yourself, and to hell with anyone else.*

Quinn's voice came quietly through the transceiver. "Careful, Focus. It's getting close to leaking through."

Charlie gave an inward sigh, knowing her brother was right. It was getting harder all the time to hide her distaste for the ilk in general, and her loathing of this one in particular.

"I think you need to go shopping," Hayley said. "For female things, because you're extending your stay."

There was no doubt about it, her sister-in-law was a genius. She needed a break from the man, and this was the perfect way to get it. And was exactly what she told Flood, in almost those words. Saw him cringe just slightly at the phrase "female things," which showed her one more aspect of the man.

Using the term *man* loosely.

"I'll send someone with you," Flood said.

"You don't need to, Max. I think I'll just walk down the block to that shop next to the cell phone store. They should have what I need."

"I'm not comfortable with you out there alone." With anyone else it would have been an expression of caring. With Flood she had the feeling it was wanting her watched at all times.

She thought for a brief moment, about what "Lita" would do. She went for her best shot. "I'm not comfortable with taking staff away from you, when you're clearly in the middle of something important."

"Ducane can accompany you," Flood said. "Since we're staying in, we won't need him."

She'd been hoping for that, another chance to assess and maybe wear down the man who clearly didn't think much of his current employer. But she frowned as if she didn't like the idea, which made Flood smile in turn, no doubt because she didn't jump at the chance to be with the good-looking guardian.

"All right," she finally said with an audible sigh. "If it will put you at ease."

"That's what I love about you, Lita dear. You're willing to compromise."

*On everything but payback, you monster.* She smiled

even as she thought it, and there was genuine pleasure in it as she thought about how they were going to wipe that phony benevolence off his face.

Quinn's voice as he spoke in her ear told her he'd followed her line of thought perfectly. "One to Five, pull out of the hotel and be ready to meet with Focus and friend. Put a little more pressure on him."

"Five, copy." Rafe's voice, ever cool.

"Take your sidekick," Hayley said. "He could tip the scales."

"Agreed," Rafe said.

It was amazing—and wonderful—the utter faith and confidence the Northwest office had in their canine operative. Especially when Rafe agreed with it, so easily. He was the most skeptical man she'd ever met when it came to anything inexplicable by either logic or math or the proper tools. And yet he obviously believed, as they all did, that Cutter had…some unexpected capabilities.

When he joined her, it seemed Cort was back in quiet mode, saying nothing, communicating mostly with nods as they walked toward the shop on the corner. She wondered if that moment when Flood had almost snapped at them had scared him, since he so badly needed this job.

Or if it was something else.

"Are you all right, Cort?" She used his first name intentionally, and it seemed to startle him.

"I… Fine. I'm fine."

"Something's obviously bothering you. Or," she added, watching his face, "you've decided I'm not worth talking to."

That got a low half chuckle out of him. "You're the only one in this crowd who is worth talking to."

The moment he said it he looked as if he regretted it. She was pondering how to keep it going when that all too recognizable awareness shot through her. She looked past Cort and down the street.

She spotted Cutter first, heading their way. With a tiny lean to the right she saw Rafe, and he did not look happy. A little jolt went through her at the idea he might be jealous. Genuine jealousy, not Flood's kind. She couldn't deny she liked the idea, but she wouldn't let it interfere with the mission. She knew Rafe wouldn't, either.

Not this mission.

# Chapter 30

"Thanks for the compliment," Charlie said, sounding beyond rueful in Rafe's ear as she waved him back with a subtle hand signal. "And I get your point. I have to admit, the best thing that has come out of this trip for me was the chance to see friends I haven't seen in a while."

Rafe slowed his pace, now that he was close enough to get there in a couple of long strides. Cutter didn't agree, but only gave him a side-eye as he slowed his own pace to match.

"Trouble in paradise?" Ducane asked.

Rafe halted and pretended to look in a store window, reminding himself the guy had a dying wife and wasn't likely to hit on his boss's...girlfriend.

"It was never paradise," Charlie answered. "Not even close."

Ducane went very still. Looked as if he regretted having said it. Charlie hesitated, then Quinn spoke in his ear. "Five? Opinion?"

He knew what his boss meant. Was Ducane close to breaking? Should she push him? He couldn't go with his gut right now, because his gut was never sane when it came to Charlie. So he risked a look, focusing on Ducane, seeing the tangle of emotions in his expression. Thought he saw not just regret but edginess, even a sort of concern.

Hell, maybe he was getting better at being...emotionally observant.

"Go for it," Rafe said.

"Focus, copy? Five, stand by to step in. If we have to break cover, it's worth the risk."

Rafe agreed. This was an in they couldn't afford to pass up. Charlie responded to Quinn's order by going on with Ducane.

"I'm starting to think Max isn't who I thought he was." *He's actually exactly who I thought he was.*

Ducane started to speak, stopped, then said in a very circumspect tone, "I couldn't speak to that, Ms. Marshall."

"I'm sorry. I shouldn't dump my worries on you. You have enough problems. How is your wife?"

"Not good today." It was gruff, rough, and Rafe felt like a grade-A jerk for his reaction to the man's simple friendliness toward Charlie. The guy had a wife he clearly loved, and he was losing her.

"I'm so sorry. Is she here? In the city?" Out of the corner of his eye he saw Ducane nod. "You should be with her," Charlie said firmly.

"Can't afford time off."

"Then let's go to her now."

Rafe turned in time to see Ducane give her a startled look. "What?"

"We'll go now, while Max is busy. I'll just find something to read while you visit."

Ducane was gaping at her now, any thought of watching the surroundings or other people clearly blasted out of his mind.

"You...you'd do that?"

"Of course."

Rafe found himself holding his breath. He sensed a tipping point, the only question was which way would the man fall?

"You," Ducane said after a moment, "are too good for him."

"I know why I'm changing my mind, but what makes you think that?"

"Because he's not the altruistic guy he presents himself as. He's just an influence peddler."

Charlie took an audible deep breath, then plunged ahead. "Yes. He is. You're right."

Ducane blinked and drew back. His brow furrowed. Rafe usually never got involved in this aspect of their cases, but he felt as if he could relate to Ducane, at least enough to have an idea about how to reach him.

"Don't give him time to dwell on that," he said quietly, knowing she'd heard him by the way her head tilted just slightly toward the ear with the transceiver. And because she immediately did exactly what he'd said. *First time for everything...*

"How much do you know about when Governor Ogilvie was removed from office?"

Rafe had turned to watch carefully now, sensing Ducane was intent on the conversation. And there was a note of sheer puzzlement in his voice when he answered Charlie's question.

"Not much." He grimaced. "It was about the time my wife was diagnosed. I do remember cheering for that detective." He gave Charlie a sideways look. "I didn't like

Ogilvie much. Never expected him to turn out to be a murderer, though."

Charlie gave Rafe a sideways look in turn. And a small nod. A clear signal.

"See to him," Rafe murmured to his companion as they started toward the other two, and Cutter gave a very small *whuff* of acknowledgment.

Ducane looked startled all over again at Rafe's approach, and he didn't give the man any time to process it; he had the feeling the best way to breach this wall was to simply blow it up as fast as possible.

"That last-minute meeting your employer—I'm not going to call him your boss—had was with Ogilvie."

Ducane's brow furrowed again. "How do you know that?" His gaze shifted to Charlie. "You told him?"

"No," she said quietly. "I didn't have to."

Again Rafe didn't give him time to process. "We think Ogilvie wants his help with the case against him."

Ducane's mouth twisted wryly. "As if anything could help that—" He bit off something Rafe guessed would have been profane. Then, looking from Rafe to Charlie and back again, he asked slowly, "Just who is 'we'?"

Rafe looked at Charlie then, who looked uncharacteristically undecided. Quinn's words went through his mind again. *If we have to break cover, it's worth the risk.* So he took the last step.

"Ever hear of the Foxworth Foundation?"

"Yeah, they helped that detective who took Ogilvie out. And once I heard some people at the hospital talking about how they helped them, that they—" He stopped suddenly, staring at Rafe. "Are you saying...you're with them?"

"Yes."

Ducane kept staring. Then, slowly, he said, "What you

said…about being prouder of what you do now… That's Foxworth?"

Rafe nodded.

"I…can see why. So what, you're still on Ogilvie, to make sure he doesn't find a way to slime his way out of murder charges?"

"We are, but that's not why we're here now." Rafe studied the other man for a moment before saying, "Right now, we're looking to take down a traitor who sold intel that nearly got our whole team killed."

"Whole team?"

Rafe nodded. "Including him," he said, with a gesture at Cutter. Taking it as his cue, the dog stepped forward. Ducane reached down to stroke the dog's head. Even as many times as he'd seen it—and experienced it himself— he still marveled at the effect the dog had. He let it happen in silence and took the chance to grab a glance at Charlie.

She was looking straight at him. Approvingly. Something he hadn't seen in a very long time.

Ducane straightened, and Rafe looked back at him. "I don't envy the guy you're after."

"Already knew that," Rafe said.

It didn't take more than three seconds for Ducane to get there. His eyes widened. He started to speak, but Rafe cut him off before he could say the name, just in case; their connection to Ogilvie was common knowledge, this was not. Yet.

"Yes. Your employer."

"You mean he's the one who sold you out?"

"He is," Rafe said firmly. "But we're still working on proof that will stand against someone in his position."

Ducane let out a low whistle. "Good luck with that."

"We're hoping for a little more than luck."

It was the first time Charlie had spoken since Rafe had joined them. Ducane turned his head to look at her.

"You're part of this?"

"She's the reason Foxworth exists," Rafe said, meaning it. And when Charlie shot him a startled yet gratified glance, he decided it was worth that little release of emotion he'd allowed into his voice.

"Let me reintroduce myself, Cort. I'm Charlaine Foxworth."

Well, there they were, Rafe thought. Charlie-like, she hadn't just broken their cover.

She'd blown it up.

# Chapter 31

"Why are you all trusting me with this? You don't even know me."

Charlie leaned back in her chair and didn't respond. It was Rafe who had the rapport with the guy right now, if only because the man knew who he was. And admired him, was perhaps even a bit awed. And Quinn clearly realized it, too, because he also stayed silent.

They were back in the suite they'd kept as a temporary headquarters. Teague and Liam had confirmed Flood and Brown were still secluded in their own suite, and with their help she, Rafe and Cutter had come in through a back entrance and arrived unobserved. Quinn and Hayley, they said in her ear, were on their way.

Cutter, who was sitting beside Cort's chair, leaned his head against the man's leg. And once more she saw the results, saw the man start to truly let down his guard as he stroked the dog's soft fur. And Rafe gently used that to get him to open up. Odd, how she'd become the watcher, and Rafe the communicator.

But the biggest surprise—to her—was how well he was doing it.

"We know enough," Rafe said. "We do our homework, Cort. We know your background, your military record." She glanced over in time to see Rafe flash a brief grin. It was clearly aimed at Cort but it was her breath he took away. "Nice job, by the way, getting the officer you punched to admit he deserved it."

Cort looked startled, but then, slowly, he smiled. "He wasn't a bad guy, for a lieutenant. He just got a little mouthy now and then."

And that quickly they were at ease, two vets who knew in a way she never would what that life was like. She'd never seen Rafe like this, and she wondered if it was because she'd never been around him when he was this at ease, or if he'd come so far since he'd walked away from what they had.

What she'd thought they had.

"We also know," Rafe said, very quietly, "the straits you're in right now. Why you need the job badly enough to work for someone you don't like or respect. We can help. It's part of what we do."

Cort stiffened despite Cutter's presence. Charlie saw him glance her way. "I didn't tell him that, either," she said.

"Foxworth already knew?"

"We've been monitoring everything since we came on scene at the party Friday night."

"Monitoring? As in...you've got us all bugged?"

"No. Just us. But our system picks up conversations." Rafe gave a wry smile. "You don't take down a sitting governor without covering all the bases. Same applies to someone like...our subject, as we refer to him."

Cutter whined slightly and nudged Cort. His hand went back to the dog's head, and she saw it yet again, the calming.

"Let me tell you why we're determined to take him down, too."

And Rafe did, using language she supposed would ring familiar, Marine to Marine.

"We've been searching for who sold us out for three years," Rafe ended with. "And now that we've found him, we have to prove it."

"He's insulated like he was still a senator. Maybe more," Cort said. "I don't know what I could do."

And that easily, Rafe had done it. Because Charlie had no doubt Cort was solidly in their corner now.

"It's more what you don't do," Rafe said, and although she was watching Cort, she felt his gaze shift to her.

"Don't blow her cover?" Cort said.

"Exactly," Charlie said. Then, with a grimace of distaste she added, "Unless I ask you to."

"I'm surprised you've lasted this long," he said.

"Word of advice," Rafe said, almost solemnly. "Don't ever underestimate her."

The words and the way he said them kicked her pulse up a notch. Then Quinn's voice announcing their arrival came through her earpiece about thirty seconds before the door opened. Cort turned to look, warily, so she smiled at him. And the smile widened when Gavin came in right on their heels. Cort gave the famous attorney that look she knew well, the one that said they recognized him but weren't quite sure why.

Quinn came over to them.

"Meet my boss," Rafe said, bringing to mind how he'd so carefully referred to Flood as Cort's employer, not his boss. "Cort Ducane, Quinn Foxworth."

"My brother," Charlie explained at Cort's reaction to the last name. "And the tactical mind behind everything we do."

Rafe introduced Hayley to Cort. She quickly went over to the table where they'd been sitting and put a shopping bag and her purse down on the floor, grabbing her phone as she straightened. She held the phone out to Cort.

"Here," she said. "Use this to call the hospital billing department."

"What?" Cort asked, startled.

"Just call them for the status of your wife's charges."

Cort glanced at Rafe, another sign of the tentative bond. Rafe nodded. The other man took the phone, and after another moment of hesitation, dialed the number he apparently knew by heart. A simple fact that made Charlie ache a little. This was a good man, caught by tragedy and thrown into a bad situation. And she felt a tremendous satisfaction knowing Foxworth would get him out of part of it, at least.

A couple of minutes later Cort had ended the call, set the phone down carefully on the table, and looked at Hayley.

"You did this?"

"Foxworth did." She smiled at Charlie. "Thanks to our financial genius."

"You paid off a six-figure bill. So I'd help you?" Cort looked bewildered.

"No," Hayley said gently. "We hope you will, but that's why we paid it off now, before. We didn't want you to think we were holding that offer over your head, didn't want you to feel coerced into helping us. It's done and paid, no matter what you decide to do."

"I...don't understand."

"It's why I told you I'm prouder of what I do now than of anything else," Rafe said, very solemnly. The words warmed Charlie inside as Cort's head snapped around to stare at him.

"I know the feeling." Gavin's words, spoken with quiet feeling, made the man look that way. Cort's brow furrowed.

"And meet Gavin de Marco," Charlie said, not even trying to suppress her smile as the famous name registered and Cort's eyes widened in shock. "He runs legal interference for Foxworth when necessary."

"You...work for them, too?"

"I do." He glanced at Charlie. "Quinn thought I might come in handy, if this all goes down over here in the city."

"Glad you're here, my friend," Charlie said, meaning it.

Cort stared at them all, one by one. And Charlie saw the moment when he broke, when he accepted.

"I'd like to feel the way you all do," he said wearily.

"We'll see what we can do about that," Quinn said, briskly now. "But right now, you two need to get back. Liam says the subject is starting to wonder where you are."

Charlie stifled another grimace. Then drew back slightly as something occurred to her. "I was supposed to be shopping."

"I know," Hayley said, grinning. She bent over and grabbed the small shopping bag she'd come in with. "Here. Girly stuff."

Charlie took the bag and looked inside to see a package of tampons, some skin lotion and a small bottle of what happened to be the only perfume she usually ever wore, the heavy stuff Flood preferred notwithstanding.

*Because Rafe loved it enough to actually say so once...*

She shoved away the memory and the crazy thought that somehow Hayley had known that. She looked at her brother instead. "Thank you," she said.

Quinn shrugged. "I didn't do it, Hayley did."

"Exactly. Thank you for bringing her into the family."

She hugged her sister-in-law, who was smiling widely now, then looked at Cort, who immediately got to his feet.

She saved her last glance for Rafe, and accompanied it with a quietly spoken, "Well done." Rafe looked surprised, which told her rather more than she'd wanted to know; he still expected her to jab at him.

They were nearly back to Flood's suite when Charlie looked up at the man beside her. She didn't think she was imagining that he looked less loaded down. Nothing could ease the pain he was going through, but at least they'd been able to remove something that was making the heavy burden even worse. Even if it netted them nothing, she would count the expenditure worth it for that alone.

But in fact, it netted them results much sooner than she would have dared hope. Because less than half an hour after they'd stepped back into Flood's realm, when Cort came to tell her they were ready to head down for dinner, he whispered something else to her.

"I heard him say something to his aide that seems... curious. He said he thought he and Bradford—that's Ogilvie's first name, right?—could reach a 'mutually beneficial accord.' And I'm wondering what could be mutually beneficial."

She got what he meant immediately. "As in what could the gov, stuck in his mess, possibly do for someone like our subject?" Cort nodded. "That's a very good question. One, you copy that?"

"Affirmative," came Quinn's voice immediately. "Definitely curious."

Cort blinked. "You really meant that about monitoring." When she nodded, he looked at her more closely. She reached up and tapped at the guilty earring. "Oh."

She laughed and followed him out to where Flood and his minion were waiting.

Rafe was pacing the suite. Big as it was, and even with Teague and Liam still out watching Flood's suite, he wished it was bigger because he wasn't wearing himself out nearly enough. Cutter was watching him go back and forth, and he knew from the dog's close attention that the moment the animal felt he was pushing it too far, he'd be herding him to a chair.

"Mutually beneficial," he muttered to himself.

He'd taken out his earpiece, thinking he couldn't stomach Charlie making nice with Flood. He was starting to worry about how long she could hold him off. And to what extremes the man might go.

He kept pacing. Quinn was over by the windows with Hayley, probably discussing their next move and what they would do if they couldn't end this before Flood was ready to leave and head back east to his rat hole. Rafe hated even the thought of this going on another day, let alone weeks.

He walked over to where Quinn's secured laptop sat on the table. It was open, and on the screen were the records Ty had sent, of the transactions run through the offshore account he had backtracked to Flood, since the day it had been set up. He wasn't really focused on entries—that kind of financial stuff was Charlie's bailiwick, not his, as so much was—he was just noting the ridiculous amount of money involved, that Flood apparently asked and got for his influence. And oddly, it hadn't really dropped much since he'd quit the Senate, so he clearly had plenty of influence left.

He stared at the screen, doing more marveling at the fact that this was simple to Charlie, while he was boggled. The numbers he did best with were velocity and range, or maybe properly gapping spark plugs, so this stuff was beyond him.

But then he was back to that phrase that was nagging at him. *Mutually beneficial.*

What could a disgraced former governor, who killed his

political opponent and was eventually going to go down for it, offer a mover and shaker on Flood's level?

His eyes were fixed on the screen, but he wasn't really seeing it as he wrestled with what didn't make any sense. He didn't know how long he'd been standing there when he felt the nudge of a cold nose against his right hand. He snapped back to reality and looked down at Cutter. He gave the dog a scratch behind his right ear.

"I'll bet you could figure this out faster than I could, buddy. It might as well be in...dog, for all the good it does me."

He looked back at the screen ruefully. Only this time his gaze locked on two entries, just three days apart. Sizable entries. He'd noticed them before, but only the numbers, which had made him shake his head. But now he backtracked on the spreadsheet line to the name on the entry. And suddenly, those spark plugs he'd just thought about started to fire.

"When was Flood's wife killed?" he asked, without looking at either Quinn or Hayley.

"Four years ago," Quinn said.

"Date, exactly."

His peripheral vision caught Hayley checking her phone. "March 27," she said a moment later.

Like a teetering pile of blocks finally collapsing, the pieces fell.

A large payment dated March 25 of that year.

A second even larger payout dated March 28, three days later.

Both payments allocated on the paperwork for something called the Lark Project.

The exchange rang in his head as if Charlie and Cort were standing right beside him. The exchange about Alondra, Flood's wife's name.

*It's Spanish for lark, my mother's favorite bird.*
The Lark Project.
*Mutually beneficial.*

Cutter let out a low, worried sound, no doubt at the sudden, shocked stillness as Rafe stopped breathing for a moment.

"Rafe? What is it?" Hayley asked.

"You spot something?" Quinn had come over to stand beside them.

He took in a deep breath. This wasn't his thing, he could be wrong. Way wrong. He could be making the proverbial mountain out of the hill their mole had built.

But he didn't think so.

He looked up at the two people he was so proud to work for and with. Hesitated, until Cutter nudged his hand, as if in encouragement. That tipped him over the edge.

"I think I know what Ogilvie could do for him." He grimaced. "Or more like, not do. As in talk."

Quinn frowned in puzzlement, but he and Hayley both waited quietly.

"I think…" It finally came out in a burst. "I think he paid to have his wife killed, and Ogilvie knows it."

# Chapter 32

"It all fits." Rafe heard Charlie whisper it, trusting Liam's device to pick it up. "I overheard the aide referring to that meeting, saying something about they'd better go see what he's got."

"And we know that's how the gov works," Quinn said.

Charlie's voice came faster now. "And I overheard something else, back at the beginning, about some chance they'd had to take, extreme measures the subject said, because it was an emergency."

Rafe's gut knotted again. He was even more certain now.

Gavin inserted the earpiece Hayley had given him before saying, "This is how the governor has managed to stall his trial so long. He's got a lot of dirt on a lot of people."

"Two of a kind," Charlie muttered. "Good job, bro. Er, One."

"Not me. Five put it together."

She didn't react to that at all. Rafe figured she was probably shocked; putting mechanical pieces together was more his style. But he didn't care if she was surprised, all he cared about was one thing.

"Focus, you've got to get out of there," he said.

"Out?" She sounded almost offended. "We haven't nailed this down yet."

"The gov could recognize you. Pictures of you with him are popping up."

"Five's got a point," Liam put in. "He probably did his research on Foxworth well before Data planted the new images."

Mentally tossing the Texan thanks for the support, Rafe searched for words to convince her. But she spoke first. "Look, it all fits too well, and I wouldn't put murdering his wife past him. But I don't think he'll break the way Ogilvie did when confronted. We need proof."

"Agreed," Quinn said, and Rafe stiffened as he stared at his boss. Quinn gave a slow shake of his head as he added, "And he covers his back better, because he's smarter."

"The bar was pretty low there," Hayley said, easing the tension a bit in that way she had.

He heard Charlie start to chuckle, but she stopped abruptly just as they heard a knocking sound. Then she spoke again, this time clearly not to them but for them. "Hello, Alec."

They heard another voice, male, but not clearly enough to catch the words.

"Meet him there? All right," Charlie said, sounding as cheerful as if it were all real. "I'll be ready in just a minute."

"I'll be on you to the elevators," came Teague's voice.

"I've got the garage exit," Liam said.

The comms devices then went silent for the moment. Rafe felt his nails digging into his palms and only then realized he'd been clenching his fists. He hunted for words, realizing that his years of being uncommunicative had a cost. When he really wanted to say something, the right thing, the discarded words weren't there.

He should be the one tracking Flood. He should—

Quinn's phone buzzed. He glanced at it, then went over to his laptop and hit a couple of keys. The screen went live, and Rafe saw Ty.

He began without preamble. "I did some research, and I think we're right. It was buried deep, but the late missus had that accident on her way to a meeting. With one of those guerilla journalist types."

"She was going to blow the whistle on him," Quinn said softly.

"I think so," Ty agreed. "Problem is, I don't know about what, specifically. They managed to quash any public mention, but it was mentioned in an old comment I found on a private message board."

*As if anything's private to Tyler Hewitt.* Rafe thought it almost numbly.

"Thanks, Ty," Quinn said.

"Just call me Data," the young tech whiz said cheerfully. "I'll keep going."

The screen went blank.

Rafe stood staring at Quinn. Remembered again his words, as close to an emotional order as he'd ever heard from the man. "I'm trusting you to set it aside when it comes to protecting my sister."

*What if I have to disobey you to protect her?*

His own Foxworth phone rang. For once he welcomed the interruption. He pulled it out, didn't recognize the incoming number. But he recognized the voice before the caller even gave his name.

"Crawford?"

"Ducane," he said.

"Yeah. Look, this is probably nothing, but—"

"Nothing's nothing," Rafe said, rolling his eyes at his own absurd phrasing. "What?"

"My employer just changed his plans at the last second. He had an evening planned with…Ms. Marshall, but now I'm supposed to drive him in half an hour to a city council meeting where he's going to speak." The thought made Rafe's stomach churn a bit, but he sensed this wasn't the real reason Ducane had called. And his next words made it clear Rafe was right. "The thing is, his aide just left with Ms. Marshall, telling her he was going to drive her to the original location. And she didn't seem to know there'd been a change at all."

Meet him there, Charlie had said.

Rafe felt a chill go through him that was almost violent.

Flood publicly on display, no doubt on video as well. A time-stamped alibi with a lot of witnesses.

Charlie alone with Brown, the guy she—and Ducane—thought was more than a little off-center. The guy that he himself had been aware of in the same way he'd be aware of every step in a minefield.

Flood would never personally get his hands dirty.

Brown wouldn't hesitate.

"Hold on," he said to Ducane, moving the phone away slightly. Then he snapped into the earpiece, "Focus, new intel. You're burned. Four, track what vehicle they take. I'll be en route. Cutter, on me."

The dog had already been at Rafe's heels. He started toward the door. Felt rather than saw Quinn's stare. And he knew it wasn't because he'd suddenly started tossing out orders when that wasn't his job.

He looked steadily at his boss. "If you're going to trust me, trust me."

Quinn's jaw was tight, but he nodded. "We'll take the subject. We still need proof, but you know what price is too high."

Rafe had already been determined, but Quinn's trust, his faith that Rafe had accurately assessed the threat and would keep his sister safe, solidified it like granite. He held up his phone, where Ducane was still on the line.

Quinn nodded again. "Tell him."

Rafe went back to the phone as he ran for the elevator, laying out their suspicions about Flood's late wife, and that they suspected he had the same in store for Charlie. He wasn't sure how the man, whose own obviously much-loved wife was down to her last days, would take it. The oath he let loose was a clue.

"Cort," Rafe said, for the first time using the man's first name, "how into this do you want to get?"

"How deep do you need me?"

"Stalling your employer as long as possible."

He heard Ducane take a deep breath. "Done."

"Stall as long as you can, however you have to. Text us when you can't delay any longer."

He and Cutter were just coming out of the elevator on the ground floor when Liam spoke again. "Five, it's the same rental they took down south. I should be at the gate before them. Oh, and she's in the back seat."

"Copy," he repeated, noting the difference; when she'd ridden with Ducane as her acting chauffeur, she'd always sat in front with him. She might not be a trained field operative, but Charlie had good instincts. About most things, anyway.

He headed for one of the back doors to the garage, near where he'd parked. Cutter was glued to him, practically brushing against his leg with every step. Knowing he didn't have to worry about the dog, he took care of one other matter.

"Data," he said.

"Here," Ty responded in his ear almost instantly.

"I know you're already recording, but double-check on Focus."

"Done," Ty said after a brief moment.

He spoke again as he and Cutter got into his car. "Focus, stay low and quiet."

"Hope you know where we're going," she said, in a teasing tone clearly aimed at Brown, but the words were meant for them.

"Oh, I know."

Now that they were in the quiet of the vehicle, he could hear Brown's voice. And if he'd had any doubts about the plan, the undertone in the man's voice would have convinced him. He'd heard that sound before, and he knew it meant a man set on his course—and with plans to enjoy it.

Fury burst free inside him. He wanted to stop this right now and blow the guy to bits. Right now he didn't care if Flood went down, even if he had almost gotten them all killed. Right now, all he cared about was Charlie, and that she was in the hands of a man who would likely have no qualms about killing her if it would keep his boss's little fiefdom intact. Cutter made a small sound as he stuck his head between the front seats, and Rafe reached out to stroke the dark head. Oddly, this time he felt not the soothing he'd almost gotten used to, but a burst of energy, as if the dog was as wound up as he was and eager to get on with it.

*I'll take you as my backup anytime, dog.*

"They're clear of the parking garage, turning south," Liam said. "I got a GPS tracker on it while they were stopped at the exit gate."

*Bless you, Liam Burnett.* "Five, copy. Keep me updated."

"Affirmative. Still heading south. Normal speed."

Every second counted, and Liam had just bought him enough to get his gear together, and he was armed with everything he might need by the time he pulled out onto the street in their wake. He fought the urge to speed up until he had them in sight; the last thing he needed was to get stopped and have to explain to a cop, who likely wouldn't see past all the armament. Even Gavin might have trouble getting him out of that one.

But worse was the thought that he might not be there in time to protect Charlie.

He wondered what Quinn and the others would come up with to deal with the pompous, too-slick Flood building his alibi. Knowing them—especially Gavin—it would be clever, dramatic and inescapable. But he shoved that out of his mind. He didn't give a damn anymore about what Flood had done to them. He only cared about stopping what he'd no doubt ordered Brown to do now.

He did wonder how Flood thought he could get away with a second dead woman. Then again, he wasn't sure anybody would look askance at the guy, not the way he'd play up a second tragedy in his life. He'd probably use it like a surgeon, something about deciding he was cursed and would have to struggle through life alone.

*Not going to happen.*

He would not let anything happen to Charlie. How they'd parted, how angry she was at him, didn't matter. Nothing mattered except keeping her safe.

Liam's voice came through again. "Five, they're turning west and…hang on…okay, now south again."

Rafe swore silently as he picked up a little more speed. He'd just spotted the car when Quinn confirmed Flood was indeed still at the hotel, preparing for his appearance at the city council meeting. "Our new friend is doing a good job of stalling. Told the subject media was gathering, so he should probably have the limo shined up for a big arrival. He bought it, and us more time."

Charlie's voice came just a couple of minutes later. "Where are we going? Did Max cancel our restaurant plans?"

"In a way," Brown said, and the way he said it jabbed at Rafe, because he knew in his gut what the man meant.

"Focus, stay cool, I've got you in sight."

At least Brown didn't seem to have any idea he was being followed. He even politely signaled a lane change, then made another turn.

"Industrial district," Rafe suddenly guessed.

"Headed that way," Liam confirmed. "Another couple of blocks."

Rafe had to fight the almost overpowering urge to catch up and take the guy out right here, but the collateral damage could be huge, and that was not what Foxworth was about. He'd meant what he'd said to Cort.

"A warehouse?" For the first time Rafe thought he heard a touch of nerves in Charlie's voice. "And it looks abandoned, with that moving and storage company sign hanging crooked like that."

*Good job, Charlie.* Because now he knew where they were going; he'd noticed the falling sign the last time he'd been through here.

"Wait until you see the surprise waiting for you inside," Brown said, not even trying to hide that predatory—and pleased—tone now.

"Focus, I'm on-site," Rafe said.

"Well, Alec," Charlie said, her voice back to her steady self, but taking on a drawl that could almost match Liam's, "there are surprises, and then there are surprises."

Despite it all Rafe found himself laughing inwardly. She was something, was his Charlie.

And he didn't even bother to dispute his own terminology as he parked in the shelter of a large dumpster that would shield the coupe from this angle. He got out, pulled on his armored and full of arms vest, grabbed his trusted, exquisitely cared for Remington M40 and opened the door for his furry partner.

Charlie knew why they were here. She was a little surprised, not that Flood would actually order her murder, but that he would do it this way. True, the city wasn't the peaceful, picturesque place it had once been, and in sad fact a murder wasn't all that unusual anymore, but this seemed a bit too blatant for the smooth, subtle Flood.

But not for Brown. If nothing else, the expression of obviously gleeful anticipation would have told her. She thought of Rafe, and how only the number of lives he'd saved had enabled him to live with the number he'd taken. He had never, ever taken such pleasure in what to him was a grim but necessary job. Because he was sane, without some twisted, convoluted ego that took pleasure in ending a human life.

The warehouse had the empty look and hollow sound of a place long abandoned. Their footsteps echoed in the void. They had only gone a couple of yards when she glanced back. And saw the glint of metal in his right hand. Her heart started to pound even faster, but she forced herself to think of a way to warn Rafe.

"Why, what a pretty little popgun in your hand," she said, too sweetly. "Expecting to have to take out some rats?"

The laugh she heard in her ear gave her all the nerve she needed. Brown looked disconcerted, and she counted that a win since the man prided himself on never showing weakness, as he'd put it to Flood more than once.

"Does he really think he can get away with two dead women on his résumé? Or are you supposed to take the heat for this one?"

Brown actually gaped at her. But in her ear Rafe hissed, "Stop provoking him. At least until he's down."

*Not if. Until. A given. That's my Rafe.*

My Rafe. The simple phrase echoed in her mind, and in that moment nothing else mattered.

"He will be," she said it aloud, putting all the faith she felt into her voice. It also changed Brown's expression from astonished to puzzled at the, to him, nonsensical words.

"As soon as I get in position." Rafe's voice sounded as if he'd heard exactly what she'd intended.

And then Brown grabbed her arm, yanking hard enough that she let out a little yelp of pain. "It's true, isn't it? You're one of those Foxworth people. The ones who brought down Ogilvie."

She saw no point in denying it, but Rafe's warning rang in her head. Especially now that Brown had her jammed up against his chest, so that any bullet that hit him would probably hit her, too. She stalled.

"Foxworth people? You say that like it's a tribe." *As we are, of sorts.*

"I saw that photo Ogilvie had. It's you."

"Focus, we're in place."

She almost laughed in delight at the sound of him, and the thought of his furry partner. And she let a bit of it show when she said lightly, "Ogilvie? Didn't he used to be the governor here?"

"Stop playing dumb."

*But I am. Dumb, stupid and a few other things for ever letting that man over there out of my sight.*

She heard a faint, metallic click. "Never mind," Brown said. "It doesn't matter now." His grip on her tightened. He jammed the barrel of the gun up under her chin. It would take the top of her head off. "Goodbye, whatever your name really is."

* * *

The instant Brown grabbed her and yanked her to him, Rafe wanted nothing more than to rip the man limb from limb. He fairly shook from the need to tear him apart. Beside him Cutter was dancing, seeming to be full of the same need. He was a man who excelled at one thing, a man whose name they put on trophies and medals for that skill. But right now he wanted to throw it away. He wanted to choke the life out of this predator with his own hands, and watch the life leave his eyes as he did it.

He mentally grabbed for that legendary cool he had lost in that moment. He did one thing better than most, and Quinn—and Charlie—were counting on him to do it.

And never had it been more important than now. Because now it was Charlie.

The moment Brown moved the pistol under Charlie's chin, a vision of what would happen if he fired it flashed through Rafe's mind. He'd seen it before. Had more than one mental video of the bloody, gory, instant results.

Cutter's head bumped him, hard enough to snap him out of it.

Now.

He let his breath out. He felt that calm some called uncanny steal over him. He settled in, mentally calculated the distance, angle, trajectory, and added in the cold barrel of the M40. For a split second he wished for the armor piercing AS50 that could take down a helicopter, but his old friend would get the job done. He planned for any move the target made. Registered on an instinctive level a cross-body shot from Brown would be less accurate than straight, so he had to be forced into that.

*He's less than fifty feet away. You'd take him down if all you had was a musket.*

When he spoke to the transceiver, his voice was steady.

"Focus, when my partner shows, drop to your left. Cutter... now!"

The dog bolted like a racehorse out of the gate. His ferocious snarl made Brown freeze. He half turned, staring. Rafe knew what Brown was seeing, Cutter racing out of the shadows, fangs bared as he sprinted toward them looking like some predator out of a nightmare.

*Come on, Charlie.*

She dropped. Brown, fixated on the dog about to jump him, moved his gun hand toward the animal. Target clear. Acquired. Fire. The shot echoed in the empty building. Brown went down. Hard. Then Cutter was atop him, snarling a signal no one could miss.

Rafe slung the rifle over his shoulder in the same moment he started running. If there was any pain from his leg he didn't feel it, he just ran. Brown was screaming at the dog, but he didn't call Cutter off. Because only one thing mattered.

And then he had Charlie in his arms, felt her warmth, her arms around him in turn as she hugged him back fiercely. He closed his eyes. Savored it for a long, sweet moment.

"Status?" Liam's voice suggested in his ear.

He opened his eyes. Somewhat reluctantly he gave Cutter the command to simply guard. And it was Charlie who answered the question. "Focus, we're good. It's over here, thanks to... Five. All yours now, One."

"Copy," Quinn said. "Get here ASAP. We've got a plan to finish this once and for all."

Rafe knew they had to go, but he still didn't want to move. Oddly, he no longer cared all that much about the man who had been one of his top goals for three years.

The only one he cared about was here in his arms.

# *Chapter 33*

Charlie never thought she would willingly pass up watching their revenge on Flood for anything, but if it bought her a few more minutes in Rafe's embrace, she would have.

But her brother's words were an order to Rafe, and she had a job yet to perform tonight, so they needed to get to city hall. Thanks to phone calls from Brett Dunbar and Gavin, plus the weight of the Foxworth name, they were able to clear out much faster than she would have expected, with the understanding there would be a nightmare of details later.

Rafe drove the three miles or so to city hall too fast, but they got lucky with traffic and made it shortly after Gavin had made his grand entrance. In the middle of Flood's grandiose speechifying, as Liam put it.

"And grand it was," Hayley said with a grin. "For almost a full minute you could have heard a pin drop. Flood literally gaped at him. And then the buzz started."

She and Quinn were watching the relayed video on Hayley's tablet in the lobby area outside the council chambers. Cort was with them, and she guessed from the way the man looked at her as they approached that they had told him that Brown had been ordered to kill her.

When they reached them, one of the first things Rafe had done was to look at the man straight on and say, "Thank you," in a tone that warmed Charlie down to the bone.

Cort had looked rather shyly pleased, but then things started to happen fast. Quinn quickly outlined the plan to them. It made sense, and as she watched the feed she knew it would work. The mayor and council were none too happy about this interruption, but on top of Gavin's worldwide standing, they were also very familiar with the Foxworth name, and fear was evident in many faces there. Enough that Charlie started wondering what they'd been up to, to so fear the famous attorney and the organization that had taken the governor down.

But Gavin's name and reputation kept them at bay long enough for them to realize this was about Flood, not them, and they appeared so relieved they didn't even try to stop him as he approached the former senator at the lectern he'd commandeered. It didn't hurt that the brother of the security guard here had been a beneficiary of Foxworth's help once, and so he had been more than willing to make sure he got this assignment and not be in a hurry to restore order.

"I see you recognize the Foxworth name, Flood," Gavin said in that smooth, slightly amused tone that gave the impression he knew more about you than you did yourself. And the lack of the honorific of even "mister," let alone "senator," registered on Flood's face. "As well you should, since you sold them, and federal witness Vicente Reynosa, out to the cartel that was trying to stop him from testifying."

Gasps went around the room. And suddenly the smooth,

casual attorney went into attack mode, rattling off the list of evidence so rapidly the usually smooth-talking Flood got flustered.

"That's not proof!" He practically yelped it. "You can't prove any of this!"

"The first disclaimer of the guilty man," Gavin said with a pitying shake of his head. "Not that it's a lie, but that I can't prove it."

Charlie heard Quinn, both in person and in her ear, tell Gavin they were here and ready. Ty chimed in with the news that several local news feeds had already picked up on the live stream and it was spreading rapidly.

Gavin smiled widely in response. And then uncoiled. "But in fact, that's not what we're here to prove, anyway," he said. "This is not a courtroom, merely an official venue—" he glanced at the now clearly fascinated city officials, the ones Charlie could scarcely believe were allowing this, but such was the power and presence of Gavin de Marco "—the council has been kind enough to lend us. What we are going to present is something more…personal."

"That's what this is, a personal, politically motivated attack," Flood fumed. "Security, throw this man out!"

The security guard made a show of taking out a phone, saying, "Gavin de Marco? I'll check on that."

Charlie was smiling now, the man was so clearly rattled. She glanced at Rafe, who was reacting as well, in a half-smile kind of way that made her want to kiss that mouth.

"What was politically motivated, Maximilian Flood," Gavin said, moving toward the man like the apex predator he was in court, "was the murder of your wife."

Flood's eyes widened, but he came back hard. "I don't care how big you are, I'll have you arrested, de Marco.

And sue you for everything you've got and more. This is ridiculous."

When he spoke again, Gavin sounded like the crack of doom. "What's ridiculous is the facade you've built. What's obscene is the way you played the sympathy card over her death. We know who you paid, when you paid them and how much you paid them to rid yourself of the woman who had discovered the truth about you and was going to go public."

For a moment Charlie thought Flood was going to take a swing at him. Even as she thought it she heard Rafe murmur, "Go ahead, Flood. You'd be in for a shock."

She remembered then that Rafe, too, had seen the man fight.

"And if that's not enough," Gavin said, letting so much disdain into his voice it almost dripped ice water, "there's one more thing you'll have to explain."

Gavin turned and looked at the big doors into the room. Charlie read her cue, and glanced at her brother, who nodded. She started to walk toward those doors, only pausing to glance at Rafe when he stepped in behind her.

"At your back, all the way," he said quietly.

Feeling suddenly invincible, she strode into the council chambers, head up, gaze fastened on Flood. And she smiled, a grimly satisfied smile, as Flood spotted her and shock registered.

Gavin's tone was nothing less than triumphant when he said, "You can only buy so much loyalty, Flood. The man you tasked with murdering her is in the hospital. And he's talking."

Flood turned white and swayed on his feet, having to grab the lectern for balance.

"And the facade crumbles," she said. Behind her, Rafe

laughed. And that warmed her almost as much as the expression on Flood's face.

And so it ended with more of a whimper than a bang.

After a long aftermath, they were finally able to pack up the suite and retreat to Foxworth headquarters for a break while Gavin dealt with the fallout. Rafe was thankful for that; he felt oddly exhausted.

Ty reported that the live stream of the meeting had poured all of Flood's many crimes out to a stunned and rapidly expanding audience. The video had hit the networks after so many outlets had it that it couldn't be stopped or squelched. A couple of city police detectives had arrived; the de Marco name still carried a lot of weight even in those quarters, and their friend Brett Dunbar had made a couple of calls as well, to officers he trusted. Even if Flood were able to wiggle out of the worst of it, the scandal wouldn't be soon forgotten.

And Charlie was giving him that look again. That soft, warm look that did impossible things to his insides. He tried to call up his usual distance, but something about seeing that 9mm jammed under her chin had blasted away every bit of the icy cool he usually carted around.

"Thank you for my sister, Rafe," Quinn said solemnly.

He started to just shrug, but he couldn't treat this as if it were just another case. "That was the most important," he said, his voice a little rough.

"Who would have ever thought Flood would be an anticlimax, and yet in a way he was," Hayley said.

At that Rafe's mouth quirked upward at one corner. "And nothing could tick him off more."

They all laughed, which gave him a strange feeling on top of all the other strange feelings. Some he was familiar with, camaraderie, the satisfaction of accomplishment.

And he liked the fact that Quinn had set up some in-depth interviews with Cort Ducane for next week. The man had stalled Flood just long enough that Quinn could be sure his sister was safe before making their move. Long enough that he and Charlie had gotten there in time for her grand entrance, which Gavin had declared topped his any day.

But the satisfaction faded when, as Quinn and Hayley were getting ready to follow Teague and Liam out the door for some well-deserved rest—they'd been running 24-7 for days now—Charlie whispered to him that she wasn't leaving until they had talked. With some vague hope of outlasting her he'd escaped to his quarters in the hangar.

When Cutter showed up demanding entrance about an hour later, he gave in wearily. He knew too well the dog was immovable when his canine brain was set. And he knew as well that if he resisted, he was going to find out the meaning of the phrase "nipping at his heels" quite literally.

This would be the last time.

Rafe practically chanted it to himself as he walked—reluctantly—toward the back door of the Foxworth headquarters. It was a little chilly, a portent of fall. His fall, too? He grimaced at the corny wordplay.

When he reached the patio he hesitated, but his companion, that darned, determined, dauntless dog, wasn't having it. He didn't just step behind him and nudge, he shoved. And made a sound just short of a growl to hurry him up.

He stepped onto the patio, even more determined now that this would be the last meeting with Charlie. She would go back to St. Louis and life would settle down here, and he'd be back to his routine of machines that didn't talk back or ask about his damned feelings. Feelings that had been out of control so often while she'd been here. Even down-range under fire he'd never felt as terrified as he had when Brown had jammed that pistol under her chin.

But he counted all the training, all the competition, all the kills before worth it for that single shot. If he never took another, that would be enough.

Cutter shoved him again.

"You're worse than a sheriff dragging somebody to the gallows," he muttered at the dog.

Cutter let out a canine sound that somehow sounded like a very human, "Enough already."

Sucking in a deep breath that he knew wouldn't be enough to steady him for this, he reached for the door and pulled it open.

The movement caught his trained eye first. Then the rest registered and he stared in shock.

"You remember."

Her voice was low, almost husky, and his breath jammed up in his throat. Remember? How could he ever forget? That dress. She was wearing that dress. That blue, silky, clingy thing that hugged every luscious curve and somehow made her eyes glow in the same shade of blue.

That dress she'd worn the first night they'd made love.

*Had sex, you mean. The hottest damned sex of my life.*

The tactical part of his mind tried valiantly to kick in, asking why she even still owned it years later, why she had brought it here, had she planned this…and noting that she'd obviously had it fixed from when he'd broken the zipper tearing it off of her.

None of it worked.

And then she was in front of him, asking in that same, sultry voice, "Do you ever wonder if it would be the same?"

*Every damned day.*

If he were the sharing sort, he might tell her that his time with her had set the standard, never to be met again. Not that he tried very often, no matter how many years it had been.

"I don't," she went on, "because I know it will be."

She was so close to him now he caught that sweet scent she'd worn back then. Different from what she'd worn with Flood, which had been heavier, screaming money, this was light, airy, fresh. She'd remembered that, too? Another memory flashed, Hayley and a shopping bag? Had she been in on this? Or had Charlie asked her to get—

Belatedly, it hit him. She'd said "will be." As if she had every intention of this night ending the way the night she'd first worn this dress had.

He knew in that moment he was doomed. If Charlie Foxworth had set her mind on seducing him, she would succeed.

Because when it came to her, all his vaunted fortitude and patience vanished.

Desperately, he made one try. "You don't have to sleep with me just because I saved your life."

She should have slapped him. At least she should have given him a furious, Charlie-like retort.

Instead she laughed. Delightedly. As if she knew they were well past that kind of nonsense. As if she recognized the desperate ploy for what it was. She reached out and cupped his cheek. Her touch seared him until he'd have sworn he felt that simple gesture down to his bones. Bones that seemed to be melting as he stood there.

"Char—"

It was all he got out before she kissed him.

At the feel of her soft, luscious mouth on his, it was as if the years between had never rolled by. The spark struck, caught, blazed. And no amount of his tactical mind saying this was a mistake could overpower the body screaming it was essential.

His will broke, because nothing could withstand a determined Charlaine Foxworth, and he was kissing her back.

New sensations collided with old memories, and the resultant inferno exploded like nothing he'd ever seen or felt.

He wasn't sure he'd survive.

He was sure he didn't care.

On some level, in some rarely used part of his mind that dealt with those feelings he never admitted to, he knew this would make it harder than ever when she, inevitably, was gone. When this ended yet again, for the simple reason that he didn't deserve anything that felt this good.

But a body that overheated at her first touch, hardened completely at that first kiss, didn't care. This was Charlie, and she knew how to blow up his walls. As she was blowing them up now.

When she went for his shirt, it was fierce and determined and very Charlie. And he didn't care if he broke the zipper on that dress, that damned enchanting dress, again.

This was happening. All the hot dreams he'd never been able to rid himself of, all the memories that cropped up whenever he let his mental guard down, were nothing compared to this reality, Charlie pulling his clothes off, touching him, stroking him, only pulling back long enough to step free of the dress that then fell to pool around their feet. He fumbled with the lacy, matching blue bra, but Charlie didn't. She was free of it in seconds, and seemingly of their own volition his hands were cupping her naked breasts. Her nipples were already taut, and when he rubbed them with his thumbs she moaned and he thought he would drop to his knees right here. And when she slid her hands down over his belly to stroke already rock-hard flesh, he nearly did.

"Don't think of anything else but how this feels," she whispered.

"As if I could," he ground out.

They somehow made it as far as the couch in front of the fire, which had come on against the chill he'd noticed outside. He would have suggested the bed in the guest room, but that twelve extra feet was too far. Way too far.

Her fingers tangled in his hair, pulling his mouth even harder against hers. He almost staggered, and for once it had nothing to do with his bad leg. They went down to the cushions, entwined now, her hands sliding over him.

"Hurry," she said breathlessly. "It's been too long."

*A lifetime.*

Hunger overwhelmed him and his last bit of caution vanished in an explosion of need. He stroked, kissed, tasted, even knowing he could never, ever get his fill. She arched against him, urging him on. And then her hand slid down to guide him into her, and the memories were seared to ash by the fierce fire of the reality. He was buried inside her, her body welcoming him, holding him, and he couldn't stop the blissful groan that escaped him.

As if the sound had triggered her she began to move, arching up to take him deeper, her fingers digging into his hips as if to keep him from escaping. As if he could. As if he would.

Some buried part of him warned this really would be the last time, and his determination suddenly matched hers, a determination to make it something neither of them would ever, ever forget. He drove hard and deep again and again until she cried out his name and clutched at him. This sign of the same kind of need from this indomitable woman was the last match to the fuse, and he barely held on until he felt her body clench fiercely around him and his name broke from her again, this time on a near scream.

Then it overtook him, and as his body exploded with exquisite pleasure, Rafe Crawford felt whole for the first time in years. The first time since the last night he'd spent with her.

He'd thought before he wasn't sure he'd survive this. Now he wondered how he had survived without it.

# Chapter 34

"This is pretty, but I like your hair straight and smooth. That's when it shimmers like moonlight on dark water."

Charlie stared at him as he toyed with the waves she'd worked so hard to get just right. The waves she herself didn't really like, but Flood had. Somehow that figured.

But those words had been almost...poetic. Especially for Rafe. It almost made her change her mind, because she so did not want to shatter this mood, this lovely peace between them.

But she wanted more and more of this, she wanted a future full of this, and to get that, this had to be done. And never let it be said Charlie Foxworth shirked what had to be done.

She steadied herself and said it. "Time for that talk."

She felt him go still beside her. They'd made it to the bed, finally. She'd vaguely noticed Cutter taking up a station at the bedroom door as if to make sure they didn't leave. Or no one interrupted them.

But that thought had slipped away quickly in a burst of renewed heat. She'd wanted nothing more but that fierce, strong body inside her again. Then she wanted to touch and kiss every new scar he'd gained in the years since, and then spend some time on the one she knew so well, the one she'd so often wished she could heal with a touch.

This night had been everything she'd hoped and planned for. Nothing had been lost in the years since, in fact it seemed to have only honed the need until it cut through all restraint. She wanted him more than ever, and she was not going to give up without a fight.

There would never be a better time.

"I want an answer. Now."

In his quieter way, he didn't respond to autocratic orders any better than she did, not when it came to personal things. Quinn could order him into a death trap and she had no doubt he would go, but this…this was a scarier place to him, this place where emotions lived. Where the heart lived.

She didn't give him time to think. Running on gut instinct now, and the new knowledge she had thanks to all she'd learned on this operation, working beside him, she didn't ask, she simply stated.

"Why. That's all I want to know. All I ever wanted to know. Why you walked away." She saw his jaw tighten. Even the cords of his neck tightened. But she kept going. "I deserve that much, Rafe. Just give me a good enough reason for why you did it."

It was a moment before he spoke, and she heard a world of apprehension in his voice. "Not sleeping with the boss isn't good enough?"

She let out a snort of laughter. "Do you really think I'm foolish enough to think I'm your boss?"

He looked straight at her then. "You're everyone's boss.

There's no one at any branch of Foxworth that wouldn't jump to do what you asked."

"Even you?"

His already low, rumbly voice dropped another notch. "Especially me."

"Rafe…" Her voice died away as he looked at her, those stormy gray eyes capturing her with the intensity of his gaze.

"Do you have any idea—" it was barely above a whisper "—how proud your parents would be of you, of what you've accomplished?"

It was so unexpected she was at a loss for words. Something rare enough that it rattled her. She felt her eyes begin to sting, was afraid she was going to cry and turn this into the very kind of emotional morass he hated. *She* hated.

Then his mouth quirked in a very Rafe-like way. "I know, I'm not supposed to be that…emotionally observant."

She recognized the phrase she'd used. It had apparently stuck with him. "Why did you tell me that?"

"Because it's true. And…" He hesitated, then, as if it were a great strain, said, "I needed to."

"There's a difference between being emotionally observant and emotionally available. What you just said was almost the latter."

"Almost?"

"It would take admitting why you felt that need to get all the way there."

He grimaced, looked away. "Just because I don't vomit it all out doesn't mean I don't feel it."

She felt an inward ache, some combination of sympathy and sadness. "Is that how you look at it? As…vomiting?"

"I look at it as pointless," he snapped. "Nobody wants to hear all that."

He didn't say "from me," but it hung in the air as if he had. Her eyes began to sting again, and she had to blink rapidly. She waited a long beat to be sure her voice would be steady, then said quietly, "I do. It's all I ever wanted, to hear that kind of thing from you. But now... I need to. To understand why."

She saw the reference back to his own need to tell her that thing about her parents that had so warmed her register in those eyes. But he didn't speak. He looked away. She'd known his walls were high and solid, but this...

She kept going. Because she had to. Foxworths didn't give up. Especially when the world—hers, anyway—was at stake.

"What could have made you leave," she said slowly, steadily, "without even an explanation? Made you walk away from what we had?"

When he still didn't answer, she knew she had to use the weapon her brother had given her.

"You were what I'd been hoping for my entire life. What could have ever made you think you weren't enough?"

"For you?" It burst from him. "How could you even begin to think I was good enough for you?"

The pure anguish in his tone, something she knew he never let show, broke her. The tears she'd been fighting welled up, and she felt the drops overflowing and then streaking down her cheeks. She didn't even try to wipe them away. She'd wept tears of happiness at Quinn and Hayley's wedding, and that had been the only time she'd cried since she'd vowed she never would again after their parents had died. Until now. Now she couldn't seem to stop.

"How...how could you ever think...you're not?"

It came out brokenly, which was how she felt inside at this confirmation of what seemed so impossible to her.

And for the first time in longer than she could remember, Charlaine Foxworth had no idea what to do.

It was impossible. Charlie was crying. The indomitable, undefeatable Charlie Foxworth was crying. Over...him.

He'd seen some incredible things in his life. He'd seen ugly things, horrible things, and a few beautiful things. He'd never seen anything that hit him as hard and deep as did the sight of her tears. He wanted to speak, to tell her he wasn't worth those tears, but the undeniable fact that she thought he was made his chest so tight he couldn't get a single word out. The pressure built, and built, until he could barely breathe.

He felt something break inside him, something so definite he was surprised the crack hadn't been audible.

He couldn't do this anymore. He had to tell her. He had to tell her, and then she'd understand, not just why he'd left, but why she was a million miles too good for him. He'd tell her and it would be over, this connection between them that had gone from heart high and soul deep but was now stretched so thin it wouldn't take much to snap it.

The truth should do it.

"I..." He had to stop, the tightness in his throat was so bad. It was like a blocked rifle barrel, and if he didn't clear it, whatever rounds he fired were going to blow up in his face.

*You're about to finally blow this up for good, anyway, so what does it matter?*

He swallowed, then told himself to settle in for the second biggest, most important shot of his life. He stared at his hands, the hands that had such skill when it came to things that didn't feel. They'd delivered death, many times.

But it wasn't his hands that would deliver this death.

Still staring at them, he ground the words out. "I'm not

good enough because I'm the reason a good, decent woman and her unborn child are dead." At last he looked up and met her gaze, made himself look into those beautiful blue eyes. "*My* unborn child."

She stared at him, her expression frozen. He'd shocked her out of the tears at least. For a moment he thought perhaps that was all it was going to take, and in that moment he was almost relieved. If he didn't have to go through it all, then maybe—

"Start," Charlie said with no intonation at all, "at the beginning."

He should have known. He wasn't going to get off that easy. Not with Charlie.

So where was the beginning? He wasn't sure, so he started with the best thing he could think of. "Her name was Laura. She was a civilian aide. She was from St. Louis, too, and we got to talking about that and…"

He trailed off, floundering in the unfamiliar waters. Silence spun out until Charlie said, with just the tiniest bit of snap in her voice, "Points to her if she got you to talk." He winced inwardly. Then, to his shock, she apologized. "Sorry. Go on."

He wasn't sure he could. It was going to take a lot of talking—especially for him—to get through this. He didn't think he had it in him. But something about the way Charlie was looking at him, something in those eyes…

He kept going. "We…got close, for the duration of her deployment. Then she was due to rotate out on an afternoon flight. I was gearing up for a mission, a nasty one, and that…that's when she told me she was pregnant."

"Timing is indeed everything," Charlie said, and he couldn't read anything in her very neutral tone.

"I…lost it. That she chose to wait and tell me then, when she admitted she'd known for at least two weeks. We were loading up, departure set for less than ten minutes on. I had to focus on the mission, she knew that. We…argued. I was pissed, and I didn't try to hide it."

That day had taught him a lot about hiding his anger, and any other emotion that might dare to try and rise up. It was not a lesson he wanted to learn again.

"Understandable." Her tone was just as neutral as it had been. "On both sides."

She said it as if she understood instinctively what Laura had had to explain to him, that she'd been afraid to tell him for this very reason. He sucked in some air, knowing he would need it to go on. And he had to go on, even though it was the last thing he wanted to do.

And the last time this woman would ever want to listen to him.

"She finally agreed to delay her departure until a flight out the next day. So we could…could…"

"Figure out what the hell you were going to do?"

"Yes." He grimaced, then let out a harsh laugh. "I was thinking, *If I survive the mission.*"

He stopped. He couldn't do this. He just couldn't. The images, the gruesome memories were all there, right there, careening around in his brain, as vivid as they had been that day. He couldn't let them out. They would destroy everything, the moment he put them into words. He never had, had never spoken of this to anyone, and he was no more ready to go through it now than he had been before.

Especially to Charlie.

And then she reached out. She took both his hands in hers. His first instinct was to pull away, pull back, but he couldn't do that, either. He wasn't even sure why he was still breathing.

"Finish it, Rafe. Let it out before it smothers you."

This time a short, sharp, bitter bite of laughter escaped him. "If only," he muttered.

But somehow the feel of her fingers wrapped around his gave him...not strength, really, but the courage to go on. It was ironic, really, that the person forcing him to talk was the one he least wanted to tell this to.

He stared down at their hands, entwined. The memories that caused, of those brief months of joy, of that revisited paradise last night, almost swamped him. He felt as if some clawing, biting creature had broken free in his chest, his gut, and it was going to leave him torn to ribbons. And the only coherent thought he had then was that it was no less than he deserved.

*So do it. Get it done. Finish it once and for all. And if it finishes you, so be it.*

He kept staring at their hands, on some level certain this would be the last physical contact they would ever have. And with an effort greater than he'd ever had to make walking into an enemy's nest, he pulled the pin.

"I survived, all right. But we came back to find the forward operating base a smoking ruin." Her fingers tightened, and he thought he heard a quick intake of breath. He kept on, knowing if he stopped now he'd never finish it. He released the safety lever on that metaphorical grenade. "They'd been attacked while we were gone. Half the people assigned there were dead. Including Laura."

"And your child," she whispered, sounding as if the tears were about to start again.

"Yes." He was hoarse now and didn't even try to hide it. "All because I...because I made her wait. She would have been gone, well on her way home, safe, but I lost my temper and...they both died. Because of me."

He pulled his hands back, knowing she wouldn't want to be touching him anymore. That she let him only proved it. He didn't have to—and couldn't—look at her to know she was staring at him in horror and distaste.

He stood up, he wasn't quite sure how. Nor was he sure where he was going to go, except away from here. Away from her, because he couldn't stand to see the revulsion he deserved in her eyes. She didn't try to stop him, but he heard a painfully choked sort of sound break from her.

"Now you know I was right," he said, his voice sounding as broken as he felt inside. He yanked on the jeans he'd picked up from the floor and turned to go, certain now she'd be glad to see the back of him. Forever.

He nearly tripped over Cutter.

The dog was on his feet, staring up at him with that fierce, amber-flecked gaze.

"Out of my way, dog," he said as he started to go around the animal who had become such a huge part of all of their lives. Cutter dodged back and got between him and the back door. "Do not," he said, "try and herd me."

Cutter growled. He took another step. The growl became a snarl, fierce and threatening. He stopped, startled. The dog's hackles were up, those lethal fangs bared, and for the first time Rafe had an inkling of what it must feel like for all the nefarious sorts they'd taken down since Cutter had joined them.

"Going to go for my throat, dog?" It came out in a whisper. "Go ahead."

He sensed rather than heard Charlie move behind him. Whatever she was going to say or do, he didn't want to be here for it. He changed direction, heading now for the front door.

Cutter launched, barreling into him. The dog hit his right leg just below the knee. It pushed all his weight onto his bad leg. At that angle it gave out. He was going down, hard.

And then there were arms around him, slight but undeniably strong. Holding on. Tight. Cushioning the fall.

Charlie.

She went down to the floor with him. Holding on tight. And now he saw her face, wet with tears that had overflowed. Were still flowing. Charlie Foxworth, the indomitable, unbreakable Charlie Foxworth, crying again. Still. Over him.

He should pull away. He tried. Cutter growled, and Charlie held on. The dog stood over them as they lay on the floor, like some supernatural guardian making sure they didn't escape. He tried again to move. Cutter growled again. Feeling suddenly exhausted, his head and shoulders dropped back to the floor.

"No," she whispered. "You're not leaving me. Not like this." He tried to speak. Couldn't. But Charlie could. "What happened was horrible. And heartbreaking. But it wasn't your fault. Do you hear me, Rafer James Crawford? It. Was. Not. Your. Fault."

He still couldn't find his voice, but he let out a harsh breath, closed his eyes and shook his head.

Charlie raised up on an elbow, and when he opened his eyes again she was looking down at him. "It wasn't her fault, either, except for the rotten timing. She was in an emotional place. Should she not tell you until she got home and you were stuck half a world away? Or maybe not tell you at all?"

His stomach knotted painfully. "I...wondered about that."

"Maybe that was her plan and at the last minute she couldn't do it. I don't know. You don't know. But it doesn't matter, Rafe. You couldn't control that any more than you could stop that attack when you weren't even there."

A tremor went through him, and he couldn't even muster up the strength to try and hide it from her.

"And look at what you've done since, the people you've saved, including me. The lives you've helped rebuild."

"That's...different."

"What's different is it's your work, which you excel at. When it gets dangerous, you're the one they want at their back. And you're always there for them. It's only the personal side you won't risk. You wall it up and lock the door." She paused, as if waiting for him to deny it. He couldn't. Because it was true. "I never, ever thought you'd be a coward, Rafe. But when it comes to your heart..."

He winced. His mouth twisted. "How did you get so smart about people?"

"I've been hanging around my sister-in-law."

He blinked at that. And because Hayley deserved it, he said quietly, "That would do it."

"And there's another thing you should know." He braced himself. "It was you who gave me the words that became a mantra for Foxworth, as we grew and expanded."

He stared at her. What the hell could she mean? When she went on, it was in the tone of someone indeed quoting a mantra.

"'No operation goes well unless all the parts are oiled, fit right and work together.'"

His brow furrowed. It had been a long time ago, but he did remember saying it. Vaguely. "I was...talking about machines."

"And is Foxworth not a well-oiled machine?"

"I..."

"I was planning a trip here, before Flood." That seeming non sequitur made the swirling waters still for a moment. "I wanted to have it out with you once and for all. I couldn't go on like this, wishing I could...not care." Her breath caught audibly, and he couldn't stop himself from looking. Tears were still flowing, from those huge blue eyes down the cheeks of this woman who never cowered, never quailed...never, ever cried.

"Charlie..." It came out like a mangled whisper. She tightened her arms around him.

"Are you going to throw us away?"

"I thought I already had." He sounded like a rusty wheel, but it was the best he could do.

"Because of a tragedy you couldn't have prevented?"

"But she...they..." He stopped, unable to go on because one of her tears had dropped onto his face. It seared him, making his own eyes sting.

"It's horrible," she said again. "And I'm so sorry this world hasn't been blessed with the presence of your child." He stared at her, startled that she chose that to focus on. "But we're here, and we're alive, Rafe. You may have thrown us away, but I never let go."

"You'd be better off if you did."

"No. No, I wouldn't. We love who we love."

He froze. Didn't, couldn't breathe as those words pounded in his head. She couldn't mean what that implied.

Charlie laughed, a rueful yet somehow unrepentant sound. "Oh, yes, Mr. Crawford. I love you."

"You can't—"

"I never stopped. I even think I loved you most when I was sniping the worst."

He took in a long, deep breath. "I just a while ago realized... I kept digging at you because it was a connection, at least."

"It's always been there, that connection. Maybe even since childhood, but certainly since the day my brother brought you into Foxworth. From the moment I saw you...

I knew. You were the one I was afraid I'd never find. And when we were together, it was so right. So very right."

"Too right," he whispered, remembered that feeling, that soaring, joyous feeling. Before all the reasons why it was wrong, why he didn't deserve it, came crashing in. "But you didn't know then."

"Not the specifics, no. But I knew you were…hurting. And Quinn warned me you were too stubborn to admit it." She smiled, rather crookedly, and through the tears it was the most wrenching yet beautiful thing he'd ever seen. "I didn't care. I just knew I'd never reacted this way to any man, ever."

She leaned down suddenly. Before he realized her intent, her mouth was on his. The kiss was hot and fierce, and flooded him with the memories and images of last night, those wild hours in the dark when he'd given it all because he'd known it would be the last time.

And yet here she was, saying she still loved him. And showing him. He was breathless when she finally pulled back.

"You know what I want?" She sounded a little breathless herself.

He couldn't find any words, so only shook his head.

"I want eighteen thousand repeats of last night." He blinked. She smiled. "That works out to every night for fifty years, give or take." Of course she'd do the math. Only Charlie. Only Charlie could make him laugh at a time like this. But his laugh faded when her voice took on that low, husky note again as she said quietly, "And know that I, as you were for me, will be at your back all the way."

There were still no words—he really was going to have to do something about that—but he did answer her. He kissed her. Long and deep. And when at last she pulled back to look at him, there was a gleam in those blue eyes he'd never seen before.

"Now, listen up, Crawford. This will only work if I assume that if you're in one of those moods, it has nothing to do with me. So if it ever does have something to do with me, you're going to have to break through that miasma you live in and *tell* me. You're going to have to do it for us."

She was saying it as if it were a given there would be an us. Us. Them. Him and Charlie Foxworth.

"And by the way," she added, "if you think you're going to walk away again, I think you'd better take into account one more thing."

He had to swallow before he could force out, "What?"

Charlie grinned at him then. "Him," she said, jerking a thumb at Cutter. "And I think you know better than to try and cross him when his mind is set."

He glanced at the dog. Cutter stared back at him, looking as wise as the sphinx whose position he had assumed. There was a world of wisdom and determination in those amber-flecked eyes. Just as there was a world of love in Charlie's vivid blue ones.

He felt muscles he hadn't even realized were tensed relax. Followed by a strange flood of warmth inside, spreading everywhere. The dam had broken, the last wall had been breached. He wasn't sure exactly how, but he knew with a gut-deep certainty that a sea change was upon him. He knew it had to happen, even if he didn't know how.

He had to walk a new path, one he'd never been on before.

And he knew that no one would be better able to keep him on that path than stubborn, brilliant, loving—and forgiving—Charlie Foxworth.

With a little help, maybe, from her brother's dog.

# *Epilogue*

"Do we need to take him to the vet?"

Quinn looked at Cutter a little anxiously. He'd never seen the dog like this, sleeping so much, barely showing an interest in anything going on. Not that he wanted something to worry about, not when he was snuggled up on the couch with his wife's arms around him, but the animal was acting oddly.

"He's eating okay," he went on, brow furrowed with concern, "but..."

"He's fine."

When he looked up at Hayley's words, he found her grinning. "What's funny?"

"He's just exhausted. And I can't blame him. This was a very long haul."

He couldn't deny the three years it had taken them to finally get to the mole who had betrayed them had been long. "At least Flood's going to pay now."

Her grin widened. "I didn't mean Flood."

Belatedly it hit him. "Oh." Slowly, a smile that held the same quality as her grin curved his mouth. "Yeah."

"You are happy about it?"

"That those two knuckleheads finally got it together? Yes. Absolutely I am. I think they're the only ones who could put up with each other."

"Now that they've figured out how," Hayley agreed happily. "With a little help. Can you believe he actually knocked Rafe down?"

He looked back at their exhausted, match-making dog. "I believe he knew exactly how to use that leg against him."

"And," Hayley added softly, "how desperate the situation was. He never would have done it otherwise."

"No, he wouldn't."

She shifted her gaze to his face, and he felt that strange quiver he always felt whenever she looked at him that way. "I hope they're having a wonderful time at the cabin."

He couldn't help the upward twitch of his eyebrows. "Oh, I'm sure they are," he said as he recalled those last moments at the small landing strip in the mountains. He'd flown them there himself and arranged for one of the locals to drive them up to the isolated lodge-style cabin.

"We'll try not to burn it down," Charlie had said, happier than he had ever seen her.

"But no promises," Rafe had said gruffly, his gaze fastened on the woman beside him.

Hayley let out a satisfied sigh. "It's wonderful to see them so happy. By the way, what did you say to him, right as they got off the plane?"

"I told him not to blow their second chance." Quinn smiled. "He reminded me that the second shot out of a rifle is always more accurate."

Hayley blinked. "What?"

Quinn laughed. "It's a sniper thing. They call it a cold

bore shot. The first shot, I mean. It warms up the barrel and leaves carbon behind, and that affects the next shot, makes the path different, more accurate."

She was laughing now. "So was that our inimitable Rafe saying second time's the charm?"

"Pretty much," Quinn agreed, grinning at her now.

She let out an obviously happy sigh. "I was afraid it would never happen for him. For them."

"Me, too." He jerked a thumb at Cutter. "But we should have known he'd never quit until it was done."

"It's not in him," Hayley agreed. "Us first, now all of the Foxworth team, plus all those clients… Not a bad track record, dog."

Cutter's dark ears twitched, and his head came up. But only his head, and he was looking at them sleepily. When he saw them still seated, he plopped back down and seemed to doze back off in mere seconds.

"Do you think she'll really move here?" Hayley asked. "We won't lose Rafe, will we?"

"I should ask you. You're the mind reader."

Hayley looked thoughtful. "I think she liked it here. And more importantly, I think she knows Rafe wouldn't be really happy anywhere else." She grinned then. "I think we're going to lose our live-in security at headquarters, though."

Quinn laughed. "No, I can't see my sister living in that tiny room."

He was quiet for a moment, as he pondered the changes that had already happened, and those yet to come.

"It all makes you wonder where we go from here," he mused aloud.

"There will always be people who need us. So we go and do whatever it takes to help them. As we did this time."

Cutter bestirred himself enough to add a small woof of

agreement, then went back to sleep. Quinn took it as the canine equivalent of "Mission accomplished."

Quinn shifted on the couch so he could look directly at the woman who had changed his life. He reached up and gently turned her chin so that their gazes locked.

"I love you, Hayley Foxworth. You are my life."

"As you are mine, Quinn Foxworth." She reached up to cup his cheek. "And it's a good, good life."

"The best," Quinn whispered, just before he kissed her.

Knowing his people were all happy, Cutter slept on, taking his well-earned rest.

Until the next time.

\* \* \* \* \*

# The Suspect Next Door

Rachel Astor

# MILLS & BOON

**Rachel Astor** is equal parts country girl and city dweller who spends an alarming amount of time correcting the word *the*. Rachel has had a lot of jobs (bookseller, real estate agent, 834 assorted admin roles), but none as, *ahem*, interesting as when she waitressed at a bar named after a dog. She is now a *USA TODAY* bestselling author who splits her time between the city, the lake and as many made-up worlds as possible.

Dear Reader,

If you love cozy-mystery vibes with a heavy dose of a certain girl detective from days past, then you've come to the right place.

Writing *The Suspect Next Door* was such a treat, with feisty and sometimes irreverent Petra Jackson taking charge of (okay, meddling in) the lives of those around her—particularly a certain neighbour, Ryan, who just happens to be the most intriguing man she's ever encountered.

Like that girl detective, Petra finds herself immersed in all sorts of entertaining and alarming conundrums...but Petra is only one part of a whole cast of quirky characters, and I hope you'll come to love them all.

Fun fact: I'm honoured that the book you hold in your hands shares the same title as the Nancy Drew Files #39, published in 1989. It feels like a perfect homage to the books I grew up reading in my grandma's basement all those years ago. I still have a few of my maternal family's original hardbacks from the 1930s on my bookshelves.

Thank you so much for picking up this book and helping make this author's dreams come true.

Happy reading,

*Rachel*

# Chapter 1

## Top 10 Worst Opening Lines for a Book

1. *It was a dark and stormy night...*
2. *Gazing into the mirror, I stared into my deep brown eyes...*
3. *In the end, it was all a dream.*
4. *My eyes refused to open as I flung my alarm clock across the room.*
5. *The phone rang.*
6. *The date was March 12, 1988...*
7. *I couldn't believe how big my butt had gotten.*
8. *Kaboom!*
9. *Storm clouds roiled above menacingly...* (aka an even worse riff on *dark and stormy night*)
10. *Once upon a time...*

I was fantastically screwed.

I'd legitimately typed—and subsequently deleted—each one of the awful lines onto the screen that kept staring at me, annoyingly blank. My muse had apparently gone for a smoke break.

Eight hours ago.

I sighed. I knew exactly *who* I wanted to write about—Amelia Jones, inspired by amalgamations of real-life kick-ass women, like Amelia Earhart, and famous fictional kick-ass women like Jessica Jones. In short, she was going to be very, well…kick-ass. She would be a fighter (and not in the "oh she's so strong emotionally" way, but more the "I'll take down a burly heathen whilst in evening wear and emerge unscathed save for a charming, dewy glow" way), be so clever she could take down any vainglorious *Princess Bride* weirdo in a battle of wits, and be gorgeous to boot, but in an accessible way, of course—no supermodel dimensions here.

Except… I couldn't think of anything for her to do. Like not a damned thing. Which was weird, because I used to be able to write and write and write about nothing in particular and then sometimes—when those elusive literary deities poured their sparkle juice into my keyboard—it turned into something great.

Or at least pretty good.

At the moment, anything other than incredible suckitude would be great. I ran my hands along my hair and held it up in a sort of mock ponytail, watching the cursor blink.

You. BLINK. Are. BLINK. A failure. BLINK.

How condescending.

Before I launched my laptop off the balcony and admired its beautiful spiral of doom—the sun glittering beatifically off its silvery edges before sailing to its final, magnificent shattering—there were a few things I needed to try.

I jumped up and went to my dresser, pulling out my favorite costume jewelry—a dazzling bracelet and a few massive ornate rings—topping them off with my pink feather boa. Maybe if I looked the part of a glamorous author, the words would start to flow.

I sat back at my desk, spitting out a stray feather and scratching the tickle from my nose. Man, those feathers really got everywhere. I set my fingers gently on the keyboard and started to…

…do absolutely nothing.

Damn.

*Why?* I wailed in my head. I used to believe writer's block didn't exist. That it was just some pathetic excuse for someone who was too lazy to sit down and do the work.

What a prime ass past me was.

I mean, sure there was a little more pressure to come up with something good now that I'd written a book that was published and actually sold well, but that was silly. That should mean I was even more confident about the magic I could weave with words, right?

Um. Apparently not.

I spit out another feather, fished an additional plume from my cleavage and shook my head. This was ridiculous.

Tossing the boa aside, I packed up my laptop and grabbed my coat. Perhaps a change of scenery would do it, and I could really use a cinnamon caramel latte while I was at it. Nothing soothed the writerly soul like the decadent scents of a coffee shop.

I stepped into Cuppa Joe on the ground floor of my apartment building, and instantly felt at home. I'd spent hours there writing my last book, and that had gotten me almost to the top of the *New York Times* bestseller list. My stomach did a little flip just thinking about it. Cuppa Joe was the reason I'd moved in once I'd been able to afford an apartment in the building.

I smiled as I took in the spicy sweet scents, the low murmur of voices, the clicking of spoons on dishes. Yes, this was the ticket. Surely the words would flow once I got my coffee and found a nice quiet corner and...*damn*. The place was packed.

Since when were there so many people who could just come to a coffee shop and write in the middle of the day? Didn't people have jobs anymore? Not that I had one, really. Well, not anything structured, like in an office or anything. Although if I didn't get some words going soon, I might have to find one. Which, from what I could recall, was decidedly not a lifestyle I would prefer to go back to. No shade to those who love being cooped up in a cubicle/practice coffin begging for time off to go to the gyno or whatever, but those were not the things that brought me a whole lot of passion, personally.

Unfortunately, writing really hadn't brought much in the last while either.

Still, I knew this was my life's calling, so I needed to find a way to emblazon some words onto that screen.

Sitting at a table in the middle of the room, I felt like I was in some kind of performance piece, even if it was exceptionally mundane. I preferred to stick along the edges so no one could look over my shoulder. It wasn't like I was writing some super confidential plot twist (as if I had any semblance of a plot twist), but sometimes, when writing some of the more…romantic scenes, things could get a little steamy. And someone sneaking a peek out of context might wonder—or, you know, faint dead away or something. I put my coffee down and set up my workspace—laptop open, note-book handy to my right and phone to my left. Perfect.

Then obviously I had to check social media—just for a second—to see if anyone replied to that comment I made this morning. And while I was at it, I may as well play a game or two of Candy Crush, just to get nice and relaxed and in the mood for typing.

Finally, I set my phone down and really got ready, leaning back in my seat.

All the other people were typing away. Some of them incredibly fast, almost frantic—like they were so filled with ideas, they couldn't get them down fast enough. One girl in the corner, who was gorgeous and had the shiniest black hair I'd ever seen, had the big-gest, beaming smile plastered on her face over what-ever it was she was typing so passionately about. I briefly wondered what would happen if I got up, calmly wandered over and slapped her right across the face.

Which of course I would never do, but it was tempting to think about getting rid of that radiant smile.

I tried to remember a time when something I wrote gave me that much excitement. There must have been a moment at some point, but I couldn't readily recall it. I mean, maybe she was just messaging with some guy or something, which led to thoughts about how I decidedly had no guy of my own to message, but I quickly banished that from my mind.

I could not go down that rabbit hole again.

Even the man in the corner, who was very serious about whatever it was he was working on with his stern look and harsh glasses, typed faster than, frankly, I'd ever seen a guy his age type.

I glanced around. These people were all so...productive.

I closed my eyes for a second.

Okay, time to stop worrying about what everyone else was doing and get to it. I stretched my neck to either side then readied myself at the keyboard once more. Here we go. Just write something.

Anything.

I blinked. The cursor blinked. I took a sip of coffee. The cursor blinked some more.

My phone dinged. *Thank god*.

How's the writing going?

Victoria. Who should know better than to bother me when I was working. Of course, she probably knew as well as I did that there was not a lot of actual work going on. She'd been an up-close-and personal witness to my writer's block for months.

It was so bad the writer's block had taken on its own persona. I called her Mabel.

Funny, I wrote back.

Well, kid. I don't know what to tell you. You've got to get out of this slump.

Tell me something I don't know.

Okay, one question. WWND?

???

What would Nancy do?

I smiled. Vic was well aware of my juvenile obsession with girl-detective books.

She'd go find a mystery for inspiration, of course, I typed.

Then you know what you have to do.

I set down my phone. Could she be right? I mean, maybe it *was* the whole "trying to think up a mystery out of thin air" that was holding me back. Surely other writers must look for inspiration in real life, right?

There was only one problem. How did one go about finding a mystery in the middle of a random Tuesday?

An hour later, my coffee was gone and my screen was

as blank as ever. The raven-haired girl had left, leaving a sense of despair in her wake. Not her own, of course. She looked perfectly fine when she left. Happy even.

The despair was all mine.

I packed up my laptop and headed out to the street—there was no direct access from inside the building to the coffee shop, which I thought was a massive oversight until the barista, Frank, had explained that it was for the safety of the residents. "You wouldn't want people off the street to be able to access the building through one of the businesses, would you?" Fair point, Frank. Fair point.

Other than Frank, I hadn't made much headway getting to know many of the people in my building. Except Annie.

Annie was quickly becoming my favorite human. I'd basically already decided I wanted to be her when I grew up. And the *gossip*, my god, but somehow it was the complete opposite of snark and more just a way to talk about her favorite people, which was to say, everyone in the building. She talked shamelessly about all of us, and yet, we loved her. There had to be a name for that. Affectionmonger? Praisecaster?

In any case, Annie was my insider. For instance, the couple in Apartment 406 was a teacher and an office manager, which at first sounds like a perfectly tame combination. Until you find out the office manager, Samantha, was in charge of the nation's largest chain of adult toy stores. I had to admit, I was pretty glad I didn't have the apartment underneath those two.

And then there was Mrs. Appleton in Apartment 105.

Until I'd moved in, I'd never even heard of a woman who'd had eight husbands. How does one even go about finding men that fast? I hadn't even had a date since Johnny and I broke up four months ago.

Anyway, Annie really was adorable, and that day was no exception as I unlocked the front door to the building and saw that she was, as she tended to be, sitting in one of the comfy lounge chairs in the lobby. Her outfit was pretty surprising though. Normally the woman looked like a unicorn had exploded on her, all rainbows and sparkles, but today she was pretty tame in a black sheath dress and black ankle boots. If it weren't for the leggings featuring cartoon characters and the electric blue wig, I would have thought something terrible had happened.

"Petra!" Annie squealed. "My gorgeous! How can you even be so spectacular with all that hair?"

I smiled, trying my best not to make a face. In the words of my favorite Nancy, compliments were not my chum.

"And this figure… You are to die for, honey. Those curves!" she said, fanning herself.

Frankly, I didn't love when people mentioned my curves. They were somewhat new—hello, slowing metabolism—and I hadn't quite gotten used to them yet. Seriously, I'd bought six different bras and they all fit just slightly wrong, though each in dissimilar, and increasingly mystifying, ways.

"Thanks, Annie," I said. "Your wig is stellar."

"Aw, thanks," she said, primping it a little. "I wasn't

really feeling any of my outfits this morning, but the wig put me right in the spirit."

I wasn't sure what spirit she was talking about— maybe the spirit of RuPaul or something—but she always put me in a better mood instantly. Annie had a way of making everyone feel just a little bit better about their day.

"Come sit with me. Tell me everything."

So of course, I sat, though I wasn't really sure what she wanted me to tell her. There hadn't been a whole lot of "everything" since we'd danced this routine yesterday.

"I don't know what to tell you, Annie. There just isn't a whole lot going on these days."

Annie tilted her head, a sort of nondescript look on her face. It wasn't quite pity or disappointment or a "things'll get better" look, but it was maybe a combination of the three. In any case, it made me feel like I had to elaborate.

"Maybe I need to take a class or something."

Annie chuckled. "You certainly like your classes, don't you, kitten?"

I smiled. "What? It's been like, two weeks since Tae Kwon Do for Beginners ended."

"And before that it was?"

"La Dolce Vita: An Exploration of Italian Pastries."

"And before that?"

"An Introduction to American Sign Language."

"Uh-huh. Exactly how many classes have you taken this year?"

I shrugged. "I'm not sure. Maybe...six?"

"Petra," she said, taking my hands. "It's only April. That's more than one a month."

"Well, some of them overlapped. ASL can't be learned overnight, you know," I explained, not sure why I felt like I had to. Because seriously, I loved taking classes. What's not to love? Learn new things. Meet new people. Sometimes there was exercise…that intermediate pole dancing class was no joke, let me tell you.

"Is any of it helping with your writing?"

Did I mention Annie had a way of squeezing information out of people? We'd already extensively covered the subject of Mabel the writer's block, ages ago.

I shrugged. "I don't know. Learning new things has to be helpful, right? And I've been meeting a lot of people, so that's good for creating characterization."

"And how much have you written because of it?"

"Um, not…much?"

"Well, if you ask me, all these classes of yours are great, as long as they're not a distraction from your real work, and I hate to be the bearer of bad news, but I feel like they might be."

She was right, of course, and I was about to tell her so, except another distraction entered the lobby at that precise moment. And heavens to Nancy, what a distraction it was.

Ryan.

He was quite possibly the most gorgeous man I had ever laid eyes on. Tall, with a smirk that said he understood things about the world. Things you were sure would come in handy in every aspect of life, including the bedroom.

Annie jumped up at the sight of him. "Ryan, honey. Have you met Petra yet?"

Which kind of made me want to duck behind the chair since I hadn't gotten particularly dressed up to, you know, go down to the coffee shop.

He came over, looking like he wanted nothing more than to escape, but Annie was not the kind of person that was easy to escape from.

"Oh yeah, hey. I've seen you around the building," he said. "I'm Ryan."

I stood and he shook my hand.

I hadn't mustered the ability to do anything but blink quite yet, but Annie was kind enough to give me a little kick in the ankle.

"Uh, hi. Petra Jackson," was the best I could cobble together.

"Nice to meet you," he said, and smirked an even more adorable smirk than before. And yeah, a smirk is not always a good thing, but on Ryan it was like he was in on some sort of secret or something. And it was utterly captivating.

As was the view as he walked toward the elevators.

After the doors had safely closed and he was out of earshot, Annie perked right up. Which was to say she went from a level three on the perkiness scale—Charmingly Bubbly—to a level eight: Enthusiastically Vivacious. "So, I see you have a little spark of interest in our floor-mate."

My stomach squeezed. "He lives on our floor?" I asked, my gaze whipping from the elevator doors to her.

"2202. Right across the hall from you, my dear. I'm surprised you haven't seen him coming or going yet."

"Huh," I said, pretending like it was the most normal thing in the world that the most magical representation of the male species I'd ever seen in real life lived right across the hall from me.

I frantically thought back through all the noises I'd ever made since I'd moved in. Had I ever farted in the hallway? Thankfully, nothing came to mind. There certainly hadn't been any raucous sex noises or anything.

It took everything in me not to beg Annie to spill every morsel she knew about the guy, but even I knew that would arouse at least as much pity as the time I got that perm in fifth grade.

Then again…maybe this was exactly what I'd been looking for—*The Mystery of the Handsome Neighbor*, I mused silently, as I fought the urge to raise an inquisitive eyebrow as one might do in a good sleuthing novel.

# *Chapter 2*

"**W**hy don't you just go over there and knock on his door?" Brandt asked.

Ah, Brandt, what a wacky baboon. Somehow Brandt and Vic and I had become an inseparable crew when we were roommates in our early twenties, even though none of us really had much in common anymore. Still, I couldn't really imagine my days without them. Or their arguing.

Victoria looked at him as if another arm had just sprouted out through his luscious hair.

"What is it with guys?" Vic said.

"What?" Brandt said, as if he hadn't just proposed the most absurd thing in the history of the world. "Guys like it when a hot chick comes on to them."

I gave him a face. "As sure as I am that it's the *fan-*

*tasy* of guys that hot chicks come on to them, have you ever seen it work in real life?"

"All the time," he said, straightening up, ready to defend his stance.

"And it resulted in a relationship, not just some hookup?"

"Oh," he said, looking dejected. "I didn't know you meant a relationship."

Vic scoffed. "You idiot. First of all, when have you ever known Petra to just want a hookup? And second of all, I can promise you that most women don't ever just want that unless they are either trying to get over someone else or have a serious need for some male attention. Neither of which guys probably really want to get involved with."

Brandt shrugs. "If a guy's getting laid, he probably doesn't care."

"Sure," I said, "until she catches feelings and starts contacting him, then it's all a big disappearing act."

"What? No one ever promised a relationship."

"Of course not," Vic says, putting her hands on her hips. "Guys don't do relationships anymore. Or if they do, they get bored after a month and pretend they were never into it in the first place. Typical."

Poor Brandt was looking a bit like one of those nocturnal little monkey creatures with the huge eyes.

I sighed. Dating had become more complicated than my uncle Marv trying to explain to a room full of women why he didn't think sexism was a real thing.

I sighed. Maybe it was just that Vic and I had reached the age where we were looking for more than just fun.

Although frankly, I couldn't really remember a time when I was only looking for a hookup. I couldn't help feeling like the whole culture of dating had changed, effectively making me feel like an old plastic zip bag, discarded hastily at the first sign of its tenant—the dreaded fuzzy cheese. Or maybe I was the cheese.

"These days guys just want to 'hang out,'" Vic said. "Whatever happened to dating? Like real dating?"

"You sure want a lot," Brandt said, seemingly bewildered. "I had no idea. I just thought all girls liked hooking up."

I stared daggers into his soul. Or at least I would have if he'd noticed I was even looking at him.

"Unfortunately, no matter how much I'd like to, we are not going to solve the world's dating problems by hashing it out among ourselves," Vic said.

Brandt was still staring into space like he was deep in thought. As deep in thought as a guy with his mouth hanging open could look, anyway. "But I mean, they always *say* they just want to hang out."

"Are you stupid?" Vic asked. "Would you ever start dating someone who was all like, 'I really, desperately just want a relationship'?"

"Probably not," he said.

"See, it is the guys' fault," Vic said. "There is literally no other choice but to pretend we all just want to hang out." She looked like she had just eaten a sardine lollipop.

"Can we change the subject for a second, please?" I asked, hoping they were finished their immature, though often morbidly delightful, squabbling.

There was never a dull moment with two best friends who pretty much hated each other. And even though it was somewhat entertaining, why did I always have to be the glue that held them together? Especially now, when my life was akin to a sad plate of nachos, which had all the components to be a glorious, synergistic taco except it really didn't have itself together.

Thankfully, Vic was desperate to change the subject. Less thankfully, she chose everyone's least favorite subject, Mabel. "So you didn't get any writing done today?"

I sighed. "No."

"I don't really get why you even care about writing another book," Brandt said, finally snapping out of his weird thinking trance.

It really did seem to take a lot of concentration for my poor associate to think certain things through. He was super sophisticated in some ways—into art and culture and friggin' loved the bloody opera, but he definitely took up residence in Clueless Town over other things. It was like I had my own little Renaissance Caveman™.

"You have plenty of money. I mean, look at this apartment. Most people would kill to have a place like this."

"Well sure, but the very fact that I bought this means that if I don't keep writing, I'll be in big trouble. Money doesn't last forever."

"Yeah, but didn't you make like, a bazillion dollars on your book?"

I gave him another look. "I made enough," I said,

"but that doesn't discount the fact that my publisher bought a two-book deal and if I don't deliver on a second book, I could end up having to pay some back."

"Look, dumbass," Vic interrupted, turning to Brandt, "money isn't everything, you know. Writing is Petra's passion, her calling. Haven't you ever had something you just felt compelled to do?"

"Makeup artistry *is* my passion."

Vic snorted. "I still don't know why you would pick *that* as a profession. You're like six-four and two hundred and fifty pounds."

"Um, hello...models," he said as if it really should have been obvious.

But the comment did little to make his case. Vic just stood there staring at him like he had neatly made *her* point.

"Whatever," he finally said. "It's not like you have some great calling."

"What does that mean? I'm an architect. I design buildings for a living. My firm created this very building you are sitting in. I make a difference."

Brandt chuckled. "Um, your bosses create buildings."

"Well, someday I'll be the one getting the credit. But you should know, the junior architects do most of the actual designing."

"Whatever you say," Brandt said, putting his hands up in mock surrender then smirking.

"Guys, seriously, change the subject."

"Do you want to talk more about your writing?" Vic asked carefully, as if she already knew the answer.

"No," I replied, my tone conveying I was as serious

as my fourth-grade teacher's obsession with spelling tests—and believe me, I am not exaggerating when I say Mrs. Potts had an alarming affection for the English language.

"Tell us more about this dude," Brandt said, shoveling chips into his mouth.

It wasn't that I didn't want to spend a little time on my new favorite subject, but the truth was I literally knew nothing about Ryan. "I wish I could, but I've got nothing for you. I've already told you what he looks like, and that's pretty much all I've got."

"Did you check online? Like Facebook and stuff?" Vic asked.

"I have nothing to check. All I have is the name Ryan. I don't even know if it's his first or last name. Or like, if he just goes by Ryan, you know, like Cher."

Vic opened her mouth as if to add another idea, then closed it again.

"So… I think I'm going to head out," Brandt said, as if it was a perfectly normal time to announce he was leaving and not right in the middle of a conversation. "Duty calls." He smiled, reading a message on his phone. "Or should I say, booty calls?" He laughed hysterically at his own joke.

Somehow Vic and I didn't find it quite as funny.

"What? I don't care what you guys think—none of my girls are complaining," he said, grabbing his coat and heading out the door with a bit of a skip to his step.

"That guy," Vic said, watching him leave.

I smiled. "Even *you* gotta admit, there's something likable about him."

She shrugged. "I suppose there's a certain…fascination that he draws, though I can't decide if it's allure, or more like a science experiment gone wrong."

I rolled my eyes.

"And that makes him all the more dangerous. It's those charmers you have to watch out for."

After Vic left, I pondered whether I should pull out my laptop. But then I realized I'd rather force a white-hot needle softly into my ocular cavity, so instead, I very productively wandered around my apartment trying to think of something to do. I mean, there was stuff I could do. There were still unpacked boxes in the spare room, certainly some cleaning that could be done, maybe a quick workout (insert laughing-with-tears emoji). But none of those things seemed to give me much of a spark. In fact, it seemed I'd been entirely spark-less for a while.

As I wandered past my front door for the third time, debating whether I might find something interesting to do outside the confines of my apartment, I heard some shuffling noises out in the hall that sounded like they might be coming from the direction of Apartment 2202, aka Home of the God. I sucked in a breath and crept to the peephole.

Ryan was most certainly coming out of his apartment. But…what was he doing heading out so late? I mean, I suppose it wasn't that late. I had, after all, just been debating going out myself. Still, I was intrigued by what might be causing Ryan to head out at an *almost*-late hour. I daydreamed for a moment that maybe he was just bored like me and wanted to grab some food or something. Yes! Maybe I should just happen to be leaving at the same time and he might ask me to join him.

I rolled my eyes. The chance that he was just heading out to do nothing was a pretty big stretch. Most people had a little more going on in their lives than the write, delete, lather, repeat that I did.

As if by some force outside myself, I reached for my coat and slipped into shoes as I continued to stare out the peephole, dropping my keys gently into my pocket. I pulled on a ball cap and tucked my hair up underneath as I cracked the door, listening for the elevator. (And yes, I did ask myself if sneaking out into the night to follow my perfect-looking neighbor was a bit, you know…stalkery, but I reminded myself that I was totally doing it for a good cause. Just a little research— That. Was. All! Seriously, you're so judgy). When the elevator doors started closing, I felt like Nancy as I scrambled out of my apartment, knowing timing would be everything. I obviously couldn't go down in the same elevator as Ryan, but I couldn't be too far behind, or I'd never see which direction he was headed. I hit the button to call the second elevator, which, thankfully, didn't take too long to get there.

The ride down felt like it took half a year, stopping on the eighth floor to pick up another passenger, an older gentleman I'd seen around the building a bit. What was with all these people heading out so late at night? I couldn't really be too mad though, since he smiled and tipped his hat at me like some jaunty fellow straight out of the fifties, which was quite adorable.

The doors finally opened on the ground floor to an empty lobby.

I raced out of the building, frantically scanning the area. Then I spotted him. He was already half a block away, but he was on foot, which gave me a chance to follow. A while back I'd taken this class on surveillance—it was part of the So You Wanna Be a Spy course. Not for the purposes of pursuing it as a job or anything, but more to lend my stories an air of credibility, and this seemed like as good a time as any to see if the techniques were any good.

Ryan slipped around the corner at the end of the block and I half ran, half walked to try to catch up. I didn't want to get too close, but I had to keep him in sight, or all would be lost. (Okay, that was maybe a little dramatic, but my curiosity certainly wouldn't have been quenched. Um, I mean, my research wouldn't have been complete.).

I followed pretty well if I do say so myself. Kept right up, corner after corner, block after block until I didn't really know where I was anymore. Still, I didn't panic. I figured I was intelligent enough to find my way home from a strange neighborhood. Plus, you know, app maps were a thing. Technology really was a godsend to those suddenly finding themselves in a strange place in the middle of the night when they were...just out for a stroll.

When Ryan walked for long stretches going straight, I kept a safe distance. There was no way he'd see me as far back as I was. Then when he turned, I'd make my run for it to catch where he turned again. I kept this up for what felt like an hour, though with all the adrenaline and excitement rushing through me, a more precise estimate would have been anywhere from twenty minutes to the end of life as we know it.

I was trying to figure out why he didn't catch a bus or a cab or something, when…suddenly, he disappeared.

Seriously, just disappeared. Vanished right into the delicate veil of the atmosphere. Wait, was he magic? Had I been following this gorgeous creature through the city only to find I was actually researching the beginnings of a paranormal novel?! The idea got my heart beating faster (hello, genre-jumping!) until I realized that perhaps…just maybe, I had been doing a bit too much reading lately and was losing my grip on the fragile boundaries of reality.

I stood and listened for a minute, hoping I'd hear his footsteps or something, but the area was eerily silent. I'd been super perplexed about so many people going out so late at night just a little while ago, but now my thoughts were more in the vicinity of, where the hell was everybody?

I wandered for a few blocks, hoping luck might be on my side, but I had apparently pissed off the ethereal beings in charge of serendipitous events (or maybe that old grip on reality was just loosening again). I spotted a man a block away and rushed to catch up, but it turned out not to be Ryan.

I felt completely ridiculous. The whole thing had been so silly. What did I think I was going to find anyway? He was probably out meeting a woman, and honestly, that was not something I was particularly keen to uncover.

I headed to the nearest corner. I'd been so busy trying to follow that I hadn't read a street sign for blocks. But it was time to give up the charade. I needed to figure out where I was and get my phone to draw me a map home. Easy peasy. I mean, I was a little disappointed, but it's not like I'd had anything else to do, and besides, I'd gotten a walk in for good measure.

Although, I wasn't sure I'd want to take another walk quite like this anytime soon. I couldn't get over how quiet the streets were. It was late, sure, but this seemed a little ominous, and frankly, I wanted out. I spotted a quick shortcut down an alley that would get me to the corner and back to my bearings. I was tired and frustrated, and apparently thinking with the clarity of a shallow pond at the end of summer after the weeds had overtaken the water and it sported that thin film of smelly, floating slime.

I scurried down the alley, my mind lost in thoughts of Ryan, wondering what he was up to at that exact moment. To be fair, I was lost in those swirling thoughts while also digging in my bag for my phone—which didn't seem to want to make an appearance, buried way down at the bottom somewhere—but still, I probably should have noticed the obvious and rather dastardly-looking illegal activity I was waltzing directly into.

Under a single light above the back door of some store or warehouse or something, several men had gathered. Which, of course, I would have noticed if I had been aware of my surroundings even a little bit—but unfortunately my brain was off gallivanting somewhere between what Ryan might look like with his shirt off and what I might wear if I was ever nominated for a big literary award. My mind only whipped back to the present after a rather ominous-sounding click, which was followed by several more. This was the moment I finally glanced up and became aware of the various guns pointed toward the approximate vicinity of my head, and I couldn't help but wonder if I might have gotten a wee bit more involved in a mystery than I had originally planned.

# Chapter 3

It's strange what goes through your head when several scary-looking dudes have guns pointed at your face. Like, for instance, how bright that light above the door seemed to suddenly be and how bold these guys must be for doing whatever they were doing right there in the middle of it.

Honestly, thoughts can be very unhelpful sometimes.

I quickly became aware of a few things. One, the boldness of the under-the-light transaction was a good indication that very few people were apt to show up in that particular spot. Two, I couldn't hear any street traffic, which meant the area was probably on the industrial side, thus lowering the likelihood of spectators even more. And three, the dude on the left had some intense wheezing going on, which, even though he had a gun pointed at me and a look on his face that said he could easily use me as a snack, I still had the urge to tell him to be quiet already. Didn't he realize everyone could hear him? I mean, not that he could probably help it, I supposed.

I also really needed to adjust my underwear, which chose that exact moment to ride into an uncomfortable position, but I decided it might be best to wait on that issue. Unfortunately, this only reminded me of which underwear I was currently wearing—the larger grannyish ones (don't judge, laundry day was a bit overdue). I tried not to think of how embarrassing it would be if these were the undies I'd be found dead in.

"Um, hi, fellas," I said, my voice sounding intensely loud, echoing off the building. "I was just out for a bit of a midnight walk and didn't realize I'd, um, run into anyone. I was just heading back to the, um, street." I pointed up the alley.

You know, in case they had no idea how streets worked or something.

Nobody moved. They all just kind of looked at each other, clearly not knowing what to do. Opposed to what you might think from the movies, people did not, apparently, stumble into secret bad-guy deals very often.

I decided I may as well try to take advantage of the lack of action. I just sort of started to walk away, continuing in the direction I was already going, hoping the street was closer this way, although I had a bad feeling I was about exactly halfway.

A sturdy-looking man stepped out in front of me. Unlike many of the others, he had a shotgun, which he

held at hip level and seemed more comfortable with—
if only a little—than the others.

"Hold on there, lady," he said. "I don't think you'll
be going anywhere."

My head began to get itchy, but I did not make a
move to scratch anything. I felt like Nancy D. must
have surely been in situations like this a time or two
in all those mysteries I'd read, but I was having one of
my CRAFT moments (i.e., Can't Remember A Flip-
ping Thing). No doubt Ned or Bess or George had come
to the rescue or something, and I suddenly felt like a
supreme jackass for not letting anyone know where I
was or what I was doing. Although I'm honestly not
sure how that conversation might have gone. *So yeah,
I'm just out following my sexy neighbor around shady
parts of town. No worries. Just, I dunno, see if you
can come find me if I don't make it back in a couple
hours. Whatevs.*

Unfortunately, I got the distinct impression I might
not have a couple hours. And honest to god, how could
the rest of these guys just stand there and listen to that
wheezing?

I widened my stance ever so slightly, hoping that
none of the guys would notice I was even moving. Then
I slowly…very slowly…started to shift my weight, bending my legs slightly to ready my stance. My fingers
began to curl.

And then BAM!

Two of them went down beside me. Straight to the
ground, so fast I had absolutely no idea how in the hell
they'd gotten there. But I decided it might be better to

process the hows later, so I sprang into action, kicking the shotgun away from my torso and punching the sturdy guy in the face. He was startled but was far from going down. Thankfully, I'd expected that and was already on my way toward the arm holding the shotgun, spinning around and heaving my full weight and momentum into the guy, knocking both him and me off our feet while at the same time taking aim as I curled into him.

A tiny inkling that a gunshot would seem somewhat loud in this quiet place and probably alert people flashed through my mind, and for some reason against all logic, that felt like a bad idea, but obviously I was in a bit of a bind. So I squeezed the trigger anyway, aiming for the leg of the other man headed my way. There was no way in hell I actually wanted to kill anyone—figuring that couldn't be too good for the old karma, not to mention mental health—so the leg it was.

He yelped and went down, clutching at his thigh. The man underneath me was already trying to get his arms around me, seizing control of the shotgun again. He was so strong I knew I'd never have a chance to get another shot, so while he was focused on the gun, I rolled away from him, already searching for a place to take cover.

Inexplicably, something jumped out of the shadows from above me, taking out the shotgun guy with a flying kick to the head. The dude folded over like a piece of tissue paper. Two guys were still on their feet and the one I'd shot in the leg was beginning to get his bearings again. He reached for the gun he dropped on his way to the ground, but the shadow guy—even more inexplicably, wearing a ski mask—had his attention focused on the two who were still in good working condition.

The ski mask guy had a piece of pipe, already swinging it with incredible speed at one of the bad guy's heads. I didn't see how it went since I was already diving for the gun the bleeding man was headed for, but judging from the sickening thwack above me, I guessed that he'd made the desired contact.

I got to the gun half an instant before the injured guy, sliding feetfirst for the last stretch as if I were sliding into home, my hands grabbing the gun as my foot careened toward the dude's head. From the several martial arts and self-defense classes I had taken— jiujitsu, kickboxing, karate and a few others—I'd learned the places to strike to take down an opponent with the least amount of effort. Not that I'd ever tried to really knock somebody unconscious, but in theory I possessed the info.

Turned out, the theory held up. Dude flopped backward like a rag doll.

Just as I was about to spring up and assess the situation, another sick thud filled the air and the night went silent.

I sat for a minute, daintily catching my breath (aka panting like a damned dog in heat) and perusing the scene. Six men lay unconscious in a circle around me. Besides the one I'd shot in the leg, none of them seemed to be injured in any way other than the bumps and bruises they would wake up with.

The man in the mask was tending to the leg of the

guy I'd just kicked in the face—and, you know, also shot—tying it off with a makeshift tourniquet.

I realized then, that even though I'd helped distract the guy whose shotgun I'd fired, I had only actually taken down one of these six men. Ski Mask had done the rest. Frankly, I felt a little like my fighting skills could use some brushing up. But I didn't really have a whole lot of time to lament my poor performance before Ski Mask strolled up and put his hand out to help me up.

So there I was, on the ground surrounded by unconscious men, trying to decide if I should allow myself to be helped up by a guy wearing a ski mask and holding out a hand covered in someone else's blood.

But he had also just saved my life. And to be fair, the blood was kinda my fault.

Needless to say, I took the hand.

He lifted me up as if I weighed nothing more than a small child. This guy was strong. This guy was also tall, I noted.

And...this guy was about to speak.

"So," he said, lifting his hand toward the mask. "Apartment 2201, right?"

# Chapter 4

My stomach seized like the assets of a Ponzi scheme fraudster.

I blinked, my eyelids apparently the only thing on my body that would move, since my brain was using all its functioning power to try to process exactly what was happening. I couldn't figure out if I wanted the ground to open up and swallow me whole, or if I wanted to pretend to faint, landing conveniently in his arms.

"Oh, um. Hi, Ryan."

Was it bad that a little jolt of relief shot through me that he wasn't with some gorgeous woman?

He stood staring at me, one eyebrow raised as if to ask what in the fiery depths of hell I thought I was doing in a place like this in the middle of the night. I thought briefly of lifting my eyebrow right back in an attempt to convey the same thing, but quickly realized he was absolutely not in the wrong in this particular situation.

No, this was all me.

I was about to start squirming and wishing I had been the one shot, and maybe not just a flesh wound, when he suddenly seemed to come to a realization.

"Listen," he said—and holy hell, his voice sounded sexy. "We need to get out of here. Someone might have heard that shot and called the police."

"Will we be in trouble?"

"It's not trouble from the cops I'm worried about. I really can't have anybody seeing me here."

"Just what, exactly, *are* you doing here?" I asked, dying to know what sort of situation I had just made much more complicated.

"Really? *You're* asking *me* that right now?"

I glanced at my feet, suddenly unable to look into those beautiful hazel eyes.

"These guys aren't going to be out forever. We've got to go."

As if on cue, a groan emerged from one of the first guys who had dropped. Ryan grabbed my arm and started walking me back the way I'd come, away from the street.

I decided not to argue, assuming he knew the way home much better than I did since, you know, he probably knew where we were. We walked at a startlingly brisk pace for several blocks and I could only hope we were getting closer to home. My choice of wedge sandals was decidedly not the best decision I had made all week, but it wasn't like I'd had time to plan or anything.

And they did seem to work pretty well for kicking that guy in the face, actually. But my feet were killing me now, and I was having quite a hard time keeping up with Ryan.

Not that I was about to complain to him about it.

Still, I wasn't particularly known for keeping my mouth shut, even under the most awkward of circumstances. In fact, that's when the old talk hole seemed to want to flap the most. "So, um. What is it you do, exactly? I mean, you saved me, so you must be a good guy but I'm just not entirely sure why you had the mask on—"

The look on his face made the words stop spewing from my mouth.

"Not that it's really your business, but I'm a private detective."

My breath caught in my throat. Already my dream guy, with the dreamy looks, but to cap it all off he had my dream job too!

"Really?! That's amazing," I said, and started in on my usual babble that seemed to burst forth every time I was talking to a guy I was interested in. "I love detective work so much. I mean, ever since I was a little kid and read all the Nancy Drew and Hardy Boys books, you know." I rolled my eyes at myself. Only I could sound that naive. "I mean, I get that in real life the mysteries are way harder to solve and stuff and the clues don't just happen to pop up in front of you magically at the right time and everything, but man, those books got my imagination going when I was a kid. Like, totally set me on the path to my detective-work obsession."

Ryan looked over at me like I'd just vomited up a chicken. Not that I could blame him, exactly. I had, after all, just admitted to an obsession with detectives immediately after stalking him. God, he had to be super pleased that I lived right across the hall from him.

"Yeah," he said, making a face like there was a bad smell in the air. "You're right—it's not really like that."

I nodded, thanking my lucky stars we were still walking at the pace of super speed, which gave us something to do besides me berating myself for being such a moron and him wondering how the hell a moron like me even existed, let alone lived in the same building as him.

We walk-ran in silence for approximately thirty-eight years until he broke the silence. "So, Petra? What exactly were *you* doing out here?"

Oh. Dear. God.

"Um…"

I couldn't believe I'd had all this walk-running time to try to think of some kind of excuse for what I was doing and I had been too dense to do so. I had absolutely no sense of self-preservation whatsoever.

"Uh, well… I was kind of…following you?" I squeaked, picking up the pace even more.

Unfortunately, being amazingly tall, Ryan had absolutely no trouble keeping up.

"And uh, why, may I ask, were you doing that?"

Shit. There was definitely no right answer to that.

"Okay, so this is probably going to sound stupid, but I'm kind of a detective too. I mean, I'm not, but I took a couple classes on the subject as sort of research for what I do for a living and I guess I was a little bored so I was kind of just…practicing."

He raised his eyebrows. "Practicing being a detective?"

"Um, yeah. Sort of." I let out a sigh. "Look, it's not as stupid as it sounds. I mean it is, but I'm a novelist and I've kind of been having trouble with writer's block lately, and I write mysteries, you know? Well, sort of rom-com mysteries. So yeah, that's what I was doing."

"Following me."

I nodded. "I guess so."

"Why, of all the people in all the world, did you choose me to follow in your little—what did you call it— rom-com mystery game?"

I tried not to be offended by his dismissal of my career research as a little game and tried to focus on some sort of sane answer. It probably wouldn't be the smartest to lead with *Well, I'm incredibly intrigued by you because you're the most beautiful thing in the world and I really wanted to know everything about you*, so instead I played it a bit more…vague.

"I don't know. I just heard you leaving because you're right there across the hall, and I didn't really think about it all that much and just went for it, I guess."

He shook his head. "Well, congrats. I gotta hand it to you. For an amateur, you really have done an outstanding job."

I smirked. "You had no idea I was following you, did you?"

He glared sideways at me, still walking at his breakneck pace.

"No. I certainly didn't, so good for you." He smiled a "you must be so proud of yourself" smile. "But that's not what I was talking about. What I meant was that it was quite spectacular that you were able to monumentally screw up the case I'm working on. So, congratulations."

Somehow I didn't feel all that pumped over my "victory."

We walked a while longer in silence. My feet were ready to fall off and all I wanted to do was cry, but I was not about to show weakness. At least...not any more than I already had.

I could finally see our apartment building a few blocks up. My feet were screaming and I was so emotionally spent I just wanted to go home and curl up in a ball. I usually didn't get so worked up, but this night had been something for the record books.

We entered our building in silence and rode the elevator to the twenty-second floor together. As we made our way to our end of the hall, he spoke. "So how did you learn to round-kick like that, anyway?"

I shrugged. "I took a class."

"Another class. You sure do like your classes."

I couldn't tell if he was making fun of me or not, so I shrugged. "I like to learn new things. Meet new people. Classes are a good way to do that."

"Uh-huh," he said, nodding. "Well, you did pretty well out there considering you were caught completely off guard. A lot of people would have just fallen apart."

"I never thought I'd have to find out what I'd do in a situation like that. I guess that's the good news," I said, smiling half-heartedly.

I still felt like a giant elephant anus for ruining Ryan's case.

"Well, now I guess you know you can kick some butt when necessary."

"I guess," I said, unable to look him in the eye. "So... what now?"

He looked at me for a moment and took a deep breath, letting it out through his nose in a long, slow whoosh. "Well...now I figure out what my next move is with the case, and you go inside and hope you never see any of those guys ever again."

I nodded, then turned to slip my key into the lock.

"And, Petra?"

I turned back to him. "Yeah?"

"Please, do me a favor and stop with the sleuthing," he said, his forehead creasing to drive home the point.

Too bad it just made him look more adorable than ever.

# Chapter 5

"Do anything exciting last night?" Vic asked at brunch the next morning.

That's right, we did brunch on Sundays, and it would take a helluva crisis for us to miss it. I don't care what anybody says, brunch is not just for soccer moms and grandmothers. There is little in life that is quite as perfect as a Sunday brunch—the eggs, the pancakes, the "perfect amount of crispness" hash browns...the mimosas. All of it spectacular. Not to mention I got to hang out with my friends for an extra three hours a week, you know, 'cause almost every other day wasn't enough.

I sipped on my pre-mimosa coffee, stalling. I wasn't quite sure how to answer what was seemingly a routine question when I definitely did not have a routine answer. Obviously, I wanted to spill everything, but I had no idea if any of what had gone down last night was like, confidential or something. Eventually, I decided I hadn't taken any oaths, and Ryan hadn't told me not to say anything, so I figured it couldn't hurt to tell my best friends. Right?

"Well, um, I sorta followed Ryan."

Vic's eyes got wide, and Brandt even turned his attention away from his menu—and believe me, not much could distract Brandt from food, unless it was a woman. Even then, she had to be pretty spectacular.

Vic leaned in. "Oh my god, tell me everything. Did he go see a woman? No," she gasped. "A man."

"No, neither of those things."

"Perfect, so he's single."

"Vic, just because he didn't go see a significant other on one particular night doesn't mean he doesn't have one."

"So he does?" she asked, disappointed.

"I have no idea. I just know he didn't go see anyone last night."

I'd already lost Brandt to his menu again and Vic just looked at me like she was wondering why I was even bothering to tell the story if I didn't have any juicy news about his personal life.

"Yeah, so anyway… I was tailing him, you know, like in that class I took."

Brandt didn't even try to stifle his chuckle. I could never figure out why everybody was always hating on my classes. I'd made some really good connections through them, and learned a lot of interesting stuff.

"And he walked forever and then I lost him."

Brandt glanced up at me like I was the saddest thing on earth. To be honest, at the time that I'd lost track of Ryan I had pretty much felt exactly that, but he could give me a *little* credit. Besides, it wasn't like I was wasting his time. I mean, what else were we going to talk about that was more interesting?

"If you're about to say, 'so then I turned around and went back home,' I'm going to throw this sugar packet at you," Vic said.

Cripes, even Vic was getting bored with me.

"If you just let me talk, I'll get to the good part," I said, shooting them my best scolding look. Which probably wasn't really all that scolding so much as it was me trying to hide the excitement of what I was about to reveal.

Vic leaned back in her seat and crossed her arms. Brandt was nose-deep in the menu.

"So then, I started trying to get my bearings and figure out how to get home when I decided to take a shortcut up an alley and sorta ran right into a bunch of dudes in the middle of some shady transaction. You know, the whole works…a bunch of guns pointed at my head and everything."

"What?" Vic yelled.

Brandt simply folded up the menu, set it down and sat up as straight as I'd ever seen the man sit.

I nodded nonchalantly. "Yeah, so it was pretty scary and everything and I had no idea how the hell I was going to get out of that mess, when this masked guy jumped out of the shadows and started taking the dudes down one by one. And you know how I've taken a few martial arts classes, right?"

They were finally both hanging on my every word. Brandt with his mouth drooping open—he really had to work on that—and Vic with her eyes wider than I'd ever seen them.

"So, I jumped in and knocked one guy over, then shot another dude with that guy's gun, and the masked guy kept taking guys down, then I kicked the guy I shot right in the head and yeah, that's about it." I let out a breath.

"What the hell?" Brandt said. At least that's what I thought he said. It was kind of hard to tell what with Vic freaking out at the same time.

"You shot somebody? Like actually shot them? With a bullet?" Her voice was getting rather loud for brunch, nevermind that the subject matter might not be entirely appropriate either.

"Yes," I said, in that strained way you do when you're trying to get someone to quiet the hell down.

"Oh my god. Oh my god," was all she seemed to be able to say.

"Okay, wait a second," Brandt jumped in, his eyes searching to piece the story together.

I couldn't help but feel a little smug at the fact that suddenly they were oh so interested in my evening.

"I would have had you pegged for a flighter, not a fighter."

Since Vic was on the same side of the table as he was, I let her go ahead and punch him in the arm instead of doing it myself.

"Ow! What?" he moaned.

"Holy crap, okay," Vic said. "So, you're there and all these guys are like knocked out or friggin' shot or whatever…" She raised her eyebrows to get me to continue with the story.

"Oh yeah, this is the good part. And then the masked guy came over and was all like, 'Apartment 2201, right?'" I finished in my best man-voice.

Vic gasped. Brandt scratched his head, not quite following as quickly. "Holy shit, it was Ryan," Vic said.

Brandt looked at her like she'd said the most absurd thing he'd ever heard.

But I nodded. "Oh yeah, he ripped off that mask and I nearly fainted. And not just because I'd forgotten just how gorgeous he was."

"Oh my god, he's your hero," Vic said, excited.

Brandt rolled his eyes.

"Well, yeah, I guess," I said, "but it was kind of more like me being a big pain in the ass because I had totally ruined his whole spy operation."

"Dude's a spy?" Brandt asked, shifting excitedly in his seat.

"Well, no, but he's a private detective. He was working on a case and well, I sorta got in the middle of it. Literally."

Brandt cringed. "Seriously. That is so bad. And what the hell is he getting himself involved in, exactly? A bunch of guys with guns is not your typical investigation shit, you know."

I nodded, the sinking feeling in my stomach coming back now that I'd revealed the whole story. I really had gotten myself into a seriously dangerous situation.

Vic was apparently thinking the same thing. "What the hell did you think you were doing? What if you'd been shot? Or worse?" She was starting to get worked up into a bit of a panic now. Well, as much of a panic as Vic ever got into, anyway. Which, thankfully, wasn't particularly panicky.

"Well, I guess I was thinking I'd follow this cute guy around for a while to see what he did on a Saturday night. I thought he'd go to a movie or meet up with friends. I admit, I hadn't really thought through every possible scenario. Such as him being on a stakeout, watching a bunch of dudes with guns."

"Okay, start from the start again. I feel like I'm missing something," Brandt said.

"Well, maybe if you had listened the first time instead of obsessing over the damned menu," Vic said in her voice that seemed to be reserved solely for giving Brandt shit, "you would have understood a little better."

"Come on, you guys, just give it a rest for today, okay? I'm not in the mood to play referee."

They both opened their mouths to say something, but thankfully thought better of it. I finally gave my own menu some attention, deciding on the French toast. Carbs felt like the right thing on a day like today.

I set my menu aside and Vic moved to put hers on top of mine. "Oh shit," she said, glancing past my shoulder.

"What?" I asked.

"You don't want to know."

"Ugh," Brandt said. "Not this douche nugget."

I turned, totally confused as to who my two friends,

who were usually very accepting of everyone besides each other, could possibly be so upset to see.

And my heart jumped into my throat, the same re-action I had every time I saw those doe-brown eyes.

Johnny.

Talk about a serious *Case of the Old Flame*.

"Petra! I have been looking everywhere for you. How come nobody will tell me where you moved to?" He got that sad, puppy dog look in his eye, which un-fortunately undid me almost as much in that moment as when I used to believe he was genuine and sincere.

"Uh, hi, Johnny."

"Hi, guys." Johnny beamed to Vic and Brandt as he began to sit down in the free chair beside me, totally oblivious to the eye daggers they were hurling his way.

Vic and Brandt didn't agree on much, but when it came to Johnny their feelings were mutual.

Johnny leaned over and kissed my cheek. "Good to see you, Beautiful. So, tell me, why all the secrecy? Why aren't you answering my calls?" he asked, pout-ing again. Somehow, he was one of those guys who could get away with it. All charm and, as I had recently found out, very little substance.

"Um, maybe because you cheated on her, you irritat-ing excuse for a human being," Vic said, kind enough to answer on my behalf.

Which was probably a good thing, since I was never quite able to actually say what I wanted to Johnny. He always found a way of making me want to take care of him. Which was exactly what I had been doing for the past two years, I was embarrassed to admit.

Johnny looked pained, like he couldn't believe he should possibly be held accountable for his actions. He was an artist (except he said it *artiste*, like a jackass), after all. He lived life by his emotions, and it was hardly his fault that the blonde waitress from the coffee shop in our old neighborhood made him horny and then she somehow accidentally landed on his penis.

While he was living with me.

Or more accurately, while I was supporting him and his "artistic endeavors." Which, incidentally, never seemed to pan out. Come to think of it, he really didn't even spend a whole lot of time creating art.

"Now, Petra," he said in that sexy voice of his, causing me to cringe over how much it still made me swoon. "I'm hurt. I can't believe you just took off like that and left me to fend for myself."

His face was so close to mine that I was having a hard time breathing over the scent of his cologne, and unfortunately, it was not in a bad way. More of an "I remember every single orgasm I had while smelling that cologne" way.

"You make it sound like I just ran off. I paid two months' rent in advance so you'd have plenty of time to find a place to live."

"But you just left without a trace."

"I left you a letter explaining everything."

"I know, but I never got a chance to properly say goodbye." He glanced down at my body, which should have made me want to slap him, but somehow got my blood moving at a slightly elevated pace.

Frankly, the only way I had been able gather enough

strength to leave him was to slip out without saying goodbye. Johnny was nothing if not persuasive.

Or perhaps more accurately, manipulative.

"Okay, that's it. Just get the hell out of here, dude," Brandt said.

I'd like to say he was defending my honor, but I think it was more the fact that having another guy at the table who might have more swagger than he did made him entirely uncomfortable.

"What?" Johnny said, putting up his arms. "What did I ever do?"

"You know, that's your problem," Vic said. "You never think you do anything wrong. You're the universe's gift to humanity, right?"

Johnny smiled, deciding to take that as a compliment.

"You think the whole damned world owes you a favor, but you know what? Your run is over, man. At least with anyone at this table. We are onto you, you freeloading dirtbag."

Johnny's smile faded quickly, and he decided he was done paying attention to Brandt and Vic, turning his full focus toward me. Which, I'm sad to say, was the worst thing that could happen. For whatever reason, I was powerless against Johnny.

"Come on, Petra," he cooed, running a finger up my forearm, which unfortunately sent shivers through me. "Just let me see your new place. We can still be friends, at least, right?"

It occurred to me that there was probably something very wrong with me that I actually thought it would be easier to be back in that alley kicking the crap out of those guys than what I was about to do. It literally took every ounce of strength in my entire body to open my mouth and say the words.

I cleared my throat. "No, Johnny. No, I don't think we can be friends." I hated myself for the "think" part, but at least I'd gotten it out.

Even Brandt and Vic looked a little stunned. And kinda proud of me.

Johnny's mouth dropped open. He was apparently not expecting to hear those words coming from me.

"But…"

"Oh no, you don't," Vic said. "Do not say another word. Petra was very clear. She does not want to be friends. It's time for you to leave."

Johnny turned to Vic, obviously only half listening.

The problem was, while Vic had the balls to say anything to anybody, she was pretty much one of the tiniest humans on earth, clocking in at about four foot eleven and maybe ninety-five pounds. Brandt, on the other hand, was a giant of a man, but was not really one to make waves about anything. If I could morph the two of them together, I'd have one hell of a badass best friend.

"Look, Petra," Johnny said, turning to me again.

My stomach dropped. Was he really going to make me say it again?

"The lady said now," Brandt uttered, calm as could be, then stood to his full height, maybe even stretching a bit for good measure. His chair screeching across the floor added to the intensity of the moment.

I could feel Johnny physically recoil beside me. "Um, yeah, sure thing, man. I was just on my way."

Johnny got up quickly and gathered his things. Unfortunately, he was one of those people that just took up space, not only with his body but with the stuff he was always setting down everywhere. He scrambled to gather his scarf, sunglasses, phone and wallet, clutching everything awkwardly to his chest when he normally would have made a big scene of putting things in their place before he left. If there was one thing about Johnny, it was that he always made a big entrance and an even bigger exit.

"And don't even think about bothering Petra again," Vic added as Johnny backed away a few steps.

"Petra," Johnny said, making one last plea. "Just... just call me, okay?" he said. And somehow the way he said it nearly broke my heart all over again.

Brandt slowly sat and picked his menu up again. "Now, can we finally eat?"

"I hear that," Vic said, and I realized I really didn't need one perfect badass friend when the two I had sitting here were both very much badass in their own perfect ways.

# *Chapter 6*

I was decidedly shaken after the little run-in with Johnny, but Brandt and Vic snapped me out of it pretty quickly with approximately four hundred and thirty-seven more questions about what had gone down the night before. Which was exactly what I needed. Once I recounted the fight again, it reminded me that I was, in fact, a little bit badass myself.

And I was definitely stronger than Johnny could ever hope to be.

The real problem was that Vic and Brandt had this theory that Johnny was the root of all evil…and the root of my writer's block. It was an idea that I absolutely did not believe because when I wrote my first book, I hadn't been in a relationship at all—in fact, I wouldn't even meet Johnny until months after I'd signed my contract with my publisher. And yeah, he was around for some of the editing process, but honestly, he'd been more of a distraction than helpful in any way.

Of course, I hadn't felt like such a loser in love back then either. I'd dated my fair share before Johnny came around and never had any issues. Although, come to think of it, as incompatible as some of those other guys had been, none of them had made me feel as insecure as I'd felt when I finally realized that I'd fallen for Johnny's games and had to get out.

But he was just so good at what he did. Helping him felt like the right thing to do—it was that satisfaction of having someone to take care of, knowing that I was responsible for something outside of myself. I was proud of the fact that I had the means to take care of us both.

Unfortunately, I realized way too late—and only at the consistent prodding from my friends for much longer than I was quite comfortable admitting—that this was Johnny's schtick. He was the kind of person who made it seem like he was helping you by letting you help him. He had a special gift for off-loading the responsibilities of his life onto others without making it even seem like it was a chore.

Until, of course, he inevitably strayed from the hand that fed him.

So really, I suppose he had two special talents: a sophisticated grasp on the art of manipulation and a magnificent lack of conscience when it came to his extracurricular activities with potential future manipulees.

And he was so magnificent at it that just having him nearby made my pulse pitter-patter, and wanna get at 'er.

Honestly, what the hell was wrong with me? And yeah, I tried not to beat myself up about it—women fall for the wrong guys all the time—but still. It was just so pathetic of me to even give the guy the time of day.

Of course, now that I was crushing on someone new, I had to admit it was a little easier to stop thinking about ol' freeloader Johnny. Ugh, I did not want to be one of those girls that has to jump from guy to guy—I loved being on my own! And in my defense, it had been over four months since Johnny and I were over—and I'd barely thought about him in weeks until he sauntered on over to our table. I just had to keep him out of sight and out of mind.

And as I headed back to my building after finishing brunch in our leisurely three-hour manner, Ryan was squarely in the forefront of my mind and Johnny almost forgotten. Which was exactly where he belonged.

Annie was at her usual spot in the lobby when I got back to my building, lounging in a low-cut tangerine pantsuit that looked incredible on her, her silvery hair sleek and shiny.

"Hey, love, out for brunch?"

"Yeah," I said, sitting down to chat while wondering if I should be worried that she had my routine down already.

Was I that predictable? I mean, all the self-defense courses I'd taken talked about switching up your routine, which I always thought was a good idea. I just never thought I was important enough to be someone to have to worry about such a thing.

The lobby was surprisingly quiet, so I took my chance,

glancing around to make sure a certain hot PI wasn't standing right behind me.

"So, Annie, I'm just curious…about Ryan."

Annie gave me a knowing smirk. My cheeks immediately warmed, and I suddenly felt like I was in seventh grade again.

"Ah, yes… Ryan."

"Well, I mean, I was just curious. Since he lives right across the hall and everything."

"Don't worry, hon, that man has caught the eye of you and every other female in this building, married or not. He is one fantastic example of maleness—there is no debate about that."

I smiled, hoping the redness wasn't as noticeable as it felt creeping up the back of my neck. "I'm sure he has."

She chuckled. "Well, believe me, I wish I had some juicy gossip on him, but he keeps pretty much to himself. He's friendly enough and puts up with my flirtations," she said, winking, "but never really gets into his personal life. I do know that he's some sort of a detective." She glanced at me with one eyebrow raised and I could tell she was thinking she was revealing some big secret.

"Right, I actually knew that already. We did have one little chat." I decided not to tell her how utterly uncomfortable it was and how it had lasted about forty blocks or so.

Not that distance counted really, since a lot of that time we had walked in silence. Tumultuous, soul-squashing silence.

Annie mock-gasped. "You've been holding out on me, Petra!" She smacked my hand good-naturedly.

I laughed. "Not really. I definitely don't know any more than you do." I left out the part where I might know a few details about a case he was working on and how dangerous his work might actually be.

"Well, that's pretty much all I know too," Annie said. "He's quiet. A good neighbor."

"Does he normally have a lot of...company?" I cringed even saying it.

"I'm going to assume you mean company of a female nature," Annie said brightly. "I've only noticed him bring home women a few times." And for some reason she stopped there. Like that was any way to end a sentence.

I looked at her expectantly.

"And well, the women those few times were quite... sophisticated looking?" She ended with an inflection like she was asking a question.

I guess that's the information I'd hoped for. I wasn't even sure. I'd just wanted more details, but now that I heard the word *sophisticated*, I knew for sure what I'd already suspected. He was way out of my league.

Sundays were usually a bit dull after brunch, and the guilt of not being able to write was getting to me.

When I first started writing I had this idea of what being a writer was going to look like.

Afternoon creativity walks.

Posh parties at sumptuous locations.

Words flowing from my fingertips as if sent from a higher power.

Mingling with fans at signings and getting recognized on the street for selfies.

What I hadn't bargained for was the constant guilt. Not being able to find the words, the hours of solitude feeling useless, the idea that I was letting so many people down. I had to figure out a way through this writer's block or start seriously thinking about what else I could do with my future.

And thing was, I loved writing...or at least I used to, before I had to write something better than the last book. Not that I didn't appreciate the success of my first book—I definitely did—it was just that surging to success sometimes meant there was nowhere to go but down.

It was enough to strike terror in me faster than a dimly lit parking lot and a dog in an eight-legged spider suit jumping on me as I exited an elevator (seriously, have you seen that stuff on the internet?).

I opened my laptop and clicked on my word processing program, opening a new file. The lovely fresh, white page popped up before me, the cursor blinking innocently right there at the top.

I formatted my document as I would any work in progress, with my last name and page number at the top. I'd learned this in one of my beginner's writing classes years ago and the habit had stuck. It was like getting something...anything on the page was at least a start.

I typed "*UNTITLED*, by Petra Jackson" as a title page, then filled in "Chapter 1" on page two.

Which is precisely where I came to an abrupt halt.

I mean, it wasn't as though this was my first rodeo. I'd started plenty of stories without much of a plot or characters in mind, and everything had always been fine. You type away to figure that stuff out, right? It had always worked before.

I sat, looking thoughtfully into space. Then tried glancing around the room. For a while I stared at that blinking cursor, daring it to mock me.

Which of course it absolutely did.

I surfed the internet for a couple hours (avoiding all things with dogs and/or spiders) and was surprised to look up and realize night had fallen, the darkness creeping into my apartment without me even realizing. I'd been super enthralled in learning about travel capsule wardrobes—you know, just in case the character in my new novel had to do any packing for a trip, I guess. *Sigh*.

After dinner, I decided to relax and listen to some music, and a nice bubble bath might be in order later.

But then I heard it. Someone coming out of the apartment across the hall.

Ryan was on the prowl again.

My heart sped and my first instinct was to grab my coat and go racing after him. But his last words echoed in my ears: *Do me a favor and stop with the sleuthing*.

Although come to think of it, I never really had been one to do what people told me to for no good reason. And I mean, he probably thought he had a good reason, to keep me safe and all, but I was a big girl. I could take care of myself. Hadn't I helped take down all those men, after all?

My eyes darted around the apartment for a quick disguise. Thankfully Brandt was always bringing stuff around from photo shoots and stuff, so I grabbed a pair of teal prescription-less glasses and flung a floppy wool hat on along with a long, shapeless coat. I was looking rather hipster/I'm-too-cool-to-care, if I did say so myself.

Against my better judgment—which, frankly, I'm not sure I really had anyway—I stepped out of my apartment on a mission to follow once more. I mean, let's be honest, no one really thought my sleuthing would ever come to an end, and if they did then they didn't know me very well.

The elevator opened on the ground floor just in time for me to see Ryan heading in the opposite direction he'd gone the night before. I followed at about the same distance, but I had learned from my mistakes. I paid closer attention to where I was this time, even taking cursory glances at street signs here and there, and I was much more cautious when coming around corners. I promised myself if I did lose Ryan again, I'd head straight back home and use only the main streets, staying in the lighted areas.

But for now, I kept to the shadows.

We didn't go nearly as far this time, and my feet had never been so grateful. I'd grabbed much more sensible shoes, some slip-on sneakers, but still, the grotesquely peeled skin and jellylike pockets of fluid on my feet definitely had not had time to heal.

Ryan made his way up an alley, and I admit I paused before I followed. But I wasn't about to come this far just to turn around and go home. The classes said the good stuff always happened right when you were about to give up, and patience was rated the highest skill to practice above all else. I stayed well back and only moved into the alley once I knew Ryan had gone pretty far in.

I moved slowly, my heart beating so hard it drowned out any noise. If I was going to keep doing things like this, I was going to have to figure out how to get a grip on my fear...and my adrenaline.

I shook my head. *If I was going to keep doing things like this?* Sometimes I wondered if I was, in fact, losing my mind.

A noise loud enough to drown out my ridiculous heartbeat came from about halfway down the alley. A ladder on a fire escape being pulled. I stopped and flattened myself against the wall of the brick building beside me, trying to control my breath, though I was pretty sure I sounded like a German shepherd after a four-mile run.

Someone up ahead, presumably Ryan, held the ladder down for a full minute or two. I assume he was waiting to see if anyone had heard the noise and was coming to investigate. I channeled my inner Nancy (seriously, that girl had one giant horseshoe up her butt), hoping to River Heights that no one was curious. Other than flattening myself against the building, I had no place to hide and was pretty sure if someone came walking past me, I'd be more than a little noticeable.

No one came a-sniffing and soon I could see Ryan's silhouette climbing the ladder to the first-floor fire escape. Then he let the ladder back up slowly, so slowly it barely made any noise this time. When it quietly shifted into place, Ryan glanced around once more, then settled into a seated position. If I hadn't seen him climb up with my own eyes, I would have thought there was just a bag of garbage sitting out there.

Now that he was settled though, I suddenly realized I was trapped. He had the perfect perch for an excellent view up both ends of the alley, and no doubt any movement, especially movement that suddenly burst out of the shadows, would have him on high alert. And the last thing I needed was Ryan to know I was following him again.

You know, after he explicitly begged me not to.

Thoughts suddenly swirled. What if I had to sneeze? Or like, got snackish? Or, what if a bunch of murderous guys were about to walk directly past me? Or worse… what if I had to pee?!

Soon Ryan pulled out a camera with a massive telephoto lens, like something someone in the paparazzi might have. I couldn't fathom where the heck he'd been hiding that ginormous piece of equipment (that's what she said), since I hadn't noticed him carrying anything. My attention to detail could apparently use some work. Strike two on the old detective work for the evening. And no, I wasn't going to let myself think about how many strikes I'd gotten last night, thank you very much.

Ryan continued to snap pictures of the goings-on inside an apartment on the opposite side of the alley. Every once in a while, I caught a glimpse of someone walking past the window and Ryan's camera would start clicking away.

The evening moved on.

And on.

My legs were getting tired from standing in the same position for so long and the need to pee was becoming less of a theory and more of a reality. I really wanted to check my phone to see what the time was, but I was pretty sure a phone screen suddenly lighting up in the middle of the alley might be a tad noticeable.

Jesus. It wasn't until that moment that I realized I hadn't turned my ringer off. I guess that was strike three.

Most of the time I enjoyed when my friends remembered I existed, but in that moment, I prayed I had drifted as far from their consciousness as a fart released in a hurricane. But then I started worrying that by thinking about someone calling me, I might accidentally be sending vibes out for them to call. Gah! I tried to clear my thoughts. Which basically resulted in me never being able to think of anything *but* that ever again.

What felt like at least another hour later, Ryan finally moved. He'd made slight movements all along, taking pictures now and again, and sometimes it looked like he was writing something in a notebook, which made me want to take out my phone and make a few notes of my own, but again, the whole screen thing. I finally understood why some people still carried a pen around in their purse. But this time he was on the move for real, and I only had one chance to get out of there unnoticed.

As he carefully lowered the ladder, trying not to make noise, I began to inch my way up the alley, my eyes never leaving his figure both because it was a very nice figure to look at, and to make sure he had no idea I was there.

When he eventually turned his back to me to climb down the ladder, I started speed walking, placing my feet carefully so I wouldn't make any noise, then turned up the street the opposite way we'd originally come.

I'd never be able to stay off his radar if I was in front of him, so I needed to hide out and wait until he got well ahead of me again. Thankfully there was a recessed entranceway for a store fairly close by that I could duck into unseen.

Ryan was startlingly quick coming out of the alley but didn't seem to catch on that anyone had been with him most of the night. He headed back in the direction of our apartment building, and this time I gave him a lot of space. I had not come this far just to get caught now.

And while the night had been exceedingly dull, and frankly the main thing on my mind was getting to a bathroom, once I got home and did my business, I made quite a few notes while addresses and descriptions were still fresh in my mind. As I finished up with the notes, a quiet knock came on my door.

I tilted my head, wondering who the hell it could be. People didn't generally just knock on my door if I didn't know they were coming—especially considering this was a secure building where you had to be buzzed in.

I debated for a moment whether to answer it—my first thought being that Johnny had somehow found me. But the knock came again, and I found myself moving toward the door, opening it a crack just as Ryan was raising his arm to knock a third time.

"Oh, hello," was all I could bring myself to say.

I was totally relieved that it wasn't Johnny, but at the

same time, I had a feeling Ryan wasn't there to borrow a cup of sugar.

"Hi," he said.

I looked at him expectantly.

"So...did you have a good time?"

"I'm sorry?" I asked, my mind swirling.

"I know you were tailing me again," he said.

My stomach dropped to my knees.

# Chapter 7

I sighed and opened the door for him, having a feeling I might have a long conversation ahead of me. He looked around my apartment like any good detective would, I suppose. I cringed at the takeout container on the coffee table and the laundry basket heaped high in the corner, but mercifully, the place wasn't too much of a disaster.

"So, since asking nicely apparently isn't going to stop you from putting yourself in danger, not to mention invading my privacy and potentially screwing up my investigation...how about you tell me what will?"

I wish I could say his voice was kind, but frankly he sounded a tad pissed off. I mean, I guess I couldn't really blame him, but it wasn't like my intentions were bad, so it didn't seem fair.

"Ryan, I just want to help."

He scoffed.

"Look, I've got skills. I've got training. You saw what I could do out there when we were fighting those guys."

"You would have been killed on the spot if I hadn't risked my own life—and my investigation—trying to save you."

He had a point, but did he really have to put it like that? "I know," I said, "but if I had known what was going on, I would never have stumbled into that situation."

"Of *course* you wouldn't know what was going on," he said, his eyes widening slightly. "Because you were secretly stalking me!"

Ouch. That stung. "I was *not* stalking you," I said, my face feeling as though it might be getting a little pink. Or, you know, burgundy. "I was just bored, and I needed something to do."

"Well, here's the thing. Following someone like that *is* actually stalking. Invading their privacy. And I get that you didn't know I was a detective or that I was on the job and things could get seriously dangerous, but even without all that, it's pretty damned reckless to just go following someone around."

"I was trying to practice my skills. It was research."

He snorted. "Yeah, research. And what makes you think I'm interested in being fodder for some ridiculous novel?"

I frowned. "My novel isn't ridiculous."

"It's a novel. And therefore fiction. And therefore ridiculous."

"You think books are ridiculous?" I was certainly

seeing a side of Ryan I had not expected. He had seemed so intelligent, so interesting.

"No, books are good. The ones that actually teach you something or present you with new and interesting ideas. Fiction, on the other hand," he said as if he suddenly had a bad taste in his mouth, "is basic entertainment. Just made-up fairy tales."

My mouth dropped open. I wanted to defend fairy tales more than anything—fairy tales were the stuff of dreams—but I figured I had a bigger issue on my hands. "Fiction is not just made-up stories," I said. "Fiction tells the emotional truth of real life. It gets us out of our heads when we need a pick-me-up. It takes us to places both real and imagined and allows us to live incredible adventures we would never otherwise get a chance to live."

He shook his head. "Whatever. It's not my thing. I get that it's yours and that's fine, but in no world, real or imagined, will I ever be interested in being some character in a ridiculous book. Aren't you supposed to figure that stuff out on your own anyway, not just follow someone around and tell their life story?"

"I certainly do not tell other people's life stories. It just helps make characters and situations more real if you have something solid to base them on. A realistic sense of a character is incredibly difficult to just make up out of nowhere."

He put his hands up to his head in frustration. "Look, I did not come here to debate the merits of literature. I just want you to stay the hell away from my case."

The last words felt like a slap in the face. Frankly,

he was a little full of himself, if you asked me. It wasn't like I was following *him* per se; he just happened to be the person who was there. You know, purely random. Mostly. Give a girl a break. It just makes sense to follow someone who actually piques your interest.

"I don't really see what the problem is. Don't all detectives have partners, or sidekicks, or whatever? You've seen what I can do. The martial arts. The reconnaissance. I'm also really good with disguises and as you already know I've read all the Nancy Dr— Uh, detective stories, and I've also watched a million episodes of *CSI* and *Criminal Minds* and *Bones* and stuff. Not to mention it's my actual job to create mysteries. Plus, you know, I'd work for free." I gave him my most hopeful look.

He sighed. "I'm sorry to tell you, but none of that makes you a detective."

I squinted at him. "What does then?"

Somehow Ryan didn't seem like the type of guy who'd gotten into the private detective business because he used to be a cop, and if he hadn't been a cop, I was certainly interested to know what his credentials were. Not that I thought it was a huge deal, I just couldn't understand the difference between what I was saying and what he was saying.

"On-the-job experience is what makes a good detective," he said.

"Oh, so did you shadow someone for a while, you know, to get your experience, or like, have a mentor or something?"

He looked a bit confused. And a lot adorable, unfortunately. "No."

"Did you take a bunch of classes?"

He tilted his head. "Of course not."

"So, we can safely say that I have more knowledge and experience than you did when you first started this job."

He opened his mouth to say something, then promptly closed it again.

"So we agree, I can help with the case?"

"Petra, no. You're being ridiculous. It's way too dangerous, and I do not need a partner. Or a sidekick." He rolled his eyes.

"What if I can prove how valuable I can be?"

"No. How would you even do that?" he asked.

"Um, I don't exactly know yet, but I'll figure something out."

"Even if you do, the answer is still going to be no."

I sighed. "We'll see."

He shook his head like he couldn't quite believe this was happening to him. Not that I could blame him. It wasn't like I'd ever forced anyone to be my detective mentor before.

"I'm going home now. And can you please just stop? I honestly can't deal with the stress of this case *and* worrying about someone else's safety at the same time. It's too much, okay?" He looked so sincere. So intense, like he was really trying to make me see his point. "It's just too much."

And with that, he headed for the door and walked right out without turning to say goodbye.

Which was so incredibly rude. I mean, I suppose spying on him for several (dozens?) of blocks and all the way into a dark alley could technically be considered rude too, so I probably shouldn't judge him too harshly, but at least I'd been rude behind his back. Of course, I realized with a slight grimace, that might perhaps be a teensy bit worse.

But you know what? He hadn't even acknowledged my remarkably solid arguments. Because I *did* have all my classes behind me. And I *did* have intimate knowledge of the ins and outs of a good crime. Planning crimes was what I did for a living! Which, granted, might not be the greatest argument. But I solved them too, which I thought was an excellent point in my favor.

I'd spent countless hours delving into the minds of bad guys, figuring out exactly what their motivations might be—and not just one motive either; no, I had to run the gamut of every possible motivation so I could pick the one that was best for the book. I had to see the story…er, case…from every potential angle, unraveling the threads that made the most sense depending on that very motivating factor. My god, when I really thought about it, there literally wasn't anyone better equipped to solve a crime than a mystery writer. Just look at Jessica Fletcher! *Murder, She Wrote* had twelve seasons. And that was back in the day when TV shows had like, twenty-four episodes every year!

Okay, even I recognized I was working myself up into a bit of a tizzy over the whole thing, but frankly, I was insulted. What right did Ryan have to tell me I shouldn't be involved in the case? Like it or not, I was *already* involved in the case. Quite personally, if the blood on my favorite shoes had anything to say about it (sidenote to self: clean brown leather wedges).

Not to mention I could already feel the inspiration flowing back toward me, and yeah, maybe it hadn't actually taken up residence in my brain quite yet, but I knew it was there, floating all around me. I just needed a little more time with a mystery to really grasp it.

I shrugged. Fine. If Ryan wanted it this way, he could have it. I'd stay out of his investigation. I'd simply do my own investigation and see who solved the mystery first. And to be honest, I was pretty confident that I could do it just as well—if not better—than he could. Sure, he'd been doing things like this for years, but then again, so had I. Sort of.

Plus, it wasn't like I had a whole lot else on my plate. You know, other than delivering a new book to my publisher. Ugh…which was yet another reason that I needed to do this. I didn't want to plagiarize the story of Ryan's case, obviously, but I also hadn't been this excited about plotting in a while. Probably because plotting a novel was pretty similar to solving a mystery. All the pieces had to fall into the right places at the right times. The highs…the lows—they all had to be there. I mean, if the bad guys only experienced highs, the crime would never get solved, right? All I had to do was make sure I had a front-row seat when these bad guys experienced their lowest of lows.

Of course, I hadn't determined exactly who all the characters in the story were quite yet, but I knew exactly where to go to find out.

\* \* \*

The next night—after a productive day binge-reading a couple of my favorite Nancy books—I went back to the alley where Ryan had settled on the fire escape to do a little staking out of my own, and frankly, I was much better at getting the ladder from the balcony down, since I'd thought to bring a handy-dandy umbrella to hook around it so I didn't have to jump and make a big ker-fuffle. I mean, I might have looked a little weird car-rying an umbrella around when there was no sight of rain, but whatever—it was dark.

I settled into the same corner where Ryan had been sitting on the fire escape, quiet as could be, to wait. And it turned out I didn't even have to wait for long. I couldn't quite believe these guys just had their curtains wide open for all to see. I mean, I guess it would only be someone in the building across the alley who would see, but still, you'd think if you were up to something illegal, you'd close the drapes.

Maybe they'd been at it so long they felt invincible or something. Definitely helpful for me.

Though now that I had a little time to really stake out the place, it didn't seem like there was a whole lot of illegal stuff going on in there. It just seemed to be a couple guys milling around. I certainly didn't know what had interested Ryan so much that he'd been tak-ing so many pictures.

But soon, the scene changed. One of the guys brought in a girl, holding her arm like she was a prisoner. Ex-cept, the girl appeared content to be there, like she was wanting something from them. Too bad I hadn't brought any listening equipment, though that would have probably cost thousands of dollars and was not the kind of thing I just had lying around. Still, it would have been top-notch to be able to hear what was going on.

Eventually, they took the woman out of the room then brought in another girl and the same type of scenario went down. The girls were obviously desperate for something—they wanted to be involved with these guys.

One of the guys (whom I'd lovingly labeled "dude with the face that looks like he was taking a whiff of his gym bag after leaving it in the trunk for two weeks in August"...I know, I know, wordy, but I was working on it) brought in a brunette. He removed her jacket as two other guys sitting at a small kitchen table— weirdly in the middle of the living room—motioned for her to turn around. In a strange turn of events, at least in the world I lived in, she did one better and gave them a striptease-like dance, crouching, butt out and moving like she was about to start undressing. The men stopped her. Which was maybe the strangest part of it all.

I sighed.

So...fun fact—I was not very good with the whole patience thing. I mean, sure, I could sit and be still if I had to, like last night when I followed Ryan, but it was not my favorite. In fact, it was, by far, the section I'd found the most difficult in my private investigation class. Frankly, I just didn't see the point when there was usually a much more efficient way to find out what you needed to know.

I slipped back down the fire escape, taking my time so no one would be alerted to my presence, then went for a little jaunt around the front of the building. I mean, nothing to see here...la-la-la. Just an inconspicuous lady out for a stroll late at night.

In a not-so-great part of town.

But I wasn't concerned. I was on alert, constantly scanning the vicinity the way I was taught in my classes so no one could sneak up and surprise me.

As I had hoped when I peeked around the building, a couple girls were loitering outside. I leaned my umbrella against the side of the building, flopped the hood of my sweater over my head, stuck my hands in my pockets, slouched and took a deep breath the way I'd been taught in my Intro to Dramatic Performance 101 class. I never thought I'd actually use the class for acting. I'd mostly taken it to help me get into characters' heads when I was writing, but I was excited to put it into practice.

"Hey," I said, walking up to the ladies, fighting the urge to use a fake accent. I'd learned a long time ago they weren't my strongest talent—what might start out as a light Southern lilt could turn into a "your mama done gone and whipped up the best sweet tea evahhhr" in about three seconds flat.

The women looked at me like they weren't very happy someone else had shown up to their scene.

"What's up?" I asked, getting a good look at the three of them.

They were all quite skinny. Dark circles loomed beneath their eyes and there was a certain glassiness to their gazes, like they'd maybe been down a path of drugs for a while.

I took a chance. "Is this the place you can get the stuff?" I asked.

"Stuff?" one of the girls said innocently.

I tilted my head, hoping the hood was casting shadows over my face so that my face looked as thin as theirs, at least a little bit. "You know what I mean."

Another girl sighed. "Yes, this is the place, but we were here first and if you think you're going to jump ahead, you've got another thing coming." Her hand moved slowly to the waistband of her glittery skirt, bringing my attention to the small, but I'm sure very effective, knife that she had tucked in there.

"Whatever," I said, already turning away, afraid one of the guys would be on his way out to collect another woman at any second. "I'm not really presentable right now anyway. I'm coming back tomorrow though." I glared at her for good measure, my heart pumping.

She sneered right back but looked relieved to see me go.

I walked at as normal a pace as I could muster, but honestly, I couldn't get out of there fast enough. I could faintly hear a man's voice then, talking to the women I had just left, but I didn't dare turn around.

"She was just walking by," one of the girls said, apparently not too excited to let them know I might be back.

The less "competition" the better for them, I supposed.

I turned the corner and was out of sight, taking off into a run as I scooped up my umbrella. Being that close to who knows what kind of a situation had affected me more than I thought it would, and I needed to shed the nervous energy. I felt like I'd just downed a gallon of coffee.

As I neared my building, I slowed. I may not have come up with much evidence on my little nighttime trek, but things had changed.

Now I had a plan.

# Chapter 8

I couldn't sleep.

And when I couldn't sleep my mind could be a bit like a hamster on speed. Did my plan make sense? Would it rain tomorrow? Was the pain in my knee from walking for miles the other night, or was arthritis starting to kick in? Did Liechtenstein have a royal family? How much would it cost to buy the internet? What would magenta taste like?

Of course, I knew I wouldn't be able to write either. Sure, my brain was buzzing, but it was spinning too fast to squeeze anything remotely coherent out of it.

I needed a distraction.

I picked up the mystery I'd been reading, but after going over the same page four times and having absolutely no idea what happened, I set it back down and sighed. I had to find something distracting enough to lull my brain out of its pointless loop, but that was also mindless enough to not require too much thinking power. I needed something to organize or puzzle out.

Ooh! A jigsaw puzzle would be perfect (yup, I could really conjure up a firecrackin' good time when I wanted to). The only problem was I didn't have a puzzle.

Wait. I'd only been to the games room upstairs once since I'd moved in, but I remembered thinking it would be a nice place to relax with friends or do one of the puzzles that resided with the books and games. I didn't necessarily want to sit up there and do a puzzle at three o'clock in the morning in my jammies, but it would probably be okay if I wanted to borrow one, right? I mean, who was even going to know, really? And I could just return it in a few days.

The games room was one floor up, so it didn't take long to get there, which was a good thing since I was hardly looking stellar in my attire of ratty bathrobe, fuzzy unicorn slippers and pajama bottoms that were cut off at the knees—I couldn't stand when the pant bottoms scrunched up when I was trying to sleep so I always just chopped them off.

Unfortunately—as I discovered when I flicked on the light—my theory that I'd be the only one around at that hour was false. Except…why were they sitting in the dark?

I took a step closer. "Hello?" I said, the sound of my voice surprising even me in the silence.

It was a woman, cradling her head in the crook of her elbow, having apparently fallen asleep on top of the puzzle she'd been working on. I was surprised that she didn't wake up when the lights came on. Honestly, I was a little jealous of how deep some people could sleep—I'd jolt awake if a neighbor three floors down discharged a big sneeze. But then I noticed something didn't look quite right. The angle of her body was... off somehow.

I took a few more steps. "Hello?" I said, tentative this time.

She still didn't move. I closed my eyes, gathering all the courage I could find and pushed her ever so slightly on the shoulder to wake her up. At least that's what I was telling myself.

Then I pushed a little harder.

And that's when I knew for sure. The woman was not waking up. She was never going to be waking up again.

It took every ounce of self-control not to scream as I stumbled back out of the room. I braced myself against the wall just outside the door where I couldn't see...oh god...the body anymore.

If I'd thought my mind had been whirling before, it hadn't seen anything yet.

*Okay, okay*, I told myself. *Calm down.* I had to do something, but in the state I was in, I had absolutely no idea what that something was supposed to be. It's not like I'd ever discovered a dead body before.

I took a moment just to breathe.

Okay, what would a normal person do here? Which made me think of Vic asking me her WWND question. Yes, good. So...what would Nancy do?

With that one moment of focus, it suddenly seemed

so simple. Because the answer was clear. I had to tell someone about this. Nancy would likely alert someone in a position of authority, right?

So off I went, down to the ground floor of the building and straight to the security desk, completely forgetting what I was wearing until I was in front of the nighttime security guard and he gave me a bit of a look. It was just my luck he had to be attractive—tall with gorgeous dark skin—and I cursed myself for not spending more time down in the lobby during the night shift. I pulled my ratty robe tighter.

"Um, hi," I said, shooting him an awkward wave. "I'm Petra from 2201. I was just, um, up in the games room on twenty-three, and uh, well, there's sort of a body in there."

The guard's eyes widened. "What do you mean, a body?" Ozzy—as his name tag stated—asked.

"Um, well, I think it's a dead one?" I said, though it came out more like a question.

I mean, up in the games room I had been completely sure the body was not of the living variety, but now that I was in the bright lights of the lobby, not to mention in the company of another human, I started to second-guess myself. Or maybe it was a last-ditch hope that the poor woman wasn't really gone.

The guard blinked, then moved toward the front doors of the building without saying another word, locking them.

"Follow me," he said, and headed toward the elevators.

When we got in, he pressed the button for the twenty-third floor.

"Oh, um. I don't think I need to go back up there," I said, really, really not wanting to go back up there.

"Well, I'm not going in there by myself!" Ozzy said, looking at me like I'd lost my mind.

Which I thought was a little funny, since Ozzy was one of the biggest, toughest-looking dudes that I'd ever seen. Then again, maybe he hadn't ever discovered a dead body either.

"Couldn't we just call the cops or something?" I asked.

"We could, but the way you said there was a dead body didn't sound all that confident, and I don't want to make myself look like a fool. So I'd like to double-check for myself."

"Right, okay. I mean, I am pretty confident though. I really don't think that lady is getting up anytime soon. Or like, you know. Ever."

And I might have been mistaken, but it looked like Ozzy was trying very hard not to roll his eyes, but I guess I couldn't hold that against him since I was kind of even mistrusting myself. Wait, was it mistrusting or distrusting? Good lord, I was supposed to be a writer.

I really needed some sleep.

The elevator doors opened, and Ozzy stepped out while I sort of just stood there.

"Are you sure you need me to come?" I asked.

"Oh, I am definitely sure," he said, and honestly, I almost felt sorry for him when I saw the look on his face. Like he was trying to be tough, but there was some definite terror behind those eyes.

I sighed. "Fine, but I'm staying in the doorway."

"Just come on," Ozzy said, as he started marching down the hall.

I got the impression he felt like it was his duty to go in there but needed to hurry up and get it over with before he talked himself out of it.

I skulked behind. Why in the hell had I thought it was a good idea to do a stupid puzzle anyway? I stood outside as Ozzy took a deep breath, steeling himself, and marched in. I stayed right where I was.

"Oh no, it's Ms. Lawrence."

"You knew her?"

Ozzy nodded. "Erica Lawrence from 2301. And you're right. There's nothing we can do for her now except call the police and make sure nobody else stumbles on the scene. I'll call in some backup from my security company to stay here in case the police take a while. I can't leave the door downstairs unmanned for too long."

He got on the phone and started making calls.

Erica... I realized then that I knew Erica too. I took another quick peek into the room and had to admit that I hadn't really taken much of a look the first time around. So much for being the excellent witness I thought I'd be. Except, honestly, I think I'd been too scared.

Shit, it was her. She was a friend of Annie's. And well, everyone was a friend of Annie's, but whenever Annie talked about Erica, it gave me the impression that they were quite close.

I suppose I could have gone back to my apartment, but it didn't seem right to leave Ozzy there all alone, so I leaned against the wall in the hallway and slid down to the floor. This was one of the most surreal situations I had ever been in. Even though I wrote about these sorts of things, I had to admit I could have been perfectly content going my whole life without finding a dead body.

When the cavalry arrived, I went back downstairs, thinking I'd try to get some sleep even though I was way more wound up than I was before I'd taken the fateful trek to the games room. When I passed Annie's door just down the hall from mine, I decided to knock on her door. I couldn't bear the thought of Annie finding out from someone who thought it might be good gossip to pass along.

When the door opened, I stood staring at Annie for a good long while before I was able to speak. First, because I thought I'd have to knock several times before she'd even get to the door—it was five in the morning, after all—but she'd opened it as if she was standing there waiting. And second because of her appearance. She wore a long, satiny housecoat in fuchsia, complete with feathery trim that directed the eye down to her pink leopard-print sandal slippers, magnificent sunshine-yellow pedicure and diamond toe ring. Her robe was hanging slightly ajar, which gave a pretty good view of her matching nightgown, though it was really more like a longish teddy. And longish was even pushing it. It was not lost on me that the woman probably had better legs than me—not that mine had ever been spectacular or anything—but seriously, Annie was well into her seventies. I guess what they say is true—the legs really are the last thing to go.

The look was topped off by a glittering sleeping

mask that would have been right at home at a formal masquerade ball.

And even though it was just Annie and me standing there, I couldn't help but feel a little underdressed in my plaid flannel cutoffs and ultrathin tank with the hole just under the armpit. Thank goodness I'd thrown on the terrible housecoat, though I couldn't help but feel a little childish with my choice of slippers compared to the kitten heel slippers Annie was wearing.

"Is everything all right, Petra?" Annie asked, starting to look a bit worried.

"Um…" I tried to formulate my thoughts. "No. No, I'm afraid everything isn't all right."

"Come in," she said, motioning for me to enter.

And for the second time in a minute, I was rendered speechless.

I wasn't sure what I was expecting. I suppose I thought the whole place might be a mishmash of wild colors—a sort of frenzied boldness to it, much like Annie's outfits often had. But her place wasn't like that at all. There were certainly bold colors, the most prominent being the lavender walls, but they weren't exactly just lavender—more like a lavender ombré treatment, that slowly morphed into a plum color near the ceiling. The furniture was tasteful and understated. Mostly antiques, with each piece looking like it had come from a different corner of the globe. The artwork and photographs, the books, the rugs, the layers of pillows on every sitting surface—all of it added worldly flair and I got the impression Annie had collected every piece with love on what must have been decades of travels.

"Your place is amazing, Annie," I said, momentarily forgetting the horrible news I had come to tell her.

"Oh, thank you, dear. That's very kind of you to say." She pointed toward a chair at the heavy wooden table and went to the cupboard to get another cup for the coffee that was already on the table in what looked to be a Royal Albert coffeepot. I realized then that Annie hadn't actually been expecting company and that 5:00 a.m. coffee out of fine china must have been a daily occurrence for her. Annie Whitlock most certainly knew how to live every day to the fullest.

Annie sat and poured coffee into my cup and looked at me expectantly. Now that I was there, I was kind of frozen. I didn't want to just blurt it out, but I didn't know what you were supposed to say to lead up to these things either.

I took a deep breath. "I don't know exactly how to tell you this, but I went upstairs to the games room. I couldn't sleep and thought a puzzle might help calm my mind and make me tired and, well, I found someone."

Annie's head tilted, confused.

"Like someone who had...died." I wasn't sure why I felt the need to whisper the last word, but that's how it came out.

Annie gasped. "You're kidding! Are you all right, dear?" she asked, gently putting her hand on my arm.

"Yeah, yeah, I'm okay, but...it was...it was Erica Lawrence."

Annie's face went pale. "Erica? But I just saw her yesterday afternoon. She seemed perfectly fine."

I nodded. "Yeah, I don't think they really have any

information yet, but I saw her myself. The police are up there now."

Annie stood like she was about to march right up there to see for herself.

"I'm not sure you want to go up there," I said. "As her good friend, maybe you want to remember her as she was the last time you saw her?"

Her eyes widened. "Oh no. Is it grisly? My god," she said, putting her hand to her chest, "was she murdered?"

I shook my head. "No, she looks okay, just—" I cleared my throat "—dead." I scrunched my face in a kind of "sorry, was that too harsh?" kind of way.

But Annie just nodded. "You're probably right." She sat back down heavily in her seat, picking up her cup, her hands shaking. "It's just so…terrible. Hasn't the poor woman been through enough? She was widowed already this year."

Right, the widow. That's the other reason I knew her. Shortly after I'd moved in, Annie filled me in on the poor woman, who had been recently widowed for a third time. I guess I hadn't really put two and two together that "the widow" and Erica were the same person.

The weird thing was that she wasn't even old—in her early fifties, maybe. And yeah, as a mystery writer, a youngish woman who'd already had three husbands die on her was basically just a plot waiting to happen, but it wasn't like they'd all happened in a short amount of time or anything. She'd lost her first husband after they'd only been married a year when he was called to duty overseas. Given that he was in the army, this wasn't completely unheard of. According to Annie, the second husband was hurt in an accident at work after almost twenty blissful years of marriage, and this last poor guy—Stan, if I remembered correctly—had simply had a heart attack. I couldn't imagine how much more one woman could take.

Of course, whenever I saw Erica around the building, which, admittedly wasn't very often, she seemed like one of the most optimistic people I knew. It was almost as if having lost so much, she had a greater appreciation of life. For the brief time I'd been acquainted with her, I'd come to admire the stories about her, and it made me doubly sad that the poor woman I'd seen upstairs was Erica.

I sat with Annie for another few minutes, but she was understandably quiet and I had run out of things to say, so we said our goodbyes and promised to keep one another posted if we'd heard any news. I trudged back to my apartment, realizing that even though I hadn't gotten a wink of sleep, morning had arrived.

# Chapter 9

After the 3:00 a.m. shock and subsequent comforting of Annie, the tired was marinating deep into my bones. It had taken a while for the police to deal with everything. I'd captured a few winks at seven and since I worked for myself, I could have technically slept in as late as I wanted, but my body had this fun thing it did where it refused to sleep past nine. I was also, inconveniently, not a napper. Or a great sleeper of any kind, really. Once I tried to stay awake all night before an early-morning flight from Amsterdam to Los Angeles thinking I'd be able to catch some z's on the plane and the eleven hours would pass in no time, but I was sorely mistaken. All I did was create an agitated Petra monster.

Cuppa Joe was my first stop. I needed that caffeine hit like Nancy needed Bess and George. Once I had my apple crisp macchiato double shot in hand, I actually needed a little rest. Or maybe I just didn't want to face that dreaded blinking cursor that awaited me in my apartment. Or, you know, that little matter of a dead body above me and all. Not that Erica's body was still there—at least I hoped it wasn't—but just knowing it had been there a few short hours ago was no small thing. To be honest, it was probably why even the little sleep I'd gotten between seven and nine had been somewhat restless.

I flopped into the nearest chair, ready to veg out until the coffee kicked in. Unfortunately, my gaze landed on the gym next door. The Luxe building was interesting—an apartment/retail combo building with the businesses on the bottom floor while the rest of the floors were apartments. The thing that wasn't so typical was that it housed the Fit Body Factory. Which I thought was an amazing perk when I first moved in— all tenants even received a free gym membership with their rent—but it kind of ended up being a constant source of guilt.

Turns out I was apparently in both a writing and a gym slump. And the gym might not have been so bad if it wasn't sandwiched between Cuppa Joe, where you could pick up all your favorite calorie-laden beverages, and Darkside Doughnuts, which made the most decadent pastry of all time. Seriously, this was not your average doughnut shop—this place was an artisanal sugar factory, churning out creations like the Chocolate Ganache Caramel Custard Toasted Hazelnut Toffee Bit Delight. While the names of their creations may have been a little on the nose, you couldn't really blame them when they sounded as good as that.

My Cuppa and Darkside time might have been a teensy bit more frequent than my time at Fit Body.

The real kicker was that the shops on the ground floor were divided only by glass so you could leisurely watch all those treadmill runners and stationary bikers while you were enjoying your delicious beverage or snack. And while it was aesthetically pleasing, what with all the sunlight the design allowed in, I'm not sure the architects anticipated who, exactly, the business tenants might end up being.

My gaze landed on Eliza, a woman who had moved into the building around the same time as I had. We'd chatted a few times in the elevator and she seemed friendly, but she definitely spent a lot more time at Fit Body than at the Cuppa Joe or Darkside. Watching her on the elliptical, it looked like she was on a mission.

Sadly, the only mission I had was to write my next book and, well...that was best done sitting at my desk. Or lounging in my bed with my laptop.

Of course, there's nothing wrong with being a little softer around the edges, but a person who dedicated that much time to exercise just somehow seemed... more focused. Like she really had her shit together. And yeah, I'd had some wins and lucky breaks in my day, but my motivation seemed to be a little less than optimal lately.

Conversations mingled with the bakery smells as I sat. I'd gotten good at tuning out the chatter, having spent so much time writing in coffee shops, but a few words caught my attention. *Investigation. Body. Suicide.* Clearly the gossip mill had been running on overtime because I had seen Erica and it did not look like a suicide to me. And I mean, I guess I don't really know what every kind of suicide might look like, but the woman looked perfectly fine. You know, except the being-dead part.

I stayed for another twenty minutes or so, kind of zoning out, mostly wondering if I'd ever be able to get another book finished, or if I was going to have to figure out something else to do with my life. I had, after all, written almost the entirety of my first book, *Desperately Seeking Fusion*—a sort of cozy mystery/romance hybrid set mostly in a laboratory—while I was killing time at the old office job. I mean, what did they expect me to do when sorting the mail and filing only took me four hours and the workday was eight? The computer was just sitting there and if I was typing all the time, at least I looked like I was busy.

Honestly, most of my coworkers thought I was the hardest worker they'd ever had in the receptionist position. Hmm…maybe that's where my motivation came from. Did I need to find a way to limit my time so that I'd *have* to write the next book within a certain window? I sat up straighter for a moment, almost ready to start scrolling the want ads when I remembered how much I hated that soul-sucking horror of an office and promptly relaxed back into my seat.

No. I would try absolutely everything else before I would ever go down that road again. On the plus side, that dreaded thought seemed to actually light a fire under my butt. I got up to head straight to my computer, vowing to write something—anything—before the day was done. I was in so much of a hurry, in fact, that as I flew out the coffee shop, I plowed right into a poor unsuspecting person on their way in. A person who was so lightweight that I nearly knocked her right down to the ground.

"Oh my lord, I am so sorry, Eliza," I said, as I grasped on to the Burberry coat of my building-mate.

Being so agile, Eliza was able to steady herself quickly and hadn't really been in any danger of going down. "Whoa there, linebacker," she said, but at least she had a smile on her face.

"Ha-ha, right, linebacker. That's a good one," I said, really hoping she meant because of the tackle and not due to any size discrepancy there might have been between us.

"What's got you all in a tizzy?" Eliza asked.

I tilted my head. Was I in a tizzy? I kind of thought I had been more in a burst of inspiration, but I suppose it may have been coming off a little tizzy-like. Especially considering the woman before me was immaculately put together in her tailored coat, slim-fit pants, hair looking like she had just gotten a salon blowout—how is that even possible when I saw her fifteen minutes ago in a ponytail on that elliptical?—and looking like she just waltzed out of a style blog. I, on the other hand, had all morning to get myself presentable yet I was gracing the coffee shop with my usual leggings and oversize hoodie combo. At least I'd put shoes on instead of slippers this time.

"Oh, um, nothing really. I'm so sorry. I just had a bolt of inspiration about the book I'm writing," I said, not mentioning that I hadn't actually started writing it. "I just wanted to get it down before it flew out of my head."

I also didn't mention that it wasn't really an idea as much as it was a desperate urge not to have to re-enter the corporate world (aka the daily assassination of joy) again, but I'm sure Eliza didn't really care about the details.

"Amazing!" Eliza said, and I wasn't sure if she really thought it was amazing or if she was just humoring me. "It's so great that you have your books. Your confidence is wonderful—you don't feel like you have to impress everybody all the time." She glanced at my outfit then kept right on rolling. "Unfortunately, I chose the professional path. Well, for as long as I have to, anyway," she said, rolling her eyes like she wondered if she had gone the wrong route—except I could totally tell she didn't actually think she had taken the wrong route. In fact, it sort of seemed like she was thinking that I had taken the wrong route. "Honestly, I envy you. Content with making your own money, such as it is. Right now, I'm dedicating everything to making sure I have enough time to work on myself so I can find the man that will ensure my financial security."

I blinked. "I'm surprised to hear a woman say that sort of thing in this day and age, to be honest."

"I know," she said, "we've really lost our traditional values. Anyway, I better not keep you—you have important writing to do," she said with a smile and a little scrunch of her nose.

"Um," I said. I really wanted to respond with something along the lines of "tradition is pretty much just peer pressure from dead people" but I wasn't sure that would go over well. "Okay, I'll see you arou—"

"Wait," Eliza said, her eyes getting huge. "Did you hear about the death in the building?"

I looked around a little self-consciously, considering the volume of Eliza's inquiry. If anyone in the coffee shop—and probably in Fit Body Factory too—hadn't known about Erica before, they probably did now. Although no one really seemed to pay much attention—most of the patrons of Cuppa Joe had headphones in while they worked…rather productively, I noticed.

"Oh yeah, it's so sad," I said, not particularly wanting to rehash all the details.

"Can you believe anyone would be so selfish? Well, I guess you can hardly blame her, being a widow and all. If I had to suddenly make my own way in this world after being taken care of, I'd want to off myself too. Honestly, I can't wait until I find my forever man and can just sit back and relax."

"Um…" was all I could seem to muster, trying to work out how she could so quickly redirect the topic of a tragic possible suicide straight back to her, before she spoke again.

"Anyway, good luck with the writing." With that she headed to the counter and ordered her skinny hazelnut iced macchiato with an extra shot, light ice, no whip.

When I got back to my floor, Annie and Ryan were

talking in the hallway just outside my apartment. Well, just outside Ryan's apartment, I supposed.

"Oh, Petra," Annie said, "I'm still just beside myself with all that has been going on."

I glanced at Ryan, then quickly glanced away. She had no idea.

Annie turned to Ryan, whispering. "It's the strangest thing," she said. "The policemen upstairs, they—I don't know—they seem to have it all wrong."

"What do you mean?" Ryan asked.

"Well," Annie continued, "Ashton from 1805 said he overheard them talking about a suicide note, but there's just no way that Erica would do something like that."

Ryan's eyebrows rose. "Well, unfortunately you can't always tell with these things," he said.

But Annie cut him off right there. "No. I would know. I talked to Erica every day. She was happy."

"Someone looking happy doesn't always mean—"

"I know what you're going to say and I'm going to stop you right there," Annie said, putting a hand up rather close to his face. "She was excited to be starting a new chapter in her life. She had just started a new job and was loving it."

Ryan cleared his throat and rubbed the back of his neck. I could tell he wanted to say something, but probably realized it would be fruitless to argue with Annie. "Well, I'll have to take your word for that."

Annie nodded once like that was the end of the matter. I could tell Ryan wasn't quite as convinced as Annie though.

"Well, I guess I should, uh…" He pointed toward his

apartment, taking a step backward toward the safety of it.

"Wait, Ryan. Before you go," Annie said, her tune suddenly changing. "Could I just ask you a teensy favor?"

Ryan swallowed, obviously scared to ask what the favor might be. "Um, sure."

"I know you have connections with the police, and I was just wondering if you could maybe go up there and see what they have to say?" She smiled and batted her eyes. And she didn't look weird doing it either. I mean, what I wouldn't give to be a woman who could literally bat her eyes at someone and not look like she was having some sort of ocular episode.

I glanced at my apartment door, wondering how awkward it would be if I just went inside. Not that I didn't enjoy the way the taut little micromuscles fired all the way up Ryan's shoulders, neck and jaw as he squirmed under Annie's questions.

"Oh, I don't think they'd want me snooping around in their investigation," Ryan said.

But Annie was having none of it. "I just know Erica wouldn't have done anything to hurt herself," she said, her voice starting to shake. "I knew her better than most people did."

If there was anyone Erica might have trusted with her problems, it probably would have been Annie. I mean, I spent at least a few minutes every day with Annie, and I would bet Erica did as well. Ryan must have sensed how much she meant to Annie too. Annie was nothing if not positive at all times—honestly, she was the most optimistic person I had ever met—and to see her upset was frankly, well...upsetting.

He let out an audible and resigned sigh. "Um, I suppose I could see if there's anyone I know up there," he said, looking like it was actually the last thing he wanted to do, but Annie had obviously found a soft spot in his heart too. "Just let me grab my credentials," he said, ducking back into his apartment.

Annie nodded, then turned to me. "I just can't believe they're even suggesting that Erica could do this."

I knew how she felt. I'd had a friend years ago take her own life and no one had seen it coming. It took me a long time to accept the truth. "You knew her a lot better than I did," I said, "but I think we have to at least give this theory some consideration."

Annie looked at me in a way I wouldn't have thought she was capable of. She was so very "live and let live"—accepting and championing everyone's choices, no matter how differently she might have done things—but in that moment she looked...disappointed in me.

But she softened and let out a long sigh. "Look, I know that you can't always tell about these things. That sometimes the people who appear happiest are the ones suffering the most. And given the fact that she's just lost Stan and everything, I get why the police think the things they do. But I know Erica. This just doesn't feel like her."

I nodded. I never wanted to be on the receiving end of that look ever again, but still, I had to say something. "Mental health issues don't always look the way we think they should look."

Annie nodded. "Of course, you're right, but I'm still not convinced. I'm not sure anything could convince me."

I nodded back. "Okay then. You knew her the best. I will take your word for it."

"Thank you, dear. Thank you. That means a lot. I just... She was starting that new job and everything. She was excited for the future."

"Of course. Whatever you need from me, just let me know."

Ryan's door opened and he stepped out. "I'll be back shortly, ladies," he said, giving us a nod and heading toward the elevator.

"Do you want some tea or something?" I asked Annie. "We can keep the door open so we can hear when Ryan gets back."

"All right," Annie said, though she looked tired.

But I knew there was no way she was heading back to her apartment before hearing what Ryan had to say. Even then, I was sure poor Annie wasn't getting any sleep anytime soon. I'd just poured the water into the blueberry tea when the elevator dinged. It was Ryan returning.

Annie and I rushed to intercept him as he made his way back.

"Well?" Annie asked, almost breathless.

"I'm sorry, Annie," Ryan said. "It looks like your friend was more troubled than you realized. They're ruling it an open-and-shut case of suicide. She overdosed on her own prescription sleeping pills."

# Chapter 10

Even after the coffee that morning, and the tea with Annie, I still needed to go down to Cuppa Joe for a midafternoon pick-me-up. And after the night I'd had, I figured a lavender sprinkle doughnut from Darkside couldn't hurt either.

On my way back up, I waved at the daytime security person, Hazel—she was kind of my favorite with her coiffed hair and broad shoulders that hinted at a gym regimen rivaling that of a professional bodybuilder even though I had never seen her over at Fit Body Factory. I suspected she had a full gym setup at her house instead, since it seemed like her workouts must have been more like a lifestyle than a hobby.

Hazel waved back with a bored expression, though I didn't take any offense since she was currently being regaled by Lessie Webster, the kid from 412 whose parents apparently thought having security in the building meant a full-time babysitter. The kid was always in the lobby bugging whoever was behind the desk. Frankly, Hazel was a superstar for putting up with it.

I rode the elevator upstairs with a woman who looked a bit like a detective in her trench coat and dead-faced lack of reaction to the smile I gave her as she entered. My suspicions were confirmed as she wheeled around to check the floor buttons with her hand on her hip, efficiently revealing her police badge. I got the feeling she'd mastered the move a long time ago and did it almost without thinking anymore. I assumed she'd be going to the floor above mine, but she didn't press floor twenty-three, and when the elevator arrived on twenty-two, she barged out and made her way down the hall.

I followed slowly behind.

She stopped in front of Ryan's place and knocked, putting more than a little oomph behind it.

Ryan opened the door in jeans and a T-shirt that looked like it was custom designed to fit his generous biceps.

"Hey, Jess," he said. "What's up?"

He glanced my way. After the little run-ins from the previous nights, I expected him to glare at me or something to let me know he was still angry, but strangely, he looked a little uncomfortable, his eyes darting between Jess and me, me and Jess.

I wondered what it meant that he was on a first-name basis with the detective. The way she looked at him—like he was something she'd like to get into her handcuffs, and not in the "you're under arrest" kind of way—made me wonder just how close they were.

I got close to my door and Ryan gave me a little nod. It wasn't a friendly nod, just...neutral. I smiled and raised my hand, almost a wave, but not quite, since I couldn't really do anything that wasn't incredibly awkward around the guy.

Jess, of course, didn't bother to acknowledge my presence as I fished in my hoodie pockets for my keys.

"So we're off," Jess said. "Again, it was open-and-shut so no need to worry, but if there's anything you need..."

I had angled myself so I could just barely see the two of them out of the corner of my eye.

Jess leaned on the door frame provocatively. "You have my number."

Ryan cleared his throat. "That I do," he said, and shifted his door an inch or two, almost as if he wanted to close it.

So. Perhaps things weren't as close between Detective Jess and Ryan as the detective had hoped.

"I guess I'll see you around," she said, turning to leave, though she looked back for several steps as she sauntered down the hall.

I wasn't quite sure how she managed it, to be honest. If I had tried to walk with my head turned that way, there was a ninety-eight percent chance I would have ambled right into a wall.

I put my hand in my pocket to actually find my keys this time and my stomach sank. Where the hell were they? I frantically fumbled in there with both hands, no doubt with a look of panic plastered all over me.

"Uh, they're tucked under your arm."

I'd almost forgotten Ryan was still standing there.

"What?" I said, somewhat distracted by *The Mystery of the Missing Keys*, my mind already whirring over where I could have left them, mentally going through the entire route I had taken down to Cuppa Joe. Had I stopped at the mailbox and set them down?

"Your keys. They're tucked under your elbow there," he said, with that smirk solidly planted on his face.

"Heh-heh," I said, smiling, but not quite able to look him in the eye. I grabbed the keys and sort of held them in the air. "Forgot I put them there for safekeeping."

I turned and unlocked my door as quickly as I could, diving into my apartment. I'm sure I heard a little chuckle coming from the hallway.

So damned awkward.

I'd just gotten settled in my bed with my laptop on my lap, about to type my first word (JK—I'd been looking up cute outfits on Pinterest for the past half hour) when a knock came at the door. I was happy for the distraction. You know, from my distraction.

"Oh, Petra," Annie said, looking relieved that I opened the door. "I knew you'd be the one I could count on to be home."

I wasn't quite sure how to take that, but Annie kept going so I didn't have to think about it for too long.

"I just can't stop thinking about Erica. She was in the prime of her life and starting this new relationship and everything. I just… I can't stop thinking about how none of this makes any sense."

"Erica was in a new relationship?" I asked. "Didn't her husband just die a few months ago?"

"It was seven months ago, but yes, Erica is one of those relationship people. She really loves sharing her life with a partner."

I nodded. The whole thing seemed to be a bit quick, but who was I to know? Maybe that was her way of grieving, by finding a way to fill that void of despair. It wasn't like the memories of her former husband were going anywhere just because she was dating someone new. It was probably nice to feel something, anything, besides grief.

"So anyway, I want to go have a little look-see in the games room where it all took place. Maybe we can spot something the police have missed."

She said it with such seriousness that I could hardly break it to Annie that the police were professionals, and we were, um, not. As if I had any right to that opinion, given my latest escapades.

"What do you think we might find?"

Annie sighed. "I know it's a long shot, but I want to at least get a feel for the room. See if there are any lingering…vibes or, I don't know, something. But I can't quite bring myself to go up there alone," she finished, her tone becoming more desperate.

"Of course, Annie. Of course I'll go with you."

What else was one supposed to say to a woman beside herself with grief? I tried not to think about the fact that if she truly didn't think Erica had done this, then what did that imply? That someone had done it to her? I glanced up at the ceiling, decidedly uncomfortable with *that* scenario, since it happened right upstairs and everything.

Still, I threw on the first shoes I could find—my unicorn slippers—and followed Annie to the elevator, secretly congratulating myself on being the kind of person who has those little sly smile moments of "oh the things I do for my friends."

As we made our way toward the games room, my stomach began to churn. Whether this was Erica's doing or not, the fact still remained that a body had been in there not so long ago—a visual I'd been working quite diligently to shove into the most secluded cubbyhole of my brain.

For being the one who was most upset, Annie definitely had more courage than me, squaring her shoulders and striding right in without hesitation. I, on the other hand, stopped at the doorway and peeked before going any farther. I couldn't afford the nightmares if it looked like anything violent had taken place in there. The irony that I was a mystery writer didn't escape me.

I opened one eye slowly, then the other. Because the thing was, the games room looked exactly like it did before. No crime scene tape, no blood, no nothing besides a few random games stacked on the window seat and a half-finished jigsaw puzzle depicting what would have been a clock tower if anyone ever decided to finish it.

"Hey," a perky voice said, nearly vacating my soul from my body.

Annie jumped even more violently as someone stepped out from behind a small alcove.

"Jesus, Eliza, you scared the hell out of us," I said, clutching my chest.

"Good lord, dear. Way to make an entrance," Annie said, closing her eyes and letting out a long whoosh of breath to try to calm her nerves.

"Sorry, didn't mean to scare you," she said. "And technically you were the ones who made the entrance. I was just standing here."

Annie was already having a thorough look around, getting up close and peering at things, bending over the puzzle, then stepping back and peering into the massive bookshelf.

"What are you looking for?" Eliza asked.

"I'm not sure, just something that might be out of place, I suppose," Annie answered.

"Yeah, I guess I'm just being nosy too," Eliza said. "I wanted to... I don't know. Maybe I thought I could make myself feel better by coming up here. It's a little discombobulating having a dead person in the building, you know?"

I nodded, though I couldn't help but think it was a little insensitive of her to essentially be calling us nosy. Annie had been Erica's good friend, after all. We were hoping to find out what had been going on in Erica's mind...trying to figure out what really happened.

"Anyway, the room seems the same as always, I guess." Eliza shrugged as she headed toward the door. "See you guys around."

"Yeah, see ya," I said, glancing at Annie, who didn't say a thing.

In fact, she seemed to be aggressively trying to ignore Eliza altogether, which was very off-brand for Annie. Maybe I wasn't the only one who Eliza rubbed the wrong way.

Unsure what else to do, I started copying Annie. I hadn't really spent any time in the games room, so I had no idea what was normal and what was out of place. Sure, if there had been a gun on the floor or a red hand-print like in *The Secret of the Scarlet Hand* or something, I might have picked up on it, but the games room was just a games room, peppered with tables and chairs and lined with shelves of books and games. Add the fact that everyone in the building had access and probably moved things around all the time, and I couldn't really see how it was possible to find a clue.

"Hey, ladies." Jamieson, another tenant from the building, popped his head in.

Every time I saw this guy, I tried not to think of the phrase *celibate monkfish*, but dude just gave off vibes. I think Annie had said he was from the twelfth floor— she mostly talked in floors—and that he was lonely, always wandering the building and looking for people to talk to. I got the feeling he was one of those people who had never really found his place in life and now, nearing fifty, he was more socially awkward than ever. I couldn't help but wonder if I was perhaps witnessing my future, which in turn prompted me to leave my body for the briefest of moments, though I recovered quickly, well acquainted with fun little flashes of existential distress.

"Oh, hi, Jamieson," Annie said, still distracted.

But Jamieson was having none of it. He was looking for someone to talk to and we were ripe for the picking. "Wild what happened, hey?"

I nodded solemnly.

In the best of times, I can be a bit socially awkward, but put me in front of another potentially awkward person and it was like I lost all concept of what social interaction was supposed to look like.

It's why I loved Annie so much. She made everything look easy—like it was no big deal. I swear, she could fall down, knock out a tooth, have blood all over the front of her shirt and still be the most confident person in the room. She just had this "life is an incredible adventure" thing going on, no matter what. I'd recently decided I'd like to be Annie when I grew up—if and when that actually happened. Of course, I'd probably have to learn to not feel like a total imposter all the time if I were ever to get myself even remotely close to Annie's realm of existence.

Jamieson sidled up next to me in that way that people who aren't in the know about personal space sometimes do. "You're the writer, right? Petra something?"

He was tall, sort of slouching over me with his questionable amount of deodorant body spray and aura of desperation.

"Yup, Petra Jackson," I said, thinking a handshake would be the most obvious thing to do, but with the way he was standing directly beside me, as if we were watching a play or sporting event or something together, I decided against it.

"Jackson, right," he said, as if he should have known, even though the two of us had never formally met. "Anyway, that's cool—you being a writer and all. We should get together sometime. You *need* to hear my life story— maybe if you're lucky I'll even let you write about it." He winked. Winked!

Sadly, this was something I got all the time. People often thought the hard part about writing was coming up with the ideas. And yeah, given my current bout of writer's block, the ideas weren't exactly flowing, but honestly, ideas were as plentiful as the oxygen in the air. The actual sitting down and writing was the hard part—but no matter how much you tried to tell someone that, they never seemed to believe it. Also, everyone thinks their life is overwhelmingly riveting, and well, let's just say everyone can't be the exception. I stuck with the tried-and-true "um, I'm a fiction writer."

"Well, even fiction writers base their material on living people, right?"

"Maybe," I said, though he didn't seem to be listening to me anymore. His focus was turned to what Annie was doing, which was standing with her hands on her hips and looking frustrated.

"Like I was about to say," Jamieson said, taking a blessed step toward Annie. "It's just so sad the way Erica lost faith like that."

Annie's expression annoyified (did I mention that, as a writer, I was allowed to make words up when I couldn't find one to fit just right?). But she was still too nice a person to say anything, though I did hear her sigh audibly—something I had never witnessed from her before.

"I guess it just goes to show that when you're doing something as boring as a jigsaw puzzle, you have too much time to think about all the terrible things in life."

Annie's gaze shot up to meet his then, even more annoyified.

I couldn't really blame her. I liked puzzles too. I found them to be the opposite of too much time to think. For me they were a way to relax, almost meditative.

But then Annie said something entirely unexpected. "Erica was definitely not the one doing this puzzle." And it was super weird, because she almost sounded angry about it.

"She most definitely was. I saw it with my own eyes," Jamieson replied, almost as if he couldn't believe anyone would question him.

Annie shook her head. "Erica didn't do puzzles."

Jamieson shrugged. "She was working on this very one just yesterday before..." He trailed off, miraculously reading the room and knowing he didn't have to finish that thought.

"I guess your eyes must have been mistaken," Annie said, standing her ground. "Erica hated puzzles, and solitaire, and anything else that was a one-person activity. She could never see the point in doing something that wasn't a social activity. People were her passion, and she believed connection to be the single most important thing in this world."

"Coulda fooled me last night," Jamieson said, sort of under his breath.

"What's that supposed to mean?" Annie asked.

Jamieson raised his eyebrows. "I tried to come in here last night and talk to her while she was *doing her puzzle*," he said, giving Annie a significant look. "But it was like she couldn't wait to get rid of me," he said.

What a shocker, I thought, though I didn't say it out loud.

"That does not sound like Erica at all," Annie said.

"I know. That's why it was so strange," Jamieson said. "She always had time for me before, but last night was...weird. It was almost like she was afraid to even have me in the room."

"Wait, was there someone else in here with her?"

He shook his head. "Nope, she was just all by herself doing her puzzle. She made it quite clear that she did not want any company."

Annie shook her head like she was dismissing everything Jamieson was saying. The only problem was the one thing I knew about Jamieson—the thing that Annie herself was always saying got him in trouble—was his almost compulsive need to tell the truth.

Annie stormed out of the room, not wanting to hear another word. I rushed after her since the only reason I was even there was to support her—not that I'd done a great job of that. Also, I did not particularly want to be alone with Jamieson.

"Annie, it's okay," I said, rushing to catch up. "Maybe he's mistaking her for someone else or something." I knew better than to argue the point that maybe Erica was, in fact, doing a jigsaw puzzle even if she wasn't fond of them. To be honest, it didn't seem like that big of a deal if someone just decided they wanted to puzzle one day.

She looked at me and stopped just short of rolling her eyes. "You know as well as I do that Jamieson doesn't lie."

"I know but…well, maybe Erica just changed her mind about puzzles or something." I held my breath, waiting for the retaliation, but it never came.

"I honestly don't know what's going on here, Petra, but there is one thing I know for sure."

"What?"

"Something smells fishy in the games room."

# *Chapter 11*

When I got back to my apartment that evening, there was a small, beautifully wrapped parcel sitting at my door. Which was weird, since I lived in a secure building. But it was like, really pretty wrapping, so without giving it much thought I tore into it, incredibly curious to see what was inside.

Chocolates. Assorted truffle chocolates, to be exact, which was even more weird, because they were my absolute favorite. But...

...why would someone leave a box of chocolates at my door? Although perhaps *how* might have been the more pertinent question. Unless it was someone from inside the building, of course.

I quickly tore open the card, which said, simply, "From your anonymous admirer."

I swallowed.

Probably it was Annie, I thought. She was the exact kind of thoughtful that would do something like this even when she was clearly hurting more than the rest of us. Of course, it could be...

I glanced at the door across the hall. No, I thought, shaking the idea out of my head. The dude pretty much hated me, and besides, he really didn't seem to be the "I leave snacks surreptitiously at people's doors" sort.

It could be as simple as a fan who'd read my book and wanted to give me something. For all I knew, my publisher could have forwarded it over. Whatever the case, I eased into my apartment already tearing into my first smooth, glorious truffle, not giving it a second thought.

"Thanks for coming," I said, opening the door for Brandt the following day.

He had a rolling suitcase in tow.

"How could I pass up an opportunity to do a full identity makeover?" he said, rather out of character with his giddiness.

Brandt was nothing if not a genius with makeup, and his favorite thing to do with his art was to make a person look entirely different. I didn't exactly call it a disguise when I'd called him—that would have raised too many questions—but I told him I felt like being somebody else for a day and he totally bought it. I mean, who doesn't want to be someone else every now and again? It didn't hurt that I told him he could do whatever he wanted either, within reason, of course. I still wanted to look like a regular woman, but special effects weren't really his thing anyway. He was a more of a "purist" with his craft, as he liked to say.

"I just want to look normal," I explained. "But maybe a little on the seedy or dangerous side. Like maybe I haven't been taking all that great care of myself."

Brandt crinkled his forehead. "What is this for again?" he asked.

Obviously, I hadn't actually told him why I needed the disguise, uh, makeover. He'd been so excited to come over and get started, he never asked. I'd never met a person so passionate about makeup as my burly co–best friend.

But that was Brandt.

"Um, it's just for this play a writer friend of mine is doing. She wanted to have some extras that looked the part, but she can't really afford to pay a professional makeup artist. And I mean, you're probably too expensive, but if she ends up liking what you do, maybe there would be more in the budget for next time."

He nodded. I knew he didn't care that he wasn't getting paid because it was me, but still, I hoped he'd buy the story.

"What friend is this?"

God, why was he asking so many questions? Usually he couldn't care less about details.

"Becky," I said, quickly pulling a name out of my ass. "You know, from that Portraiture in Oil class I took a while back?"

"Oh yeah, Becky. Right," he said, already digging into his suitcase of goodies.

I suspected he often had to pretend he remembered

stuff that he didn't, since he had a habit of not actually paying attention to the conversations he was around for.

Thankfully that was the end of the grilling since once he began, his focus was incredible. An hour later and the magic was complete.

I was an entirely different person, complete with a disturbing nail polish job—light bluish lavender with black tips—that made me look a bit corpsey.

"Wow," I said, as he held a mirror for me to get a look. "Um, my friend is going to be so impressed and really excited, I think."

"Who, Becky?" Brandt asked.

"Right, yeah. Becky." Cripes, why are names of fake friends so hard to remember?

"Oh, I'm not done yet," he said, turning the suitcase around and unzipping a compartment I didn't even know existed.

He pulled several fake hairpieces out.

"I'm not sure a wig is entirely necessary," I said. "I mean, I'm supposed to look less healthy, not more with some high-shine hair."

He scoffed. "Ye of little faith," he said, pulling a large strand of clip-in extensions from the bunch.

He was already digging into my hair before I could protest, so I just went with it. Thankfully it wasn't a real play, and I wasn't on a time limit, or it might have been a complete disaster. But for the thing I was actually working on, the later I showed up, the better, probably.

He held the mirror up again ten minutes later and I'd been incredibly shortsighted to have questioned him. What he'd done to my hair was an appalling miracle. Usually, my hair was pretty healthy-looking, and a rather generic shade of brown, which I always thought was good since I liked to blend in, but now it had these straggly pieces of slightly lighter and redder throughout, making it not only look like I had a supercheap haircut, but also like I had done some horrible home-color hack job on it too.

It was perfect.

"Brandt, this is really great. Thank you so much."

"You are more than welcome," he said. "Now I just need to get a picture for my portfolio," he said, whipping out his phone.

I wasn't entirely sure it was a good idea to get this look on record, both because I was supposed to be in disguise, and because it was certainly not the best I had ever looked. Brandt had made me gaunt and pale with darkish circles under my eyes as though I hadn't slept in about three weeks. I was a magnificent disaster.

But I figured helping with his portfolio was the least I could do after he just spent all that time working on me for free.

"Damn, we forgot to get a before picture. Next time I come over, can you put that shirt back on and get one taken? No one will know it was taken on a totally different day."

I laughed. "Yeah, sure."

"Great," he said, packing everything back up.

I loved watching him work. There was a lightness… an excitement to him that wasn't normally there. I couldn't help but wonder, since his work crew got to see him in this giddy state all the time, whether they knew him as a totally different person from the one Vic and I got to see. Mr. Vivacious Effervescence Who Wows You with His Enchanting Charm and Bubbling Personality vs. the He Who Shall React in a Completely Irrational Manner if You Deign to Interrupt His Meal for Any Reason Even If You Are Trying to Save His Life (or Cranky Pants for short) that we got to encounter on the daily.

We never could figure out how he managed to beguile so many women, and I suddenly couldn't wait to tell Vic my theory of *The Strange Case of Dr. Asshole and Mr. Charisma*.

After Brandt left, I read a chapter of *The Whispering Statue* to help get into the dark space I would need to be in for the character I was about to play. Was it completely ridiculous to think I had any chance of pulling this off? I mean, for a person obsessed with mystery and gore, I was about the most boring person anyone was apt to find. Seriously, for someone who made my living as an artist, whenever I got around real artists— or pretty much anyone with an interesting personality really—I felt about as blah and vanilla as a tub of plain ice cream.

But then I caught another glimpse of myself in the mirror as I searched my closet for something to wear and it gave me an extra boost of confidence. Brandt really was a genius—I was pretty much unrecognizable. If someone who wasn't in my inner circle had seen me walking down the street this morning and then again this evening, they would never in a million years imagine me to be the same person.

I miraculously found something to wear buried deep in my closet. My wardrobe tended to be on the nonflashy side, kind of like the rest of me, so the look I would need wasn't particularly in my wheelhouse. I decided to use my shapewear as a skirt, which was basically a supertight slip designed to hold everything in instead of what it was meant for—underwear. It was black, so you couldn't really tell it wasn't supposed to be a skirt, other than the fact it was skintight and way too damned short.

Once I had the outfit on, the character I was playing came more to life. I was completely and utterly self-conscious due to the skimpy nature of the clothes, but it was certain now; no one in the world, even those closest to me, was ever going to recognize me.

Not that I planned on running into anyone I knew or anything, but still, anonymity was always a good thing when one was about to embark on a dangerous journey into a crime ring. I mean, I assumed it was a crime ring, anyway. It's not like I had a whole lot of experience with these kinds of things.

The realization that this might be a really poor decision charged through my mind again, but I quickly shoved it right back out. I just had to own the character and not even think about my real life. I was a girl who would do anything for her next fix. That's it, that's all.

I grabbed a faux-fur vest from an old Halloween costume…then decided against it. The girls last night had been dressed overtly sexy, but not as ridiculous caricatures. They looked like normal girls out clubbing or something. Other than the slightly unhealthy aura about them, of course.

I was finally ready, and it was time. I put on some highish wedges, but not so high that I was uncomfortable. I didn't want them to hinder my running if the night came to that. Safety first, right? My feet still hurt a bit from walking with Ryan the other night, but I was pretty confident that the adrenaline was going to kick in right about the time I reached the building, so I decided not to worry about it.

I left my apartment puzzling out the details of my character description.

A twentysomething girl, yearning for a taste of something more, leaving her hometown of Channing's Cross (a town brimming with blow-up lawn decorations for every holiday/season/mundane moment) the day after graduation, hungry for all that life had to offer. Joyful and wide-eyed, she wished for a life big enough to match her dreams. But once she had gotten to the big city, something was missing. A new romance? Career? Lipstick? But in the end, it was the sweet acceptance of the wrong crowd and the floating bliss of drugs that she found. And the never-ending chase for that first taste, that first high, was the only thing that kept her going...

I glanced up, nearing my destination way sooner than I was quite ready for. I figured I'd have the whole walk over to psych myself up, except I got lost in my characterization and, as I neared, I felt very far from ready.

But, like they taught me in the acting class, I took a deep breath and went for it. Three girls loitered outside the building, but none of them were the same ones as the other night, which was good. I didn't think they would recognize me, but I didn't need to be worried about what-ifs either—I had enough chaos and freaking out going on in my mind as it was.

The girls weren't much for chatting and it seemed like none of them really even knew each other so they weren't talking. One by one they were taken inside by the same man I'd seen last night. I'd been worried there was some kind of appointment needed or something, but no one seemed alarmed or even acknowledged that there was an extra girl, so I just stood there and made as little impression as I could.

Some time later, another girl showed up and stood behind me and I marveled that for as weird a situation as this was, it was all very civilized. Everyone was waiting their turn and being very respectful.

I was at the front of the line and nearly peeing myself waiting to see what was going to happen. Twice I almost lost my nerve, ready to take off, but I forced myself to stay, channeling the anxious feeling in my gut into the character I was playing. I imagined that a person in need of a fix would be a little fidgety and whatnot, so that's what I did.

Then the man came. He looked me up and down, his expression completely blank, and took my elbow the way he had done with each of the girls ahead of me. I suddenly realized—too late—that none of the girls who'd gone into the building had come back out. My stomach started to churn. How had I not realized something so significant until the very second it was too late to do anything about it?

Good lord, this detective stuff was a whole different ball game in real life than it was in old-timey sleuth books. Nancy always seemed to have nerves of steel and never got herself into situations she couldn't get out of. Well, she did, but she always found a way out because she was so resourceful.

Surely I was as resourceful as a teenager from the 1930s, given the fact that I had the benefit of having consumed all the mystery books and crime shows, right?

The stairwell was dark but the man at my elbow wasn't rough in the slightest, which put my mind at ease slightly. Maybe these weren't such bad guys after all.

I was led into the room. The same two men sat at the table once again.

"Name?" one of them asked.

"Um…" For some reason I hadn't expected that. How did I not figure that out in my whole character exercise?! "Um, Becky," I answered.

"Okay, Becky, so you're looking to do an exchange of goods and services, correct?"

I couldn't help but think this all seemed rather businesslike. Which was somewhat reassuring. "Um, yes."

"Okay, please take off your jacket and turn around for us."

This part didn't feel quite as businesslike. I took off my jacket and turned slowly but didn't do any ridiculous dance moves like the one girl had the other night.

"Okay, fine," he said, in a matter-of-fact way. "You'll do."

I tried to look relieved, only guessing that's what someone in the situation would feel. "Okay," was all I could spit out.

The man asking the questions nodded to the man who had led me in, and he took my elbow again, leading me to another room in the back.

Which turned out to be a bedroom.

My mouth dropped open as I saw other women, the ones I'd been standing with outside, draped around the room, all seemingly passed out.

Before I could register what might be going on, I felt a pinch in my upper arm and the room began to blur.

# Chapter 12

I knew nothing.

I had no idea where I was. No idea when it was, and only the faintest recollection of how I had gotten the worst headache of my life. Fear slithered through me as things started coming back slowly. Brandt doing my makeup. The hair extensions. Standing outside the building.

Ryan's case. I spent a moment savoring the thought of Ryan. I needed to focus my mind on something good for a second…the way he walked, the way he grinned all crooked and adorable. The way he told me to mind my own business.

Damn.

I was beginning to suspect that I maybe should have listened.

The room was dark, with a faint red glow to it. There

were red curtains in the room. Was the sun trying to fight its way through the curtains? Could I have been out all night and the sun was already shining?

My mind shot to the worst-case scenario. If something unthinkable happened to me, not a soul in my life had any idea where I was. My god, hadn't I been through this already with the walk the other night? I hadn't left a note, a clue, nothing. Some kind of Nancy fan I was supposed to be. If I never came home, no one would ever know what happened to me. Who would ever imagine I was out investigating some random criminal case? Why would I?

I would just…disappear.

I stayed as still as possible, afraid to make any sudden movements. One, I didn't want to draw attention to myself in case someone was watching, and two, I honestly wasn't sure if I might be injured. And maybe three, because I was afraid it would make my head hurt even worse than it already did. Which seemed impossible, but I wasn't particularly anxious to find out.

It hurt a little to even move my eyes, but I needed to get a sense of what was happening. What I was up against.

Shapes started to form in the blood-colored shadows. A table and one chair in the corner and a bed against the far wall, like a hotel room. It was something of a dump and smelled like it hadn't been cleaned since weekly musical sitcoms had been the hot new thing.

I let out a shaky breath. Two other people shared the room with me—one on the bed and one in the other chair. I could only assume they were the same women

I'd seen just before my world went dark. Strange that I would come to first, since they'd obviously been knocked out before I had, but maybe that was because I didn't have any drugs in my system to begin with. I wondered if they were sleeping it off nicely in their haze instead of the excruciating hammering that was gracing me with its presence.

I was somewhat distressed to discover I was duct-taped to a chair. Memories continued slowly sifting back to me. There had been another couple girls behind me in line. Where were they? Were there other rooms in this place where more women were kept?

I wished I knew how long I'd been out. I just felt so discombobulated. Knowing what time it was might help me find my bearings. Maybe. My head hurt so much, and I was fighting a sort of dull dizziness, one that almost let me focus, but not quite. I took a deep breath, which sent a searing pain into my head, but did clear my mind a little.

I had to admit, I sort of wanted to cry. Sure, I'd gotten myself into this to see what would happen once I got inside, but this was way more than I had bargained for. I don't know what I thought would happen. Maybe they'd give me a thumbs-up and tell me a location to go next, which of course I would have staked out before actually going. I sure as hell never imagined being knocked out and tied to a chair. Blood pulsed in my ears as my panic rose.

I took a breath. *Slow down.*

Go back. Back to the beginning of this whole mess. *What would Nancy do?*

Was Nancy a product of a rampantly sexist society? Yes. Was she stopped at every turn—told she should let the big boys handle it? You bet your tea-length shirt-waist dress she was. Did that stop her from solving every gosh darn mystery in town (and sometimes inter-nationally?). Heck no! If Nancy wanted to solve a mystery, she put on her favorite hat, grabbed her best chums and found those clues—in spite of...nay! *Because* of the raging underestimation that society has always had for teenage girls and women in general!

Okay, yes, this was working. Self-preservation was starting to kick in and I suddenly remembered the great thing about duct tape. Once you got it started it was fairly easy to rip. I glanced around for something to try and gouge it with. Sadly, the criminals had been too smart to just leave a pair of scissors or a razor lying around the room.

Jerks.

There did seem to be a bit of a rough edge to the TV stand, from which a TV was mysteriously absent. I couldn't help but wonder if at some point in the past one of the women had woken up and freaked out, smash-ing it to try to free herself. A jagged piece of glass would be quite handy at the moment. But that probably would have resulted in slightly more than the maximum threshold of noise to sneak away undetected.

Which was exactly what I was planning on doing.

I shimmied over to the TV stand, trying to be quiet, but every move I made seemed to be ginormous and echoing. My legs were also bound, each taped to a front chair leg, and the maneuvering was not the easiest thing in the world. Especially considering that my head felt like it had a tiny little boxer in there trying to jab his way out.

Eventually I got myself into a position where I could start rubbing the edge of the tape against the rough part. It was a cheap piece of furniture with that faux-veneer coating over particleboard. Luckily for me, a chunk of that laminate had broken off at the corner, thus making for a nice little edge for my escape.

If all went according to plan.

It took longer than I'd hoped, and I was sweating more than my uncle Jack that time he tried to impress his date by entering an impromptu county fair Macarena contest, which was to say, *quite* a fair amount. That stuff was flinging everywhere. But eventually I wore the bottom of the tape until there was a jagged little slice and I began to wriggle, trying to get my wrists to bend so that the tape would rip more and more. As the rip lengthened, it got easier and soon my arms were free. Exhausted, but free.

And that's when I heard the noise. Someone was coming up the hall.

*Shit.* I wasn't sure if I was making too much noise, getting careless and cocky toward the end of my struggle to get free, but whatever the reason, someone was coming.

I shimmy-hobbled (shobbled?) back to the spot I'd been sitting when I woke up and sat myself and my chair down as quietly as I could, sticking my hands behind my back again the way they'd been before. I could only hope the long strand of tape still hanging from my wrist wasn't obvious. I hung my head as if I was still passed out, which was actually kind of a relief for my neck.

The door opened. I tried to breathe as slowly and quietly as I could, hoping I could fake the relaxed state of someone sleeping, but the way my pulse was racing, and with how badly I wanted to take a peek, it was not the easiest task. But the stakes were too high to fail, so I sat, head flopped like the actress I had been trained to be (thank you, Intro to Dramatic Performance 101).

I guessed the person at the door was a man, both because of the heaviness of the footsteps and the fact that it didn't seem too likely that many women would be involved in this type of crime. When he grabbed me by my hair and lifted my head up, it was confirmed—not only by the size of the hand, but also the stench of way too much cologne. I'd never relaxed into anything more in my life, letting my head flop back down lifelessly when he rudely let my hair go again. I mean, I certainly hoped it looked lifeless. I honestly wasn't sure how to act something like that other than being as floppy as possible. It was all I could do not to contort my face in pain as the tiny boxer in my head decided to switch to kickboxing during all the commotion. The floppy act seemed to do the trick and the man moved to the other girls, giving them the same treatment of making sure they were still passed out. They each passed the test, of course.

The entire time, all I could think about was the tape stuck to my arm and how I was immensely thankful that it was so dark in there, but even still, it seemed impossible that I hadn't been found out.

Soon the door shut again and all I could hear was the heavy breathing coming from the other girls in the room.

I couldn't risk any more noise, but I knew I had to work quickly. I had to get out of that room. I moved to untape my legs, peeling it this time instead of ripping, thinking this might be quieter, but I was very, very mistaken. The sound was somewhat similar to an alley cat brawl. I tried to rip it, but without something to make it jagged, it was totally impossible. I'd seen people use their teeth to get it started before, but that was going to be a bit difficult. I wasn't the least flexible person in the world, but I certainly wasn't the most, either.

So peeling it was. I was forced to go painfully slowly, wondering what my chances were if I were to just rip it fast and loud to still make it out of that room in one piece. Except... I didn't actually have a plan to get out of the room, so I pulled, one painful millimeter at a time, wondering how long it was actually taking and if it was anywhere near what it felt like. After about five hours, or probably a few minutes in real time, I finally got both legs free.

I stood quickly, got a giant head rush (the boxer was really going at it) and sat back down, using all my focus not to make a huge noise when I hit the chair again. I took a few deep breaths and the dizziness passed quickly. In maybe ten seconds I was back up again, searching for a way out.

There were two obvious choices—the door that the man had come through to check on us, and a single window. I quickly peeked out the curtain.

Still night.

I figured darkness was my friend at that point, so that was good—the window, however, was old and looked like it might be hard to open.

But I couldn't think of any other way. I opened the curtains wide to get a better look at what I was dealing with. At this point if someone came in, I was screwed no matter what. I had to chance it and hope I could outrun them if they did come in.

The first thing I noticed was that the window faced the same alley I'd been sitting in just the other night, watching this horrible place so innocently. The second thing I noticed was that there was a balcony—thank goodness, it might have been a deal-breaker if there hadn't been one—and third, I also noticed that I was not the first person who had tried to escape this way; the lock was obviously tampered with. The thing was old and the windows had obviously gotten damp over the years, so the locking mechanism rusted over like it hadn't been maintained at all since it was installed. The real problem though was that it looked like the window itself might be painted shut. Not that I was going to give up.

I pushed up on the wooden crossbar. It didn't budge. Like, at all. I pushed harder, starting to get worried that I was going to have to break the glass. Which would certainly solve my immediate problem, though that pesky little problem of the noise would bring me an even bigger—and more deadly—problem.

I sighed.

I needed something to scrape the creases of the paint.

Something thin and sharp. I wished I had worn some sort of a ring or sharp pendant or something, but I had specifically left anything that might allow someone to remember me, and later identify me, at home.

I thought I was being so smart.

I turned and surveyed the room, my hands moving to my hips, which they always seemed to do when I was in thinking mode. Writer friends always looked at me funny when I sat at the table at the coffee shop, super rigid posture with my hands on my hips. I don't know what it was—it just helped me think.

Thankfully, it worked. If I could get another piece of that laminate to break off the TV stand, it would be sharp and hopefully strong enough to get the job done. I moved as stealthily as I could, setting my feet carefully, walking on my toes, back over to the stand.

I couldn't have asked for a better situation. Because of all the rubbing I'd already done, I'd actually ended up loosening one of the broken edges. I grabbed the loose piece and, putting my hand over the spot I wanted it to break to try to dampen the sound, I pulled until I felt the snap.

Then I froze, listening for any movement in the hall and desperately praying to any god who would listen to keep them away just a while longer.

No one came.

I scurried back over to the window and began to scrape as quietly and quickly as I could, stopping to listen every now and again. There wasn't a whole lot I could do if someone came, but I couldn't help myself.

This part didn't actually take as long as I thought it

might—that piece of laminate was really quite sharp—
and soon I was able to move the window ever so slightly.
Remembering back when I'd been at my grandma's old
house when I was little, I pressed on either side of the
wood frame as hard as I could, with all my weight behind it. I did this a few times in various spots up and
down the frame, which loosened it even more.

I wondered how long it had been since this room
had felt fresh air. It had to be decades.

Slowly, so slowly, the window started to give a little. Then a little more. Soon I had it open about a foot,
maybe a bit more, and decided to risk it, thinking there
was a good chance I would fit through.

I squeezed one leg through, then realized I'd have
to go both feet first, like I was in some sort of limbo
contest or something. The legs went through without
much problem, then my butt, although I had to shimmy
a little to get that through, then I was out up to my
chest and was thankful for the first time in my life to
be relatively flat-chested. It got a little awkward trying to balance myself, my abs shaking from the weird
angles that I was holding myself at, but soon it was just
my head, the window looming above my neck like a
guillotine. I turned my head sideways, scraping one
ear as I tried to rush through.

But I didn't care.

I was out on the balcony, and I was free.

In an act of utter foolishness, I decided to take one
last look back through the window, my gaze landing
on a pair of icy blue eyes with a very angry-looking
dude attached, charging through the doorway. I turned

and pushed the fire escape down as fast as I could, not worrying about noise anymore. Thankfully the window slowed him down too—he was much bigger than me—and my foot touched the ground just as he was making his way out onto the balcony.

I ran.

I didn't really pay too much attention to what direction I was going. My only focus was to get away. I don't know if he even chased me. Maybe they didn't really care about some junkie who'd decided to change her mind and get the hell out of Dodge. Or maybe they did.

I had no idea.

All I knew was that I had to run as fast as I could as far as I could, which I think might have been pretty far considering the adrenaline pulsing through me, until eventually I fell into a heap, somehow ending up down by the river that meandered through the city. I lay there for a while, more than happy to be alone, even if it was in the middle of the night and in a place I didn't particularly know.

I was free. And I was safe, relatively speaking. And I knew that once I regained a little of my strength, I'd be able to follow the walking trails that lined the river until I found something that looked familiar.

I made it back to my apartment just as the sun was peeking over the horizon, more exhausted than I'd ever been in my life. Also starving, given that I couldn't even remember how long it had been since I'd had any vital nutrients like protein or vitamins or Chocolatey Fudge Pop-Tarts.

# Chapter 13

After a long shower, made more complicated by the hair extensions, I fell into bed. I was worried the countless disastrous catastrophes that could have taken place during my escape would have sent me straight to my old friend, the Hamster Wheel of Thoughts, but I was asleep the second my head hit the pillow.

I was so dead to the world that I may have never woken up if it hadn't been for the incessant pounding on my apartment door. The noise came to me as if in a dream, but eventually my brain stumbled out of its comatose state long enough to realize I wasn't in my usual recurring dream of stealing an old-timey train (don't ask) and that the knock was real.

I got out of bed slowly—I had never been one to wake up in a jolt—and made my way to the door, forgetting to notice what I was wearing, or to be in any way alarmed that someone had gotten into my building and was now pounding on my door. It would take several more minutes, or at least a cup of coffee, for my recently slumbering brain to arrive at that train (see what I did there?) of thought.

I opened the door.

"What?" I asked, annoyed, with my eyes still half-closed.

"What are you doing?!" Vic asked, seemingly very, very angry, or at least exasperated.

"What?" I managed to get out, trying to melt the frost from the windowpanes of my brain.

"Why haven't you been answering your phone? I've been calling for hours. You've never not answered your phone for that long. Like, ever."

Even for me this was a little ridiculous. Was this what it was like to be drugged? I hadn't noticed it so much last night during my escape, but could there still be traces of something in me? You'd think I would have run it out of me, but I didn't really know about these sorts of things. I made a mental note to look into it—if not for personal interest, then it might be useful for my writing.

"What time is it?" I mumbled, my brain still struggling to catch up.

"It's four in the afternoon," Vic said, apparently noticing my pajamas.

"Obviously you've just woken up, but…were you still sleeping from last night?"

"I had kind of a late night," I said, finding my sofa and sprawling on it, my eyes drooping shut.

"Kind of a late night? I'd say so. Brandt said you were in some sort of play or something. How come I didn't know anything about this?"

As if on cue, the buzzer rang.

"Oh yeah, how did you get into the building?" I asked. "Didn't you have to buzz?"

"Annie let me in. She was down in the lobby like always and knows I'm your friend. She's worried about you too."

"You talked to her about me?" I said, not sure how I felt about that.

"We talk about lots of stuff. But obviously I asked her if she'd seen you today. She could tell that I was frantic. I think I might have worried her."

"Can you get the buzzer? I'm just really sleepy right now," I said, just wanting the thing to shut up.

"It's Brandt," she said, opening the apartment door a crack so he could come on in.

There was something about safety that twigged in my memory, like the door probably shouldn't just be left open like that, but I couldn't quite remember why it was so important. I let my eyes close again.

"I'm going to make some coffee," Vic said. "What the hell is wrong with you, anyway?"

"I don't know. Something. Maybe I'm sick."

"You don't look sick," she said. "Just tired."

I tried to mumble something in reply, but even I didn't know what it was.

When I woke again, Brandt and Vic were whisper-fighting on the other side of the room.

"Well, you were the one who got her all excited about

going out to do this stupid play," Vic was saying. She sounded even more angry than she usually did when she talked to Brandt.

"How the hell was I supposed to know she'd go out and get all hammered or whatever this is?"

"Why didn't you go with her?"

"Why would I go with her? She didn't ask me to. It seemed like a private thing. Besides, I had other stuff to do. Why would I go to some stupid play?"

"Um, because your friend was starring in it, apparently."

"She was not starring in it. She said she was like, a bit part or something. I don't know."

"Right. Of course you don't know, because it's not like you actually listen to anything anyone says." Vic was really getting on a roll now.

"Guys," I said.

But they just kept on, like they hadn't heard a thing.

"If she wanted us to be there, she would have told us to be there," Brandt was saying.

"Guys," I said, louder this time.

Vic stopped midword and came over to me.

"Are you okay? Did you like, do drugs or something?" She handed me a cup of coffee, still hot.

"Um, not exactly," I said. "I don't think." I mumbled the last bit into my coffee.

"Wait. Did you just say you don't think?" Vic said, turning to look at me, her expression exasperated.

I nodded, the coffee suddenly very, very interesting. And since it was the first thing I'd put in my body since supper last night, it was also very, very welcome and delicious. *Wait...except... Pop-Tarts? Was there something about Pop-Tarts?*

"What the hell kind of play was this?" Brandt asked.

He must have already known he was going to be in trouble with Vic, but I had a sense that wasn't where his worry actually ended. It was like he almost cared, which made me feel pretty loved, since Brandt did not show that sort of thing easily or often.

But then I felt even more terrible, since, you know, I'd totally put myself into a giant heap of trouble and didn't even let anybody know where I was going or what I was doing.

I sighed.

"I wasn't in a play." I said, staring aggressively at that beautiful cup of coffee.

"Well, what a shocker," Vic said, obviously a little suspicious the whole time.

Brandt, on the other hand, looked downright hurt, like he couldn't quite believe I had used him like that. Which was a totally fair point. I felt like I wanted to puke, and it had nothing to do with any aftereffects of drugs that might still be in my system.

I could tell they both wanted to yell at me, but they just sat staring instead. Which might have been worse. I tried to think of a way to tell them what happened without freaking them out more than they already were, but I couldn't think of a single way to phrase *I voluntarily went to a place known for its shady connections and then got drugged and, you know, held against my will* that sounded adequate. Or smart. Or like I hadn't just announced I had no regard whatsoever for my personal safety.

So I just decided to tell the story from the start, hoping they would at least understand my thought process while I was in the thick of it. Maybe, if I was lucky, they'd be so impressed by my dazzling escape they would completely forget I'd put myself into the horrible situation in the first place.

Unfortunately, that little detail seemed to be stuck in the forefront of both of their minds.

"Are you kidding me, Petra?" Brandt said.

I was fairly certain it was a rhetorical question and there was no right way to answer it, so I kept my mouth shut.

Vic was pacing. Every so often, she'd turn and open her mouth to say something, then change her mind and start pacing again.

I sipped my coffee at a weirdly constant speed until it was gone—way too soon—then wondered if I should just keep pretending there was still coffee in there and fake drink it or what. I certainly couldn't put the cup down; it had become my only shield.

And then, as they tended to do, Brandt and Vic started screaming at each other.

"If you wouldn't have done the makeover, none of this would have happened!" Vic yelled.

"Are you kidding me right now?" Brandt retorted. "Like I'm her damned keeper or something? If Petra wants to lie to us and then go out there and practically get herself killed, that is not on me."

This went on for a while. I wanted to stop them, but

my headache was coming back with a vengeance and I could barely concentrate. Then, as they were sort of winding down and looking like maybe they were finally going to get to yelling at me instead of each other, my buzzer went off.

Everybody froze.

Brandt looked sick, clutching at the arms of the chair he was sitting in. "They found you. What if they found you?" To say he looked panicked would be a wee understatement.

"Holy shit," Vic said, her eyes going wide.

"Guys, I'm sure it's not the—" I had no idea what to call the men who'd had me tied up "—um, bad guys."

Brandt snorted. "Bad guys. Jesus." He raked both hands through his hair as he got up and paced.

"But what if it is?" Vic asked, not really making me feel any better. "If you were drugged, I doubt you would know if someone was following you."

"Look, I was really careful. I took every precaution I've ever learned from all the classes I've taken. You know, the detective course and all the self-defense ones. I remember being very conscious about it. I can't see how they would know where I was."

"Okay, okay. Let's just not answer the buzzer," Vic said. "They won't be able to get into the building. We'll be safe up here."

I smiled.

"What the hell is there to smile about?" she asked.

"It's just that...you said 'we.' Like we're in this together."

She rolled her eyes. "Well, to be honest, I wish right

now that I wasn't your friend since you're so determined to put yourself in danger, but you know as well as I do that we're always all in it together."

Brandt looked up at Vic, almost like she'd said something completely profound, which to me it kinda was. I just didn't think Brandt would have felt the same.

It was a lovely moment.

Until a very loud, very urgent knock sounded at the door.

Brandt squealed in a very unmanly way and Vic clutched at my arm. "They found us," she whispered, shaking a little.

Or maybe it was me that was doing the shaking. It was kind of hard to tell.

None of us moved.

"Delivery for Petra Jackson!" a voice came from the other side of the door.

"Are you expecting a package?" Vic asked, still digging her fingernails into my skin like she was trying to permanently fuse us or something.

I started to pull one claw at a time from my arm. "Not that I can think of, but I'm sure it's no big deal. This is a secure building—people can't get in or out unless they're a delivery guy," I finished as I started toward the door.

"Or masquerading as a delivery guy," Vic said.

My arm froze halfway to the door. I peeked through the peephole instead, only to find a bored-looking dude with a massive arrangement of flowers.

*Flowers?*

I turned back to my friends and stage-whispered, "He has flowers."

"Behind which he's probably hiding a revolver or something."

I closed my eyes and sighed. My friends really could lean toward the dramatic end of the spectrum when they wanted to. Unfortunately, they were also successful in amping up my paranoia.

"Um," I yelled. "Could you just leave them by the door?"

I peeked through the door again to see the guy roll his eyes and give a little shrug before he set them down and wandered off down the hall, the annoyance showing in his stride. I suppose he had been hoping for a tip, which I gladly would have given him if I hadn't, you know, been afraid for my life. Maybe I could phone the shop and give them one over the phone.

I heard the faint ding of the elevator, then waited a few seconds longer, just to make sure he was gone. When I opened the door, I popped my head out before the rest of me to make sure the coast was clear.

"This girl has absolutely no self-preservation skills," I heard Brandt whisper to Vic, which was annoying since I was totally taking precautions the way they'd taught in my ALERT: Awareness Leads to Evasion of Risks and Trauma training class.

Since the delivery guy had really left—and wasn't hiding around the corner with a deadly weapon as my friends would have me believe—I grabbed the flowers, shutting and locking the door behind me.

"You seriously just brought those in here without

a second thought, didn't you?" Brandt said, shaking his head.

"Um, they're flowers," I said, making sure to give the word *flowers* an extra sassy inflection to drive my point home.

"How do you know there's not some kind of poison gas that's going to start leaking out of the paper wrapping or something?" he asked, as if that were the most normal thought in the world.

I sighed, heading to the kitchen for a vase. Of course, I was intercepted by Vic about five steps from my destination. I thought she was going to make me throw them back out in the hall or something, but she simply snatched the card right out from under my nose, ripping the envelope open as if it wasn't a felony to open someone else's mail or, in this case, package.

"'From your anonymous admirer,'" Vic read aloud.

"Anonymous," Brandt said, his eye going comically wide. "What the hell is that supposed to mean?"

"It's nothing," I said, heading for the kitchen again. "I got another one of these—some chocolates—the other day. It's just a fan or something."

Miraculously, the two of them left me in peace for the two minutes it took to climb up on a chair and grab the vase from the top shelf of my cupboard. But I soon discovered they were not about to let me off the hook that easily. As I stepped back into the living room carrying the vase, which I thought would look quite nice on the coffee table, they stopped their frantic whispering to each other and both turned to stare.

Vic cleared her throat. "So, let me get this straight.

You've now received two anonymous gifts from a stranger—in your secure building—*and* you are currently wanted by some evil bad guys. And you don't think this is a big deal at all?"

I shrugged. I mean, of course I was a little...jarred by the whole thing, but it was chocolate and flowers... What could be more innocent than chocolate and flowers? After my book had been released, I'd received dozens of gifts like this from fans. Maybe I should have been a little more worried, but frankly, I liked chocolate and flowers, and they both just seemed so...innocuous. "I don't know. I'm guessing my publisher is forwarding them to me or something," I said.

"Okay, so how about you phone them up and see?" Vic said, and the way she set her shoulders I could tell she was not going to let this one go.

I mean, there was a little twig of worry in the back of my mind. But didn't other people sweep those twigs into the back of their minds hoping to never think of them again like I did?

Sadly, the looks on Vic's and Brandt's faces seemed to point to not so much.

I let out a long, annoyed sigh and pulled out my phone.

But as I started scrolling through my contacts, the pounding started again. Since we were already at the most precarious of edges, we all pretty much shot straight out of our skin.

"Oh god, the delivery guy came back to finish us off!" Brandt said.

I gave him a look. "When did he start us off?" Somehow, Brandt didn't seem to find my question funny.

The pounding on the door continued. "Come on, Petra, I know you're in there!"

We all breathed a collective sigh of relief. It was just poor, harmless Johnny. Well, mostly harmless, anyway.

Brandt still clutched at his heart, like there was an invisible string of pearls holding his hand there, and Vic let out a slow, whooshing breath, trying to calm herself from her approximately sixty-foot jump in the air. I moved toward the door.

"Are you sure you want to do that?" Vic asked, flopping onto the couch beside Brandt, looking a little spent.

"Well, I guess I should figure out how he found me," I said, deciding not to add, *So that I can determine how hard that might be, since, you know...bad guys.*

I took a deep breath and opened the door. "Hey, Johnny."

"Petra! I knew you had to be here."

"Indeed," I said, my tone a little chilly.

I couldn't help but notice he had a rather large duffel bag in tow. I made myself a promise then and there that he was absolutely not going to be staying the night. No way, no how. I was over this guy.

Unfortunately, I also knew how hopeless he was and how he probably didn't have anywhere else to go either. But I wasn't going to do it. Johnny was not my problem anymore. And in fact, now that I thought about it, no guy ever should be. If I met someone great... I mean, not that I had anyone specific in mind, and it was pure accident that I glanced across the hall toward a certain neighbor's door, but whoever I dated next was going to be able to take care of his own damned self.

"You going to invite me in, or what?" Johnny asked, flashing that famously Petra-melting smile.

I sighed and moved out of the doorway, motioning for him to come in. *If you have to*, was the general vibe I was trying to project.

Brandt and Vic both stood, giving the place an even more unwelcoming aura.

"Oh, uh. Hey, guys," Johnny said, his smile faltering a little.

He knew as well as I did that Vic and Brandt had been instrumental in helping me find the strength to get away from him in the first place. I mean, I would have been able to do it eventually, but they probably saved me a ton of time and most likely a lot of money too. The guy was a leech. It was just too bad he knew it and I knew it and everybody knew it, and yet he still found a way to get to me.

"How did you find me, Johnny?"

He dropped his huge bag near the entrance to the hallway and came over to sit across from my friends. *Subtle, Johnny, real subtle*, I thought, but was more determined than ever not to let him stay. Wanting to send a clear message, I picked the bag up and hauled it back over near the front door. Johnny made a bit of a pouty face, but then smiled and turned back to Vic and Brandt.

"So, have you guys been good?"

Vic was shooting a death glare that would have made most men faint, but Johnny was well versed in people disliking his presence, so he seemed to shake it right off.

"Johnny, how did you find me?" I asked again, sitting in the other chair, wishing it was farther away from him.

"Oh, you know," he said, waving his hand. "I just did a little asking around."

"Who did you ask?" I demanded.

He looked a little taken aback. "You know, a few people."

"Johnny, you better tell me right now *exactly* how you found me. I am not in any way finding this amusing, or in a mood to be given the runaround."

In a bit of excellent timing that was out of character, Brandt leaned forward and crossed his arms, his giant biceps looking even more menacing.

"Um…" Johnny stuttered, "I, uh, after I saw you guys at brunch, I figured you must still be sorta close to the neighborhood, so I started looking around at some of the classes in the area, 'cause I know how much you like your classes," he said, his voice picking up speed, "and then I just kind of made friends with some of the people who worked at some of the community centers."

I narrowed my gaze. "So you flirted with the poor girls who were on shift until you could scam your way into finding me on one of the registration forms."

"Geez, what did you do, man, hack the computer?" Even Brandt looked scandalized.

Johnny shrugged. "I was just being resourceful."

I sighed. "Well, I guess that's good."

Johnny's face lit up and he started to smile.

"No," I said, putting my hand up. "Not good for you—you're still in my bad books—but at least the other bad guys probably won't be able to find me the same way," I said, turning to Brandt and Vic. "It's not like they know my name or anything."

"Bad guys?" Johnny asked. "What bad guys?"

"Never mind," Brandt said, standing. "It's time to go now."

"Well, it sure was great to see you," Johnny said, leaning back and putting his hands behind his head, settling in and getting comfy.

"Oh no, you don't—you're the one who's leaving," Vic said, grabbing him a bit more forcefully than was absolutely necessary, dragging him up out of the chair.

"But I haven't even gotten to talk to Petra yet," he whined.

"We have nothing to talk about, Johnny," I said. "I just wanted to know how you found me. And now you can forget that you did."

"Don't even think of coming back," Brandt added. "Ever."

"But, Petra…" Johnny turned to me, looking like he was in shock.

It was totally an act, but I could feel myself starting to falter. He was just so helpless and I always had so much trouble watching someone in distress.

"Come on," Vic said, draping the duffel bag handle over Johnny's shoulder, nearly knocking him over.

"Do not let him back in," Brandt mumbled as he passed me.

"Of course I won't," I said. And I meant it. If he was out of my sight, that puppy-dog pout gone, I knew I'd be okay. Johnny was toxic and I was not interested in living in that environment again—and it had been toxic, very toxic, even before I found out he cheated on me.

I was actually starting to get a little annoyed that he'd even tried to knock on my door again. I mean, who did he think he was? More importantly, who did he think I was? Someone who was part of whatever world he thought owed him a favor.

No.

I was finished.

And thankfully, I had a couple of great friends to back me up. I didn't even wince as Brandt gave Johnny an earnest little shove out the door before he closed it with a firmness that wasn't quite a slam, but definitely sent a message. "That should stop him from sending the stupid little gifts," he said, wiping his hands, as if ridding himself of the entire situation.

"Oh my god, you're right," Vic said. "It probably was that little weasel that sent them."

"Oh probably," I said, though as hard as I tried, I couldn't stop a little shivery twinge from shuddering through my stomach, because I was fairly sure if the flowers had been from Johnny, there'd be no way he'd leave without making sure he'd been given full credit for his generosity.

# Chapter 14

I was going stir-crazy. We're talking straight-up cabin fever. Fidgety. Antsy. Fantsy, as it were. I hadn't left the house in two days and couldn't stand being stuck for even one day. I needed excitement, I needed people... I needed the hell out.

But Vic would have my head if she found out I was out and about on the streets. Brandt and I tried to convince her that my disguise had been a good one and that none of the thugs (what Brandt had taken to calling them) would ever recognize me, but Vic was adamant. The stupid investigation class had taught us to stay indoors with the curtains shut for at least a week if you thought your cover was blown or if you were in any sort of danger, so that's what I had foolishly promised her I would do. She vowed to de-friend me due to her high stress levels if I didn't "at the very least" (her words) do this for her.

So I promised. And I was totally keeping my promise too, even though I was sure she wouldn't have approved of the fact that I was sitting in the lobby chatting it up with Annie.

"You've been around here a lot lately," Annie mused.

Fair, since I'd been sitting with her practically every waking minute and she'd probably had it up to her peacock-feather fascinator hat with me intruding on her space.

"I know, sorry. Just let me know if I'm bugging you too much. I'm just, um, laying low. Ex-boyfriend issues. You know how it is."

"Boy, do I," she said, chuckling and shaking her head. "I have been there. And you are certainly not bugging me. I like the company."

Truth be told, even with the literal feather in her cap, Annie was still not herself. She wasn't as chatty, spending much of her time sort of staring into space, no doubt thinking about Erica and how unfair the whole situation was. Especially since I knew she was still skeptical about the police's suicide theory.

"Okay, good," I said. "You're like an icon in this city—people want to come through and visit with you, not me."

"An icon!" Annie said, delighted. "Well, that would be something, wouldn't it?" She was laughing, but still looked pretty pleased.

"You are," I insisted. "It's an honor to even live in the same building as you do."

She swatted my hand. "Well, you're exaggerating," she said, "but thank you. You do know how to make an old woman feel good about herself."

"If there is anything you are not, it's old," I assured her.

She smiled again. "You flatter me too much."

I shrugged. "Just saying what's true."

"I guess age is just a number," she said. "Honestly, I don't feel any older than I did when I was thirty."

"And why should you?"

"True enough," she said. "True enough."

We settled into a comfortable silence. Since I was down visiting so much, we'd pretty much covered every topic imaginable, but found we were pretty comfortable with each other just sitting and chilling too. It was a kind of lovely relief not to have to constantly worry about what to say next (someone tell my nonexistent manuscript, please).

After a while though, Annie announced she had an idea.

"I feel like I need to do something. Maybe we can plan a little get-together? Something to celebrate Erica." She perked up at the idea. "We should do it this weekend."

"I'm not sure I should leave the building for a little while longer."

"That's what I mean—you won't have to leave the building. We'll do it on the roof."

"We have a roof?" I shook my head. "I mean, obviously we have a roof—every building has a roof—but we have a roof that you can have a party on?"

"Have you really never been up there?" Annie asked, shocked. "Oh, it's beautiful. You can see half the city up there. Didn't you get a tour of the building when you viewed it?"

I shrugged. "I just sent the deposit in without even seeing the place. I was kind of desperate to get out of my old place."

She nodded. "The guy, right?"

"How did you guess?" I said, shooting her a crooked smile.

Annie stood. "Well, let's go," she said, already headed for the elevator. "You are in for a treat."

It turned out Annie was not exaggerating. I couldn't believe I hadn't discovered this wonderful sanctum before. It was gorgeous. There were outdoor couches and rugs and tables and everything you'd ever need to relax. And the view was unbelievable. You could see half the city and all the way down the river.

"And don't worry about the cold," Annie said. "All those tall metal things are heaters and this place really gets quite comfortable, even when it's chilly out."

"It's amazing," I said.

I was already having all sorts of gatherings in my mind, especially summer ones. The barbecues were especially intriguing. I'd always wanted to take the Learn to Grill Like a Pit Boss class down at the community center, and now I had the perfect excuse to go ahead and sign up.

Of course, thinking about classes made me think of Johnny, which was super irritating, but what was I going to do? Not go to any more classes? Inconceivable.

"So, let's do it tomorrow," Annie said, excited.

"Tomorrow? Isn't that kind of short notice?"

Annie shrugged. "We live in an apartment building with over a hundred units. I realize people love to make plans these days, but surely we could find a handful of people to come out. It doesn't have to be big. The smaller the better, actually. More intimate. More opportunities to get to know a few of the neighbors."

"I thought you already knew all the neighbors."

Annie grinned. "Most of them. I'm sure there are a few newcomers I haven't met yet," she said with a wink.

And if there was anyone who could pull off a wink without looking ridiculous, it was Annie. In fact, it made her even more charming somehow.

"It's so great of you to do this, Annie," I said, already excited for tomorrow night. "I hope it's not a lot of work."

She shrugged. "No work at all. I'll put up a poster in each of the elevators, we'll make it bring your own booze. I'll whip up a few appetizers, and voilà! Party on the roof!"

Honestly, the woman was incredible. I had never left a conversation with Annie where I hadn't felt better when I walked away than when I'd said hello.

The next day was taking longer than a sloth's dive into Ativan, so I decided to make a bit of food for the party too. I couldn't go out for ingredients, so I had to make do with what I had in the pantry. That meant a no-go on a fancy appetizer, but I was able to whip up a pan of my favorite puffed wheat cake. I mean, I know puffed wheat cake is more of a kiddie snack, but I swear, it was impossible to pass up, probably because the chocolatey, sticky goodness took me straight back to my childhood.

I decided to head up to the roof a little early with my puffed wheat cake and a bottle of wine in tow, trying to decide if I was the world's most juvenile party guest ever, or if I had just discovered the world's best new breakup ritual. I almost wanted to get dumped just to see.

In the elevator, I admired Annie's poster, which was adorned with glitter glue and colorful stickers. I should have known Annie was not one to half-ass anything— not even a simple poster. And it certainly got the point across. If I hadn't known about the party already, there was no way I would have wanted to miss it.

As I pushed through the roof door, I was not surprised that Annie had absolutely outdone herself again. She'd somehow made a flurry of streamers look less graduation circa 1993 and more classy chic, and had bouquets of tasteful balloons in the corners, making the space seem even more intimate than before. It was a little chilly, so I spent about ten minutes mulling over the idea of turning the heaters on. This required quite a lengthy assessment since I felt like any adult-like person should be able to do that sort of thing, but also machines that spewed gas generally shot waves of terror through me. I considered the approximately 3,683 catastrophic scenarios that could happen with a misfire. But after visualizing the entire building imploding, I put my scaredy pants away and gave it a shot.

Turned out they were easy to run, really, just a simple dial to turn them to the appropriate temperature, and a button to light them. I set them all fairly low, figuring I could always turn up the temperature later if it wasn't warm enough.

I relocated my puffed wheat cake from a chair to a more sensible empty table, which looked like the perfect place for a food area, and sneaked behind the bar in search of a corkscrew. There wasn't a ton of stuff back there, but it had all the basics a good bar should have, and I quickly opened my wine, realizing I hadn't thought to bring up a glass. Fortunately, the bar had glasses and even a dishwasher for easy cleanup at the end of the night.

I settled under one of the heat lamps, wine in hand, feeling more relaxed than I had in days. A few other folks decided to come up a little early too, and I had a nice chat with a couple from the twelfth floor whose guacamole-and-salsa platter made my puffed wheat cake look like it belonged at a toddler's bouncy castle birthday. But the woman, Ella, squealed when she saw it.

"It has been so long since I've had this," she said, digging out a piece. "I used to love it so much."

"Me too!" I smiled.

Soon Annie arrived, bringing the largest platter of puff pastry appetizers I had ever seen.

"Have you been cooking all day?" I asked.

"Oh goodness, no," she said. "The only cooking I do is the shortcut way. I made these with ready-to-bake pastry and a few other simple ingredients. Took me twenty minutes."

I couldn't help but feel a little like my twenty minutes of cooking was a bit uninspired compared to Annie's. Although I supposed she did have several decades of entertaining experience on me. I vowed that the best thing I could do for myself was try to learn from the master. Maybe in forty years I would be the charming older lady that people made a point to stop and visit, though at that moment I felt more like a wobbly baby platypus. Parties, amirite?

Luckily, everyone in the building was so nice and quite a few people made the trek up. The food table was full, with some dishes even overflowing onto the bar. It had been a while since I'd eaten anything other than takeout, so I indulged way more than was necessary.

I couldn't help but think we should try to make this a monthly affair. Maybe I'd even find someone in the building to go to a class with, or maybe just coffee. How had I not thought of this before? Of course, no building I'd ever lived in had a handy-dandy entertaining space ready to go like that, which was a pretty big part of what made it so easy to put together.

"I'm so glad we decided to do this," a voice came from behind me.

I turned to see Eliza, sipping on a complicated-looking drink with both a maraschino cherry and what looked like a dried hot pepper of some sort sticking out of it. I wasn't quite sure what she meant by *we*, but I supposed she just wanted to be a part of a community, which, after all, was the whole point of the gathering.

"Oh, hi, Eliza," I said, sipping my wine.

She was, as always, very put together in her jeans/blazer combo with all the right accessories and hair looking like she had just left the salon.

"So how is the book coming along?" she said, glancing around behind me.

This was a move I was familiar with. I tended to be approachable or nonthreatening or something, because people would often use me as their "conversation buddy" until someone more interesting came along.

"Um, yeah, it's good," I lied. I certainly wasn't going to confide in Eliza of all people that I had absolutely no mystery for my heroine to stumble into.

"That's great," she said, suddenly spotting someone superior behind me. "Oh, there's Axel," she said, already stepping away. "Great chatting with you."

She was off before I could say, *Yeah, you too.* Not that I was complaining. After the weird conversation about her wildly traditional values earlier, I honestly wasn't sure we had a single thing in common.

Annie made her rounds across the rooftop, eyes sparkling more with each new person she talked to. She put everyone at ease, making them all feel like the most special person in the room. She flitted over to a couple leaning on the railing close to the entrance to the roof, where the door was opening.

My breath caught. I hadn't imagined that he'd come. Although, by the way Annie beelined straight for him, I had the sneaking suspicion she'd invited him personally. I also couldn't help but notice how she sneaked a quick glance my way before motioning him toward the food and the bar.

Ryan's glance followed hers and our eyes met for the briefest of moments, making my heart do a kind of whirligig sort of thing. Which was ridiculous. What was I, some love-struck teenager in the eighth grade? My first instinct was to find somewhere to hide—my nerves cracking like a glass case in the climax of a heist mystery. Instead, I found a place to sit alone, you know, just to see if he might stop over to say hi.

Immediately after I sat, I silently scolded myself over how passive-aggressive I was being with such a loser move, but it was too late to stand back up without looking ridiculous. And so I sat, nursing my glass of wine as if it were my lifeline, which, in the moment, I kind of felt like it was. Unfortunately, all the situation did was make me drink faster than normal and before I knew it my glass was half-gone. And since I did not particularly want to make a drunken-schoolgirl impression on all my new neighbors in a building I was beginning to adore more each day, the next sip I took was a very, very small one.

But then I started getting quite bored. And when I was bored, my thoughts usually leaped around wildly like an unattended toddler after scarfing a family-sized bag of cotton candy. Soon those thoughts were bounding into Ryan's case, spinning through ideas of what might have happened to the poor girls that had been in the room with me.

"Something troubling you?" a sexy voice asked.

My stomach tensed and I set my wine down reflexively on the nearest surface, a rustic tiled coffee table in front of me. By some miracle it just wobbled a bit on the edge of the grout and didn't come crashing down.

"Uh, no, not really," I said. "Just daydreaming, I guess." Somehow, I managed a smile.

He sat down. Which was good, but I instantly felt bad that I hadn't invited him to sit, which probably would have been the polite thing to do, right? Ruminating about that, then wondering if it had been the rudest thing he'd ever witnessed, I made an even bigger idiot of myself by not paying attention to what he was saying.

I blinked. "Sorry, what?"

He laughed. "I just said that must be a hazard of the job."

I tilted my head, confused.

"You know, the daydreaming. Being a writer, I imagine you're probably always dreaming new stuff up." He paused. "For your stories?"

Leave it to me to transform a nice normal situation into its most awkward possible iteration. "Um, right! The daydreaming. Ha-ha. Yes, definitely part of the job," I said, pretty much sputtering the whole thing out.

Why was it so incredibly hard to impress the people you wanted to most? I mean, not that I needed to impress anyone, but if there *was* one person I'd hoped to dazzle, he was sitting directly beside me. So close, in fact, that it suddenly felt a lot warmer since he'd sat down. Although that totally might have been because of the mortifiery (aka flaming-hot blushing) over how ridiculous I was.

My mind spun with things that might be good conversation starters, but every thought seemed to be more ludicrous than the last. My classes? No, he already knew about those. My job? No, we'd covered that, lord help me. His job? Hell no! Way too volatile.

I cleared my throat, successfully bringing even more attention to the awkward silence we had been experiencing for way too long already.

Finally, I gave up and just grabbed my glass of wine.

"Jesus!" he yelled.

I froze. "What?"

He grabbed my hand, pulling it closer to him. If I hadn't been so taken off guard, I might have even been excited by the sudden physical contact, but by the look on his face, it was not something I should get too excited over. He looked downright…angry?

"What?" I asked again.

"You're her."

I squinted. "Her who?"

"The girl from the other night. In the apartment."

*Oh. Shit.*

# Chapter 15

I tried to think of the best way to pretend I didn't know what he was talking about, but the guy was trained to spot a lie. He was searching me now, his eyes roaming over my hair…my face.

"Christ, I knew there was something…off about that girl," he said. "Something I wasn't putting my finger on." He squinted. "You were in disguise."

"I, um, don't know what you're talking about."

He shook my hand, not violently, but in a way that certainly got my attention.

"The nail polish," he said. "It's not like there are a hundred women out there walking around with this particular manicure," he said, finally dropping my hand.

It flopped to my lap.

"I'm sure there must be other women who like to

do their nails like this," I said, trying to sound as innocent as possible, though knowing damned well I wasn't going to get away with it.

Ryan put his head in his hands. "How did I not figure it out?" He looked up then, straight into my eyes. "I guess I thought you wouldn't be that foolhardy. Or, you know, you might listen to me or something." He shook his head.

After I tried—and I'm pretty sure, failed—to process the fact that he'd just used the word *foolhardy* with absolutely no hint of irony, shame washed over me. I mean, as if I didn't already know how dangerous the whole night had been, I really didn't need him treating me like some kid that he caught stealing cookies or something.

Suddenly, Ryan seemed to remember something. He looked around, frantic. "Shit, we've got to get you out of the open." He grabbed my arm and pulled me up from the couch. He was gentle but firm, a sense of urgency fueling him. He led me off the roof and in a moment we were in the elevator on our way back down to our floor.

"I was kind of having a good time up there," I said, knocking him back into the present moment.

"Do you have a death wish?"

I figured he wouldn't believe me even if I told him I didn't, so I just shrugged.

"Because pulling a stunt like you pulled the other night is a really good way to get that accomplished. Hell, you practically did get yourself killed. Or maybe worse."

I didn't really know what might be worse than getting killed and couldn't help but think he was being a little bit dramatic.

"I wasn't going to get killed."

His mouth dropped open like he couldn't believe I was going to argue with him about it. "You were knocked out and tied to a chair."

I shrugged again. I mean, the jig was obviously up, but I still didn't particularly want to admit to everything that had gone down.

"I wouldn't have been killed." I said. "I'm sure those other girls are just fine."

He balked. "Okay, maybe they're not dead, but I can guarantee you they are far from fine."

"I can take care of myself," I insisted. "I'm trained in self-defense. You saw what I could do the other night." I unlocked the door to my apartment and went in.

I was both excited and a little freaked out that he followed.

"And that's all well and fine…when you're conscious," he said, staring me down, knowing I wasn't going to come up with some great argument about that.

"I was fine. I got out. I think pretty well on my feet."

"And now they're going to be after you. They know what you look like."

I tilted my head. "Obviously they don't. Even you didn't recognize me."

He narrowed his eyes, his jaw clenching and unclenching like he didn't quite know what to do with all the angry energy coursing through him.

I was starting to calm a little though. If there was anything I was sure of, it was that he would never hurt me. Or anyone else, for that matter. You know, unless it was a bad guy and he had no choice in the matter. He was the kind of guy who saved lives. Like mine, for instance.

"You need to get that nail polish off," he said, then stared at me until I got up to get the polish remover.

I came back into the room where he was pacing.

"Look, this case is a lot bigger than I thought. It's drugs and forced prostitution and runs way deeper than I ever imagined when I started. These guys work like well-oiled machines. It's going to be a while before I have enough to be able to bring them down."

"Um, okay," I said, not really sure where he was going with all that.

I started to wipe the polish off.

"Look, you can't stay here. It's too dangerous. Especially with me being in this building too. Any one of them could be onto me at any moment and could easily follow me here. And my god, if they found you here too, the whole building could be in danger."

"Well, I obviously don't want to put anyone in danger, but it's not like I have anywhere to go."

"Go to one of your friend's houses. That girl. Or that big guy, whatever."

"Um, Ryan? I'm not going anywhere. This is my house. This is where I feel safe."

"You have to go," he insisted.

"Um, no. Actually I don't. Besides, you're putting everyone at way more risk than I am."

"This is my home base. My office is here. All my stuff."

"Yeah, well, same."

"But I'm actually trying to solve a case."

"Well, duh, so am I. What the hell do you think I was doing that night? Just out having a little fun?"

He started to pace. "I can't believe this is happening. I have never in my life ever had anyone stick their nose into my life like this."

"I'm not sticking my nose in your life," I said, insulted that he still thought this was all about him. "Obviously this is at least as much about me as it is about you at this point."

His eyes opened wide. "Because you followed me!" His voice was getting louder, more disbelieving.

I sighed. "Okay. I get it. I got involved with something that wasn't really my business. But it wasn't like I thought in a million years that I would stumble upon something like this."

"Yeah, well. I guess you never know, right?" he said calmly, then his voice got louder again. "Which is why you don't just go around following people!"

He sat down, exasperated, like he seriously didn't know what the hell he was going to do with me. Which may have been a valid point, since no matter how much he might have wanted me to stay out of it, I definitely wasn't going to stay out of it. But I also didn't need him worrying about me.

"Look, it's nobody's fault," I said, even though it was maybe a little my fault—which was exactly why I had to help fix it. "It's not even a problem."

"Not a problem? How can you say that? You were *abducted* the other night. You don't think that's a problem?"

I shrugged again. "No. Now we know more about how they work than we did before, right?"

"Not really. I'd seen them drug the women before."

"Well, now we know more about how secure they are and stuff. And—" I hesitated to say it, but I knew we'd have to get to the real issue eventually "—now we know how to get back inside."

His eyes looked like they were ready to pop right out of his skull. "Get back in?!" His voice cracked and sort of squealed at the end, which I'd kind of anticipated, but nonetheless it made my nether regions do a little flip.

I nodded. "You said yourself that this case was taking longer than you'd expected." I figured it was best not to mention that I was actually doing him a favor. "But with me helping, we can get in there and get what you need and get out. And hopefully with a bunch of arrests and stuff."

He was much calmer than I expected, sitting there just looking at me with those gorgeous eyes of his. Staring, I might add, just a little longer than I was particularly comfortable with.

It was starting to get a little uncomfortable, actually.

After an eternity of infinitude, he spoke. "You have got to be out of your mind if you think I'm going to be on board with you helping me on this case. Especially considering you're self-destructive enough to be doing things like you were doing the other night."

"Why does everybody keep saying that? I am not self-destructive. I mean, maybe my tolerance for danger is slightly higher than an average person's, but that's only because I am confident in my abilities. I'm trained."

"Yeah, yeah. The self-defense. The spying," he said pointedly, looking me in the eye.

I could see again why he made such a good detective. In one stare, he had a way of making me want to disclose all my secrets...and I didn't even really have secrets. Though the way he was looking at me, I kinda wished I did so I could spill my guts like a guilt-ridden six-year-old. Except I suddenly realized I had a lot more gumption when I was six. Right...gumption. I just went ahead and did stuff for the hell of it even when I knew it wasn't "allowed." People seemed to think it was cute, actually. And you know what? It *was* cute. It was goddamned adorable. I decided then and there to adopt the mindset of my past cute self and be the Emperor of My Own Domain. Who the hell was this guy (no matter how exquisite he was) to tell me what I could and couldn't do, anyway?

"Look, I know you don't think I'm capable or whatever, and that's fine. I'm used to being underestimated, and people always make fun of my classes, but at the end of the day, I've spent hundreds of hours gathering knowledge and gaining practical experience."

"Not in detective work," he retorted, though I could see I was starting to wear him down a little.

Or maybe just exhaust him.

I tilted my head. "A lot of it is, actually. It helps with my work as a writer so I've taken a lot in exactly that sort of thing... Elemental Weapons Design for Dummies, my Kickass Combat workouts, this one class called The Authentic Art of Disguise, although Brandt is much more of an expert at that."

"But...why would you want to risk your life like that?"

I shrugged. "Why do you do it?"

"Money, for one," he said, exasperated. "And you haven't mentioned one word about getting in on that."

"I don't want your money," I said. "I just want experience."

"I thought you already had all the experience you need," he challenged.

I sighed. "Fine, whatever. You're obviously not interested in doing this together, but like it or not, I'm in this now. Do you think I can sleep at night knowing those guys are still out there? And that maybe some of them might even be looking for me?"

"That's exactly why you should have never gotten involved."

"Maybe, but it doesn't change the fact that I am involved and that's not changing until these guys are found and hopefully arrested."

"And that's precisely what I'm trying to do."

I nodded. "And we could probably do it twice as fast if we helped each other out, but if you're not up for that, just try not to get in my way, okay?"

He nearly choked on his own spit. "Petra, you *cannot* keep trying to catch these guys. What will you even do if you do get back in there, which, by the way, is about the stupidest thing anyone could do? Even if you can get inside, what's going to happen then? Do you have a plan? Someone you're going to call?"

I bit my lip. "Honestly, I was hoping that person would be you or that you would, I don't know, be on the other end of the secret wire I would be wearing or whatever, but I can see that's not going to be the case, so I'll have to find someone else to help me."

"Oh my god, drag some other poor innocent soul into this already out-of-control situation? You really have no sense of who these people are."

"So fill me in."

He sighed and ran his hands through his hair again roughly. I couldn't remember a time when I had gotten someone so worked up before. I was a little disappointed in myself that it felt kind of...powerful. How awful was it to be gratified that I was making someone else miserable?

"Look, by now you probably already know almost as much as I do. There are bad guys, and from what I can gather, they have this ingenious and well-organized prostitution ring."

I nodded, things clicking into place.

"They find the girls by preying on their drug addiction so they don't even have to kidnap them or do anything against their will," he continued. "The girls just willingly waltz right on into the madness. I've heard rumblings around town that the girls get bid on at some sort of horrible auction for rich dudes."

"So why don't the cops just find out where the auction is and take it down?"

"The police," he said with a despondent look of doom. "The police don't know anything. They just have a bunch of missing girls. And frankly, probably only half of them have even been reported missing. Most of them are assumed runaways by their families. In a lot of neighborhoods, it's often a relief to have one less mouth to feed, you know?"

The thought made my stomach turn. "So what's your plan?" I asked.

"I'm still working on that. Surveilling. Trying to figure out who all the players are and how all the pieces fit together."

"And then what? Take down the bad guys?"

"We don't really use the term *bad guys*."

"Well, I do," I said. "I'm not about to run around calling them perps or something. I seriously cannot get away with that kind of lingo."

He actually chuckled.

"Run this by me one more time. Exactly what kind of training and experience do you have?"

And with that I knew I had him.

# Chapter 16

I'd love to say he agreed to let me help right then and there, but it took another hour and a half of convincing (I wouldn't call it hounding, exactly). Eventually I wore Ryan down, deciding not to tell him about the True Visionaries in Negotiating and the How to Debate Like a Genius classes I'd taken.

But I knew the idea of a dazzling and crafty sidekick was beginning to grow on him when he finally filled me in on the specific details of his case.

"I was hired by this woman…the mother of a missing girl. It has taken me a while, but I've tracked down this group, the one you oh so gracefully stumbled upon the other night. They're pretty bad guys," he said, shooting me a "why the hell did you have to go and do that?" look, even though we were so past that already. "Like *bad* bad. As bad as it gets. They run a prostitution ring where they take girls off the streets…the fresh, younger ones, like Kathleen, my client's daughter, and give them the drugs they want."

"Jesus," I said.

He nodded. "The thing about these guys though is they give the girls a life that isn't half-bad. I mean, it's not good. It's forced prostitution, the girls are totally coerced. But word on the street is that it's kind of like the luxurious spa version of prostitution and drugs. They apparently get to live in this big mansion and get treated pretty well. The catch is that they have to sleep with old rich guys, but they get their fix and a safe place to stay."

"Huh," was about all I could muster. I mean, sleeping with random guys who were paying for it was not number one on my "fun things to do on the weekend" list, but for someone who'd been living on the streets, it kinda sounded like a rescue of sorts.

"The other catch," Ryan continued, "is that no one seems to know what happens to the girls once they are no longer useful. Once they get older or too far into the drugs and lose their looks or what have you. They just…disappear." He said the last word ominously. I could only assume he meant that they get dead.

"That…doesn't sound good," I stupidly said.

"Exactly. So we can't half-ass any of this," he finished.

And even though he didn't say *like you've been doing so far* at the end of his sentence, I felt the sting of the implied words anyway.

"Look," I said, "I'm really sorry about all of this. I know how stupid it was to be following you in the first place. I don't want you to think that I just go around following people all the time. I just... I've had this writer's block for a while now and I guess I was curious about you."

"Curious?" he asked, raising an eyebrow.

Of course that would be the word he focused on. "But mostly," I said, shooting him a look that I hoped would suggest we were just casually going to skip over that part, "I was desperate. Desperate to find anything even remotely interesting for my heroine to get into."

Ryan looked weirdly thoughtful for a moment. "You're putting a lot of pressure on yourself for this next book."

I sighed. "I know you think it's just silly fiction, or whatever, but it's important to me."

He shook his head. "That's not what I meant. I just... I think it's nice that you're worried about what people will think of the next book."

"Not just any people. The fans. The ones who spent their hard-earned money on my first book. It's like... I'm so grateful to them for making it the success that it was. There are so many choices out there and the fact that even a single person picked up my book and thought it looked interesting is a huge deal. I just—" I swallowed "—I just don't want to let them down, you know?"

Ryan nodded. "I read it, you know." The words were quiet, barely audible.

A viselike knot gripped my stomach. "What do you mean?"

"Your book," he said casually, as if it were the most normal thing in the world.

My god, I had a hard enough time when complete strangers came up to me and said they read my book, but someone I knew? Someone I was hoping to get to know better? That was too much. It was funny, when I was writing my first book, I guess I hadn't really thought the whole thing through. I hadn't imagined what it would feel like for people to read it…and then come up to me and want to talk about it. For as cool as I thought it might be, it ended up being an exercise in that whole "leaning in to discomfort" thing that people were always talking about. I wasn't sure how to describe the feeling really, other than maybe over-exposed? Like someone had waltzed in and taken a leisurely stroll through my brain. And does one really want a bunch of people loitering around in there? I still didn't know if the answer was yes or no, but either way, it was something that I still found…disconcerting.

As I was trying to come to terms with the fact that Ryan was now one of my brain-loiterers, he continued. "You know, *Desperately Seeking Fusion*? It was… good."

I distinctly did not like the little pause near the end of his sentence.

"Good?" I said, crossing my arms over my chest.

He nodded. "At first I was just going to look up the blurb, but the premise was original—it piqued my interest, actually." To say he sounded reluctant to say the words was an understatement. "I guess I never imagined a cozy mystery set in a science lab. I was very impressed with your research. It must have been quite a challenge to make sure all the tech and terminology, not to mention the science, was correct. I bet there are people out there just waiting to tell authors they've screwed up some tiny detail that doesn't matter the slightest for the plot."

"There definitely are," was all I could say, my mind still reeling.

"So I started reading a bit in the store, you know, for my own research," he said, shooting me a sheepish grin, "and I guess I kind of got sucked in."

"Your own research?"

Ryan shrugged one shoulder. "I needed to see what kind of a person I'd gotten myself tangled up with," he said. "And I figured, what better way to get a read on a person than to actually, you know, *read* a person."

I rolled my eyes. "Wait. You said you read it. Like, the whole thing?"

"I…did," he said, still weirdly pausing between words.

I wasn't sure whether he was trying to go slow to spare my feelings, or if he was trying his hardest not to compliment my book.

"When did you have time? We just met the other day."

"Yesterday."

"You read the whole thing yesterday?"

"Yes."

"In one day."

"In one sitting, actually. Well, besides the first few pages I read in the store."

"And you just couldn't stop?" I said, still not sure if he was messing with me or not.

He let out a low growl of sorts then and looked like he was regretting life at the moment. "I was just so sure I knew what was going to happen and wanted to see if I was right."

"Huh," I said, not quite sure how to respond to that little tidbit.

He'd just explained the exact thing I'd been trying to do with the book. Have the reader sure they were going to guess what had happened, what was going to happen and why it all came together that way. Of course, the better mysteries are the ones that the reader is sure they know the ending to, but in the end, is utterly wrong.

He fidgeted with the collar of his shirt.

"Well...?" I asked.

"Well what?"

"Were you right?"

He broke out in a crooked grin then, like he was conceding something. "I have to say, I absolutely did not see the ending coming. I was so damned sure too." He looked down and shook his head, still smiling. "It's pretty rare when I don't see the twist coming."

A feeling washed over me—a shot of energy filling up my torso and spreading to my limbs like a burst of white light. Was this...pride?

"You thought Reggie was the one that did it, right?"

"One hundred percent, and I was feeling pretty confident about it too," he said. "And then when Monique, oh my god, it was like she came out of nowhere, except then—when I thought back over the whole thing—it almost seemed inevitable. I don't know how I didn't catch it."

I was smiling like I'd just been handed an Academy Award. Except, you know, not for acting or whatever. "That was exactly what I was going for."

"It was great. A damned good mystery, really," he said, his smile growing.

I sighed a big, happy sigh, the goofy smile still plastered all over my face. "So...does that mean we're ready then? You have a newfound trust in my wit and ability to be involved in a damned good mystery?"

"Oh, hell no," he said, his smile fading fast. "I mean, I have no doubt you can craft a good mystery, but I'm not really sure it translates into real-world skill."

My smile faded even faster than his. "So, being a mystery reader doesn't help in solving real mysteries, and neither does being a mystery writer?"

He shook his head. "The bad guys in novels are usually clever, outsmarting the detective time and time again."

"Until they don't," I piped in.

"Right. But that's not the way it is with real criminals. Real criminals get emotional, often doing stupid things. Real criminals also get lucky way more than those of us in law enforcement would like to admit. Real criminals don't have a neat and tidy motive all the time— hell, sometimes I don't think they even know why they do the things they do."

"So, we have to be smarter than them," I said.

"Sometimes, yeah, we have to be smarter than them. But sometimes we have to also try to be as emotional or out of control as them. Or at least think that way.

We have to be irrational, angry, scared…all the things real people are."

I had to admit, this was a fascinating trek into the mind of criminals, and I couldn't help but think this whole conversation was going to come in very handy if I ever got the motivation to sit down and write my next novel. A task, I suddenly found, that didn't feel quite as daunting as it had yesterday. I mean, it still felt like I was trapped on a set of railroad tracks just down the line from an oncoming train that I had to somehow stop before it ran over me. But honestly, it was an improvement from where my mindset *had* been—which was somewhere in the vicinity of stopping a world-ending asteroid streaking toward Earth with my bare hands.

The next day, Annie and I decided we should have a debriefing tea session after yesterday's party—though mostly I think she wanted to talk about the part where Ryan dragged me out of there. So when I opened my door and was instead greeted by a construction worker in full gear—tool belt, orange vest and, most oddly, a hard hat—I was somewhat taken aback.

I glanced at the ceiling, thinking my friends really had been unfair when they claimed I didn't have any self-preservation skills. I mean, seriously, one glance at a hard hat and immediately I was surveying my surroundings for any and all potential threats. I took a step back as I tried to wrap my head around this unexpected caller.

And that's when things really careened toward the weird.

The guy set down what looked like a speaker, pushed a button on his phone, calmly placed it into his tool belt and proceeded to start dancing to the music emanating from the speaker at his feet.

Just as my thoughts started going *I'm sorry, what?* the elevator doors opened. Out of the corner of my eye (I mean, obviously I wasn't about to take the fronts of my eyes off this, I now realized, quite attractive stranger in front of me), I saw Annie begin to stroll toward my door.

But my mind was so occupied with the situation in front of me that I couldn't even figure out whether I should be relieved that I was no longer alone with this stranger, or weirded out that she was witnessing this… spectacle of human strangeness that was unfolding.

But that's when the weirdness began to multiply. Tenfold.

Because as Mr. Construction Worker Man began a slow spin, gyrating the whole way, inch by inch he started removing his brightly colored vest. Which was so unanticipated, it even stopped Annie in her tracks. The man did not seem to mind the additional audience.

Maybe I was in shock or something, because I kind of just stood there watching this guy twirl the vest in the air, eventually flinging it off to the side. This was followed by a similar production with his shirt.

I realized I should probably try to find out what in the wits of Nancy D. was going on, but to be honest, I was a little caught off guard by the chisel-y-ness of his abs and couldn't quite find the fortitude to speak.

Just as the gentleman's tear-away pants were being

whisked off in a flourish—which, I might add, showcased an impressive bulge beneath a vibrant orange G-string, complete with caution symbol on the front— Ryan decided it was the perfect time to mosey on out of his apartment to see what the hell was going on.

To the stranger's credit, his performance didn't falter as he finished with a couple more spins and a move that perhaps might best be described as a full-body shimmy-shimmy.

The dude cocked one eyebrow and spoke for the first time. "If you want this to go any further, I'm afraid we'll have to take this inside your apartment."

"Um…" Clearly, I was still searching for my coherence. "I think we're good?" I said, not sure why my voice rose at the end like it was a question.

He shrugged in a sort of "suit yourself" way and fished a card out of his tool belt. I couldn't help but think it was an awfully handy accessory, and briefly wondered why the fashion world hadn't figured out something similar for everyday wear.

"From your anonymous admirer," he said as he handed me his card, gathered his clothes and speaker in a bundle, then simply walked away, waiting patiently for the elevator in his G-string and work boots as the three of us stood frozen, still not quite sure what we had just witnessed.

Not surprisingly, it was Annie who finally broke the silence once the elevator had whooshed our new friend away and we all continued to stare at its doors a few moments longer.

"Well," she said, pulling an accordion-style hand fan from somewhere in the depths of her complicated multipatterned, pocket-heavy pantsuit, which she proceeded to flick open like a pro, fluttering it lightly at her face, "that was certainly invigorating!"

Finally, I glanced at the card, which simply said, Jack P.'s Strip-O-Grams with his number listed neatly below, and honestly, I had to admire the no-fuss, no-muss attitude of both his performance and his marketing materials.

"Anonymous admirer?" Ryan said.

Of course that was the part he would latch on to.

"It's nothing," I said, kind of waving the thought away. "Ready for tea?" I added, turning to Annie, hoping Ryan would just drop it.

Unfortunately, as I headed into my apartment, both Annie and Ryan followed.

"It's not nothing," he said, his tone amplified with a bit of a growl as he said each word. Which should have been frustrating but was honestly damned sexy. "Someone just sent a complete stranger to your place of residence to do a strip show and you think that's nothing? Is this the sort of thing that happens to you a lot?"

I gave him a look. "No, I can honestly say I've never had a strip-o-gram delivered to me before, and frankly I thought the whole notion of a strip-o-gram was one of those urban legend things, but I have to say, Jack *was* kind of entertaining."

"And how!" Annie piped in, fan still in hand, fluttering away.

"Whether your—" Ryan seemed to be mustering up

the fortitude to say the words "—strip-o-gram was entertaining or not, is not really the point here. The point is that someone sent an anonymous—"

The poor man seemed to be at a loss for words again.

"Gift?" I said, helpfully.

He took a slow breath, closing his eyes. "Fine," he growled, "an anonymous *gift*—" he spit out the word like it pained him "—which means we have a very big problem."

"Gifts, actually," I said.

His eyebrows rose and I swore I detected a hint of a tremble in his body, which kind of made me regret saying anything.

"I'm sorry?" he asked.

"Not to interrupt, lovelies, but I think tea might be better some other time," Annie said, moving toward the door.

"Annie, you don't have to go."

She looked from me to Ryan, then back to me, then again to Ryan. "I really think I do," she said, her fan becoming a little less fluttery and moving more into the manic oscillation category as she eased herself out the door.

I watched her go for as long as I could get away with, then turned my attention back to Ryan, who was waiting with alarming patience for me to explain.

"I don't know, I got some chocolates and some flowers," I finally said, my entire insides cringing in wait for his reaction.

"Show me."

I scrunched up my face. "Well obviously I ate the

chocolates, but the flowers are over here," I said, pointing to the coffee table.

"You ate...the chocolates," he said, all stuttery, like he couldn't quite believe it.

"What? They were really good chocolates."

He stood blinking for what seemed like a lifetime, his mouth hanging open a little like he was trying to figure out what to say.

But I held fast to the belief that anyone with a pulse and some taste buds would have absolutely eaten the chocolates.

"Didn't you ever go like, trick-or-treating or whatever as a kid? Didn't we all learn about candy safety?"

I shrugged. And honestly, all this talk about chocolates was kind of making me wish I still had some of the sketchy chocolates because I really could have used a hit of sugar right then.

He gave me a look out of the side of his eyes that told me he once again thought I could use some work in the self-preservation department. He marched over to the flowers and whipped the card from the stems with a flourish.

"'From your anonymous admirer,'" he said, and seriously, that growl was really starting to get to the bottom of things. The bottom of my nether regions, that was.

I shrugged again. "It's just a fan or whatever."

"Or whatever," he deadpanned.

"Yeah," I said, crossing my arms.

"I don't even know what to say to you. Your recklessness is going to get us all in trouble."

"Or," I said, raising my eyebrows, "maybe it just might solve this mystery."

He closed his eyes and shook his head ever so slightly, taking a little pause for composure. "I'm taking this," he said, lifting the card he held in his hand. He moved toward me and plucked Jack P.'s card from my grip as well, then headed for the door.

"In need of a gift for someone special?" I asked. I mean, how could I resist, right?

But he just let out a final, low growl and headed on his decidedly unmerry way, which of course made me smile all the more.

The next day, Ryan insisted on testing some of my battle skills, and quite frankly, I was not going to argue. Mostly, because I might get to see some of his skills too, but more importantly, observe him in his workout gear, which, lord willing, would be shirtless.

Sadly, he showed up to our rooftop workout in a full tracksuit. I mean, sure it was cold out and everything, but way to let a girl down, dude.

Still, the exercise was far from a loss considering the three milliseconds it took for a shivery heat to build down my spine when his gaze met mine as we lined up for sparring. The way he stared…so intense, searing… almost like…lust? But the moment broke too soon, and he was rushing me, my mind jumping into fight mode as he charged.

Muscle memory kicked in as I sidestepped the blow, but he was so fast, and before I could get my bearings, he had me in a choke hold with one arm, his other hand planting itself around my waist—a move that felt so familiar, the graze of his thumb across the bare skin under the hem of my hoodie igniting a turbulent fire deep in my belly.

Fortunately, one of the first moves they taught in my Always Be Aware self-defense class was how to get out of the exact situation I'd found myself in. I grabbed the arm he had around my neck with both hands and took a step forward, launching my leg back to kick out his knee. As he started to buckle, I used the momentum to flip him over my head, quickly straddling him while he was still stunned, readying my arm for a blow in case he wanted to continue.

He let out a low groan, causing my thighs to tingle in response.

"Nice move," he said, panting and rubbing the back of his neck, then relaxing back into the floor, his hands coming down to rest on my legs with that same, familiar touch, like we'd done this a hundred times before. The smirk that accompanied his words nearly undid me.

And maybe that's why I just sat there, straddling him (dear god) and gazing into his eyes. And for a while, he gazed right back. Suddenly, I had a hard time catching my breath.

Of course, Ryan seemed to come to his senses before I did, since I felt him tense up in that way you do when you're not sure what the hell to do. Like he was frozen, not wanting to disturb the moment, or perhaps, more likely, not wanting to embarrass me by asking if I was ever going to, you know, stop straddling him (to which the obvious answer should have been absolutely not). But, being a gentlewoman—or, at least, as gentlewomanly as someone who just upended a grown-ass man over her shoulder then straddled him like he was her prize can be—I eventually heaved myself off the poor man.

"Again," Ryan said as we climbed to our feet, and he shed his light jacket.

Sadly, he was still not shirtless, but what I wouldn't give to be a piece of that T-shirt clinging to him in all the right places like it was custom-made. Honestly, even with the chill of the wind, it really was getting rather hot up on that rooftop. I peeled my own hoodie off, a moment of self-consciousness flowing over me and my exercise bra. But I didn't have much time to think about it, since Ryan was already headed my way.

I quickly moved into a defensive stance, stepping out to give myself a wide base, both front to back and left to right with my legs diagonal from each other. It didn't stop Ryan's momentum though, and before I knew what was happening, he'd taken us both down.

There were plenty of maneuvers I could try to gain control of the situation, but there was one little problem. The weight of him on me felt more like it was always meant to be there instead of something akin to an attack. With the distraction of this thought, it only took a moment for him to pin both my hands above my head, holding them with one hand while the other rested gently close to my neck in a sort of gentle mock-strangle as proof that he'd bested me, but without being too threatening.

Frankly, it was one hell of a turn-on.

His face was inches from mine, our breath heavy with the exertion…and maybe something else.

"I guess we might have to work a little more on this one," I said, not meaning for it to sound as suggestive as it did.

Perhaps because I'd said it as I stared directly at his delectable lips.

I quickly snapped my eyes back to his, but he'd definitely caught me staring.

He cleared his throat and lifted himself off me, holding out his hand to help me up, which I accepted only after I took a moment to catch my breath and try to pretend the last minute or so hadn't actually happened.

Way too soon—and with great sorrow—the hand-to-hand portion of the day was complete as he pulled out a few of his Tasers and hand combat weapons to show me how to use them—as if I didn't already know (you'd be surprised at how many licensed weaponry classes were out there). I think I may have impressed him, which only annoyed me slightly. Most of the time I was more than happy to be underestimated—frankly it usually gave me the advantage—but one doesn't really want the guy she's crushing on to underestimate her.

I didn't want to get into a real fight or anything, but I couldn't help but think that that might be the only way to show Ryan what I could really do. Although, it would probably say more for my acting and improvisation skills if I were to be able to avoid a fight altogether. Either way, I hoped to shimmy further toward the "impressed" side of the old sliding scale by the time this operation was complete. I tried not to think about the whole "I could also end up on the dead end of the scale" possibility, but unfortunately, the notion did manage to wiggle into my mind once or twice.

# *Chapter 17*

Ryan had pointed out, quite correctly, that I couldn't very well go back to the apartment looking even remotely like I had looked the last time I had, you know, escaped and whatever. We were both pretty sure the bad guys weren't going to look all that kindly on my waltzing back in again.

So we called in Brandt for a consultation.

At first, he wanted to go full-on living dead, but Ryan countered that they only took the girls who still looked half-decent, so I'd have to pass their initial attractiveness test just to get back into the scary room, tied up like I had been the other night. They'd had plenty of time to look me over and knew very well what I looked like—at least what I'd looked like in that first disguise. And while it was a good one, we all agreed this one had to be even better, making me look completely different from both myself and the, er, less put together version of myself.

"We've got to go complete opposite then," Brandt said. "Brown contacts. Dark hair. I can maybe do something with makeup to change the shape of your eyes."

A strange wave of calm washed over me. I'd seen Brandt perform miracles with his skills. He used to work with a photographer who specialized in temporarily altering regular people to look like their favorite celebrities, and I felt oddly secure in his hands.

As we made final preparations, Ryan tested the listening device he'd gotten, which would allow him to hear everything I heard. It was a cheap-looking pin, like a promotional button, but he assured me it was top-of-the-line. Totally wireless and no one would ever suspect it was a bug.

Brandt thought it was ridiculous at first, but in the end, he ended up designing the entire look around it. Kind of like an old-school Madonna look, but his plan was to make a more modern look, like an on-purpose '90s retro thing. He even found a few more of the old-school buttons to make a nice little cluster out of them, which I thought was kind of ingenious, but Ryan just rolled his eyes. It didn't seem like he was having as much fun as the rest of us at the makeover party.

"I cannot believe you are calling this a makeover party," he said, his jaw clenched.

"What? The situation has enough tension and drama as it is. Is it really so bad to try to have a little fun with it?"

He sighed and went back to his apartment to "double-check his supplies," whatever that meant. For a steely private eye, he sure seemed to have a lot of nervous jitters.

Brandt got to work on my face while Vic poured us each a glass of wine.

"Make sure to hide mine," I said, taking a quick sip. "Somehow I doubt Ryan would approve of me going in drunk."

Vic quickly grabbed the glass away. "Shit. I never even thought of that."

I rolled my eyes. "Vic, I'm not going to get drunk. I am, however, going to have a single glass of this lovely wine you brought to calm my nerves a little. No more, I promise."

"Okay," she said, handing it back over, "but this is it."

I nodded. "Thanks, Mom."

She gave me a look. If there was ever anything Vic always said she wasn't interested in, it was being anybody's mom.

As Brandt worked his magic, Ryan popped in every few minutes to see how the "disguise," as he insisted on calling it, was going—apparently, in his mind, makeovers were for teenagers and divorcées. The whole thing was making it rather hard to enjoy my wine, since I had to quickly ditch it every time the door opened, though in truth, I was somewhat torn—I really did enjoy watching the guy enter a room. I don't know if Brandt could feel my heart speed up or what, but he sighed and shook his head every time I spotted Ryan.

"Okay, I'm almost done. Just your lips are left,"

Brandt said. "If you want to finish that wine you better chug it, because you can't be drinking until they are set, and it's gonna take a little time."

I shrugged and downed the rest of the glass. Not that there was much left anyway. Vic whisked the glass away and put it directly in the dishwasher in case Ryan got all detective-y and decided to count how many used glasses were hanging around. I could just see him canceling the whole thing based on something super insignificant, just to have an excuse not to do it.

"Okay, guys," Brandt said, "I think we're done."

As he was talking, Ryan came in for an update.

"Wow," Vic said, glancing over at Brandt. "You are actually really good at this." Her mouth hung open for a second as she looked at him.

"Um, yeah," Brandt said, acting offended, though I knew he got it all the time. Nobody expected his big ol' self to be a genius artist with a makeup brush.

"My god," Ryan said. "That is amazing."

He sat staring at me for a moment and I gladly stared back, but it got uncomfortable pretty quickly. And it's not like he was staring at me, like Petra me; he was staring at whatever concoction Brandt had come up with.

"Do I get to see or are you all going to sit there and make me feel like a freak?" I asked.

"Right. Sorry," Brandt said, sneaking a glance over at Vic.

Which was so entirely weird it almost made me forget that I was about to embark on a dangerous mission.

Ooh, I liked the idea of calling it a dangerous mission. Maybe I could use that in my book.

Brandt held a mirror up and I gasped. "Holy crap," I said, although the words were not coming out of my mouth.

I mean, they were, obviously, but it was certainly not the mouth I was used to seeing when I looked in the mirror. My lips were suddenly fuller, but somehow also seemed smaller, more delicate. Almost heart shaped.

And the rest of me was not any more recognizable than the lips. My face was pale with hints of dark circles under my eyes and a bit of a sunken look to my cheeks. I wore a straight black wig with long bangs, covering even my eyebrows, which were normally one of my more distinctive features.

But perhaps it was my eyes that were the most changed. Somehow Brandt had lined them to look completely different, more almond shaped, but only slightly—nothing over-the-top that would have anyone guessing this had not been my look since birth.

"Wow," was honestly all I could say to the reflection in the mirror, my voice completely weird coming out of the face of a stranger.

"Shit," I said. "My voice. What am I supposed to do about my voice?"

"Did you speak to them before?" Ryan asked, suddenly looking concerned all over again.

Sigh. Those ten seconds without that look had been nice.

"Well, yeah," I said. "They asked me a few questions.

Had me agree to work with them, you know, before they knocked me out."

"Damn," Ryan said. "I don't suppose..."

"What?"

"Well, your acting classes? Was there ever any accent work or anything like that?"

I raised my eyebrows. "There was. The only problem was I was really kind of bad at it."

He looked worried. And suddenly I felt worried. I couldn't believe I hadn't thought of this before that moment, which was very close to when we had to get going.

Vic piped in, "Maybe you could just pretend to be kind of meek or whatever and just nod and use gestures as much as you can. And if you have to answer something, just do it really quiet, like you're scared and just want to get the hell out of there."

I raised one eyebrow. "That shouldn't be too hard. I mean, not that I'm scared, but I'm sure it wouldn't be too far of a reach, at least."

Ryan was nodding. "Yeah, that's not bad. Change your demeanor, your personality. The voice isn't as big a part as the way you present yourself. Just speak softly if you have to speak." He nodded a kind of kudos at Vic.

I couldn't help but feel pretty proud of my friends at that moment. Without Brandt, none of this would be possible, and Vic just ended up solving a major problem in about five seconds.

Someone knocked on the door, making me jump. All eyes turned to me, but I had as much of an idea about who it might be as they did.

"Come on, Petra, open up!" a very familiar, and irritatingly whiny voice came from the other side of the door.

"Again with this bloody guy?" Brandt said, as he finished packing up his gear.

"What bloody guy?" Ryan asked.

Vic sighed. "Petra's idiotic ex," she said, then turned to me. "Sorry, no offense."

"Oh, don't worry, none taken."

"Well, he can't see you like that," Ryan said, looking more and more stressed out by the second.

"Actually," Brandt said, puffing his chest a little, "I wouldn't mind testing out my work."

"What do you mean?" I asked.

"I want to see if he recognizes you." He grinned. "This guy lived with you for months. I know he's an idiot, but still. Let's see if he figures it out."

"This isn't a game, you guys," Ryan said.

"Actually, I kind of want to see too," I jumped in. "If we can fool him, I'll know we can fool anybody, and I think it will help me feel a little more confident about the situation. Besides, I should probably practice my new personality."

Ryan shook his head in defeat and sat, leaving Vic to open the door.

"She's not here," Vic said in the "I hate your guts and everything you stand for" voice she reserved for Johnny.

Johnny immediately barged in and looked everybody over, quickly deciding Vic was right. "Well, where the hell is she? Like in the bathroom or something?"

"She went out," Brandt said, crossing his arms and looking altogether menacing.

"Why are all you guys here then?" he asked, unable to keep that whine from creeping into his voice. It was like he was a petulant five-year-old that never grew up.

What had I ever seen in him?

"And who's the new girl?" he asked with a couple of eyebrow pumps.

Ugh.

"And I don't even know this guy," he went on, gesturing at Ryan, as if it was impossible that someone he didn't know could be in my house. "Who is this guy?"

It was more than a little obvious that Johnny had taken an immediate dislike to Ryan, which was basically how he felt about any good-looking guy. The competition sent his tiny ego reeling.

"Why are you here?" Brandt said, his voice slightly lower and a little more booming than usual.

"I just… I need to talk to Petra." He was slowly inching toward the couch that I was sitting on, and I did not want him to get any closer.

"Like we said," Vic said, blocking him from the path of the couch. "She's not here. And how in the hell do you keep getting into the building, anyhow?"

He shrugged. "People are nice. They let me in."

"Christ," Ryan whispered under his breath, obviously less than pleased at the security in the building.

I threw Vic a pleading look.

She jumped into action. "Okay, well, we'll tell her you stopped by." She grabbed his shoulders and pivoted him around toward the door, pushing him slightly toward it, and then a few moments later the pushing intensified.

"I can just wait for her," he said.

"No," Brandt boomed. "You can't."

"But you guys all get to be here when she's not." The whining had reached high-level patheticism.

"Yup, we sure do," Vic said, just to add a little salt to the wound.

She opened the door and gave him one last good shove.

"You know what?" Ryan said, suddenly getting up from his chair and walking at a somewhat alarming pace toward Johnny.

The look on Johnny's face was a fairly hilarious mash-up of stunned and afraid.

"I wouldn't bother coming back to this building if I were you," he said, stopping just inside my apartment as Johnny backed out. "I'm going to make sure no one lets you in again." And with that he slammed the door in his face.

I wasn't sure if I should be pleased or insulted. I mean, Ryan didn't even know if I wanted to see Johnny again or not. But I couldn't help but feel a lovely warmth radiating through my stomach.

And you know what? I did have a feeling it would be the last time I'd see Johnny, at least for a very long time. More importantly, I realized I was pretty pleased about that and couldn't help the tiny smile that crept across my face.

Ryan stood facing the door for a moment, then slowly

turned. "Sorry about that." He cleared his throat. "But we really do need to be going."

I nodded and took a deep breath.

"Okay. Let's do this."

# Chapter 18

I waited in the alley until Ryan was in position on the fire escape across from the apartment where I'd previously been held. He signaled me with a quick wave and I was off, around to the front of the building.

I stood in line again, but this time there was only one person in front of me. I didn't speak at all and didn't even get a strange look.

Things were going perfectly.

I stood in front of the table just like I had last time, although this time I may have been slightly sweatier. Not my face, thank goodness—Brandt had powdered the whistling Dixie out of that so the makeup would all stay in place—but under my armpits had that tingling, moist feeling when your body is about to pull a *Case of the Disappearing Deodorant*.

It also took everything in me not to look out the window into the back alley. Knowing Ryan was there this time made me ten times as nervous—although that may have helped as I was being questioned, because I was sure I was way more nervous this time, which naturally made my mannerisms different. The fact that I knew what was coming this time might have been a wee bit of a factor too. I kept thinking they were so dense for not figuring out who I was, but then I'd remember how amazing Brandt was at his job and I relaxed into my weird little performance.

In a flash, they scooted me past the first hurdle and led me down the hallway toward the same room I'd been kept in previously. The door swung open, and like before, a couple girls were already there, passed out and tied up.

I quickly remembered I was supposed to be taking the scene in for the first time (actually, this wasn't so quick—I'd one hundred percent been focused on my acting and had forgotten what I was really there for... you know, just for a second though). I gasped a teeny gasp—subtlety was the main thing they grilled into you in acting class, and did my best to look startled and confused, my gaze quickly moving from one girl to the other, then I made a move like I was going to try to get away. And before I could even feel relief that I didn't even really have to act that part—I was out cold, flopping to the floor in a lifeless heap.

Except, of course I wasn't.

I played dead while the guy picked me up off the floor and pretty much threw me on the bed, putting one half of a pair of handcuffs around my wrist and the other around one of the metal headboard rails. I thanked my lucky stars this hadn't been my fate the other night.

Our plan worked. Ryan had found a prosthetic sleeve thing that went over my arm and worked like a "dummy" limb. It was extremely realistic, fitting snugly over my real arm, the inside of it anatomically accurate enough to fool someone into thinking they were giving you a needle, when really the drug emptied harmlessly into the prosthetic. Don't even ask me where he found it. In fact, I didn't really want to know because I was picturing a supersecret spy store that only proper spies were allowed access to, like some kind of Spies R Us situation with retinal scans and everything. I would have been breathtakingly disappointed if it was just like, Amazon or whatever.

Both the girls in the room were out, although one was moaning softly as if she was in some sort of blissful haze. My gaze shot to the window, and I couldn't help but smile, knowing we were already getting one over on these assholes, and that this time I wasn't alone.

Unfortunately, things got real boring real fast and I wished the mic in the button was a two-way deal where Ryan and I could have a conversation. But while that definitely would have made the time go faster, talking was probably not the safest thing for me to do.

If only I knew he was out there. I mean, I knew he was, and was fairly certain that he wouldn't leave me, but still, it would be nice to have some sort of confirmation. Being in that room, even if it was with two other girls, was as lonely as the poor Ténéré Tree—

famous for being the only landmark in two hundred fifty miles of Sahara Desert, and also famously knocked over by a drunk driver (which is honestly pretty impressive—what are the odds?). Unrelated, but did I mention that my mind tended to wander when confronted with boredom?

Time crawled to a resounding halt. I tried not to think about what came next. I'd been so worried about getting to this point, I hadn't really thought much past it, and now that I had all the time in the world, I was seriously starting to get a little anxious.

I thought about Ryan out there, wondering if the wait was worse for him or me. Knowing the way he was taking on all the responsibility for my safety, a good gambler might have bet on him. Of course, wondering how he was feeling got me thinking about all kinds of Ryan-related things. I couldn't help but remember the moments we'd touched when we were sparring. The tension. The spark. What the moment might be like just before he kissed me, you know, if that ever happened. What other…things might be like with Ryan. And honestly, I had a *lot* of time to kill so things got a little R-rated. And yeah, I knew he'd barely given any indication that he might possibly be interested, other than a certain…tension whenever we were in a room together, or maybe that was only on my end. A thought that catapulted me back to the time Annie said Ryan tended to have more sophisticated girlfriends.

Sigh. Daydreaming was frustrating business.

Finally, there was shuffling outside the door. I kept my head down as if I were passed out like the other girls.

Two guys came in and grabbed the first girl from a chair against the wall where her hands were tied up over her head around a sconce. I felt a little sorry for her. The way her arms were, it seemed like it must be terrible on the shoulders for any length of time, but then again, she wasn't fake passed out like I was. She probably wasn't feeling a thing. They hauled her out of the room, then came back for me. I did my best to play dead, though it took everything I had not to flinch when one of the guys whipped something out of his pocket. I'm sure I tensed, but they didn't seem to notice and thankfully all it ended up being was the key to release the handcuffs.

I stayed as limp as I could as they hauled me down a different set of stairs, which led out into the alley. I fought the urge to look up at Ryan's balcony, hoping he was invisible up there. Thank Nancy for people who had too much stuff and used their balconies for extra storage.

Propped up on a bench seat, they duct-taped our legs. Seriously, these guys loved that stuff. Ryan's car was at the other end of the alley. I hoped he'd be able to get to it quickly enough to follow. I had the tracker on me, of course, but I'd seen more than a few spy movies in my day and right before the big climax, the technology always seemed to crap out.

The men left the back of the truck, and I sneaked a quick peek at my surroundings. The other girls were propped up on the opposite side. We were in a tall vehicle, more like a box truck than a van, which would hopefully make it easier for Ryan to follow. I quickly shut my eyes as one of the men got back into the vehicle.

There was very little else about the truck that gave me any clues to what might happen next. No windows, not even a smell besides a bit of stale dust.

This was when I was reminded, yet again, how difficult it was to play the part of someone passed out. Every instinct in my body screamed to open my eyes, which would have been a disaster. I tried to focus on relaxing my face, since every movement and noise around me made me want to flinch.

I hadn't anticipated how exhausting it would be. I wondered if I could get away with a catnap, then realized that this was probably the part where I should pay attention. Try to get a handle on which direction we were going and how far we drove—just like they'd taught in my online class. Sure, Ryan would be taking care of that, but then I started thinking about trust. God, my mind could have some terrible timing. Because when I really thought about it, I didn't know that much about Ryan. I mean, my instinct was that he was exceptional, but now that I had a merciless eternity to think about it, I had no actual basis for this conclusion. Could I really trust myself to be impartial considering how attracted I was to him? Because, let's face it, my track record in the trusting-men department was not spectacular.

And honest to god, did one of these guys really have to sit in the back with us? Because I had a huge crick in my neck. Keeping my head flopped to my chest was no joke, but that was the position of the other girls, so that's what I went with. The other guy went up front with the driver. Or maybe he *was* the driver. I supposed it didn't really take an army to haul around three passed-out chicks.

The truck finally moved, and I caught myself holding my breath. I let it out slowly, super freaked at the guy sitting beside me, but he didn't seem to notice. I tried to relax and not think about the kink in my neck, which was obviously impossible. It was the only thing I could think of. Well, except Ryan and whether or not I could trust him and, more importantly, if I'd ever get to see him without his shirt on. And I guess I kind of had this anticipatory worry thing going on about what might await me once the truck stopped. Also, why did I have "Super Freak" in my head all of a sudden?

What felt like an hour later, we finally stopped, but then again, time had done that thing where it lollygags for days, then rushes, then lollygags again until time means nothing, so it may have been much less. Or more. I really had no idea. From what I could tell, the road changed about halfway through the drive, like we were on gravel instead of pavement, and I wondered how Ryan was supposed to follow on some remote road without being noticed. In my private investigation course, they'd taught us to drive without any headlights on, but I wasn't even sure cars could do that anymore. Seemed like anything from this century had automatic running lights. Although, I supposed that was something that could probably be doctored. Still, if he was driving without headlights, it would have been pretty dangerous considering the speed that we seemed to be going.

Ugh, I needed to relax and trust Ryan to be there for me. He was a professional. I was pretty sure.

As they dragged me out of the truck, I risked a quick peek, acting as if I was groggily fighting to wake up, and caught a tiny glimpse of our destination—a huge mansion, apparently in the middle of nowhere. From the bit I was able to see, it wasn't some creepy old place either—it was new, as if it had been built in the past few years.

I wondered if it had been built specifically for this horrible purpose.

# Chapter 19

The other girls and I were put into a bright room where they continued to sleep off whatever drugs were pumping through their system. One girl was a bit more conscious than the other, which I figured was a good thing. I could probably get away with being slightly more awake if I needed to.

I started stirring. Several additional girls were in the room with us, though they were more alert. Oddly, a few of them were in full-on evening gowns—the kind I'd always wanted to wear, but unless you were a movie star or millionaire, you'd never really have the occasion. I mean, the fanciest events I ever went to were weddings, and sparkly evening gowns were certainly not a thing with the crowd I hung out with. Was it bad that I was a little excited that I might get to wear one of them?

And then…things got super boring again. And yes, all the classes I had taken had pointed out that surveillance was more sitting and waiting than it was rushing around the countryside finding clues every five minutes—Nancy had mismanaged my expectations on that one—but still, I couldn't have imagined the absolute atrophy of my will to endure. I really thought fear and danger would be the hard part, but a bit of jeopardy would have been absolute life candy right about then. I honestly didn't know what the hell was up with my personality—a massive disaster could strike and I'd flutter like a delicate butterfly into problem-solving mode, all graceful and elegant…then the one time my zipper gets stuck on my coat, I'm thrashing around like certain death is nigh.

Perhaps the whole situation was giving me too much time to think. Maybe I could get into a comfortable position and indulge in a little catnap. I mean, it wasn't like I was getting any good surveillance in anyway— I was stuck in another damned room, and I'd already taken mental pictures of all the girls in there with me. Besides, I was a superlight sleeper, so if anyone came in or went out, I'd be able to catch it.

Approximately twelve years later, I blinked my eyes open. Apparently, the adrenaline of the day made me more tired than I realized. Wiping the drool from the corner of my mouth, I realized a few of the girls were missing from the room, and even more disturbing, an emerald green evening gown was laid out on the couch five inches away. I'd missed someone setting it down RIGHT BESIDE ME. The gown was definitely meant for me, since the other girls who'd arrived with me had gowns beside them too. The girl who'd started coming out of her trance before my nap had already started undressing.

"Are we supposed to put these on?" I asked, hoping my words came out sounding kind of slurred. Was that what drugs were supposed to do to a person? I mean, I knew alcohol did, but I wasn't sure about drugs. I hadn't been around them much.

The girl just nodded kind of lazily. "That's what someone said."

I started to undress as quickly as possible, hiding myself like I was in a high school locker room. It had been years since I'd been forced to change in front of strangers and the experience wasn't one I missed. I scrambled into the dress and struggled with the zipper. Eventually, I got it up, but my neck was not a particularly willing participant after all the head hanging (way to go me that my head flopped the same way during my li'l nap). Also, the dress was a little tight. At least I wouldn't have to act uncomfortable, since I was, in fact, aggressively uncomfortable. I could barely sit in the thing but managed to sort of lounge-lean into the couch without the dress digging into my guts too much.

I kept my eyes and ears open for any clues, then suddenly realized now that I'd changed, I was no longer wearing my wire tracker thing.

Damn. Who would have thought we'd have to change clothes? I grabbed my shirt, pretending to start folding it, seeing if I could find a way to somehow get the wire off and back on me somewhere, but a man came into the room and told us we needed to be ready in two minutes. The fact that a man had barged in was to be expected, I supposed, but I couldn't help but be surprised at the women who were still changing and half-naked. They barely flinched at the sight of him. Good thing I was already changed since I probably would have reacted quite differently, like screamed or flailed to cover myself or something equally discreet.

Note to self. Do not react to anything.

I could not figure a way to get the wire off the shirt, particularly without wrecking it. What looked like a simple button had wires out the back that continued down into the shirt, sewn in place. With the short amount of time I had, not to mention all the people milling about, I'd never be able to pull it off.

I needed to let Ryan know that I didn't have it anymore, and the only thing I could think of was to try and destroy it so that maybe it would go dead. I hoped it would be obvious if it went out of service, like a warning signal would come up or something, but there was a very real chance that the thing could just go dead and Ryan would think I was just being really quiet. Or like, napping.

Still, what choice did I have? I started picking at the button, pretending like it was a nervous habit I was doing to help try to calm my nerves. One of the other girls was pacing around anxiously, so I figured it wasn't a huge stretch. Soon, I had the front of the button nearly yanked right off, along with a good portion of my nail polish.

I only hoped it was enough to make the thing go black.

A few minutes later most of the girls were ready to go, although I wasn't sure where. A man (I'd have been shocked if his name wasn't Igor) herded us into a line and led us through a series of hallways. I made a mental note of which directions we turned the way I was taught in Everyday Surveillance, even though I wasn't sure why I'd want to go back to that dressing room. Except that my clothes were still there—not that they were likely clothes I'd ever wear again. Still, out of habit, or maybe just to help keep my mind occupied, I marked our steps in my mind and tried not to panic. Things were already starting to go wrong, and I wondered if I should be planning an escape route, just in case. I glanced around, making sure not to look too alert though no one seemed to be paying attention to me anyway, and compiled mental notes.

The mansion was set up as a house would be, not an institution, so there weren't clearly marked exits. Still, there were windows on the south walls of a grand room we were being herded through, so there was a good chance any doors on that wall led outside.

They herded us into a smaller room, this one dimly lit. The shadowy atmosphere lent an even creepier vibe to the place, and since I already knew I was in the middle of nowhere with a bunch of criminals, that was saying something.

My nerves began to twitch, and my heart beat a little faster. I took a few deep breaths to calm myself. The other girls started looking a little uneasy as well, which did not help deter my brain from performing its favorite little catastrophe disco.

A door opened on the opposite side of the room and an elegant woman in her own evening gown—much more tasteful than the rest of ours with a high neck and long sleeves—made the rest of us look like a bunch of prostitutes. Which was probably the point.

The man who'd led us into the room put his hand around the arm of the first girl and guided her toward the door where the woman stood. She gave the girl a once-over, nodded and went back out the door. The man and rather terrified-looking girl followed behind.

Soon the man and woman returned, the two of them leading the next girl out, and then the next. I tried to breathe, feeling more alone than I'd ever remembered feeling in my whole life.

Maybe half an hour later, I was at the front of the line, quaking like Jell-O on a roller coaster, trying to balance in my heels. It was bad enough I felt like I was going to topple over in the tight dress, but heels too? I mean, seriously, what was the point of all this? I desperately wanted the woman to hurry up and get back so I could just get whatever this was over with, but at the same time, I willed that damned door to stay closed forever.

Unfortunately, it didn't.

And then I was being pushed through the door and almost immediately toward a flight of stairs. The space was completely black except for a couple of dim lights on the stairs, like in a movie theater to guide you in the dark. I could hear voices, like the murmur of a small crowd somewhere nearby.

My pulse jackhammered as the woman gripped my

arm, forcing me up the stairs. She was much less gentle than the man had been, almost as if she was angry with me, although I couldn't fathom what on earth I might have done to her.

She shoved me through a black curtain and into an explosion of floodlights. I blinked and raised my arm to block the searing glare, trying desperately to see something, anything.

I was on some kind of a stage—the murmuring I'd heard loud now. I blinked again, my eyes adjusting a little. Below the stage was a small crowd, though I still couldn't see much. I got the sense they were sitting, but my eyes had begun to water from the abrupt change in light.

I had absolutely no idea what I was supposed to do.

A voice came from my left, maybe twenty feet away. "Okay, gentlemen, we'll start the bidding at one thousand."

*Bidding?*

I'd been to a few charity bachelor auctions, so I knew right away what must be going on. I was being auctioned off. *Jesus.* Somehow, I didn't think the winning bidder was just going to expect a nice dinner out of the deal. I guess the whole prostitution ring theory was confirmed. And I was the current item up for bids.

In the depth of my guts, my inner anatomy decided to hold a twerking contest. *What the hell had I gotten myself into?*

And I had no way of knowing if Ryan was anywhere that he could help. Without my wire, he probably didn't even know what was going on. Had no idea there might be a limit to how much time we had before I was "sold" and taken who knows where.

My mind started whirling with possible ways to escape. I couldn't shake the deep sense of dread telling me I had waited too long.

I put my arm up again, trying to see something, anything. An exit, preferably—although in the heels I wasn't really sure how far I could make it even if I was able to find a way out.

The audience was all men, all dressed in expensive suits and tuxes. The only women I'd seen since I'd left my apartment were the drugged ones and the horrible lady outside the stage. I wondered how she could justify being a part of all this. Money, I supposed. People did some really terrible things in the name of good ol' cash. Still, this was pretty extreme. Of course, I had to remind myself that I was supposedly here of my own accord. Perhaps not for money, but for what it could buy. Drugs. The twerking amped up to a full-blown dance party.

The bidding continued and the unwelcome question of how much I was worth took a wander through my mind. Ugh. No matter what the bid came to, I reminded myself, I was worth more than all of this. All these girls were.

I tried to look at some of the faces in the crowd. Especially the ones raising their paddles to bid. Could I take them in a fight? Would I be able to slip away without anyone knowing?

My eyes had more time to adjust, and I started to see much better. A man at the back lifted his paddle to place a bid. He caught my eye, and my heart skipped a beat.

Ryan.

I let a huge whoosh of air out, my whole body relaxing with relief.

I wasn't alone! And honest to goodness, that was the only thing that mattered in that moment. Except for the little issue of the tux he was wearing—and might I add, looking hotter than a foot-long row of flame emojis. The attire was an interesting surprise, and a bit of a puzzle—somehow I doubted they handed out tuxes at the door—but who cared! Ryan would simply bid on me, take me to wherever the people who won these things went and we'd simply slip away.

I was so relieved that I forgot what we were trying to accomplish and almost smiled at him, catching myself just in time. I quickly looked away and made sure not to look in his direction again. I mean, it wasn't likely these people would ever realize we were in this together, but then again, I had absolutely no idea how Ryan had even gotten in there.

But none of that mattered. Everything was going to be okay now.

Except, something weird was happening. The bidding was starting to slow down and now that I thought about it, Ryan seemed to have stopped raising his paddle. I stole a glance his way, but his face was unreadable. Staring straight ahead and not catching my eye, his jawline was set as if it were made of stone.

"Sold!" the auctioneer said loudly, banging the gavel onto his podium hard, knocking me back into the bleak reality of the present.

*What in the actual bloody hell*, was all I could think.

I took a deep breath. Okay. Ryan must have a good reason for doing what he was doing. Maybe he didn't have the kind of money these other guys were playing with. Come to think of it, I had absolutely no idea what I had even sold for. Which was probably a good thing.

What wasn't as good was when my stomach whirled out one last grievous tango as, out of the corner of my eye, I spotted Ryan being led away by two guys that were so immense and neckless they could have only been one thing.

Security.

# Chapter 20

I stood in a luxurious bedroom, complete with a very creepy-looking older gentleman smoking a cigar. And honestly, I don't usually get angry (unless you beat me at Monopoly), but the fumes were enough to make my already churning stomach want to relieve itself of its contents.

But I had to keep it together. Not only did I have to figure a way out of this room, but now I needed to figure out what was happening with Ryan and possibly even rescue him too.

And I had no idea how I was going to do it.

Especially in the damned heels.

The man had risen from his perch on the end of the bed as I was ushered in, then nodded to the guy who'd led me in. The jerk had the nerve to friggin' leave, making it just me and Cigar Man.

I cleared my throat and tried a smile, though I was pretty sure it didn't come out like I was super happy to be there. I choked back the excess saliva that invaded my mouth, both because of the churning stomach and the sickly sweet scent of the cigar.

He, however, was able to give me a full smile. And if I thought he looked creepy before, it was ten times worse now that he was looking me up and down and licking his lips. I fought the urge to shiver.

He set down his cigar and moved over to me, running his hands down the length of my arms. It took every ounce of self-control I had not to run screaming out of there. I couldn't quite bring myself to look him in the face, hoping the "too shy to talk" thing had a bit more mileage.

Not that he seemed very interested in talking.

As he circled behind me, I fully understood that I was on my own. Who knew what had happened to Ryan after he was escorted out?

I closed my eyes. *Okay*, I told myself. *First, I need to get out of here, then I can figure out what to do about the rescuing Ryan situation.*

I had to hatch a plan, and ideally it would happen in a somewhat brisk manner.

*So, WWND?*

As the carcinogen of a human continued his circle around me, I forced a smile, catching his eye for half a second and giving him the best knowing look that I could muster. He stopped in front of me, and I unbuttoned his suit jacket, pretending I was concentrating very hard on the task at hand. He looked like he had just swallowed a goddamned canary.

I held on to the lapel and began to walk around him, as if I was about to peel off his coat, then in as swift a move as I could manage, I reached around and pulled the other side of the jacket around his back as well, jerking both sides hard so that his arms were forced backward, still tangled in the jacket. I held the jacket in place with my left hand and curled my right arm around his neck, putting him in the sleeper hold I'd learned at Marge in Charge: A Woman's Guide to Self-Defense.

And people made fun of my classes. Honestly.

Everyone should take more classes. They really did come quite in handy.

Cigar Man struggled, but he wasn't a very big dude, and it didn't take long before he passed out from the lack of oxygen. I didn't want to hold the move for too long because I didn't want to truly hurt him, but unfortunately, my expertise on the matter was a tad flimsy, so I had to hope that instinct would come through. He flopped into my arms, and I held him for a few seconds longer, quickly realizing that he likely wouldn't be out for more than a minute, so my best bet would be to tie him up and maybe find a way to gag him.

I gently set him on the floor, which was more than the bastard deserved, but I couldn't bring myself to just drop him.

My eyes darted around the room searching for something to tie him with. Sadly, there didn't seem to be a rope conveniently nearby. In my fave amateur sleuth books, there was always a handy-dandy implement for whatever the situation called for.

*Sigh. Why did real life have to be so hard?*

I went back to the guy and undid his belt then wrangled the jacket off his arms. I cinched the belt around his wrists as best as I could, heaving him over to the bed. I raised his arms over his head and lifted a corner of the bed, dragging it just enough to hook his arms underneath so his arms were essentially above his head and looped around the bed leg. It wouldn't be impossible to get out of my makeshift trap, but hopefully by the time he woke, he'd be in too much pain and fatigue to fight his way out easily.

But I needed to keep him quiet too.

I ripped a pillowcase off one of the pillows and tried ripping it apart, wanting to make a strip of material to shove in his mouth and another to tie tightly around it so he couldn't just spit it out. Sadly, the bedding was really good quality, proving impossible to rip.

I let out a groan and glanced around one more time, looking for something sharp. Then it hit me. The heels.

I ripped off one shoe and held the fabric taut, shoving the stiletto through the material and ripping as hard as I could. Once I got the hole started, I was able to tear the material easily and soon had a fairly large chunk along with one strip. I shoved the chunk into his mouth and tied the strip around his head as tight as possible, then listened to make sure he was still breathing. I didn't particularly want a death on my hands, to be honest.

Kicking off the other shoe, I made a beeline for the

door, pausing to listen. When I didn't hear anything, I cracked it open a sliver and peeked out. The hallway seemed deserted.

Easing it open a bit more, I stuck my head out and peered around, but the coast was clear. I darted through the door and headed to the right, hoping my sense of direction wouldn't fail me. The house was a maze of hallways and I was probably completely turned around, but I ran anyway.

My mind swirled.

Now that I'd gotten out, I had no idea whether I should just find a way to get the hell out or sneak around to try to find Ryan. Ryan could take care of himself, but his situation had looked slightly dire the last time I'd seen him. Still, I knew that he'd kick my ass if he found out I had a chance to escape and didn't take it.

Okay, first, find an exit. Someplace that would lead me outside…then, once I had an escape route planned, I'd reassess the situation and see if it was safe for me to go back in. Or maybe I could actually get all the way outside and start peeking in windows. *I wonder what the chances were that they'd have Ryan in a room with a window?* But as I was thinking it, I realized I had yet to see a window that wasn't covered by heavy, impenetrable drapes.

I sighed. I swear, Nancy never had such troublesome dilemmas.

I slowed a bit as I approached a corner, my ears straining, but I was met with silence. I turned the corner at a fairly good clip, thinking I was close to the outside perimeter of the house. Maybe one more hallway and an exit door would appear.

Unfortunately, something very tall and very solid and dressed in a very alluring tux clotheslined me around my waist, stopping me mid-stride. I bounced back from the momentum I had going and stumbled, though my captor pulled me close.

"What are you doing?" the voice whisper-yelled at me.

My breath hitched. Up close, the man smelled even better than I imagined.

"Um, hi, Ryan."

He stared into my eyes. I held tight to his arms, which felt even more muscular than they looked. That same feeling of familiarity rushed through me—like tea and a good mystery, like the sun on your face on a perfect spring day, like curling up under the covers and starting a favorite movie.

It felt like home.

He blinked, startled, but much to my disappointment, he took a step back, keeping his arms out to steady me, which was probably a good thing, since I was suddenly feeling a bit woozy.

"You can't just go running around like that. There are security guys everywhere," he whispered, looking rather angry.

"I was listening for noise," I whispered back harshly, annoyed that he still didn't think I could do anything by myself.

"And how'd that go for you?" he asked, raising an eyebrow.

I narrowed my eyes. "Whatever. You're very quiet."

He closed his eyes and sighed, then took my hand. I'd like to say that the skin-to-skin contact didn't affect me, but my mind did go somewhat foggy, I was embarrassed to admit.

"How did you get out, anyway?" he asked.

"I have skills," I said, and gave him a look that hopefully conveyed that he really needed to stop underestimating me. I put my hand on my hip. "Besides, I could ask you the same thing."

He shot me a little smirk that sort of made my heart melt, then dragged me down the hall. Unlike me, he stopped to peek around the next corner.

Show-off.

We made it to what seemed to be the foyer, a huge room with a grand staircase and, blessedly, a set of large double doors on the other side.

"We're going to have to make a run for it," Ryan said. "We've been lucky so far but I'm going to assume they have cameras on this area."

"Okay," I said, supposing I could just follow his lead.

"Go!" he said and shot off in a sprint.

Which took me by surprise to say the least, but I was off in an instant, headed straight for the front door. He grabbed the doorknob and flung the door wide, turning to guide me out ahead of him, which made my heart do a little stutter flutter. I thought he'd been thinking it was every man for himself, but now I realized he wanted to get a head start to get the door open for me. What a gentleman.

The only unfortunate part was that instead of flying gracefully through that door, I spluttered to a dead stop.

Mostly due to the three guns pointed directly at my head, a circumstance that was becoming kind of an alarming pattern.

## Chapter 21

My hands flew above my head without even having to think about it and I'm sure my eyes were as big as the barrels of those guns. Seriously, they looked really friggin' huge from my vantage point.

"Ryan Kent," Ryan's voice uttered calmly beside me. "Private investigator. I'm the one who called this in."

I nearly gasped. Ryan was his first name. And holy mother-of-pearl, there was just something about a guy with two first names. Or two last names. Or, whatever... two great names in any case.

"Someone take these two out for questioning," one of the men holding a gun said.

My mind seemed to start working again, at least a little, and I finally registered that the gun-pointing dudes had uniforms on. SWAT and police uniforms to be exact.

For being the good guys, the police certainly weren't overly gentle with us. I wasn't sure if they thought we were lying about who we were, although I wasn't quite sure why else we'd be making an escape, but in any case, we were soon led to a "safe zone," where ambulances were arriving and official-looking people—some in uniforms and some in crumpled suits—waited for the police to do their job inside the mansion.

Additional police surrounded the perimeter of the building, which was a good thing, since several people in various stages of undress were trying to make their escape. If it hadn't been such a terrible situation, the whole thing might have been kind of funny, considering how obvious it was that some of the men had never run more than three steps in their lives.

Emergency vehicles continued to show up. Some of the men were secured in the backs of large trucks, several at a time. There was a chorus of "Don't you know who I am?" and "My lawyer is going to have your badge."

I shook my head. It always amazed me how certain people honestly thought they were entitled to get away with anything no matter who they hurt or what laws they broke. I suddenly got a sick feeling some of them probably *would* get off with a slap on the wrist at best.

I sighed. I liked money as much as the next person, but when too much of it was put in the hands of people like these guys, it became dangerous.

Girls were being led to the ambulances to be checked over.

"I hope they get the help that they need," I said.

Ryan nodded. "I'm sure they will for tonight. Hopefully at least some of them will be able to stay off the streets." He held the picture of his client's daughter in his hand, scrutinizing each girl as they were led past us.

I couldn't get over the sheer size of the operation going on around us. All because of Ryan and me. Well, okay, mostly Ryan—I may have been the bait, but knowing how to get this many people to come out into the middle of nowhere in the middle of the night was not one of my skills.

Eventually, the girl in the picture, Kathleen, made an appearance. A female emergency medical technician was leading her down the lawn toward our group. Ryan went to her, rechecking the picture several times.

"Kathleen?" he asked.

She glared at him. I supposed it had been a while since she'd had someone come up to her who wanted to help. I expected her to smile. To be relieved. Instead she glared even harder.

Ryan turned to me. "Can you give us a minute? I need to talk to Kathleen about a private issue."

"Uh, sure," I said, stumbling away in the too-tight dress and trying to understand what kind of issue would be too private for one of her rescuers to hear. I'd thought I'd kind of earned my way into the circle of trust or whatever, but then when Kathleen let out a wail, yelling at Ryan about being a bastard and a liar, I was embarrassingly relieved that I hadn't been there.

"Is she okay?" was all I could say as he wandered back over to me.

"Um," he said, clearly searching for what to say, "unfortunately, it's not the first time I found someone who didn't want to be found."

I shook my head. Being a private investigator in real life did not seem to have the warm fuzzy feelings that usually came at the end of my Nancy novels.

"Her mother will be relieved though," I said.

But Ryan just nodded absently, staring after Kathleen. He pulled out his phone and dialed, walking a few paces away for privacy.

A few minutes later he came over. "Come on," he said, hanging up. "Let's grab your clothes and get out of here. We've given them all they need."

I nodded, wondering why no one needed to question me. But it didn't really seem like the time to ask—Ryan just looked so...sad or something—so I just followed him back into the mansion where I retrieved my clothes and quickly changed in one of the many powder rooms, ditching the wig and wiping off as much of the makeup as I could.

We drove in silence for a while until eventually, I couldn't take it anymore. "So uh, I'm sorry that Kathleen was kind of...well, not happy, but you did a really good thing, you know."

He nodded. Then it was his turn to clear his throat. "Yeah, and um, I want to thank you for your help. I couldn't have done it without you." I could tell it was a little difficult to spit the words out.

I smiled. "You're welcome. It was fun."

He shot me a look that conveyed that I should definitely have *not* thought any of the past few days had been fun.

"So, why didn't any of the cops need to question me?" I asked.

In every movie and TV show I'd ever seen, every witness was thoroughly questioned, especially the ones that had played a major part in the takedown.

"I told them you worked with me." He said it quick and terse, like he was not exactly keen to add anything to that little tidbit.

So I just smiled.

When we got back to our building, things got quiet again. The old tension was back, especially in the elevator. What was it with elevators that turned you into a beacon of dumbassery with absolutely nothing to say? I stared at the numbers as we slowly rose to our floor.

Ryan cleared his throat. "So, uh, I know we've had kind of a long night, but I was just thinking... I could really use a drink and I'm wondering if maybe you do, too?"

I tilted my head, then nodded. "Yeah, actually I could but I don't have anything at my place right now." I couldn't imagine there was any of the wine left from earlier. Brandt and Vic liked their wine as much as I did.

"I've got a few things if you want to stop in for a bit," he said, actively avoiding eye contact.

"Um, yeah. That sounds nice," I said, trying my best not to let on that my stomach was suddenly hosting a gymnastics floor routine competition.

It was strange following Ryan to his door instead of heading to mine. I wondered if Brandt and Vic had stayed, waiting for me to get back. It wasn't like they hadn't slept over before if they'd had a bit much to drink or whatever, but I was sure that wasn't the case tonight. I'd texted them both to let them know it was over and that everything was okay, so it wasn't like they'd be worried or anything.

Strange. Come to think of it, neither of them had texted me back. Oh well, they'd probably fallen asleep. Either way, I wanted to have a drink with Ryan way more than I wanted to debrief my friends.

For being in the same building, Ryan's apartment was very different from mine. While mine was mostly white with pops of color in the artwork, rugs and cushions, his was sleek, polished wood and plenty of smoky gray and metal. So much more moody and dark than mine was, but I loved it anyway.

The walls had some black-and-white photography, but just architecture-type pieces. No personal or family photos to be seen anywhere.

"So, what do you feel like?" Ryan asked, taking off his coat.

"Whatever you're having. I'm not picky."

He went to the fridge and grabbed a couple bottles of import beer.

"Perfect, thanks," I said as he handed one to me.

I wandered the apartment a bit, stopping in front of a gleaming metal bookcase.

"Shit," he whispered.

For a second, I didn't know why he'd said it, but then I saw. A huge collection—maybe the entire series—of Hardy Boys books.

As a writer, I knew the English language had a word for pretty much everything. A *snollygoster*, for example, was a dishonest and corrupt person. Then there was the word *tessellate*, which was to form or arrange in a checkerboard pattern. Specific, right? But in that moment, I could contest that there were still words we hadn't suitably invented yet, such as a collective term for nieces and nephews, or a monumental-enough word to describe the feeling that was enveloping me.

I turned toward him, letting loose my best "seriously, you were heckling me about my Nancy books?" look.

He rolled his eyes, looking rather sheepish. "Okay, okay. I'm sorry. I get it."

"I am never going to let you live this down," I said, running my finger along the spines.

"I have no doubt," he said, laughing a little.

I studied the titles, marveling at how similar some of them were to my treasured Nancy books. *The Clue of the Broken Blade* was so similar to Nancy's *The Clue of the Broken Locket* and *While the Clock Ticked* made me instantly think of the very first Nancy book, *The Secret of the Old Clock*.

A strange feeling twigged in my mind. A flash of... something. I felt like I had noticed clocks more than average lately, like there was something I should be remembering.

Of course, the thought didn't have much chance to take hold considering I was occupying space with Ryan. I shook my head again, still a bit stunned with the whole Hardy Boys discovery and flopped onto the couch. Ryan quickly took a spot close to me. I'd expected him to sit in one of the chairs but was absolutely not going to complain that he wasn't.

"So, listen," he said, sitting upright and looking slightly uncomfortable. "I just wanted to officially say thank you for all your help with the case."

I smiled. "No problem."

"Seriously, Petra. I don't think I could have finished this one without you on the inside. And I'm still sick about how much danger you were in, but I also get that you can handle yourself. You're pretty great, actually."

My heart flip-flopped. "That might be the best compliment anyone has ever given me," I said.

He sort of smiled shyly, quickly taking a sip of his beer.

I'm not sure if it was the adrenaline of the day or finally being safe and sound in my own building, but suddenly I was very, very tired. I tried to sip my beer and just relax. Ryan finally leaned back too. We were sitting so close our arms were nearly touching and I could feel the warmth of him.

"I don't know about you," I finally said, "but that was one exhausting day."

"One for the books," he said, and let out a yawn.

I took a big gulp of my beer and sat up, setting it

down on the coffee table. "I should probably get out of your hair."

He sat up too, and suddenly his face was inches from mine. He reached out to set his beer down beside mine.

His lips. Those gorgeous lips were so close. I couldn't take my eyes off them, hypnotized. He smelled so good, and I wanted nothing more than for this moment to never end.

Then he leaned in and...promptly leaned back again. I wasn't sure my heart could take it—one second it looked like he was about to kiss me, and the next he seemed almost disgusted.

"I'm sorry, I can't do this," he said.

There were absolutely no words. What in the hell was someone supposed to say when something like that happened?

He ran his hands through his hair, some sort of internal struggle clearly taking place behind those hazel eyes.

"Ryan, what's going on?"

He sighed. "There's something I haven't told you."

"Oh god, are you married or something?"

Honestly, it was the exact sort of thing I would have written into one of my novels to send the tension through the roof.

"No," he said, though by the look on his face it almost seemed like he wished it was as simple as that. Which was to say, not simple at all.

"I... I haven't exactly told you everything about Kathleen's case," he started.

"Okay," I said, drawing the word out.

"I haven't told you who hired me to find her."

"You said it was her mother."

"Right, but I haven't told you who her mother was."

I tilted my head, questioning.

He swallowed. "It was Erica."

# *Chapter 22*

To say that I was shocked would be to say that my pal Nancy fancied a little mystery every now and then. "Erica from upstairs?"

He nodded.

"The woman who hired you to find her daughter is the same woman who died by suicide a week ago in this very building?"

"That's right."

My mind raced as I tried to breathe. "The one that Annie is completely positive did not actually die by suicide, but potentially by something else altogether. Maybe even by some*one* else altogether."

He nodded.

"And you're only now getting around to telling me this?"

"I know. It was stupid, and I'm sorry. I was just so freaked out about how deep you had already gotten involved in this whole thing and I thought I could protect you by keeping your part as small as possible." He shook his head. "Not that it was at all small, mind you, but I would have liked it to have been."

"Why are you telling me now?"

"Because..." He dropped his gaze, unable to look me in the eye. "Because when I sat down beside you just now, I wanted to kiss you, but I couldn't do that knowing I had this huge secret I was keeping from you."

And it was so stupid, and it probably happened mostly because I was so damned tired, but my eyes welled up. Or maybe it was because I was feeling so unworthy lately—unable to write, unable to do anything productive with my life—certain that this man in front of me was so far out of my league with his "put together" dates...except here he was telling me he wanted to kiss me and it just felt...well, nice, I guess.

Or maybe I was processing the fact that Kathleen, this poor girl who had just been freed from a drug and prostitution crime ring, had to be told that her mother was gone too. Oh, that's probably exactly what Ryan was doing when Kathleen screamed.

"That poor girl," I sort of whispered, my mind wandering over the cruelty of it all.

Ryan nodded.

"Obviously Erica's death has to be connected to the whole thing. I mean, I suppose a parent could conceivably want to end everything if their child is gone, but there was always hope that Kathleen would be found, right?"

Ryan nodded. "Yes, I think they're probably connected."

"Why haven't you talked to the police about any of this?"

"I have." He shrugged. "They know about Kathleen being missing and they believe—just like you said—that's the very reason that Erica decided to end things. That she'd given up hope on ever finding Kathleen alive. They're rationalizing that she just couldn't deal with it anymore."

"But Erica hadn't given up on Kathleen. She hired you, for crying out loud."

"I agree, but the police said the evidence of suicide is just too overwhelming. There was a note."

I rolled my eyes. "That's the oldest trick in the book. Suicide notes are easy to fake or coerce—anyone who's ever read a mystery knows that."

Ryan nodded. "I agree."

I could feel my anxiety starting to rise. "So what? Now Kathleen just comes back, and we're all supposed to say, *So sorry, but your mom's gone, here, have a little life insurance money to make it all better*?"

Ryan let out a breath, almost like a humorless chuckle. "We can't even do that much," he said, the pained expression returning to his eyes. "I talked to a friend at the police department. Shortly before her death, Erica rewrote her will and left everything to her new boyfriend."

My mouth dropped open. "That doesn't make any sense."

"The cops think it does, since their theory is that Erica thought Kathleen was gone forever."

"Except you knew that wasn't true."

"I *suspected* it wasn't true. That's a long way from knowing."

"Jesus. That is so messed up. And who is this boyfriend, anyway? Her husband just died, but all of a sudden, she's so close to this guy that she leaves everything she owns to him?"

Ryan shrugged. "After Kathleen, I don't think there was anyone else to leave anything to."

"But Kathleen is alive."

"Yeah," was all he said.

He didn't have to explain how awful the whole situation was. That much was more than clear. I could not stop thinking about how Kathleen was supposed to take this news. Being trapped inside the crime ring, she would have had no way of knowing her mom was even gone, let alone that she'd changed her will. Kathleen was essentially going to have to restart her whole life all alone and without any money to even get herself back together.

"Who was this guy, anyway?"

Ryan shook his head. "I don't know."

"But do you think he's legit? Was Erica really in love with him?"

"I don't know, Petra. I never saw the guy. I didn't know about any of this until after they found Erica."

"It's just…it's just not right. We have to tell Annie."

"I'm not sure that's a good idea. I'd like to close the

case on my own and then break the news to her once we know exactly what went down."

"Ryan, you know how much Annie cared about Erica."

"I know," he said. "I just don't want anyone else more mixed up in this than they have to be."

"But Annie might know something we don't."

"Petra," he said. "It's over. There's nothing we can do other than hope Kathleen can bounce back from this."

"Well, isn't that just...bullshit!"

I stood, not knowing what to do with myself. I had to move.

He nodded. "I know. I'm sorry."

I started toward the door.

"Petra, you don't look okay."

"That's because I'm not okay. This can't be it. This can't be the end of Erica's story."

Ryan sighed. "What are you going to do?"

"I don't know. I just need some time to think."

"There really isn't anything to think about. Is it terrible? Absolutely," he said, answering his own question. "But there's a lot of shitty things in this world that we can't do anything about, and unfortunately, this is one of them."

I let out a breath. "Fine. Then I guess I just need time to process. Time to try to get my head on straight again. I need some air."

I opened the door and stepped into the hallway, half expecting Ryan to try to stop me. But he didn't, which I took as a good sign. A sign that he trusted me enough not to do something stupid. Which was quite nice considering I didn't even trust myself not to do something stupid.

I headed to the roof. I really did need some air. Even though Ryan's apartment was minimalist and spacious, it was starting to feel like the walls were closing in on me. And I knew my apartment would be no better.

As I flung the door open, the air hit me like an ocean wave. The night was chilly, and I didn't have my coat, but something about it felt right. Like I wasn't supposed to be too comfortable in that moment. The breeze was strong and blew my hair back from my face, taking my breath away for a moment, but at the same time, it felt good. Like an invigorating freedom after being stagnant too long.

I walked to the edge of the roof, leaning on the rail, looking out onto the city.

Lights twinkled as far as the eye could see. It really was the most spectacular view of the cityscape I'd ever seen. So much life going on out there. It seemed perverse, that the world could just go on like nothing happened, even though someone's life had just utterly fallen apart. I suppose that was how it always worked. One person thrived while the next got kicked in the groin.

And then the cycle continued.

But thinking about that made me wonder why some people hardly ever got kicked, while the rest could barely get up before getting slammed right back down again.

I thought about Kathleen. The world was not a fair place.

A tear crept into my eye, quickly getting whisked across my temple by the wind. I wiped at the coolness of it, then laid my head on my arms as I leaned into the railing.

Somewhere a clock began to strike the hour.

I'd loved that sound as a kid. It was always strange to me to have a clock on the outside of a building. It was kind of an old-fashioned thing from a world before the time of digital watches and smartphones. I supposed there was probably a time when the average person couldn't even afford a pocket watch and depended on those sorts of public clocks to let them know when they needed to be somewhere.

I glanced around to find the source of the chimes. Several blocks away stood a tall building with an even taller tower. Probably a municipal building of sorts, something that taxpayer dollars kept maintained. It was a beautiful stone building, and I couldn't help but think I had seen something similar recently.

The puzzle.

There had been a clock tower like the one I was looking at on the puzzle that Erica had been working on right before her death.

Except Annie swore Erica would never be doing a puzzle. And didn't it seem strange that someone would feel the urge to do something they had never shown any interest in right before they were about to end everything? Especially something as mundane as a jigsaw puzzle? I tried to run through Erica's thought process of deciding things were so terrible that she just couldn't take it anymore, but then heading to the games room. Why didn't she just stay in her apartment to do what she needed to do? And why the puzzle?

Something didn't add up.

I forced myself to think about something I really did not want to think about. The way Erica looked that night, with her head slumped on the table, one arm above her head. One finger sticking out, almost... pointing.

I shook my head. I was sure that must have been a coincidence, had just been the way she had fallen. The police said that Erica had overdosed on her own sleeping pills. But again, why not just go to sleep in your own bed? The whole thing was just strange.

So strange that I decided I wanted another look at the puzzle. If it was even still there. I doubted the police had spent precious time cleaning it up, but maybe they needed it as evidence. Of course, if there was no suspicion of foul play, what kind of evidence did they really need though?

I moved quickly, on a mission now, heading to the games room, taking a moment to pause outside the doorway to take a deep breath and compose myself before stepping inside. I flicked on the light and my heart soared. I don't know why I thought it was so important that the puzzle still be there, but something wouldn't stop niggling at my brain.

The puzzle was only partially done, and if the box hadn't been sitting off to the side, I might not have known what it was supposed to be a picture of. The full outer edge of the puzzle had been completed, but there was only one other section started.

The clock.

Again, I tried to picture how Erica had been lying.

Maybe it was just my imagination, but now that I was picturing her again, I could almost swear that she had been pointing directly at that clock.

I started to pace.

This had to be nothing, right? But something about the whole situation didn't quite add up. I mean, maybe it was Annie getting into my head, but the thing was, Annie was not someone who spoke willy-nilly. She was thoughtful. She was careful. People didn't always take her seriously with the way she dressed, but that was only until they knew her. And that's what was bothering me so much.

I trusted Annie. Which also meant I was very much leaning toward believing her when she said she knew Erica well enough to know she wasn't in a place where she'd be willing to do what the police were saying she'd done. And that meant that Annie must be right about Erica hating puzzles too.

I paced some more. What would have brought Erica to the games room in the first place? Was it possible she was meeting someone? No, Jamieson had seen Erica in there alone. But then, if she was alone, why would Erica treat Jamieson the way she did? I mean, a lot of people would try to get rid of Jamieson—he was a bit of a dung beetle, honestly, but Jamieson himself said that Erica had always been good to him and it was out of character to act the way she did. Of course, if the police were to be believed, she wouldn't have been in a normal state of mind, but still. Wouldn't she have seemed sad, or upset, or something? But Jamieson said she just seemed like she wanted to be alone.

So…what if she had good reason to want him out of there? Like maybe because he might be in danger. Because the long and the short of it was that if Erica hadn't taken her own life, then absolutely there was danger lurking around very close. But…where?

I stopped pacing and turned to the table. Then glanced beyond it.

The alcove.

That day that Annie and I had come in here, Eliza had scared the absolute shiznit out of us because she'd been hiding in that alcove. And she hadn't even been hiding on purpose—there was just a lot of space back there. A person could easily have been hiding, waiting for Jamieson to leave.

Of course, then the question became, why would Erica stay?

I needed more to go on. I needed a damned clue.

It took me a moment to work up the nerve to sit in the chair Erica had been sitting in when I found her that night, but I wanted to get a sense of what things looked like from her perspective. Maybe if I could see what she saw, something would stand out. I sat and peered around the room. The alcove was almost a natural place for someone to be sitting, or maybe standing, if they were talking to Erica. Especially if they had an idea about what they were about to do.

I took a deep breath, letting the idea wash over me. Was I really sitting here by myself thinking murder? I swallowed.

Okay, this was fine. This was the kind of stuff I had an interest in. Although if I was being honest, it was more the puzzling things out that got me going than the actual catching of criminals. I always thought that sort of thing was best left to the professionals. Except in this case, the professionals had given up.

And hadn't I proved to myself over the past few days that I was more capable than I ever thought?

I nodded, having sufficiently talked myself into pushing the potential danger out of my mind and focusing on the one thing I could focus on. Finding clues and figuring out what really happened to Erica.

Unfortunately, sitting where Erica had been sitting wasn't really making any giant clues jump out at me. I got up and went to the alcove, searching the floor to see if there were any shoe prints or, even better, seeing if anything had been dropped. Of course, if there had been anything obvious, the police would have noticed it and I wouldn't be the only one still searching for the truth.

I sat back down.

The puzzle was literally the only thing I had to go on, and it wasn't much. I mean, what did Erica doing a puzzle even mean? Maybe she was just trying to distract her mind from the danger in front of her. Or maybe, in some desperate long shot, she was trying to leave a message behind.

And if I had any chance at deciphering it, I needed to enlist some help.

# Chapter 23

"I'm sorry to show up so late," I said, as a concerned-looking Annie opened the door. The woman was truly a miracle. Here it was, two in the morning and she was the picture of radiance. Unfortunately, I was pretty sure the same could not be said for me considering I was still in my disguise clothes, my hair was likely inexplicable and I had no makeup on. You know, except for the dark and probably smeared eyeliner that I couldn't quite get off completely back at the mansion.

"What's going on, dear?" she asked, ushering me inside.

Bless the woman's soul, she didn't even ask why I was knocking on her door so late.

"Annie, have you been inside Erica's apartment?"

Annie tilted her head in question. "Of course, why?"

"Does she have a clock?"

"That's a strange question. Doesn't everybody have a clock? I believe I have about seven of them myself."

I nodded. "Of course, yeah. I was just wondering if there was ever anything significant about Erica and a clock."

Annie crinkled her brows together. "I don't really think so. I mean, she did have that gorgeous antique on her mantel, but she never told me how she got it or anything like that."

I nodded. "I suppose it would be bad form to break into the apartment of someone who had just died, hey?" I said, joking.

Annie raised her eyebrows. "Well, we wouldn't really have to break in, dear. I do have a key."

My eyes went wide. "Have you been in there since she's been gone? Is anything out of place?"

Annie's eyes glistened over. "I... I know I should go in there and make sure everything is in order. Her plants are probably way overdue to be watered but..."

"I'm so sorry, Annie. This must be incredibly difficult for you."

She nodded. "Maybe it wouldn't be so difficult if I had someone with me when I go. Would you be willing to go in there with me?"

"Of course," I said quickly, hoping I didn't sound too eager.

We made our way to Erica's apartment and the silence that met Annie's knock at Erica's door was absolute.

"I'm not sure why I'm even knocking. It doesn't

seem right to just walk in, I guess," she said, sadness filling her voice.

As Annie turned the key, the excitement I'd had about possibly finding more clues had waned and the realization that Erica would never step foot in her apartment again hit me in the guts. Whether Erica was responsible for her own death or not, the whole thing was just so unfair.

Annie paused in the doorway, taking a moment before she could continue inside. Eventually she flicked on a switch and the apartment was instantly bathed in muted light. The place was decorated elegantly, stark but cozy, and the scent of spiced fruit and cedar subtly filled the air. I mean, I wasn't one for fancy fragrances (for me, essential oils were what dripped down your chin whilst eating saucy ribs), but this was nice, not too chokey.

"It's strange that the curtains are all closed. Erica always had everything wide open, though I suppose that night she'd probably already closed them for the evening."

I nodded, not sure what to say. "Maybe we should leave everything the way it is," I said.

"I'm not sure that really matters anymore," Annie said, implying what both of us already knew. That there would be no further investigation.

I glanced around, admiring Erica's taste. The place was minimally decorated, and the few pieces she did have on display were obviously well taken care of and loved. I couldn't help but notice the antique clock sitting on the fireplace mantel and it took everything in me not to run over to examine it.

"I'm surprised Michael hasn't been around yet to collect his things," Annie said.

"Michael?"

"Erica's new beau, Michael Turner. They made such a beautiful couple. So different, yet both so attractive in their own ways."

"Erica was beautiful," I said. "So put together. She always seemed so full of life…" I trailed off, cursing myself for choosing those words.

But Annie nodded. "She was. That's why none of this makes any sense," she said, her voice cracking on the last word. She cleared her throat. "And Michael, he was a real looker with those striking blue eyes."

"Striking blue eyes?" I asked, wondering if maybe I'd seen him around the building with Erica. I felt like I had seen eyes that matched that description recently…

"They're quite marvelous, really. He has this dark hair, which is such a contrast to those eyes. The kind of look that's not easy to forget."

I furrowed my brow trying to place where I'd seen someone exactly like that.

Annie moved down the hall and into what I assumed was Erica's bedroom, and my attention moved back to the clock, but as the light flicked on down the hall, Annie let out a little scream. "Oh my lord, Michael, you nearly scared me half to death."

*Michael?* My mind spun as I followed Annie's voice. Why was Michael here? More importantly, why hadn't he answered the door when we knocked?

Dread crawled up my insides, taking hold of my heart as a heavy clunk sounded from the bedroom.

I rushed in to find a man standing over Annie, who was, oddly, lying on the ground. In the moment it took me to process what had happened, the man turned, meeting my gaze. His eyes. Those steely, ice-blue eyes.

The same eyes that my gaze had locked with during my escape from the apartment Ryan had been staking out.

"You're Michael?" The words fell out of my mouth before I could catch them.

But Michael didn't say anything. He did, however, begin moving toward me—slightly less stunned about the whole situation than I was. Still, I was able to turn and take a few steps, moving toward the front door, but Michael was too fast, his viselike grip clamping around my arm, flinging me back hard. I stumbled but stayed on my feet.

"Okay, okay," I said, putting my hands up to show I wasn't going to run.

He pointed to the sofa. "Sit."

I hated that I followed his command, but I wasn't especially in control of my reactions in that moment, fear having apparently moved into my brain and evicted everything else.

Finally, I got myself together enough to speak. "What did you do to Annie?" I asked, fearing the worst.

I hadn't seen any blood, but it wasn't like I'd had a whole lot of time to process the scene.

He shrugged. "I'm sure she'll be fine. Might have a

bit of a headache later though," he said, kind of sneering like he was proud of himself.

"Shouldn't you be skipping town or something after the big roundup of your buddies?" I asked.

It was nice to see it was his turn to be surprised. Given the disguise that day I'd escaped the apartment, it was clear that he didn't recognize me.

He blinked a few times, then said, "I don't know what you're talking about. I was just gathering a few of my things before building maintenance cleans out Erica's things."

"Right," I said, nodding. "That's why you're lurking around in the dark and knocking out harmless ladies in the bedroom." Honestly, the moron didn't even deserve one of my signature eye rolls.

He shrugged, then went to a drawer in the kitchen. I guess since he'd been dating Erica he knew exactly where she kept the duct tape. Or maybe it was his—lord knew the dude loved the stuff.

Michael sat me in a kitchen chair, wrapping my wrists with the tape, then moved to my ankles. He really did have a knack for it.

Once I was secured, he resumed rummaging around, this time in the kitchen.

"What are you looking for?" I asked. "Don't you already know where everything is?"

He shot me an exasperated glare.

"No, seriously. I mean, you already have everything you want, right? Except...why wouldn't you have left town by now? Being here is a pretty big risk. Anyone could walk in on you at any time, and we can certainly assume you've got a warrant for your arrest out there."

He shook his head. "They probably have an arrest warrant for Michael Turner."

"Exactly," I said.

"The only thing is, my name isn't Michael Turner."

My stomach dropped. "But... Erica called you Michael. She would have named Michael Turner when she changed her will."

"Nope. She put my real name."

"Which is?"

He grinned. "Nice try," he said, then continued searching.

"Okay, so if you have this will with your real name on it, and I presume since you belong to what seems to be a long-standing crime ring, you probably already have a way of getting the money into some offshore bank account or something, which you'll be able to access once you've skipped town." Honestly, I wasn't sure I was pulling off all the lingo like *skipped town* and *crime ring*—I mean, I didn't even know if people used those phrases in real life, but Michael didn't seem to think anything of it. Or maybe he was just trying to ignore me.

Michael continued searching while I did a little searching of my own. Searching of my brain, that is, to try to come up with some idea of how to get someone from outside that apartment to figure out Annie and I were in there and that we were in danger.

I thought of my favorite girl detective again. She would have probably come up with at least three different solutions for alerting someone to our situation, and she didn't even have cell phones to rely on back then. Unfortunately, my brain had become too dependent on my damned phone, and it was literally the only thing I could think of to use. And yeah, I could think of about seven ways to use it—text someone, have it make loud noises, send out a tweet or, you know, dial emergency services. The only problem was the small matter of my hands tied behind my back.

*Okay, channel Nancy*, I thought. Back in the days before cell phones she always found a way to alert people to danger. Maybe I could start a fire and get the smoke alarms to go off. Of course, that would be somewhat challenging without the use of my hands. *Come on, think.* Then I had it. I stood, super awkward and crouched over with the chair attached to my ankles and everything, but thanks to my yoga classes, I was pretty well versed in chair pose. *Okay, here goes*, I said in my head, as I sat down as hard and as loud as I could. I did it again. Stand. Sit. Stand. Sit. The chair clanged as the legs met the floor. I knew it was a long shot—everyone in the building was probably asleep—but I couldn't sit there and do nothing.

Unfortunately, Michael didn't love my little performance and abruptly came over and smacked me right in the face. In the face! I mean, how much ruder could you get than smacking someone open-handed right across the cheek? What a jackwagon.

Once I straightened back up, I gave him my best glare to let him know I did not appreciate his reaction. I mean, I guess he hadn't appreciated my reaction to what he was doing either, but I don't think there was any question as to who was in the wrong.

Michael started pacing, doing less searching and more...I don't know, getting worked up like a hyena in heat (absolutely no idea if hyenas go into heat, but it paints a picture, yeah?) and part of that was probably my fault, but I think it also had to do with the fact that he was not finding what he was looking for.

And then it hit me.

Another will.

That had to be the piece of the puzzle that I'd been missing. If he already had it all worked out with the offshore account and all that, the only thing that would have been holding him there was the possibility of another—perhaps more recent—will.

My mouth dropped open. "She told you there was another one, didn't she?"

Michael's head whipped around to face me. "What do you know?" he asked, breathing hard through his nose like an angry bull.

"Hey, man, don't look at me. I'm just figuring this out as we go. And the only thing I can think of that would explain you still hanging around is that there must be another will stashed somewhere." I let out a humorless chuckle. "And it seems like you might be having a little trouble locating it." I shook my head like he was pathetic. And yeah, it wasn't like I had any idea where another will might be either, but I barely knew the woman.

"Oh, shut up, would you?"

I shrugged as best as I could with my hands tied

behind my back. "Erica must have been pretty smart. Planting that seed of doubt, probably right when you were about to murder her. Or maybe after you had already poisoned her with her own sleeping pills. How did you get her to take them anyway? I mean, I assume you crushed them up in her tea, but how did you get her to write out the note and drink it?"

"You're so damned smart, why don't you tell me?"

I had to say, I was getting really tired of this asshat.

"It had to be Kathleen, didn't it? Erica knew you had her. She was willing to give up her own life to save her child. The child that you no doubt lulled into that life with the drugs and the rest of it."

He tilted his head. "You'd be surprised how easy it is to get troubled young women to go down the wrong path. There's a lot of pressure on kids these days. Pressure to be perfect. Pressure to perform. When you grow up on social media, your whole life is about what people think. How many views and likes you get. And when nobody is paying attention to you, it's easy to believe that you're not worthy of people's time. That you're not interesting. That, in fact, you're not worthwhile at all."

"And that's where you come in. How very predatory of you. So…how do you do it?"

Michael sighed. "Once someone is already feeling like they're worthless—which, to be honest, is most of the younger generation these days—all you have to do is pay them a tiny bit of attention."

"But why would any young woman care about attention from some old guy like you? No offense," I added—I mean, I wasn't a monster.

"They wouldn't. We have recruiters for that. Gorgeous young people. Men and women who spend time on social media getting attractive young women to meet with them. Eventually most of them do, they're so desperate for attention. By the time they get to them, they're primed to do almost anything to impress the one person who really gets them." He chuckled. "So frail. So gullible. All it takes then is a little push to try the drugs—just a little convincing that it's no big deal, and voilà, after a time or two they're hooked."

I shook my head, bitterness flooding my mouth. To use people's insecurities against them was a special kind of evil, and these bastards had made a whole damned industry out of it.

"So what then?" I asked. "Why mess with Erica too? Wasn't destroying her daughter enough?"

"For years we didn't bother with the parents. But then we acquired some contacts in the police force and found out how desperate these people were to get their kids back. They would do almost anything."

"Really? It took you having an insider to figure out that parents love their children? Some personal life you must have."

"Actually, it was *not* having a personal life that made the idea come to me. You see, the thing about beautiful young women is that often the mothers are beautiful too. And some of them are single," he said, pumping his eyebrows.

Honestly, what a skeev.

"And the thing with the older generation of single women is that sometimes they have a whole lot of cash to part with—you know, in case something tragic were to ever happen to them."

The bile rose in my throat. "You're disgusting."

He turned to me. "You know, that's something that I am perfectly fine being. I like the company of women and I like money. Besides, I've been told they quite like my company as well," he said, those icy blues twinkling.

"Gross."

He tilted his head in a "perhaps, but it works for me" kind of way.

"Too bad Erica was a little too smart for you." I grinned.

He shook his head, clearly annoyed that I kept interrupting his progress. He looked around some more, which gave me time to think about what my next plan of action would be since clearly the banging the chair against the floor hadn't done much. Although, now that I was thinking about it again, the tape around my ankles had gotten somewhat looser above my right foot. I wiggled my ankle around, realizing that the tape had stuck more to my sock than it had to my jeans on that side. If I could just keep wiggling until my sock came off, I might be able to get my foot free.

With one eye on Michael, I wiggled that foot like my life depended on it, which, I was beginning to think, it probably did.

I wiggled and twisted until it felt like my ankle was about to pop out of place, and then suddenly the hem of my jeans came loose from the tape completely, my sock pulling down around my heel. A few more wiggles and my foot was free.

I glanced around, twisting a bit and shimmying my chair as quietly as I could. Thankfully, Michael had other things on his mind as he began throwing items out of the kitchen drawers, seemingly more desperate by the second.

I was about five feet from the window, so I shimmied a bit closer then stopped to double-check if Michael was paying attention. I mean, if I was being completely honest, the wiggling might have worn me out more than I cared to admit, and I might have enjoyed the tiny break it gave me to catch my breath.

I took a deep breath and shimmied even closer. Four feet now. Another glance over my shoulder, then another shimmy. Three feet. A couple more feet and I could... Well, I wasn't sure, but I hoped something would miraculously come to me in the next few seconds.

Two feet away.

"Hey, what are you doing?"

Without thinking, I kicked my foot out, smashing through the window, the glass scraping my bare foot as it broke through, pain jolting up my leg.

And then the chair I was in was being whipped around and the last thing I saw before everything went black was a look of absolute contempt on Michael's face.

# Chapter 24

Shuffling noises were the first thing I noticed. The pain behind my right eye was the second. There was no third, since the pain was pretty much all that was on my immediate radar after I'd discovered its existence.

I slowly tried to blink my eyes open, squinting at the light.

"She's coming to," a voice said. And goddamn, it was a sexy voice. "Petra, are you okay?"

I tried to nod, but that made me close my eyes again, trying to fight off the angry jolt that blazed through my head. After a careful, shallow breath—I'd tried a deep one, but that was no good for the head either—I opened my eyes once more.

"Hey," I said, though it was more of a croak.

"Hey," Ryan said, tucking a piece of my hair behind my ear.

And it was so gentle, his fingers grazing my jaw-line, his eyes filled with concern.

It was only then I remembered where I was. Against my better judgment, my eyes darted around the room, trying to figure out what had happened.

Annie was sitting on the couch. She was holding an ice pack to her head, but besides that she looked as good as ever. I breathed a sigh of relief.

"Michael?" I asked, worried.

"We have him, Petra. Thanks to you, we have him."

Another layer of stress left my body.

I tried to sit, Ryan helping me. "Watch your foot," he said.

My foot. I'd forgotten all about my foot, which seemed to be oozing quite a lot of blood. The chair I'd been taped to sat—still upended—a few feet away. Ryan must have cut me free.

"How long was I out?"

"Just a few minutes," Ryan said. "The paramedics aren't even here yet. Don't move too much, okay?"

I nodded, which sent another wave of pain through my head. I raised my hand to my head, feeling for the goose egg I already knew was there.

"What happened?"

"I heard a smash and rushed out to my balcony to see what was up, and there were still a few pieces of glass raining down to the street. Which got me thinking about the thumping sounds I'd heard earlier. It hadn't occurred to me that they were coming from Erica's apartment. But somehow the falling glass made me realize."

My eyes widened. "Was Michael still in here?"

"He was racing down the hall, trying to get away."

I smiled. "But you stopped him."

"No," he said, shifting a little. "I just kept wondering about the glass and the thumping and I thought Annie, or maybe you," he said, meeting my eyes, letting me know how worried he'd been, "had been in here."

"You risked letting him get away to help me?"

He nodded. "And I would do it again."

My smile widened, then fell away. "But you said you had him."

Ryan nodded. "Hazel from security came to the rescue. She was just coming on shift and saw the glass too. She headed for the stairs to see what was going on and since Michael had seen me coming off the elevator, he took the stairs instead." He shrugged. "Poor choice on his part. Hazel knew right away that he was up to no good and detained him."

"I always liked that girl," I said, moving my jaw a little, testing how far the pain went.

The paramedics came in then and pulled Ryan away so they could shine lights in my eyes and press a bit on my goose egg—basically doing everything that would make me hurt just a bit more. In the end though, they said I would be okay and that I didn't need to go to the hospital.

They checked out Annie and gave her the same prognosis.

By then the cops had arrived and were taking everyone's statement, sitting us one by one on the couch to do so.

I was oh so lucky enough to be questioned by Jess, the detective who clearly had a history with Ryan, but I relayed everything that went down without letting it affect me. Much. I told them all about how he'd hurt Annie and then started rummaging through the place.

"I think I was kind of annoying him," I said. "I was doing it on purpose, trying to distract him from what he was doing."

Detective Jess glanced up from her notepad. "And what was he doing?"

"Just rummaging around in everything looking for the..."

And I'm not sure why my eyes chose that second to land on Erica's fancy clock on the mantel above her fireplace at the exact time I was saying those words, but they did. And that made it all click. The way Erica's hand had been pointing to that clock in the puzzle. I always knew my Nancy love would be the thing that saved me.

Well, okay, I had already technically been saved, but the full mystery had yet to be solved.

Detective Jess stared at me, no doubt wondering if I was having some sort of medical issue, but in that moment, I couldn't think about her. All I could think about was the very first Nancy novel—*The Secret of the Old Clock*—because the clock in that book had a secret compartment.

I held my breath and fought through the pain as I

got up and limped over to the clock, pulling it from the mantel. It was heavier than I thought it would be.

I turned it around so the back was facing me but couldn't see any obvious openings or compartments. Which I suppose was good or else Michael may have found it, but I did encounter my first niggle of doubt.

I flipped it upside down. Same thing.

Then I shook it, and I was sure Annie was about to tell me to put the poor thing down—it probably wasn't super constructive to shake an antique clock after all—but then she heard the same thing I heard.

A distinct rustle of paper.

"Is there something in there?" she asked, moving closer.

I nodded. "I think so. I just have to figure out how to get—"

I'd been fiddling with the face of the clock, wondering if perhaps it might somehow flip open when...it did! The entire face hinged open to reveal the compartment that I had hoped beyond hope existed.

I reached in and withdrew the few sheets of paper hidden inside, unfolding them to see perhaps the most beautiful words in the English language.

"Last Will and Testament."

"We need to get this to whoever is dealing with Erica's estate," I said.

Annie nodded, speechless since the clock had revealed its secret. Finally, she spoke. "I'll call Kathleen."

I relayed the rest of my story to the police, including my suspicion about the double wills, and how Erica had been coerced into the first one, but had been smart enough to write a second, hiding it.

"There's just one thing I can't figure out," I said. "I don't understand why she would tell Michael about the second will."

"She must not have had time to tell anyone else about it before Michael got to her," Ryan said. "Maybe she thought if her apartment was ransacked from his searching, someone might clue in as to what he was looking for. It might have been the only way anyone would know they should even be looking for something."

"Right, that makes sense," I said. "Still, that was a risky move."

He nodded. "It must have been the only move she had left."

A moment of silence fell over the room then, until Detective Jess cleared her throat. "Well, I guess we're about done here," she said. "Ryan, can I walk you back to your apartment?"

I had to admit, I did not love the way her eyebrow rose in a sort of "come hither" way.

Ryan looked from Jess to me, then back to Jess. "Actually, yeah," he said, and I hated to admit how much my heart sank in that moment. "In fact," he continued, gently grabbing hold of my elbow, "you and I are both going to make sure Petra gets back to her place safe and sound."

It was all I could do not to jump up and down and squeal. Which probably would have hurt quite a lot, so I just did it in my mind instead. I wish I could say the look of disappointment on Jess's face didn't affect me, but honestly, I was feeling extraordinarily gloaty. Of course, then I started wondering why, exactly, he wanted her there when he walked me back to my place.

"You guys go ahead. I'll make sure everything's locked up tight," Hazel—who'd been up there observing since the cops showed up—chimed in.

"Thanks, Hazel," Ryan said.

I was so aware of his hand on my lower back, gently guiding me out of the apartment, I don't even remember how we got to the elevator, but as we stepped in, he let go and I regained my ability to think.

"Are you sure you're okay?" he asked.

"Yeah, I think so," I said. "I think I just need some sleep."

"Did the paramedics say that was okay? No risk of concussion or anything?"

I nodded. "I asked. They said sleep would probably do me good."

"Okay, good," he said as the elevator doors opened on our floor.

We headed down the hall, a little twinge of disappointment zipping through me that he didn't put his hand on my back again.

And way too fast we were at my door, me fiddling to find my key, as was my way.

"Before you go in," Ryan said, "there's something we all need to discuss."

"I really don't know, outside of what just happened upstairs, what the three of us would have to discuss," Jess said.

And as much as I didn't want to be, I was definitely on the same page as Detective Jess about that.

But Ryan continued. "Normally I would agree, and this certainly isn't a conversation I ever envisioned myself having to have, but there is the little issue of a certain anonymous admirer."

"Ugh," I groaned. "Do we really have to file a report? Or can we at least do it some other time? My head is still killing me and honestly, I'd just like to relax," I said.

But then I noticed the tension in the hallway had increased about a millionfold and that Jess had gone unnervingly still. Ryan hadn't taken his eyes off her.

And I couldn't, for the life of Nancy, figure out what the hell was going on.

But something definitely was.

"Shit," Jess finally said, sort of under her breath.

"No kidding," Ryan said. "What the hell were you thinking?"

My eyeballs bounced between Ryan and Jess like they were playing Ping-Pong. "Um, not to get in the middle of something, but can someone tell me what's going on?"

"Oh, you're definitely in the middle of it whether you like it or not," Ryan said, though from his tone, he was decidedly not happy to have me in the middle of...whatever this was.

"I've been doing some research on your 'anonymous admirer,'" he said, using air quotes and everything.

"Okay..." I said, the word trailing off like a question.

Ryan turned to Jess and stared. "Are you going to

tell her or am I?" he asked. As hard as I tried, I was absolutely not catching on.

And then Jess opened her mouth and I thought she was about to, I don't know, do something police-y, but then she said, "I'll stop, I promise. Just don't go to the captain with this."

*Wait. What?*

"That will be up to Petra," Ryan said, and it seemed like this whole conversation was starting to mean that Jess was the one who had been sending the gifts, which made absolutely no sense at all. Still searching the ground for an answer that clearly wasn't going to be found there, my body spit out the word "Why?" before I could even stop it.

Jess let out a long sigh and scratched her forehead. She looked like she would be much happier if the building would just go ahead and crumble all around us.

"I don't know. I just, ugh…" She winced as if she were in pain. "I guess I didn't like the attention you were getting. I wanted it to seem like maybe you were unavailable, and…I don't know, make things a bit uncomfortable for you in the process." She glanced at Ryan.

And that was the moment he started looking like he was kind of in pain too. Or maybe it was more like that awful secondhand embarrassment you get when you're watching the auditions of a singing reality TV show and the person thinks they're amazing when they're clearly not.

"Look," Ryan said, "we've been over this, Jess. I'm

sorry about that one night, but I've told you, I'm not looking to get into anything."

"With me, anyway," she said, turning to stare daggers into me, which seemed kind of uncalled-for.

He sighed. "Yeah, I guess with you, Jess. Are you happy? Is that what you wanted to hear?"

And then the hardened detective's eyes welled up, and I really, really don't do well when someone else's eyes well up because it always makes my eyes want to well up and then I start thinking about what it must be like to be in their situation and lord knows I'd had my fair share of dating rejection all the way back to Jacob Corby in seventh grade when he made me think he was into me, except what he was really into was someone else doing his English essay for him.

But then she covered her tears by getting even angrier, this time aiming her resentment at me. "Are you going to press charges, or not?"

"I... I..." I stuttered, still in shock that my anonymous admirer was a woman who was, what? Jealous of...me? That was definitely something I needed a minute with. But now that the identity of said admirer was out in the open, I was fairly certain the gifts would stop. Which, to be honest, was kind of a shame. I mean, this woman knew how to send a gift, I thought, wistfully wondering how Jack P. was doing. But then I pulled my shoulders back. "No. I'm not going to press charges."

"Okay then," Detective Jess said with a nod. She turned and walked away, unable to even glance at Ryan again.

And then she was at the elevator, and it took forever for it to get there, and Jess stared so hard at those doors I was afraid she might burn a hole through them, until finally the doors opened and she got on. As the doors were closing, I couldn't stop myself from yelling, "They were really good chocolates!"

And then she was gone.

I turned slowly to Ryan.

"Um, that was unexpected."

"It was," Ryan agreed. "I, uh, I'm sorry for being mad at you about the anonymous-admirer thing."

"Because…" I let the word trail off.

I knew he felt responsible, and after all the grief he'd given me, I couldn't help but make him squirm a little.

He ran a hand through his hair. "Because I slept with her, okay? And it was a long time ago and it was just one stupid night when I was on a stakeout with her since we were working the same case. We ended up catching the bad guys and went for drinks to celebrate and one thing led to another, and well, it was stupid. Because she got attached. And didn't seem to want to let it go. But mostly, I could avoid her. Until this thing in our building. Which I guess…set her off again."

I nodded, trying my best to process that little bout of word vomit.

"I thought you said you didn't use the term *bad guys*."

"That's what you got out of all that?"

I shrugged. "I'm still processing."

"How long do you think you're going to need for that?" he asked.

I tilted my head one way, and then the other, my head feeling surprisingly better. "I think I'm good. There's just one thing I don't entirely get. Why did she fixate on me?"

"It was because..." he started to say, then paused.

That look of uncomfortable pain came over him again and I decided the poor guy had been tortured enough for one day.

"Well, thanks for everything," I said, finally moving my key toward the lock.

"Thank you," he said. "Without you, I'm not sure anyone ever would have found the other will and Kathleen would have been out of luck. Maybe even out on the street."

I shrugged one shoulder. "I didn't really do anything."

Ryan gave me kind of a stern look then, like he was going to lay into me about not giving myself enough credit or something, but then, he apparently decided to do something different.

He moved in close. "It was because she was always able to tell when I was into someone else."

And then he leaned down and kissed me.

And I nearly fell to the floor.

But somehow, I remained upright and even found a way to ease into the kiss as if it had been expected all along. His lips were warm and soft, energy flowing through them straight into me, swirling to my toes. He put his hand on the back of my neck and pulled me closer—gentle but somehow also urgent.

I'm embarrassed to say I may have moaned a little.

But the moan only seemed to get him more fired up

as he pulled me tighter, then put his hands under my butt, hiking me onto his hips.

Funny how certain things—adrenaline, a shock of surprise, a concentrated shot of longing straight to the nether regions—can make the exhaustion of an impossible day completely disappear.

Ryan pulled back and looked at me, though all I wanted was to feel his lips again, for them to never leave mine. He moved toward his apartment door and had it open in three seconds flat.

Show-off.

"I'd really love to take this to the bedroom," he said in a gravelly voice. "But I don't want to rush if you don't want to."

My head nodded rapidly and of its own accord, like some kind of bobblehead, hopefully a sexy one (ooh, sexy bobblehead. New Halloween costume?). "Bedroom, yes, please. Rushing can be good sometimes," I said, even though I'd imagined the moment so many times it hardly felt like rushing.

My limbs were heavy, wholly relaxed, as he eased me onto the bed, then stood to tear off his shirt and holy moly, was *that* worth the wait. I scrabbled with my own shirt, arms flailing like I'd grown an extra set and all they wanted to do was tangle. Finally free, his hand found my waist and he closed the gap between us, the heat of our skin threatening to ignite a fire as my legs wrapped around him. He pressed against me, crushing his hips to mine, easing the exquisite pressure, but only for a moment before it built again, tenfold.

He kissed my neck, and up under my ear, then began to work his way down, tasting his way—an explorer mapping new worlds—my breath catching as he moved to my breast, lips grazing over the lacy fabric of my bra, my body reacting immediately and intensely. I fought to release myself from the cloth prison, flinging the offending annoyance across the room, running my hand through his hair as he took my breast into his mouth, an epicenter of pleasure pulsing shock waves through me.

My hands uncovered all the mysteries of his body—I couldn't get enough of his arms, his strong back—and then as he rose, his chest…his zipper. All the clothes had to go, a frantic flurry of rushing, hurrying, racing…then everything slowing as our bodies came together again, tumbling onto the bed, taking a moment just to look at each other and breathe.

Ryan tucked a strand of hair behind my ear and kissed me again, gently this time, though the gentleness didn't last long as I wrapped around him, rising to him, a wave of need. His weight, his mouth, his hands. I wanted him more than I wanted to breathe. And then he was inside me and everything blurred, fell away. That feeling of home again.

His mouth found mine and we lost ourselves to each other in a haze of movement—hips, hands, legs. Time somehow moved both too fast and too slow as the desire, the demand, the hunger built until finally, I cried out in release. He tensed, his own release crashing through him.

He collapsed onto me as we both trembled, my arms weak and falling away as we tried to catch our breath, my mind taking its time coming back to my body, having vacated to another plane of existence somewhere along the way.

Eventually he managed to roll off me and pulled me close.

"Sorry, I'm a little dazed," he said, his signature smirk playing at his lips.

I nodded. "I know the feeling. Dazed but utterly satisfied."

"Yeah," he said, breathing hard.

He leaned up on one elbow, running his hand across my stomach. "I think I'm going to enjoy being right across the hall from you."

"It really is lucky," I said, raising an eyebrow. "You'll be able to consult with me on all your cases now."

His smirk tugged the corner of his lip a little farther up. "Not exactly what I meant," he said, leaning in for a long, slow kiss as he slid his hand up my side.

It took another round for the exhaustion to finally catch up with us. I wasn't quite ready to spend the night—it seemed like too much too soon, and I wanted to savor every moment of whatever this Ryan and me thing was going to be—so, half-dressed, we found ourselves at his door.

He looked at me and smiled.

I smiled back.

"I'll see you tomorrow?"

"Absolutely." He leaned down and gave me one last, sweet kiss.

"Mmm…good night," I said, eventually tearing myself away.

It took everything in me to wait until I made it safely into my own apartment before I jumped up with a fist pump and let out a little squeal.

But then, when I glanced up and noticed the state of my apartment, all thoughts of Ryan shot straight out of my head.

Because there was something much, much more shocking happening on my floor.

Two entangled bodies, naked and barely covered with my tiny couch blanket, were sprawled in the middle of my living room.

What was even more shocking was that those two bodies belonged to very familiar people.

Brandt and Vic.

I nearly dropped my keys.

After a moment or two of utter astoundment— opening and closing my mouth like a fish—I blinked, and then smiled. Man, was I going to heckle them when they woke up.

Stepping over my two best friends and into my room, I crawled into bed.

But instead of dropping into the longest sleep of my life, I found I suddenly wasn't tired.

I had also suddenly come to a realization. The character I wanted to write—the Amelia Jones in my head— was so complete already, so kick-ass in every way, that there was nowhere interesting for her to go. No room to grow.

Maybe I needed her to be…a little flawed. A little unsure. A little more real.

A little more like me.

And suddenly my mind filled with ideas. With potential. With stories.

I pulled out my laptop and began to write.

\* \* \* \* \*

# *Romantic* Suspense

## Danger. Passion. Drama.

## Available Next Month

**Colton's Secret Stalker**  Kimberly Van Meter
**Hunted Hotshot Hero**  Lisa Childs

**Deadly Mountain Rescue**  Tara Taylor Quinn
**Undercover Cowboy Protector**  Kacy Cross

 LOVE INSPIRED

**Lethal Mountain Pursuit**  Christy Barritt
**Kidnapping Cold Case**  Laura Scott

Larger Print

LOVE INSPIRED

**Protecting The Littlest Witness**  Jaycee Bullard
**Undercover Colorado Conspiracy**  Jodie Bailey

Larger Print

LOVE INSPIRED

**Witness Protrction Breach**  Karen Krist
**Sabotaged Mission**  Tina Radcliffe

Larger Print

Keep reading for an excerpt of a new title
from the Intrigue series,
HELICOPTER RESCUE by Danica Winters

# *Chapter One*

The man stepped out of the ditch, a stuffed lobster dragging on the ground behind him. The orange bailing twine was looped around the animal's neck, and the lobster bounced like it was hoping for the sweet release of a figurative death—if only it could have been so lucky. Instead, it was the perpetual stuffed clown of a man who seemed to have as much apathy toward the thing as he did self-awareness.

Kristin Loren glanced down at the man's Bermuda shorts, one leg markedly longer than the other and tattered and torn, with a strip of hibiscus-printed cloth flapping against his leg as he teetered toward them.

From what she had been told about the man, he was in his eighties, was a former dean of the physics department at CalTech and suffered from Alzheimer's. Seeing him now, his ripped and dirty clothes, and stumbling gait, she had a hard time seeing him as the powerful authority on astrophysics that, according to the internet, he had once been. He was proof of the ravaging effects of the disease, and how it could even bring an intellectual juggernaut to his knees.

Perhaps one day in the not-so-distant future, due to her own family's history of Alzheimer's, she would be found like this man had been, confused and disoriented and smelling of sweat and urine. She hoped not, but it made the ache in her chest for the man intensify.

"Wh-where am I?" the man stammered, a look of uncertainty in his eyes. "Who're you?"

"I'm Kristin. What's your name?" she asked, hoping the man was capable of answering.

"I'm Hugh." He pointed at the flight crew as the nurse approached. "Who are they?"

"We were sent out here to help you get back home. That is Greg," she said, motioning toward the pilot, "and he will be helping to make sure you make it home safely. This lady here—" she indicated the thirtysomething brunette woman at her side "—is a sweet nurse who wants to get you medical assistance. Okay?"

The nurse smiled up at Hugh. "Is it okay with you if I check your vitals really quick?"

The man frowned but nodded, then pulled the lobster into his arms like he was not an eighty-seven-year-old man and was instead a seven-year-old boy. The nurse set to work, slipping on her stethoscope.

"How are you feeling this afternoon, sir?" the nurse asked.

"I'm fine," the man said, shrugging. The man seemed not to realize they had spent nearly a day looking for him, or that the nurse appeared to be slightly alarmed by his condition.

According to his son, the man had managed to

escape the confines of their home and disappeared into the night. They had only noticed he was missing when they woke up and found the man wasn't in his recliner watching reruns of *The Price is Right*.

She could almost imagine Bob Barker yelling "Come on down…" as this man with a stuffed lobster rocked away, engrossed. Then again, at the thought, she could understand why the man would have wanted to get up, slip out and disappear into the scrubby landscape of the rimrocks.

"You look nice," the man said to Kristin, seeming to forget about the nurse as she worked. A droopy, sad smile adorned his lips like forgotten party streamers left to the rain.

"Well, thank you. You look nice yourself." She sent him the closest thing to a real smile as she could muster. He deserved some respite from the chaos in his mind, if even just for a moment, thanks to her fleeting grin.

Kristin had been on so many of these types of calls for search-and-rescue that most didn't really faze her anymore, but there was something about this old-timer that pulled at her. Perhaps it was his utter lack of understanding, or the way he had seemed to look into her soul when he spoke. He reminded her of her grandfather in the last years of his life, when she was small enough to pull on his beard and whisper Popsicle-stick jokes into his failing ears.

She missed him.

"Do you remember your full name, Hugh?" she

asked, glancing over her shoulder at the double-bladed helo that rested in the pasture behind her.

The man's gaze slipped toward the helicopter. "I used to fly in the war," he said, not bothering to acknowledge, or not knowing the answer to, her question.

She'd long ago learned that the best way to get answers from someone who was aggressive or confused was to take a round-about approach. The wrong style of communication in fragile situations only led to undesirable results. For now, it was imperative that she handle him gently so that they could get him into the helicopter and transport him to the hospital in Billings, and hopefully then get back into the hands of his family.

"Which war were you involved in?" Kristin asked.

He stumbled as he took a step and she put his arm around her shoulder, helping him to walk. "Vietnam. Did two tours." He glanced up at the sky, then covered his eyes as if he was staring into the midday sun. "I should have never made it out."

She wasn't sure if that was a statement or a wish; either way, the agony of his tone set against the precariousness of his situation made her want to sob, but she couldn't pay heed to her emotions when there was a life to be saved.

"His BP is pretty low. We need to get him some fluids and get him stabilized so the doctors can sort him out," the nurse said as she moved to the other side and helped to walk him toward the helicopter as Kristin tried to keep chatting with the somewhat listless man.

By keeping him talking about the details of his war years, it didn't take long to get him loaded. They spent the next forty-five minutes pushing IV fluids while she and Hugh chatted about her job at FLIR Tech and their forward-looking infrared equipment that they had used to locate him in the field near the edge of a sage-lined cliff. Every time she tried to get him to answer more questions about his identity or where he lived, he avoided them and turned the conversation back to his younger years.

She watched as the nurse on the flight took the man's blood pressure as they neared the helo pad outside the hospital. The nurse's face pinched, and she took it again.

"Everything okay?"

The nurse seemed not to hear her, and instead glanced over at the EKG monitor. The green lines on the screen were jagged and irregular, like the thrusting peaks and valleys of freshly shorn mountains. Kristin didn't know a great deal about the line on the screen, but she knew enough to realize that with a heart rate at 43 bpm and a read like what she was seeing, it didn't point at anything good.

The nurse took out a syringe, then glanced down at her watch and turned to the pilot. "How much longer until we touch down?"

The pilot pointed down at the ground, where Kristin could just make out the red circle with an *H* in its center. As they got closer, she saw a group of personnel waiting near the doors of the hospital with a gurney.

Reaching down, Kristin took Hugh's hand. He looked up at her, his actions slow and deliberate, as though he was struggling to control his body. "It's going to be okay, Hugh," she said, positioning the lobster deeper into the nook of his arm. "We're at the hospital. They're going to take you from here and get you the help you need."

He answered her with a broken nod and an almost imperceptible squeeze of her fingers. The chill of his skin made her wonder if this simple exchange would be one of his last.

"Tell my son..." He took in a gasping breath as the nurse plunged the needle into his arm. "Tell him, I'm sorry."

The man closed his eyes just as the helicopter touched down. Before the blades even stopped rotating, there was a rush of nurses and hospital staff, and Kristin was pushed out of the way. Hugh was pulled onto the pad and put on the gurney, then he was whisked out of sight, into the belly of the industrial building.

She wanted to follow him, to make sure that he would be okay and that she had been wrong in her thoughts. The man hadn't been hurt, only left in the elements for too long. He couldn't be dying...not on her watch. If anything, she had just let her fears get the better of her. There had been dozens of other rescues she had taken part in where the persons they had rescued were in far more precarious medical states and had pulled through.

Hugh would be fine.

Yet, she couldn't help but step out of the helo and make her way inside the hospital in hopes of hearing good news. The staff had disappeared into the triage area, so Kristin made her way to the waiting area. It was empty, aside from a couple holding a small, ruddy-cheeked baby who was pulling at his ear and starting to cry. The poor mother had dark circles under her eyes and the father was pacing, as if each step would bring them closer to relief for their child.

She wasn't a parent, but there was no amount of pacing that could quell another's pain—she was well-acquainted with that concept.

After ten minutes or so, she was unable to watch any more of the parents' struggle and she made her way to the check-in area. "I'm part of the flight crew that came in with Hugh Keller. I was wondering if you have an update on his status?"

The secretary behind the desk nodded, the action stoic. "Hold on for just a moment and let me check for you."

As the secretary headed for the glass doors leading to the ER, the automatic doors at the entranceway slid open and a man came rushing in from outside. He was wearing blue-tinted Costa sunglasses and a tight-fitting, gray V-necked shirt that accentuated all the muscular curves and bumps of his body. Though she couldn't explain why, she caught herself catching her breath as she stared at him. He definitely wasn't bad-looking; in fact, she could safely say he was the hottest man she had seen in person in a long time. But standing here and waiting on a man's medical status seemed like the last moment that she should have found herself stunned by a handsome brunette.

The man walked up beside her and she caught a whiff of expensive cologne, made stronger by his body heat. If she had to guess, it was Yves Saint Laurent or some other haute scent, but as quickly as she tried to name it, she noted how out of place it was in the industrial austerity of where they were standing.

"Is there anyone working here?" he grumbled, tapping on the counter.

"She just ran to check on something for me. I'm sure she will be back in a sec," she said, her initial attraction somewhat dampened by the man's annoyance.

The man grumbled something unintelligible under his breath, but she was sure it was a string of masked expletives and she frowned.

"Sorry," the guy said, finally seeming to notice that she was a real live person and not just a source of information. "I'm not trying to be an ass... It's just..." He ran his hands over his face and bumped against his sunglasses, realizing he still had them on. He gave a dry chuckle as he took them off, then looked up at her with eyes that were even more blue than the lenses on his glasses. She thought he was handsome before, but now he was absolutely stunning and she found herself unable to look away. "It's been a long day."

"Uh-huh. I get it." She glanced at the little line

next to his mouth, a crease that came from a life of smiling—which seemed at odds with his current mood.

"My father. Yeah…" He paused. "They recently brought him in."

Just like that, she was whipped back to reality. She couldn't just ask who he was because of privacy laws, but even without knowing his father's name, she could tell from the shape of his eyes and the curve of his nose that he was Hugh's son. She wasn't sure how she could have missed it until now. There was no denying that the man before her was a younger version of the man whom she had found deep in the middle of nowhere.

"I'm sure your father is going to be okay."

His face darkened, but she wasn't sure if it was because he feared that it was an empty platitude, or if he was actually angry at her for her attempt to mollify him—either way, she wanted to make that look disappear.

The glass door through which the secretary had disappeared reopened and she walked out. She glanced over at the man at Kristin's side, then back to her. The woman raised her eyebrows, a silent question. Kristin gave her a furtive nod.

"The man you accompanied, Hugh, is currently with the doctor."

"Hugh? Hugh Keller?" the man asked.

The secretary nodded.

The man gripped the edge of the counter. "That's my father. I'm Casper Keller. I'm going to need more information. What's the doctor saying? Is he going to be all right?"

The secretary's mouth opened and closed, as if she was hoping the right words would just magically appear on her lips in this challenging situation. "I... I'm afraid I can't speak to—"

"But you have an answer. Please, if this was your father..." Casper pleaded, making Kristin's chest ache. "Please."

The secretary wrung her hands and looked down at the desk. "I'm sorry, Mr. Keller." There was an agonizing pause before the woman finally looked up. There were tears in her eyes. "I heard the doctor say he didn't think your father will survive. I'll try and get you back to see him." The secretary turned and slipped back through the door.

Kristin didn't know what to do to comfort the man when her heart was breaking for both Casper and the man who had reminded her so much of her grandfather. Something about this situation made it feel like she was losing the patriarch of her family again.

"I'm so sorry, Casper."

He looked at her, but there was no recognition in his eyes, and the look was so much like his father's that she was thrown off balance. "Yeah."

In that single, breathless word, she felt every ounce of his loss...and it tore her to pieces.

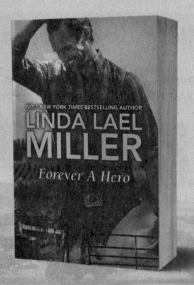

# MILLS & BOON

## Want to know more about your favourite series or discover a new one?

Experience the variety of romance that Mills & Boon has to offer at our website:

## millsandboon.com.au

Shop all of our categories and discover the one that's right for you.

**MODERN**

**DESIRE**

**MEDICAL**

**INTRIGUE**

**ROMANTIC SUSPENSE**

**WESTERN**

**HISTORICAL**

**FOREVER**
EBOOK ONLY

**HEART**
EBOOK ONLY

**f** @millsandboonaustralia  🐦 📷 @millsandboonaus